THE WONDERLING

Songcatcher

THE WONDERLING

Mira Bartók

WALKER
BOOKS

First published in Great Britain 2017 by Walker Books Ltd
87 Vauxhall Walk, London SE11 5HJ

This edition published 2018

2 4 6 8 10 9 7 5 3 1

This book has been typeset in Dante MT

Printed and bound by CPI Group (UK) Ltd, Croydon CRO 4YY

British Library Cataloguing in Publication Data:
a catalogue record for this book is available from the British Library

ISBN 978-1-4063-7990-7

www.walker.co.uk

For Doug, for love and wonder;
for Jed, who helped to build my flying suit;
and for Jen, who gave me wings to fly

THE
WORLD
OF
THE
WONDERLING

THE SEA

KESTREL HALL

FALCON HALL

OWL HALL

HAWK HALL

THE HOME

CONTENTS

PART THE FIRST

Part The Second

In Which the Wonderling Learns Much
About the Precarious Life of
Wayfarers, Peddlers, Slyboots & Thieves

121

Part The Third

In Which the Wonderling Finds That
Which Once Was Lost & Discovers the Truth
About Some Things Along the Way

287

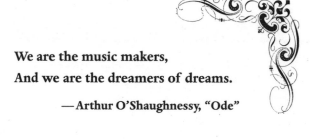

We are the music makers,
And we are the dreamers of dreams.

—Arthur O'Shaughnessy, "Ode"

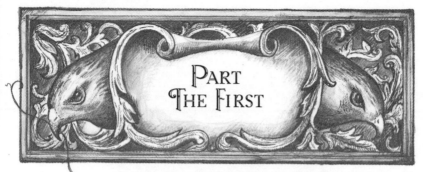

Part the First

On the Mysterious Origins of the
Wonderling & His Arduous Life
at Miss Carbunkle's Home
for Wayward & Misbegotten
Creatures

CHAPTER 1

An Inauspicious Beginning

EFORE HE WAS CALLED THE WONDERLING, he had many names: Puddlehead, Plonker, Groundling and Spike, among others. He didn't mind these much, not even Groundling. The name he truly disliked was the first he ever remembered being called: Number Thirteen. It wasn't a name, really. Just a number, written in red, on a piece of paper, filed in a drawer, in a room full of hundreds of files and drawers. It was embossed on a small tin medallion attached to a piece of cord he wore around his neck at a home for unclaimed creatures. It was sewn inside his tattered grey shirt and shabby grey trousers. And it was painted on his hard, narrow bed in a room full of the beds of other unclaimed creatures who had at least been fortunate enough to have been given the gift of their own names at birth.

He looked like a young fox but stood upright like a child and had no tail to speak of. His eyes were a lovely chestnut brown and flecked with gold. But there was something about them that gave one the sense that, although he had not been in this world very long, he carried within him some inexplicable sorrow.

He was a creature with an innocent heart. What kind of creature, though, who could say? Despite his fox kit face, his snout was more dog than fox, and there was something rabbity about him too, in the way his nose twitched when he sensed danger, and how he trembled when he heard the loud clang of the orphanage bell. But the most singular thing about him was that he had only one ear.

How he had lost his other ear (or whether he was born without it) he did not know. His right ear, the pointy ear of a fox, was velvety soft and covered in reddish-brown fur like the rest of him, but for a small white spot on his chest shaped like a leaf. Except for his missing ear, Number Thirteen had nothing out of the ordinary about him, at least not outwardly, for he lived in a world where the line between animals and humans was not so clearly defined. Nevertheless, people thought him strange. "Bad luck, that ear!" they whispered to one another. "Must be deaf as a doorknob, that one! And that name – Number Thirteen! Bad luck indeed!"

At night, he comforted himself, as frightened children

do all over the world. He'd reach beneath his pillow and pull out something soft and blue: a fragment of his baby blanket. Embroidered on one of the corners was what looked like the initial *M,* although he couldn't quite make it out, for some of the threads, which had once been brilliant gold, had faded or fallen out over time. Wrapped inside the scrap of blanket was a tiny gold key. He didn't know what it opened, or if it had ever opened anything important at all – just that the key and the blue scrap were the only things remaining from his very first home.

But Number Thirteen – one-eared, nameless and small of stature, for he never grew taller than three feet high – could not remember where he came from. Everyone comes from somewhere, and yet there he was, his origins unknown, even to himself. He could not remember being tucked in at night, or if he had ever been truly loved. What he did recall, however, was a sound from long ago: a beautiful, lilting song, floating through a sky full of stars, landing inside his fledgling of a heart. Other than that, he couldn't remember a thing.

When asked about his early years, Number Thirteen could recall only the terrible place he had been sent to.

CHAPTER 2

The Home

THE ORPHANAGE where Number Thirteen was abandoned shortly after his birth (by whom, he did not know) was called Miss Carbunkle's Home for Wayward and Misbegotten Creatures but referred to by its miserable occupants as, simply, "the Home." It was located in the country, far from city or town. The Home, which had been built centuries ago in the shape of a giant cross, had been many things – first a monastery, then a prison, then a workhouse for the poor and finally an asylum for unclaimed creatures.

On the front of the Home's brochure was a happy-go-lucky creature with the head of a rabbit and the body of a little girl, wearing a polka-dot dress and bow, clutching a bouquet of daisies. Beneath the picture, the caption read: *Have you been unexpectedly burdened by a recently orphaned or unclaimed creature? Worry not! We have just the solution for you!*

The advertisement boasted of "a warm and welcoming place, nestled in an idyllic valley, surrounded by fields of buttercups, bluebells and heather." But none of the orphans ever saw a single flower or felt a blade of grass beneath their feet once they walked through the Home's ominous front gate. In fact, the only green they saw was the moss that grew on the massive stone wall surrounding the place.

And Miss Carbunkle's Home was anything but welcoming and warm.

The high black gate that rose to an arch in the middle stood a hundred feet from the entrance. Through it, any carriages came and went. Each of the gate's iron bars was topped by a spike that resembled the tip of a medieval spear, so sharp that birds never perched there. Hanging from its apex was a rusty metal sign with faded black letters announcing the name of the wretched place. So many of the letters had worn off over time, the sign now read:

M   UNKLE'S H ME F R AYWARD AND M B TT N E T R S

On each side of the sign was the profile of a hawk. Someone or some force of nature had dislodged the sign long ago, and it dangled from a single nail, causing it to clank loudly against the gate whenever the wind blew or whenever someone entered or left the grounds.

Let us just say that more entered than left, and leave it at that.

Two dim-witted mastiffs the size of calves stood chained together in front of the gate, barking incessantly and salivating so much that small puddles of drool gathered at their feet. At night, beneath the eerie glow of the gaslight, the guard dogs resembled a slobbery Cerberus, the three-headed guardian of hell – minus one head, of course. The dogs responded to one voice only, that of the headmistress, Miss Carbunkle, who ruled over her dominion with a cold, impenetrable heart.

To enter the orphanage itself, one had to pass through a heavy oak door, built into the wall and impossible to open without Miss Carbunkle's big brass key. Carved into the door was the figure of another hawk, clutching a tiny mouse in its

talons, a reminder lest anyone forget their place. The only way to pass from the Home to the outside world was through that door. There had been other doors built into the wall that surrounded the three-storey building and grounds – ancient arched doors with beautiful pictures carved and painted on them – but Miss Carbunkle had sealed them all off when she bought the place. Along the formidable wall, only the ghost image of each original door remained – a palimpsest of an exit to the outside world.

The wall, built centuries ago from thousands of rough-hewn stones, was three storeys high and six and a half feet thick. As with "the Home," the orphans called it simply "the Wall." Except for the top of a tall white birch, the orphans could not see a thing over the Wall – not the lush valley, nor the rolling hills that embraced it, nor the farmlands beyond the hills, the blue mountains beyond the horizon, nor, beyond that, the glowing spires of the Great White City of Lumentown.

And so the shy one-eared creature adapted to his surroundings and grew. Like so many others who have never known solace or love, Number Thirteen said little, kept his head down and did what he was told. He felt that he knew nothing at all about himself or about the mysterious world beyond the towering wall and gate. What he *did* know in his heart of hearts was that he hungered for something. But what that something was, he had yet to find out.

CHAPTER 3

Number Thirteen

EVERY DAY BEGAN exactly the same at Miss Carbunkle's Home for Wayward and Misbegotten Creatures: Wake up at five a.m. to the Home's earsplitting bell, followed by Miss Carbunkle's screeching, "Roll call, groundlings! Rise and shine!" over the loudspeaker. Next, wash face and mitts in shared basin of dirty grey water left over from yesterday's laundry. Then remove tattered grey pyjamas, pull on tattered grey uniform (which looked identical to aforementioned pyjamas), and rush outside with the others for roll call – all of this accomplished at breakneck speed.

One bleak December morning, toward the end of the eleventh year of Number Thirteen's strange and lonely life, he and the others gathered outside in Kestrel Courtyard at dawn, as usual, for roll call. The orphans stood in rows of ten in front of the Wall that towered above them, closing them in on all four sides like a castle fortress.

It was Monday morning, less than a week before Christmas *and* Number Thirteen's birthday, for both fell on the very same day. Not surprisingly, Number Thirteen was completely unaware of this fact. And besides, celebrations of any kind were strictly forbidden at the Home.

A damp mist swirled above the courtyard, slowly creeping into the orphans' threadbare coats and bones. All the wayward and misbegotten creatures – the orphans, the foundlings and the street urchins doing penance for petty crimes – stood at attention. They were the "groundlings" of the world – a hybrid mix of animal and human, or of animal and animal, that, in the hierarchy of the day, inhabited a place very close to the bottom. They were skinny and squat, furry and feathered, some nearly human if not for a rat tail or jackrabbit ears, a piglet face or wings and webbed feet. Most were half human, half animal, but not all. Some appeared to be all animal, or reptile, or bird, but for the fact that they spoke and acted like human beings.

The one thing they all had in common, besides the numbers they wore around their necks, was the dread they felt when Miss Carbunkle appeared, dressed in her black hooded cloak and carrying her hawk-headed cane, her mouth drawn in a permanent line of disapproval.

That morning, like all mornings, Miss Carbunkle leaned forward on her cane, pursed her lips and glared down at the young waifs before her. She was a tall imposing woman, and her astonishingly large flaming-orange wig (one of her few indulgences in life) made her appear even taller. Her bespectacled assistant, Mr Sneezeweed – sour-faced, shoulder-stooped and long of limb – stood scowling beside her, his greasy black hair clinging to his forehead and the sides of his long pale face.

The headmistress began calling out names in a shrill, clipped voice:

"Hershel!"

"Here, ma'am."

"Cecil!"

"Here, ma'am."

"Gaffer!"

"Here, ma'am."

"Dimble!"

"Here."

"DIMBLE!"

"H–here?"

"Here, MA'AM!"

"Here, ma'am."

"Glover!"

"Here, ma'am."

"Joop!"

"Here, ma'am."

And so on. All the little groundlings, with names like Morris and Stanley, Nesbit and Snook, Twinkles and Nigel, Rufus, Tweeter, Moe and Baby Tizer (who refused to grow larger than a hedgehog), answered in turn. There were ever so many, with more coming each and every week. They stood there shivering, staring up at Miss Carbunkle, whose face looked ghoulish in the grey morning light.

Miss Carbunkle had been a beauty in her youth, but as time went on, she became so unfeeling toward the world that her heart, once so full, had become brittle and small. Her expression had shrunk as well, and always looked angry and pinched. Except for the two blotches of rouge on her cheeks, Miss Carbunkle's face resembled an angry ghost's.

Miss Carbunkle paused to check her list. She could never keep the names of her wards straight, for although each of them looked so very different from the others, they seemed all very much the same to her – freakish, ill-formed and wild. As Miss Carbunkle read off the names, her assistant absent-mindedly stroked a small downy patch below his left nostril. Mr Sneezeweed dreamed of one day sporting an extravagant handlebar moustache, but alas, at thirty years of age, he had yet to produce any facial hair whatsoever, save for the spot of fuzz.♦

Sneezeweed, who was nearly as tall as Miss Carbunkle, was for ever sniffling and blowing his aquiline nose into a dainty white handkerchief that his doting mother had embroidered with his name. The orphans called him "Sneezy" behind his back. Now, as always, Sneezy was alternating between blowing his nose and stroking his non-existent moustache. In his other hand, he gripped a long wooden paddle, at the ready should anyone step out of line.

Number Thirteen was far more afraid of Miss Carbunkle's cane. She was known to strike a groundling's backside at the slightest provocation. At the top of her cane was the head of the same sinister hawk carved on the Home's oak door and painted on the Home's unwelcoming sign. Its resemblance to the headmistress, with its piercing eyes and beak-like nose, was not lost on him. Sometimes, in the dim and sleepy light of morning, he swore he could see the hawk's amber eyes blink.

Miss Carbunkle opened her mouth to speak just as Sneezeweed, who was allergic to nearly everything – fur, feathers, mould, dust and most every kind of food – let out a succession of explosive sneezes. The groundlings stifled their

♦ "Fresh as a newborn babe, my Mortimer, fresh as a newborn babe! His mama's favourite, he is," his mother would say to anyone who would listen.

laughter as best they could, because laughter, like most other things, was strictly forbidden.

The headmistress gave Sneezeweed's foot a sharp stab with her cane and said, "For pity's sake, man, control yourself!"

Sneezeweed winced and said quietly, so as to not be overheard, "I beg your pardon, ma'am, but ... but ... it's the *spores,* you see; spores are everywhere! And—"

"Oh, shut it!" said Miss Carbunkle, and continued rattling off more names: *Seymour, Petey, Queeg and Pocket! Buttercup, Tillie, Millie and Schmoo!*

Clearly, it was a Non-Alphabetical Day.

On Non-Alphabetical Days, Miss Carbunkle read off her list in no particular order to keep the groundlings on their toes. Sometimes she read the same name twice. But none of that mattered to Number Thirteen, for even on Non-Alphabetical Days, he was always called last. Being only a number made his status lower than an *X,* a *Y,* or even a *Z.*

Miss Carbunkle scanned the rows before her and called out the final name. "Number Thirteen!"

But before he could answer, someone kicked the back of his knees and he fell onto a small rabbit groundling, causing them both to tumble to the ground. "S–sorry," he stammered, and helped her up.

He could hear Mug and Orlick snickering behind him. Mug, a bulldog groundling, and "Smelly" Orlick, an opossum groundling who, for some inexplicable reason, always smelled like pond water, were the one-eared orphan's most frequent tormentors at the Home. As far back as he could remember, they had bullied him. Once, when the headmistress and Mr Sneezeweed had rushed out of the courtyard to catch the groundling that had set fire to Miss Carbunkle's desk, Mug grabbed his ear and shouted in it, "Is anybody home in there, you stupid plonker?" His ear ached for weeks afterward. Mug and his friends had called him "Plonker" or "Plonky" ever since.

He got used to it, though, just like he got used to everything else. *Better to be a name than a number,* he said to himself, *even if it is an unpleasant one.*

"Number Thirteen!" Miss Carbunkle shrieked once again into the cold, misty air.

He struggled, as usual, to get out the words, but the words wouldn't come. It felt as if a large rock were lodged deep inside his throat.

All of a sudden, someone pulled his ear really hard. Number Thirteen spun around to see who it was. Next to Mug and Orlick stood an imposing new arrival: a tall, grey, bristly-furred rat groundling with a long snout and two sharp incisors protruding from his mouth. He had large yellow-clawed feet and a long wiry tail. His shoulders were so scrunched up that it seemed his head was attached to them and that he had no neck at all. His eyes were small and shrunken and black as night.

"Delighted to meet you," whispered the Rat, who promptly belched right in Number Thirteen's face.

The poor creature almost passed out from the smell – a bouquet of dirty socks, fetid meat and the flotsam and jetsam of dark sewers.

Great. Now he had three bullies to worry about instead of two.

Miss Carbunkle roared his name like a wild beast. He stammered out an inaudible "H–here."

In a voice as smooth as silk, the Rat whispered in his ear, "What's the matter? Rat got your tongue?"

Number Thirteen began to tremble from the tip of his ear to his furry toes.

"Number Thirteen, do you want the cane? Or would you prefer Mr Sneezeweed's paddle?" snarled Miss Carbunkle.

He tried again, a little louder, but the headmistress still could not hear him.

"NUMBER THIRTEEN!" she boomed. "Are you here or not? Make up your mind!"

Finally, Number Thirteen, known to the world only as an unlucky number, forced the words out from behind the rock in his throat: "Here, m–m–ma'am."

The orphans let out a collective sigh of relief, and off to breakfast they marched, led by Mr Sneezeweed. Fortunately, Mug, Orlick and their new ratty friend were farther back in line.

And Number Thirteen, who shuffled along with his head down as usual, wished he had a nice warm cap with which to hide his ear.

CHAPTER 4

The Secret

NUMBER THIRTEEN trudged along as Mr Sneezeweed led his wards down the long narrow corridor of Kestrel Hall. "One, two, one, two! Keep up, you worthless little beasties!" snapped Sneezeweed, holding his paddle above his head.

They were heading off to the same place they went every morning: the dreary dining hall at the far end of the Home. And after that, two hours of Miss Carbunkle's illuminating lectures on topics such as "The Necessity of Groundling Obedience in the Service of Progress and Industry" would be followed by more hours of tedious backbreaking chores: scrubbing floors, washing clothes in freezing-cold water by hand (or claw or paw), repairing broken desks and chairs, mending blankets and socks, and, more often than not, soul-squelching factory work.

Sunday was the only day that deviated from the rest. The orphans awoke early for roll call and did their work, but to their immense relief, there were no lessons at all. That December day, however, was *not* a Sunday. It was just another Monday, and there was nothing special about it.

Number Thirteen's stomach wouldn't stop growling. It seemed to take for ever to get to the dining hall, for the orphanage was immense. Four long corridors radiated from the centre of the cross-shaped building, each named for a bird of prey: Hawk, Kestrel, Falcon and Owl. Kestrel Hall, which ran from the centre of the cross to the back, was where the orphans slept and where they gathered for roll call each morning in the courtyard. The schoolroom and dining hall were in Hawk Hall, which ran from the centre to the front, where, outside the thick oak door, Miss Carbunkle's dogs growled and drooled and barked.

The sides of the cross were made up of Owl and Falcon Halls, which contained dozens of workrooms, including the Home's very own steam-powered factory, where the orphans assembled strange little widgets under the direction of an ill-tempered foreman named Mr Bonegrubber. The widgets looked like small black beetles. What they were used for, nobody knew.

No one knew what was on the very top floor either, for it was off limits to everyone except Miss Carbunkle and her staff. The orphans had their theories, of course: these ranged from medieval torture chambers with pots of boiling oil in which to dip naughty groundlings, to nasty cells where wicked creatures were forced to eat bowls of big furry poisonous spiders. As for the cellar, everyone was certain that it was full of gigantic black rats who liked to nibble on toes and would make a meal of you if you stayed down there long enough.

"Look sharp! Snap to it!" hollered Mr Sneezeweed. His foot was still sore from Miss Carbunkle's cane, and he wasn't happy about it.

They were in the Grand Hall, where Miss Carbunkle's office was located, the centre point where all four corridors met. Sneezeweed slowed down in front of the headmistress's office, struck with a surge of envy. Her office was enormous, as were her living quarters, and his were not. The office was soundproof and made from a special kind of glass that allowed the headmistress to see out but prevented anyone from seeing in. It rose up through all three floors of the Home. A circular stairway led to her private chambers on the top floor. From there, she could access her panoptic observatory tower on the roof, keeping watch from all sides with her spyglass and telescopic goggles. Her chambers were not lavish but they were modern and clean.

Mr Sneezeweed slept in a poorly furnished room barely big enough to fit a bed and a dresser. He was sequestered in Kestrel Hall, next to the infirmary and across from the dormitory, as it was his job to monitor the groundlings at night, which meant he barely slept at all. *A babysitter for freaks, that's what I am,* he said to himself as he passed by Miss Carbunkle's magnificent office in the Grand Hall.

Outside Miss Carbunkle's office, a giant cuckoo clock stood sentry. Number Thirteen looked down so he didn't have to see what came next, right at the top of the hour, just when they were all marching past. A bright-yellow bird appeared from behind a door above the clock face. The mechanical bird chirped and danced for exactly ten seconds. Then a large beak popped out and swallowed the bird up with an awful *SNAP!*

Finally, they arrived at the dining hall. "Get your bowls, sit down, and shut up!" yelled Mr Sneezeweed. He tugged hard at the thick greasy rope that hung from the rafters, and a loud clang announced the beginning of the meal.

The Home served only breakfast and dinner to the poor

creatures, and the meals were almost always the same: porridge in the morning, watery pea soup at night and a piece of stale, coarse bread. At dinner, there might be a piece of raw turnip, a small carrot, or a boiled potato too, but these luxuries were rare. By breakfast each day, Number Thirteen was famished.

He sat down at a long wooden table where the smallest groundlings congregated – Baby Tizer (a good-natured spiny little fellow), Twinkles (part pig, part pug), Nigel (*mostly* dachshund), Nesbit and Snook (rabbity twins), Morris and Moe (sloth groundlings) and Rufus (*mostly* wombat). Nesbit and Snook looked at him kindly and mouthed "hello." Number Thirteen forced a shy smile and tucked into his bowl of cold

grey gruel. The Sloth brothers, Morris and Moe, greeted him too, but it took them so long to open their mouths that he didn't even notice.

The dining hall had a large vaulted ceiling and high arched walls. In an earlier incarnation, the room had been decorated with colourful frescoes, and monks had held choir practice here. But the walls and ceiling had long since been painted over in dull gunmetal grey. However, unlike the rest of the Home, which was devoid of decoration save for a big white clock on every wall, the dining hall had its own particular form of adornment.

There were signs everywhere, crammed from floor to ceiling. They were printed with Miss Carbunkle's favourite sayings, such as: *Know Your Place! It's at the Bottom!* and *Time Waits for No One – Especially You!* and *Blessed Are Those Who Serve and Obey!* and *Music Is the Root of All Evil!*

Number Thirteen glanced at the sign that hung above his table: *Why Reach for the Stars When the Stars Are Out of Reach? Good question,* he said to himself, and sighed.

His two adversaries and their new friend sat down at a nearby table. Who was this creature with his black pebble eyes and sewer breath? Number Thirteen could feel the three of them staring at him behind his back, which made his ear all twitchy. *I'll just pretend I'm invisible,* he thought, and ate his watery porridge in silence.

Silence was what was expected of him anyway, for it was the first and most important of Miss Carbunkle's Golden Rules.

Noise, including conversation, was barely tolerated. It was strictly forbidden in the dining hall, except when absolutely necessary. This was difficult for some, who couldn't help but make little snuffling sounds as they dipped their snouts, claws and paws into their gruel. Those who spoke or misbehaved at mealtime, or who were foolish enough to beg more food from Mr Bunmuncher, the Home's disgruntled cook (whose big bald head resembled a pink, gleaming ham), received several hard whacks across their backside.

Singing, humming, or making music of any kind whatsoever was also prohibited. In fact, in Miss Carbunkle's eyes, music was the worst offence of all. The culprit was sent to the cellar (otherwise known as the "rat dungeon") for a month of solitary confinement, followed by weeks of toilet-scrubbing duty.

Number Thirteen noticed that the two small groundlings next to him were passing notes back and forth beneath the table. Even in this wretched place, the orphans managed to communicate. They spoke in hurried whispers or facial gestures, or in a secret code of foot, hand and paw tapping. They passed tiny notes, stories and pictures. It was impossible not to talk or laugh with one another even in a clandestine manner, for the desire for companionship far exceeded the fear of punishment, regardless of how severe.

The one-eared orphan longed for companionship too. But whenever he gathered the courage to approach someone, he spoke so softly and stuttered so much that it was hard to understand him. Some of the groundlings, not to mention the headmistress and Mr Sneezeweed, treated him as though he were deaf. How could that stammering creature called Number Thirteen possibly hear with just one pathetic ear?

But he *was* listening.

He was listening to everything around him. If he concentrated hard enough and went to a quiet, secret place inside himself, he could sometimes hear extraordinary things.

He could hear the secret movements of insects, busy at their work beneath the floorboards and inside the walls, and he wondered if they could hear him too. He could hear the old donkey in the stables softly braying itself to sleep at night, and the two carriage horses swatting flies with their tails in summer. He had never seen them, but he knew they were there. And in winter, he could even hear snow falling in the courtyard. The worst weather produced the loveliest of sounds: *pfft, pfft, pfft, whoosh, pfft, pfft, pfft, whoosh,* and he wondered if this was a kind of song, this melody of snow.

And if by chance in spring, a bird, small and delicate of wing, was singing in the tree outside the Wall, Number Thirteen could hear her clear as a bell from inside the Home.

He could hear the quiet snap of every twig, the gentle flutter of her wings as she flew from branch to branch. Loveliest of all, he could hear her tender nesting song as she soared through the air to her new home. And when he did, her song filled him with such unbearable longing, he thought his swollen heart would burst.

This thing – this gift, or curse – whatever it was, for he didn't know – had been growing inside him ever since he could remember. But why was it so? And did others have it too? He didn't think so, and thus, afraid to stand out, never told a soul.

In spite of Miss Carbunkle's Golden Rule of Silence, the room gradually filled with sound – the clatter of tin bowls upon tables, the forbidden whispers among friends, Sneezeweed screaming "Silence!" every few minutes and honking and blowing his nose, and the ever-present *tick-tick-tick*ing of clocks on every wall in every room on every floor.

After he finished eating, Number Thirteen closed his eyes, focused his mind and listened. Not to the rising din around him or the heartbeat of a thousand clocks but to something from deep within the bowels of the building. It was the fidgety little mice that scurried between the walls.

Number Thirteen was used to their scuffling sounds and squeaks. But that day was different. That day, he heard something very peculiar – something wondrous and new.

For the first time in his life, he could hear the mice talk.

Am I going crazy? No, he decided. *Those are definitely mice. And I can understand every word they say.*

What did this mean? Number Thirteen thought only humans and groundlings could talk. But mice? Mice were what humans called the "dumb beasts of the earth," even lower in status than groundlings. Did the fact that they could talk make them groundlings too? And if not, why could he hear them and not the others? No one else seemed to be noticing the lively conversation going on behind the walls.

He leaned closer to the wall and tipped his ear to listen.

The mice seemed to be discussing one of their favourite topics: food. Their banter was fascinating. In just a few minutes, he discovered that mice were: (1.) connoisseurs of French cheese, particularly a kind they called Brie, (2.) extremely polite (to a fault) and (3.) possessed of strong opinions about something called poetry. The mice seemed very passionate about it, whatever it was.

Then another conversation started up behind the wall. It grew louder until it drowned out the squeaky voices of the mice, who scurried away. He surmised that the two speakers were rats, the large black ones that scampered through sewer pipes to the dark, wet cellar where Miss Carbunkle sent naughty groundlings. Number Thirteen eavesdropped on their exchange, which, for the most part, was diabolical, but in a courteous sort of way:

RAT ONE: I say, did you see that deliciously dead thing I found last week?

RAT TWO: Oh, yes, a fine catch indeed! Bravo, my friend, bravo!

RAT ONE: Well, *I* thought so. But not everyone did. And you *know* of whom I speak.

RAT TWO: Quite! I say, he *is* a jealous fellow, is he not? You know what they say: envy is ignorance!

RAT ONE: Right you are!

RAT TWO: So, my fine friend, whatever did you do about it? Rats like that need to be taught a lesson, I daresay.

RAT ONE: Indeed! I jolly well had but one alternative, as you can imagine. I ate him. He quite deserved it.

RAT TWO: Quite! Well done! Bravo, old chap! Bravo!

Number Thirteen shuddered. *They're probably related to that awful rat friend of—* Suddenly, he felt something cold, wet and sticky hit the back of his head and dribble down his neck. He turned to see Mug and Orlick grinning from ear to ear. Their new friend sat between them, smirking. He set down the spoon with which he had flung the cold gruel and yawned, revealing his razor-sharp teeth.

Number Thirteen wiped the mess off with his sleeve. Now his sleeve was dirty and wet. He sighed. He had only one shirt, and there was simply no time to clean it.

Don't think of them, he told himself. *Think of something else.*

He rested his head on the table, and in the few minutes remaining, he let his mind drift to his favourite sounds: falling snow, birds, the gentle drumming of rain upon the roof. The world fell away – its greyness, its cruelty, its pettiness and fears. And the song from long ago that still nestled deep within his heart stirred inside him once again. He wished he knew what it all meant – the song, his lack of a name, and this secret ability to hear things no one else could hear.

The harsh sound of the bell startled him out of his dream. He queued up with the rest of the groundlings, and they headed out the door to the schoolroom for Miss Carbunkle's Monday morning lessons, Mr Sneezeweed leading the way.

There was no time now for futile wishes or birdsongs or the music of snow. No time to muse about the lovely little mice, their French cheese and poetry, for it was *not* a special day after all. It was just the beginning of yet another week at the Home. And as on all the days of Number Thirteen's life thus far, there was ever so much work to be done.

CHAPTER 5

What Happened on Cheese Sunday

INSIDE THE HOME, time crept monotonously along. But outside the impassable Wall, life raced toward a great and glorious future. Wars were fought, kings and queens were crowned, inventions invented that changed the course of history. Men and women built machines that could project moving pictures on walls. They built steam-powered bicycles that could fly, and chronometers, barometers, aerometers and many other incomprehensible things with names ending in "meter". Most miraculous of all was a secret machine that could capture the most beautiful sounds and songs in the world and play them back to you in your dreams.

But Number Thirteen had little knowledge of the world, except for snippets of stories he heard from new arrivals to the Home. For *his* world was eternally the same: roll call, porridge, lessons, chores, widgets, pea soup, bed.

But Sundays, ah, Sundays! Instead of two hours of mind-numbing lessons after breakfast, the orphans were allowed outside of Kestrel Hall. Each hall had its own courtyard, but Kestrel Hall was the only one where the groundlings could, for one precious hour a week, be free. (The second hour that replaced lessons was taken up with extra factory work, but that was to be expected.)

On Sundays, they were even allowed to run around and play (within reason), and although there was nothing on the grounds that resembled a swing set, sandbox, or ball, the little ones invented many games on their own, despite the fact that exercising one's imagination was emphatically discouraged at Miss Carbunkle's Home for Wayward and Misbegotten Creatures.

It was Christmas Day – not that one could really *tell* it was Christmas, for there were no tinselled trees or shiny gifts or trays of little cakes and sweets lying about the place. It was also Number Thirteen's eleventh birthday. But he was unaware of these two important facts. So rather than eating birthday cake and Christmas tarts, or opening presents and singing holiday songs, he stood shivering in a corner at the far end of Kestrel Courtyard, pretending to be a bug.

He imagined himself to be like the ones who lived below the floorboards in the dormitory, just a tiny thing that hid in darkness and made hardly a sound. *That's me,* he told himself. *I'm just a little bug. Too small to even bother with.*

Then he thought about the charming little mice he had heard behind the wall and decided to be a mouse, sharing a morsel of cheese with another mouse, having a chat about poetry (whatever that was) over a cup of tea.

Outside the Wall, a gentle snow began to fall. But inside Kestrel Courtyard, it began to rain. It almost always rained inside the Wall, and always a thudding sort of rain, devoid of rainbows or bursts of glorious sun in its wake.

What capricious magic was this that caused bad weather in one place and perfect weather in another a hop, skip, and jump away? No one seemed to know. Naturally, Number Thirteen wondered if it was *his* fault. After all, his name was so very unlucky.

Soon the courtyard was slick with mud, but the groundlings didn't care a toss. Some were jumping and splashing in puddles, others were playing tag, while still others pretended to be explorers, pirates, fairies, goblins, balloonists and adventurers at sea.

In short, they were playing, for once, like children.

In Number Thirteen's small corner of the world, life was as good as it could be. High above him was one of the Home's massive stone gargoyles, hiding him in its shadow. Water spilled from the roof onto the gargoyle's eyes and face, from which it, in turn, poured into the yard, but away from Number Thirteen, who stayed safe and dry behind the gargoyle's watery veil. On one side of the waterfall was a narrow gap, in case he needed to slip through without getting wet.

Each of the four courtyards had four medieval gargoyles, remnants of the Home's monastic past. They were not birds of prey, like Miss Carbunkle's ever-present hawk, although there was something birdlike about them. They mostly looked like sad monsters, with misshapen snouts, large ears, mournful droopy eyes and droopy wings, their faces worn down from weather and neglect. When it rained very hard, water poured out of all sixteen gargoyles in the courtyards of Hawk, Kestrel, Falcon, and Owl Halls.

It was as if the orphanage itself were weeping.

Number Thirteen pulled out a small piece of cheese from his pocket and nibbled on it slowly. He had saved it from the Sunday before, which had been, to the delight of all, a Cheese Sunday. Cheese Sunday meant that an official from the Department for the Protection of Wayward and Misbegotten Creatures (the D.P.W.M.C.) had visited the Home. They did this from time to time to make sure everything was running smoothly. At the end of the visit, each orphan was rationed a piece of cheese. The cheese was usually green and so hard that many creatures lost a tooth or two when they bit into it. And yet, it *was* cheese, after all, and once in a great while it wasn't so old and green but nearly fresh.

If the cheese was indeed fresh, some of the creatures used their ration as currency: a piece of cheese could be exchanged for two carrots, a scrap of paper or a pencil, part of a broken toy, or a handful of straw for one's bed. Even stories were bartered for, and news from the outside world.

But no one dared barter for songs. *That* was way too dangerous.

Miss Carbunkle had a very important meeting with a mysterious high-ranking personage in Lumentown and had left Sneezy in charge. He had wanted to be home with his mother, dining on Christmas goose and pudding. But that was clearly not going to happen, and Mr Sneezeweed was quite upset.

Despite his peevish and often threatening demeanour in front of the groundlings, Mr Sneezeweed was actually terrified of them, not to mention repulsed. He didn't like policing "those filthy creatures" any more than he liked smelling them, or eating in the same room with them. *My word, the way they slurp their food! Absolutely no etiquette! What are they, anyway? Half this, half that? Vermin, that's what they are! And who has to deal with them day in and day out – even on Christmas? Mortimer Sneezeweed, that's who!*

Mr Sneezeweed took a quick survey of the yard and slipped back inside. He found a nice warm spot away from the cold, draughty door and pulled up a rickety old chair. The door was at the end of the hall, right next to his private chamber, and oftentimes, when Miss Carbunkle was away, he would sneak into his room for a few minutes to retrieve a book or put on a dab of Professor Mifflebaum's Miracle Moustache Pomade.

How much trouble could they cause in one hour? he asked himself, ignoring the wild antics brewing in the yard. He blew his nose, tucked his dainty white handkerchief back inside the cuff of his crisply starched sleeve, cracked open a thick volume titled *The Secret Lives of Accountants* and began to read.

Meanwhile, Number Thirteen was pretending to be a mouse. How he longed to play with someone! But he stayed in his corner. He was a mouse, after all. He finished off the last of his cheese and nervously patted his ear, as if by doing that, he could push it down and make it less noticeable – not that anyone could see him behind the veil of water.

What *he* noticed, however, when he peeked out of his hiding place, was that, in front of what used to be one of the exits and was now the ghost image of a walled-up door, Mug, Orlick and the Rat were tossing something back and forth and laughing loudly. It looked like a small brown ball, about the size of Baby Tizer, which is to say, about the size of a hedgehog, or, if you will, a small cabbage. Number Thirteen wondered how they had acquired this ball – from some kind benefactor? Did such kind benefactors exist? Or had some child beyond the Wall accidentally kicked it into the yard?

Strange, he thought. *I've heard of kickballs but never fuzzy ones, but then, there are many things I've never heard of.* He remembered something about cats, though, how they spat up a terrible mess called a hairball, and he pondered what sort of cat could be so large as to spit up a hairball bigger than its own head. Then he pondered why he had never seen a cat groundling before and came to the conclusion that maybe there were very few of them around. For wasn't he the one and only fox groundling at Miss Carbunkle's Home?

The laughter in Mug's group began to grow louder.

The Rat nodded to Mug, who kept tossing the ball higher and higher. Every time he tossed the ball up, it squeaked. *It must be a squeaky ball,* thought Number Thirteen. *I'm sure they must make all kinds on the Outside.*

"Toss it here!" cried Orlick, glancing at the Rat for

49

approval. The ball flew back and forth and back again, and each time it did, the groundlings looked up at the Rat, their newly appointed leader.

Whenever the ball flew into the air and someone caught it, Number Thirteen heard the sound. He decided it was more of a peep than a squeak. *Yes, definitely a peep.*

The game went on for several minutes until the Rat stepped into the centre of the circle. He made a swift gesture with his hand, as if he were about to conduct an orchestra. The group abruptly stopped, each groundling frozen in place. They looked up at him expectantly. There was something elegant – and chilling – in the way he moved his grey bristly hands when he spoke.

"Which one of you lot thinks he can toss her over the Wall, hmmm? Who wants to try? A prize to the first to do it. A very large piece of – wait for it, my friends – *fresh cheese.*"

The group cheered wildly.

"Let me try!"

"No, me!"

"Me!"

"I was first!"

Everyone wanted to have a go at it, but Mug pulled rank. "Back off, you clodpoles! I found her. She's mine."

The Rat concurred.

In a flash, Number Thirteen understood – the little fuzz ball was not a ball at all, or the hairball from a giant cat with indigestion. It was some poor creature, rolled into itself like a terrified hedgehog. But it wasn't a hedgehog – he could see that now. It was something, or rather *someone,* else. Someone with a tin number around her neck, just like him.

Number Thirteen poked his head out and scanned the yard for help. Sneezeweed was nowhere to be found, and no other groundlings seemed to be paying attention. For once, Number Thirteen wished Miss Carbunkle were there, for she would certainly put a stop to their cruel game, if only to restore order.

He placed one foot forward, through the gap in the waterfall, but quickly drew it back. What could someone like him do, anyway?

Orlick passed the balled-up creature to Mug, who held her high in the air, ready to toss or kick her or who knows what.

Number Thirteen watched in horror as Mug threw the poor thing as high as he could. But Mug failed to throw her over the Wall and so caught her once again in his grubby mitts. The Rat ordered him to pass the furry ball to Orlick, who was next in line. Mug growled at Orlick, who grabbed the creature and lifted her up for the big toss.

"St–st—" Number Thirteen stammered. "S–stop!" But no one heard him through the waterfall, the peals of laughter, and the rain.

Orlick threw the creature up in the air, but he couldn't throw her high enough either.

Finally, Number Thirteen stuck his head out in full view and shouted at the top of his lungs: "S–STOP! Let her g–go!"

He had never screamed before.

Screaming felt good.

The Rat turned around and held a hand up in the air. The laughter immediately stopped. *Uh-oh,* thought Number Thirteen. He quickly slipped back into his hiding place.

"Who speaks?" sneered the Rat. "Who dares to challenge *the Wire*?"

Number Thirteen quivered in the shadows. Now, of all things, he had to pee too. "Please don't find me, please don't find me, please don't find me," he muttered to himself.

"Speak up," said Wire, and added nonchalantly, "or I shall eat you." His face was as unreadable and hard as stone.

Number Thirteen's heart pounded in his chest. Could this creature be related to the rats he had overheard behind the walls? The ones who ate their own friends? He shuddered. Then he thought of the poor little creature. If they threw her over the Wall, it would break all the bones in her body. *You can do it. Come on.* He took a deep breath, stepped sideways through the gap and pulled himself up as tall as he could. He walked forward a few steps and said, "You p–put her d–down! Right now!"

"Well, well, if it isn't Number Thirteen." Wire came closer. "The little twit *can* talk! What *do* they call you around here, anyway – Plonker, is it? What's your real name, whelp?

Or did your mummy and daddy just number all their freaky little runts before they left you to die by the side of the road?"

The group burst into hysterics.

Number Thirteen said nothing. What could he say? That his name really *was* just a number – the unluckiest one of all? And that he had never known his parents, and maybe they did just number him and leave him behind?

Wire sighed. "I'm getting *so* bored. Let's finish this." He snapped his fingers and nodded to Orlick, who was still holding the trembling rolled-up creature. "If you want something done right, you have to do it yourself. Let's give her a little kick, shall we?"

Orlick threw the creature to Wire, who caught her in mid-air.

"St–stop!" cried Number Thirteen. "Or I–I'll... I'll..."

"Or you'll what?" Wire's pebble eyes gleamed. "Go on. We want to hear what you have to say. Really, we do."

"J–just ... just let her go! You're hurting her."

"We have ourselves a hero!" The Rat turned to the others. "I think we should give him a hand, don't you?" The groundlings clapped slowly in unison, thumping their feet and tails on the muddy ground. They began to walk toward him, and Number Thirteen stepped back.

"P–please let her go," he begged. "P–p–please."

"What a polite little whelp!" Wire smiled coolly. "Did

your mummy teach you that?" He made a *tsk*ing sound and rolled his eyes. "Oh, I forgot! She left you in the street. Well, I'm sorry to say I have other plans for this—" he examined the small animal in his hands "—this disgusting hairball of a thing." He placed his long leg back and readied himself for a big kick.

"Kick it! Kick it! Kick it!" the group chanted.

Suddenly, Number Thirteen heard the most beautiful sound in the world: the Home's loud clanking bell, telling the groundlings they had only a few minutes left and they had better start queuing up. Mr Sneezeweed was back in the courtyard and was now peering in their direction, motioning them to hurry.

Wire looked with disgust at the poor fuzz ball and dropped her on the ground. She landed with a soft plop in the mud. He turned to Number Thirteen. "I have a new name for you, Plonker! We're going to call you Puddlehead. Because that's just where you belong."

Wire nodded to his two minions, and Mug and Orlick shoved Number Thirteen facedown into a mud puddle.

"By the way," said Wire. "I've got my eye on you, Puddlehead. Everywhere you go, I'll be there. Got that, mate?"

He turned and walked back across the courtyard, Mug and Orlick trailing after him like sheep.

CHAPTER 6

Arthur and Trinket

NUMBER THIRTEEN pulled himself up and patted his ear. *Thank goodness no one had bitten it off – at least not today.*

He carefully lifted the small creature out of the mud. It was impossible to tell where her head was or if she had a tail. She let out a sharp peep, unfurled her body and went limp, belly up. But she was still alive. Number Thirteen could hear her tiny heart racing.

He gently touched her head. She wasn't covered in fur at all but in dark-brown, mud-soaked feathers. She was a bird – a bird with no wings, just two feathery appendages sticking out from her sides, and no tail feathers either. One of her winglets was bleeding, though not too badly, considering how she had been batted about. At the end of each of her mustard-yellow feet were three long toes. Her beak was long, slender and curved.

The bird groundling's eyes fluttered, then opened. She looked up at the one-eared creature, who, in turn, looked down at her. In that fleeting moment, Number Thirteen felt something pass between them, although he wasn't sure what. It was a lovely feeling, however – warm, mysterious and grand. "It's–it's okay now," he whispered. "They're gone."

The bell rang again, signalling that their time was up. "Shall I c–carry you?" asked Number Thirteen. The Bird shook her head no. He placed her back on the ground. One leg seemed a bit wobbly, but otherwise she looked surprisingly fine.

Number Thirteen knelt down beside her. "Are you all right?"

"I'll be fine, really."

"I wish I c–could have done more."

"Oh, no," said the Bird. "You were so brave! My name's Trinket, by the way. What's yours?"

"I d–don't really have a name. P–people just call me Number Th–Thirteen or…" He winced. "I suppose they'll all call me P–Puddlehead now. Did you just arrive? I haven't seen you at roll call."

"Well, it's easy to miss me. I am pretty small."

"Oh, yes, you are; I mean … in a g–good way," said Number Thirteen. "Shouldn't we g–get you to the infirmary?"

"No, don't bother. Nothing a little hop and skip can't cure," said Trinket.

The last bell rang, which meant "Queue up or else!" Most of the orphans, including Wire and his gang, were already at the door. Mr Sneezeweed was waving his paddle, rounding up stragglers.

"We have to go right now!" said Number Thirteen.

"Well, I certainly can't call you Puddlehead or some silly number, now can I? Let's see…" Trinket went on, as if they had all the time in the world.

"We have t–to hurry! We—"

"What did your family call you, then?" interrupted Trinket.

"I–I don't really know. I never knew my family, b–but we can talk about this another time because—"

"I'm so sorry! I lost my family too, about five years ago. This is the third orphanage I've been to since then. Well, never mind. You do need a name that suits you. Let's see. I shall call you … I know! I shall call you Arthur! That's it!" Trinket flapped her winglets up and down, she was so excited. Had they been full-fledged wings, she would have been up in the air.

"B–be careful!"

"It only hurts a little," said Trinket. "Anyway, now you have a name! Do you like it? I think it's perfect! But you have to like it too."

"Arthur? Why Arthur?"

"He was only the greatest and bravest of all the kings!"

"He was?"

"Of course! Don't you know the story?"

"What story?"

"About King Arthur and Guinevere and Merlyn the magician, and Camelot, and Lancelot and the brave Knights of the Round Table, Excalibur, and the Quest for the Holy Grail and – it's, well, it's a long story – many stories, actually. There's not really one way to tell it."

Number Thirteen was completely bewildered. "W–what's a q–quest?"

Mr Sneezeweed was screaming at them from across the courtyard and pointing at the door.

"I better tell you some other time," said Trinket. "But for now, I'm going to call you Arthur!" They started walking toward the door.

"I don't think you should c–call me that, really. I mean, I'm not a k–king and I'm not brave and why don't we just stick with Puddlehead? It's not such a bad name."

"Because you are *no* puddlehead." She went on breathlessly, "You stood up to those hooligans! And so you are a king among men – or rather, among creatures."

Number Thirteen shrugged. "Well, I suppose one name is as good as another."

"One name is *not* as good as another. So it's decided. I shall call you Arthur, and that's that."

Despite the fact that Mr Sneezeweed was now waving his paddle wildly above his head, Trinket stopped in her tracks and hopped in front of Number Thirteen. "If you had a sword and armour, Arthur, I would have taken you for a knight," she said, bowing low.

Number Thirteen, embarrassed but secretly pleased, was also quite exhausted, for he had never had such a long conversation with anyone in his entire life. "W–we'd b–better go!"

And the two bruised and battered creatures – one small and one very much smaller – hobbled back together in the thrumming rain.

CHAPTER 7

The Wig

IT WAS WIDELY RUMOURED among the orphans at Miss Carbunkle's Home for Wayward and Misbegotten Creatures that Miss Carbunkle had no hair. Her foot-and-a-half-high helmet of a wig (nearly as tall as many of the orphans in her charge) was beset with rows of sausage-like curls on either side and was the colour of a freshly plucked clementine (which happened to be Miss Carbunkle's first name, though no one was allowed to say it out loud lest they suffer the consequences). Perhaps the only good thing one could say about her wig was that its colour, as hideous as it was, was a flash of brightness in a dim grey world.

Sometimes, when the mood struck her, she wore a small white hat made of rabbit fur, with a brown-and-black hawk feather poking out from the side. (Needless to say, the rabbit groundlings felt rather nauseated at the sight of it.)

When Miss Carbunkle moved a bit too vigorously at the blackboard, the Wig, that great orange monstrosity, and its companion, the tiny Hat, slid slightly to one side. The orphans were thrilled to no end when it did, and basked in a rare moment of joy, hoping that one glorious day in the future, the Wig would slide off altogether and reveal what they imagined to be lurking underneath: Miss Carbunkle's shiny pink globe.

The orphans sometimes even called Miss Carbunkle "the Wig" behind her back, as if she were that horrendous thing itself. It was her armour going into battle, along with the large brass whistle she wore around her neck, her hawk-headed cane, the telescopic goggles she used for spying on groundlings and her small leather purse full of chalk – *her* chalk and no one else's, as she frequently liked to point out. Heaven forbid any of her charges dared to draw a picture or write something of their own on the board with it instead of their daily calculations or rote copying from *The Essential Manual for the Vocational Training of Errant Groundlings,* the Home's "bible," which Miss Carbunkle had penned herself.

Miss Carbunkle believed that every creature had a purpose. In the case of her bedraggled wards, who relied on her for food, shelter and schooling, she believed that, given their lowly status as groundlings, they should be prepared for a life of suffering and toil. And toiling, without questioning or complaint, was what Miss Carbunkle aimed to teach them.

It was a Wednesday morning near the beginning of February. The headmistress – aka the Wig – stood in front of her giant steel-plated desk, scowling down at her wards. (Her previous desk had been made of wood, but a rebellious groundling had set it on fire the year before.) Her desk now sat bolted to the floor in front of a long narrow blackboard covering most of the wall. Like the rest of the Home, everything in the cold, cavernous room was gunmetal grey. There were several leaks in the ceiling, and, as it was raining yet again, there was a steady *drip drip drip* upon the desks.

The headmistress pounded the floor three times with her cane, signalling the class to sit down, which everyone did, with military precision.

The Wig delighted in military precision.

Arthur sank down in his seat along with the others and obediently folded his red furry hands. Unfortunately, his desk was smack in the centre of the front row, but such was life. His only consolation was the fact that he now had a friend in the room. Trinket was right behind him, perched on someone else's desk, for she was too small to justify having her own.

Although they had only known each other for only a few

weeks, he and Trinket had become fast friends. She told him about her family, how they had perished when she was only five – her parents, six siblings, and grandparents – all of them lost to influenza.

He felt safe and comfortable with her, and really, really happy. If he had known it was both his birthday and Christmas the day he met her, he would have said that Trinket was the best present ever. For one, she had given him a real name, *Arthur*. Then there were the stories. Every day she filled his head with wondrous tales she had learned from her mother.

Just that morning, she had whispered to him at breakfast the story of how, when King Arthur was a boy and had the silly nickname of Wart (at least in one version of the story), the magician Merlyn transformed him into a kind of falcon so he could feel what it was like to be a bird.

"My mother," she had said to him in hushed tones in between dainty sips of gruel, "was quite a respected storyteller among our people."

Arthur thought of this and smiled. But when he looked up and saw the headmistress, his smile quickly faded.

In Miss Carbunkle's version of school, there were no stories at all. No storytelling, no picture drawing, no play-acting, no dancing and most important, *no singing*. Trinket had told Arthur that there were schools that did allow such things – some classrooms even began each day with a song! – but he had a very hard time believing that was true.

At the Home, class always began with announcements. Miss Carbunkle would list any and all new rules and regulations. In fact, she created so many new ones that she was forced to make countless addenda to her sacred *Manual*. After that, she commenced with lessons. She grilled the orphans with the same questions each and every day, and the orphans responded with the same answers each and every day.

She always began thusly: "Why are you here, groundlings?"

Their voices, mechanical and flat, would respond in unison, "To be educated."

"What else, groundlings?"

"To learn a useful trade."

"What else, you wretched whelps?"

"To toil…"

"And what else?"

"…and suffer?"

"And? You lazy miscreants, you ungrateful sow bugs, *what else?*"

At that point, an oppressive silence would spread throughout the room. Some of the little ones, such as Arthur, would tremble in their seats. They felt they were supposed to answer the last question and yet – they knew they weren't supposed to at the same time. It was all so confusing!

Finally, Miss Carbunkle, a cruel smile upon her lips, would say, *"Exactly,* my good-for-nothing imps, my disgusting little bottom-feeders. *Silence. Beautiful, serene silence.* To toil. And suffer. In silence. *That* is the greatest lesson of all."

And so, that Wednesday, Miss Carbunkle discreetly touched the back of her wig, adjusting it ever so slightly, and, as on every other Wednesday for the past thirty years, she opened up her big black notebook and began listing the new rules of the day.

As Arthur sat there, trying not to doze off, his whiskers began to twitch. Something seemed different. He sniffed the air and detected a familiar bouquet: mildew, *Eau de Faucon* (Miss Carbunkle's favourite perfume), and Smelly Orlick's boggy stench in the back row. He could smell Wire too. It was hard to miss Wire. But there was something else, something he couldn't quite discern. He quickly forgot about it, though, and let his mind drift to other things while Miss Carbunkle, the Wig, droned on.

There was only one window in the room, and it was always shut tight. Outside, it was raining, steady and hard, and had been for days on end. Still, he loved the sound of water playing on windows and eaves, on the stone walls and roof, and the *ping ping ping*s from the leaky ceiling above.

That day, he heard four distinct sounds – the *pings*, a low *thwup THWUP, thwup THWUP* from the roof, a higher-pitched *pitta pitta pitta* melody on the gutters, and a gentle *ticka-ta-ticka-ta* beat against the windowpane.

Just like a song, he thought. *I shall tell Trinket.*

Arthur told Trinket things he had never told anyone before – he had shown her his blanket scrap and key, and had told her about the strange memory of the song and the stars. But he still hadn't told her his deepest secret of all, how he could hear things others couldn't, and how it made him feel at once special, awestruck and happy, and sometimes terribly sad, although he didn't know why. He had hinted at it but was a little afraid to tell her, for what if she thought him strange? Or didn't believe him? Especially the bit about understanding the mice and rats. But sometimes he felt like he would explode, with all these feelings bottled up inside his impatient heart.

Miss Carbunkle went on and on about some harsh new rule, the result of several serious infractions that year, as well as the infamous "burning desk incident" from the previous autumn. No one knew what had happened to Nancy, the reptilian rebel who'd done it, for she was never seen again.

Arthur decided that he would tell Trinket his secret later that day, before they went to bed. He thought about how nice it was to look forward to having a real conversation with – dare he say it? – a best friend.

"And let that be a lesson to you all." Miss Carbunkle's piercing voice concluded her speech. "And now we shall commence with lessons."

Everyone sat at attention, except for one.

I shall tell Trinket everything, especially about the birds and their songs. She'll like that. I'll even tell her the unpleasant things. I shall say, Trinket, sometimes I hear rats talking behind the wall and they're really quite scary.

Miss Carbunkle – the Wig – scanned her roster for a random victim to torture. That day, instead of drilling the entire class, she thought it would be fun to surprise someone. Why not the last name on her list?

"Ahem. Number Thirteen?" she said.

Well, rats aren't always scary, Arthur said to himself. *They're funny too; in fact, the other day one of the rats was saying…*

"Number Thirteen," she repeated slowly, gritting her teeth.

Trinket let out a worried peep. But at that moment, Number Thirteen was a bird. An owl, to be precise, like the Wart in Trinket's stories about young King Arthur. Trinket had said the Wart had been an owl, a goose, a fish, an ant and other creatures besides. *How lovely to be so many things!*

The headmistress was leaning over his desk now, but

he was still floating above the clouds, looking down at the Castle of the Forest Sauvage. He conjured a stag in his mind, and a questing beast, and a unicorn racing through the trees.

Miss Carbunkle was in a particularly foul mood that day. An incident had occurred in the middle of the night involving a rodent. A small grey mouse had climbed inside her wig, which she stored on a special shelf in her closet before bedtime. The mouse had had a litter of tiny pink babies, and in the morning when Miss Carbunkle placed the wig on her head, all the wee pinkies came tumbling down her dress.

I shall not tell you how she disposed of them.

Miss Carbunkle shouted Arthur's number again and smacked his desk with her cane. Arthur practically jumped

out of his seat. He thought he saw the hawk eyes on Miss Carbunkle's cane blink, then flicker bright red. He was all ears now – or rather, all ear.

He stammered in a quiet, timid voice, "Y–yes, ma'am?"

"Are you deaf and dumb or just plain stupid?"

He could hear Mug, Orlick and Wire snickering in the back of the room.

"I ... I... No, I'm, I'm not..." His voice trailed off.

"Well then, let's begin, shall we? So *tell me,* Number Thirteen," said Miss Carbunkle in a very loud and deliberate voice, as if he were either very thick or hard of hearing, "why ... are ... you ... here?"

"T–to b–be educated."

"And? What else?"

Trinket made an encouraging little peep from behind. He went on, more boldly. "T–to ... to learn a trade?" he said, gulping air. *Nearly done now, nearly done.*

"And? What else, Mr Thirteen? What else do you have to tell me?"

"To toil?"

"Go on! Go on!"

"To toil ... and..."

"*And,* you miserable little pusball?" Miss Carbunkle gripped the hawk on top of her cane so hard her knuckles turned white. "AND?"

When Arthur glanced up, he saw a mouse peeking out

from one of the orange curls on the side of Miss Carbunkle's head. *That's* what smelled different before! The mouse stuck its head and upper body out of the curl and began sniffing the top of Miss Carbunkle's ear. It looked like it was going to climb right in. She absentmindedly waved her hand at her ear, as if shooing away a fly.

"If—if you p–please, ma'am … you … you have a…"

"What? I have a *what?*"

"Well, the th–thing is … um … there is a, um, well, it's hard to ex–explain, I m–mean…"

"What in the world are you talking about, Number Thirteen?"

"It—it's your ear," said Arthur. "You see … you have a … well, it's a m–m–m…"

The Wig's voice got very quiet. This was never a good sign. "What did you say?"

"A m–mouse… Your ear … I th–think—"

"Mouse? My ears?" She was almost whispering now. More of a quiet, slow hiss, really. This meant an explosion was imminent and there was nothing anyone could do about it. "Did you say I have *mouse ears*? Answer. Me. NOW."

Everyone braced for the worst and waited to see what would happen.

A tall creature in the back row cleared his throat and raised a grey bristly hand. Miss Carbunkle noticed him out of the corner of her eye. "Yes?" she snarled. "What is it?"

"Beg your pardon, ma'am," said Wire, his voice dripping with false humility. "I feel as if I must say something regarding the fox groundling. A terrible crime has been committed."

"Well, speak up," said Miss Carbunkle, still glaring down at Arthur.

"If you please, ma'am, the one known as Number Thirteen has been making fun of your ears for weeks now. And that's not all he makes fun of."

Miss Carbunkle's face was a storm cloud. She leaned over and screamed right in Arthur's face. "How *dare* you, you stupid one-eared freak! How dare YOU of all creatures insult *my* ears! What impudence! You shall pay for this, you vile little maggot pie!"

"Oh, Arthur," Trinket whispered.

Arthur's ear trembled. He began to shake all over.

With one monstrous hand, which was bigger than Arthur's head, Miss Carbunkle seized his beautiful red fluffy ear, twisted it hard, shook it vigorously, then let go. For a moment, he thought she had pulled it right off, for the pain was excruciating. He put his hands up to stop her, but she wrenched them away and took hold of his ear again, this time twisting it even harder.

"Stop! P–please!" cried Arthur.

"This will teach you to insult your superiors!" she bellowed.

She gave his ear another twist and, still holding on to it, dragged him across his desk and lifted him up in the air. He dangled there, his nose nearly touching hers. The headmistress fixed her eyes on his and said under her breath, "You little monster, you … you … putrid dog's bottom – just wait till I—"

All of a sudden, the frightened little mouse that had been burrowing in the headmistress's curl jumped out of its hiding place and landed right on Miss Carbunkle's substantial bosom. It clung on for dear life.

It looked up at her, blinked and let out a terrified squeak.

Miss Carbunkle – aka the Wig – glanced down at the mouse and screamed.

With one great swing of her powerful arm, she threw Arthur up and away and swatted at the creature on her chest. The mouseling went flying across the room while Arthur catapulted into the Wig's giant desk and toppled to the floor.

The last thing he remembered was a searing, earth-splitting pain and Trinket crying out his name. Then the room faded to darkness.

CHAPTER 8

Bread and Butter

"ARTHUR! ARTHUR! It's me, Trinket."

Arthur awoke to find two sapphire eyes staring into his face. The sun was just coming up. He must have missed roll call! He began to panic. He was going to get a walloping from Miss Carbunkle, he was sure of that. And how was it that Trinket was here?

Here?

Trinket was perched on his chest. "Wh–where am I?" he asked.

"The infirmary." Her voice sounded muffled and strange. "I'm so happy you're awake. I was so worried! I've been here all night." She started bouncing up and down.

"P–please stop jumping about, Trinket. It really makes me dizzy."

"Sorry!"

"You sound all fuzzy, Trinket. What happened?"

"Don't worry! It'll be fine! It was just a little scratch. Well, maybe *scratch* isn't the best word, but … oh, bother! It was awful, just awful!"

Arthur felt a deep, burning ache in his ear, as if someone had poured hot embers inside. He reached up to touch it and felt a thick bandage, which was wrapped all around his ear and the top of his head. "Oh," he said. "I see." Something else felt strange, but a good kind of strange. He realized that he was lying on something soft for the first time in his life – it was a four-poster bed with a real mattress, with covers that were soft and warm. In Kestrel Hall, you were lucky if you found a handful of straw for your hard, splintery bed, which was really an old piggery trough. Arthur slept, like all the others, in an unheated room with only a burlap sack filled with pebbles for a pillow, covered by a thin, scratchy blanket that smelled like coal dust, dirty feet and pee.

But this – this was luxury! He wiggled his red furry toes under the blanket. They had never felt so warm before.

"Isn't it lovely?" said Trinket. She hopped off his chest and sat beside him on the bed.

Arthur glanced about the room. Was he dreaming? He

had heard that the infirmary was a terrible place, so dreadful no one dared to complain if they got sick. His whole life, he had avoided it. But if that were true, where was he now?

To his left was a small table that held a red jar shaped like a rooster. Stuck to the jar was a note that read, *Have a cookie! They're tasty!*

"Trinket, what's a cookie?"

"What's a cookie? Oh, Arthur, you certainly have a lot to learn. I haven't even told you about pies yet."

"Pies," said Arthur. He lifted the lid of the jar and took out a cookie. He sniffed it first, then tentatively took a bite.

"Lovely!" he exclaimed.

It was just a simple oatmeal cookie with raisins, but Arthur had never had one before, and he was ecstatic. He chewed it slowly so he could savour it until the end. When he finished, he let out a happy sigh and looked around some more.

Across from the table was a window with blue-and-white-flowered curtains. On the windowsill was a vase filled with silk flowers. Everything was colourful, cozy and warm. There was a rocking chair in one corner with a pretty red-and-blue throw on it; in another corner was a bed just like his but unoccupied. The walls were buttercup with cherry trim. Hanging from the rafters were bundles and bundles of herbs. Arthur breathed in. The room smelled mysterious and wonderful.

There was even a picture in the room, hanging on the wall

near his bed. It was a beautiful hand-coloured engraving of two smiling girls, twins, wearing big straw bonnets, standing hand in hand beneath an apple tree. The landscape looked as if it were bathed in golden light. It was the loveliest thing Arthur had ever seen. In all his years at the Home, he had never actually seen a *real* picture – that is, a painting, drawing, or print made by a real artist. He had seen *some* pictures – the little drawings the groundlings managed to make in secret. But this was different. He felt as if he could step right into the frame and say hello to the two girls beneath the tree.

"Arthur?" Trinket needled him gently with her beak.

"Sorry, Trinket. I didn't mean to ignore you."

"How are you feeling?" she asked.

"Would you mind speaking up a bit? And by the way – how in the world d–did you get in here? The d–dormitory's locked at night."

Trinket gave Arthur another poke and said, "Picked the lock with my beak. Well, not by myself, of course. Some others – Baby Tizer, Nigel, Nesbit and Snook, you know, the *nice* ones – piled one on top of the other so I could reach it." Arthur imagined what this must have looked like and laughed. "I'll tell you everything later," continued Trinket. "I better get to roll call or you know what will happen."

Just then, a lovely young woman dressed in a blue-and-white nurse's apron and cap appeared in the doorway. A long ginger braid tied with a periwinkle bow fell down her back. Arthur looked up at her. Her face seemed to radiate kindness. "How's my little patient?" she said, speaking loud enough for Arthur to hear her through his bandage. "Oh, I'm sorry. I'm your nurse, Linette. And I still don't know your name."

She glanced down at her clipboard. "There was only a number on the note I received from my aunt. I mean Miss Carbunkle." Trinket and Arthur exchanged looks. "It says Number Thirteen," she continued. "But that can't possibly be right."

Before Arthur could respond, Trinket jumped up and said, "His name is Arthur, and, and I'm Trinket, and I'm just visiting my friend whose name is Arthur, and, oh, I already said that. Yes, well, there you have it!"

"Thank you. Glad we cleared that up. By the way – I'm not sure how you got in here last night, Trinket ... but I won't tell a soul." She smiled at them both and placed a soft, cool hand on Arthur's forehead to check for fever. "You have a very devoted friend, Arthur."

Linette gently undid his bandage and examined his ear. She put a clean dressing on, this time leaving a small opening so he could hear better. After she finished, she said, "You'll be back to – well, to everything – in no time at all. So worry not."

"Ex–excuse me ... the p–picture..."

Why did he always have to stutter whenever he met someone new? Arthur pointed to the print of the girls beneath the tree. He couldn't imagine Miss Carbunkle approving of any pictures at the Home, let alone blue flowered curtains, yellow walls and silk flowers.

"Oh, that!" Linette laughed. "Well, you see, this is all new." She made a sweeping gesture with her hand. "The old infirmary was – let's just say it wasn't that nice of a place. And I heard the old nurse was a tyrant. But now I'm here, and besides, Miss Carbunkle never comes in. I don't think she ever will. Not too fond of infirmaries, my aunt. Anyway, one must have at least a drop of beauty or one would perish, right?"

"Sh–she, I mean, Miss C–Carbunkle – she's your *aunt*?" asked Arthur.

"Yes, she's my mother's sister." Linette pointed to the engraving. "That's her on the left, my mother on the right." She shook her head. "It's quite sad, really. Haven't spoken in thirty years, those two. I'm surprised she even hired me; she hates my mother so much. My mother says Miss Carbunkle has some ulterior motive for hiring me, but I like to think it's a sign of goodwill and reconciliation. At least I hope so," she said wistfully, fluffing up Arthur's softest-thing-in-the-world pillow.

"Ex … cuse me, b–but … but she looks so—"

"Happy? I know. Not quite the person she is today."

"How d–did she grow up to be so…?" Arthur looked down in embarrassment. "S–sorry."

Trinket piped up. "Yes, please tell us!"

Linette sat down on the edge of the bed and put her hand on Arthur's. "What you must remember, little ones, is that even the biggest person was, at one time, very, very small. It helps to remember that when dealing with the Miss Carbunkles of the world. You'll understand someday." She leaned over and gently touched Arthur's soft, furry cheek. "Now, enough of this sad talk! You both must be ravenous!"

Arthur was confused – confused about what Nurse Linette had revealed about Miss Carbunkle, confused about her kindness toward him. No human had ever been kind to him before. He was even more flabbergasted when she left the room and returned a few minutes later with two plates – one large, one bird-size – stacked with pieces of freshly baked bread smothered in butter.

"Breakfast!" she announced, then added, "And Trinket – don't worry about roll call or the rest of today, for that matter. I'll make up an excuse for you. Arthur could use a little company this morning, and I could use the help."

Arthur had never had butter before, nor bread as fresh as this. When he bit into the soft, buttery bread and felt the salty, comforting goodness warm his body from head to toe, he wanted to stay in that room for ever – bandaged and bedridden – just so he could eat butter every day and stare at Nurse Linette's kind, beautiful face. In one bite of bread, all the misery that bore down upon him had melted away.

"I really must get injured more often," he said to Trinket after Linette left.

"Well," she said, tickling her friend's armpit with her beak, "I might have an even better idea than that!"

CHAPTER 9

A Curious Proposition

ARTHUR RESTED in the infirmary for one delicious week. No widgets, lessons, work, paddles, bullies, or hawk-headed canes. Trinket broke out of the dormitory every night to tell him stories before he went to bed. On his last night there, Trinket gave him a present she had made in the wee hours of the night after he fell asleep. It was a toy mouse she had assembled with odds and ends she had found or bartered for over many weeks and had hidden in her bed. The mouse was a clockwork wonder on wheels – it rolled around and made a squeaking sound whenever he pulled its string. "I thought you might like it," she said. "I know how fond you are of mice."

He named the toy mouse Merlyn, in honour of the magician Trinket had told him about. And Linette tended to his ear so well that week that by the time he left, it was almost completely healed. He was sad to leave the bright, cozy infirmary with its soft bed and tasty bread and soup, its curious picture of the two little girls, and, of course, his kind and gentle nurse.

Life at the Home trudged drearily along as usual except for one thing – Arthur now had someone with whom to share his thoughts. Trinket had opened up a whole new world for him with her stories about brave princesses and knights, and firebirds, flying horses, mermaids, witches, fairies and even clever magical foxes that apparently looked a lot like him. He also had learned much about the amazing things that people Outside experienced in their everyday lives. The ones that most intrigued him were ice cream, carousels, cheese toasties, music halls and pie.

"Pies are the best of all," Trinket confirmed. "They are buttery, sweet, and filled with every kind of delicious thing imaginable. But it's not the sort of thing one can actually describe. You just have to taste it."

They spoke as much as possible, despite Miss Carbunkle's Golden Rule of Silence. And one night, finally, the Fox orphan opened his heart to his friend and told her about his peculiar gift. It was ridiculously easy. He spoke in hurried whispers, and she listened attentively, her small head cocked to one side. He also told her about how he could understand the mice and rats now too.

"Can *you* understand them?" he asked.

She shook her head. "No, Arthur. This is something special – something really, really big. I'm sure it has to do with your destiny." Then, in true Trinket fashion, she began hopping up and down.

"One of these days," said Arthur, "you'll get so excited you'll jump up through the ceiling. Or fall down. Or something, I don't know what. But it could be dangerous."

Trinket laughed. And then she pointed out to him that whenever he spoke to her, he barely stuttered at all. In fact, he stammered less and less, and spoke a little louder to everyone with each passing week. Everyone except, of course, Miss Carbunkle, Sneezeweed and Wire.

One fine Sunday evening in April, a gentle breeze caressed the surrounding hills and fields. In the mysterious world Outside the Wall, the days were growing brighter and warm. That night, the air Outside was thick with the musky scent of deer and the rich, damp earth of spring. But inside the Home, Arthur could smell only mildewy walls and unwashed feet. Inside the Wall, it still felt like winter. The temperature had dropped below freezing, a phenomenon no one understood but everyone accepted as a fact of life.

Still, there were sounds. Wondrous sounds.

From his bed, he listened to the birch tree humming in the wind and the croaking of frogs. He heard the calls of owls and bats and other creatures of the night, drunk with spring. He could hear it in their voices, their nocturnal hunting songs, their songs of adventure, exaltation and love.

In Kestrel Hall, the groundlings went off to sleep that night, as they always did, in their cold, hard beds arranged in tidy rows. Trinket's bed – a simple rough-hewn box, for she was too small for a real bed – was on the floor across from Arthur's. He wished it were even closer. He believed she had helped his nightmares go away.

Until Trinket arrived, Arthur's nights had been filled with loneliness and dread. He'd wake up from nightmares sweating and shaking all over. The dreams were dark, feverish things, full of crashing sounds, clouds of smoke and ash, with animals circling around him, then running away, howling. The details changed from time to time, but one image always remained: an enormous pillar of blazing-red light moving toward him like a faceless monster born of fire.

Tonight, in the darkness, Arthur could hear poor Baby Tizer crying. Before Trinket came, how many nights had Arthur tried to push back his own tears? He'd clutch his baby-blanket scrap and stare up at the one thing that brought him solace in that bare, frigid room – a small round window across from his bed, near the top of the wall. It was always kept shut, but at least through it he could see a patch of sky.

That night, he could see a brilliant scattering of stars and a silver moon with the figure of a rabbit etched on it. He held his small blue bundle tight against his chest, his other hand wrapped around Merlyn, his beloved clockwork mouse. Then he fell asleep, shivering beneath his thin, scratchy blanket but comforted by moonlight and the knowledge that his friend was fast asleep in the very same room.

Arthur awoke in the middle of the night to someone poking him in the side. "Trinket? Is that you?"

Trinket jumped up from the bed onto Arthur's chest. "Arthur! You're not going to believe this!"

"Believe what?" He rubbed his eyes and squinted at one of the clocks in the room. "Trinket, it's two a.m."

"What luck! What luck!"

"Shhh!" said Arthur. "Talk softer!"

The moon shone down upon Trinket as she waved her winglets up and down wildly. "Hooray for me! Hooray for us! Just wait till you hear what I found!"

"Hush! Do you want us to get c–caught?"

Outside the room, there was the sound of footsteps, and then a flicker of candlelight beneath the door. Arthur held his breath. The footsteps echoed back down the hall.

"That was close!" he said. He rubbed his ear anxiously. Talking was forbidden after lights-out, punishable by cane, paddle, or a week without food. Wire and the older groundlings slept in the room next door, but still, that didn't mean there weren't spies among the little ones.

Arthur tried to sit up, but Trinket was still standing on his chest. He could feel her long sharp toenails through his thin blanket. He let out a frustrated grunt. Arthur was feeling quite cranky. He had been dreaming a wonderful dream about the infirmary and a giant piece of bread and butter.

"Tell me what in the world you're talking about, but you have to whisper, okay?" he said.

"All right already," said Trinket. "Just listen. The big news is..." Trinket couldn't contain herself and began hopping up and down again. "I found a hole! A hole, Arthur! Can you believe it? Right in the Wall!"

Arthur tried again to sit up, but Trinket was jumping

so much he fell back against his hard pillow. "T–Trinket, you really have to stop hopping about." Trinket jumped off his chest and plopped down by his side. "There we go," he said. "Now, t–tell me, why are you so excited about a hole?"

"It's a tunnel, really, and it leads to something absolutely brilliant. Guess what it leads to!"

His face lit up. "Does it lead to … to pies?"

"*Pies?*" Trinket shook her head. "No, Arthur. Not to pies! This is better than pies."

Arthur's eyes grew wide. "Better than pies? Where does it lead to, then?"

"To the most splendid place of all, Arthur. A magical, marvellous place, beyond your wildest dreams."

He thought for a moment, then said, "The infirmary?"

"No, Arthur! *Not* the infirmary!"

She stretched up as tall as she could and whispered in his ear, "To the *Outside.*"

Arthur was stunned. Except for the top of the birch tree and the sky, he had never seen the Outside, or rather he couldn't recall what it looked like, for he had been at Miss Carbunkle's Home for all of his remembered life. There must have been a time when he *had* seen the Outside. He tried to remember *something* about it, but nothing came to mind.

Trinket explained how she had found the hole during break time. It was behind a pile of rubble a few feet to the right of where the old door used to be before Miss Carbunkle sealed it up. She hadn't realized until now that it led to a tunnel under the Wall. "Arthur," she said, "when no one was looking, I crawled down there and peeked out. I had forgotten how beautiful the world is!"

They heard footsteps again in the hall. Whoever it was stopped right outside their door. Arthur tossed his blanket over Trinket, closed his eyes and pretended to sleep.

The door creaked open, and a shadowy figure holding a candle stood for a moment, surveyed the room, then retreated, shutting the door behind him. The figure made a honking sound, sneezed, and crept back down the hall. Arthur let out a long breath. "That was close," he whispered. Then, more urgently, "Go on."

Trinket's words came spilling out. "Everything's so green, Arthur! Golden green, not like that disgusting pea soup we're forced to eat. And remember the flowers in the infirmary?"

"Of c–course," he said.

"Imagine fields and fields of real ones, as far as you can see."

"That's imp–possible. How is that possible?"

Trinket continued in a whisper. "Just on the other side of the Wall, there's a road that leads to Lumentown. I've heard that the towers and streets there are made of some kind of magical stone. And in the market, they have mountains of cheese and pies – two storeys high! And there are toy shops everywhere, and jugglers and magicians, and flying machines, and music halls just like I told you about, and ... and there's a river with big wooden boats with bright-coloured sails, and the river goes all the way to the sea. To the sea, Arthur! Just think of it!"

Arthur felt terribly unsettled. Trinket wouldn't lie to him – then again, this sounded like one of her made-up stories. But if it wasn't...

He listened to the steady breath of orphans sleeping in their tidy rows and the persistent *tick-tick*ing of the clocks. He heard a small creature two beds down cry out "Mama" in his sleep. *This is what is real,* he thought – all of them, together in this room, in this cold, unhappy place. And tomorrow morning was real. Miss Carbunkle screaming out his last-on-the-list unlucky name. Mr Sneezeweed swinging his paddle was real, and Wire, Mug, or Orlick, it didn't matter which, tripping him on his way to breakfast, one of them putting something slimy down his trousers. *Real* was scrubbing toilets and washing laundry in cold grey water by hand, and making beetle widgets for the rest of his life. At least in the Home he knew what to expect from one minute to the next, one day to the next, one week, one year.

And yet ... hadn't he himself heard the birds singing and building their nests? Hadn't he heard the sound of bees sipping nectar and summer breezes and the music of trees? Trees from far away? Hadn't he wondered what that world was like, just out of reach?

Trinket went on for a few more minutes, telling him other wondrous things she had heard about this completely fantastical place. When she was finished, she let out a huge sigh. "There! I said it! All of it!"

"Well done, Trinket. Well done."

"There's something else too," she said.

"What's that?"

"I think I still have family out there. In fact, I'm sure I do."

"What?"

"I have an uncle, a tinkerer. My mother's brother. He lives west of Lumentown, near the sea. At least he used to. It's where my people come from. Shouldn't I try to find him?"

Arthur thought about this. What if *he* still had family out there, out in the wide world of cities and mountains and faraway towns and fields? What if there was something amazing beyond the impassable Wall and gate – a road that led to where he came from? To who he really was and where he was going – the road to his destiny?

Did he even have a destiny?

Fear seized his heart. This kind of thinking would get him nowhere. It was dangerous, even – for to dream was to hope. And to hope was just as useless as the beetle widgets he and the others made every day. He shook his head.

"Oh, Trinket" was all he could say.

Trinket hopped up close to his ear. "Arthur," she whispered. "Shall we?"

"Sh–shall we what?"

"Go!"

"G–go where?"

"To the Outside, of course!"

"You mean … me too? How c–can we?"

"The hole, Arthur! Think of the hole I found as a *door*. Doors are for entering and leaving. And we definitely need to *leave*." She paused, then added, "And never come back."

Arthur watched the moon disappear behind a cloud. In the distance, he could hear the *whoosh* of wind through the trees, the invisible trees he couldn't and might never see from his small dark corner of the world. Soon it would be the cold grey damp of morning. He thought of the courtyard outside Kestrel Hall, with its stone gargoyles weeping in the rain. He tried to imagine not a hole behind a pile of rubble but a real door in the Wall, one that opened to some magical place. But all he could see in his mind was a great stone fortress with a bolted, impenetrable door. And unbounded darkness beyond.

After a long pause, he spoke. "It's late. We should go to sleep. The Outside sounds brilliant, really it does. And I know you'll make a wonderful tinkerer. But as for me … g–going—" he could barely get the word out—"p–please don't ask me again. I'm sorry, but I just c–can't."

"But Arthur … why?"

He looked down at Trinket and, full of sadness and regret, said, "I don't *want* to go. Why reach for the st–stars when… Well, you know the rest."

"I'm not so sure about that, Arthur," said Trinket, her voice a complicated mix of disappointment, frustration, anger and love.

"Why? What do you mean?"

"Because last night I heard you singing in your sleep."

CHAPTER 10

A Change of Heart

WAS THIS TRUE? Did he really sing in his sleep? Did he, unknowingly, commit such a forbidden act, an act so heinous to Miss Carbunkle that it could earn him a month in the rat dungeon? And if so, what in the world did he sing? For there was only one song he really knew, and he couldn't remember the words to it at all – at least not when he was awake.

But none of that would matter if he ever got caught. Any kind of music was strictly forbidden. So at night, before he went to sleep, he tried to will himself not to sing. But each morning that April, Trinket told him that she had heard him singing away.

And did this revelation make our young hero dream of escape? Did he try to imagine the Great White City? Of course he did. But what could he compare it to? To him, it was just a muddled vision from Trinket's tales. He imagined it like Camelot – a magic castle and town perched atop a hill, surrounded by an enchanted forest of unicorns, nightingales and dragons. A nice fancy, he thought. But nothing to hold on to.

Arthur's refusal to leave caused a slight tear in the fabric of their friendship. Trinket seemed quiet and moody at times, which was completely uncharacteristic of her usual cheerful self. But she refused to give up and began plotting their escape anyway. She worked on her plan night and day, always refining it, shaping it into something magnificent and bold. By the end of the month, she knew exactly what they had to do.

May burst forth in all its glory, and the groundlings, though they couldn't see the Outside, could feel it explode with life. On Sundays during break time, they were lured to the far end of the courtyard by the scent of lilacs floating over the Wall. The poor creatures just stood there, sniffing the air, a euphoric look upon their faces. Some had no idea what the scent was, but the effect on them was powerful. It caused a pang in their hearts, filling them with an insatiable longing – especially Arthur, who could not only smell the lilacs on the other side of the Wall but could also hear bees sipping nectar from the blossoms. He could hear birds singing in trees far from the white birch, and within those trees he heard the rising of sap, heard it rush upward like a stream trickles over rocks and little stones. The air was his library, and it was rich with sound. And when he caught these sounds, or "songs," as he called them to himself, he could hear his blood rise to his heart like sap, and he imagined himself a tree, his arms its branches, full of singing birds.

And still, Trinket could not persuade her friend to leave. At the mere mention of it, he'd look away, clear his throat and say, "I'm sorry, Trinket. I just can't."

One day, they were working side by side at the end of a long conveyor belt in the vast, windowless Widget Room. Against the steel-plated wall behind them was a huge pile of beetle widgets, discarded for not being up to the standards of the foreman, Mr Bonegrubber. The pile looked like a mountain of dead bugs, as if an exterminator had just paid the Home a visit.

Unlike the other rooms at the orphanage, the Widget Room was hot and clammy, and not pleasantly hot either. The groundlings were forced to endure long shifts with scorching steam blasting in their faces, making it difficult to see or hear.

The sign above Trinket and Arthur read WIDGET QUALITY CONTROL. It was their job that day to inspect the beetles that the rest of the line had swiftly assembled before the shiny black bugs travelled into the mouth of the Monster.

The Monster was what the groundlings called the massive steam-powered machine that swallowed thousands of widgets every day. The Monster itself looked like a gigantic plate-metal version of the tiny black bugs it devoured.

This machine, whose gaping mouth the orphans lived in fear of – for what if one of them fell onto the conveyor belt and was sucked into that dark tunnel of doom? – sat in the middle of the room. It was the only room in which one could not hear the clocks, for the sound of the Monster was relentless and excruciatingly loud.

The groundlings worked at breakneck speed to keep up with the Monster as it hissed, screeched, snorted and belched. Every five minutes, it let out a screaming whistle and a blast of steam. When it was full to the hilt with beetles, its mouth clamped shut with an earsplitting bang that made Arthur jump no matter how many times it happened. Then it started to shake as usual. Above its "mouth" were two glass globes that glowed bright red. These "eyes" turned from red to greenish white, and the machine made a horrible crackling sound. Sparks flew from the eyes and a bulbous globe on top of the machine, falling on the groundlings like hot embers.

Even though this happened on a regular basis, it never ceased to frighten most of the groundlings. All of them, including Trinket and Arthur, turned at that moment toward it, like people who can't stop looking at a lightning storm when the safest thing to do is run for cover. But where could the little groundlings go? At that moment, whatever covered their bodies – fur, feathers, or scales – stood up on end as a fierce jolt of electromagnetic energy zapped into the belly of the beast and reverberated throughout the room.

With another loud blast of steam and a blaring whistle, the mouth opened again and from the other end of the Monster (its backside, so to speak) a metallic net appeared. In it were hundreds of beetles, quivering like tiny black fish pulled from the sea. Except for a strange white-green glow emanating from their eyes, the beetles looked exactly the same as before, but now they were electromagnetically charged.

Arthur wondered if they were toys for children in the Great White City. If so, what kind of child would ever want to play with them?

Mr Bonegrubber, or just "Bonegrubber," as the orphans called him, was marching around the room, barking at the groundlings, "Go faster, faster! Put yer backs innit, varmints!" as they frantically assembled beetle after beetle after beetle and pushed them down the line.

He was a squat, bowlegged man with a large lumpy head like a cabbage. In the harsh light of the Widget Room, the top of his head seemed to glow a pale green.

He ate only cabbage soup and peas, and spent so much time indoors – for, as he put it, "The Outside's only for thems that's wild and uncivilized like" – that his face, so long concealed from the sun, had taken on the colour of an old turnip. His demeanour also resembled that of a cruciferous vegetable: bitter and exceptionally gassy.

Every fifteen minutes, Bonegrubber made his rounds, breathing down the necks of the workers, growling at them to speed up. After each round, he retreated to his office to have a few swigs from the large brown bottle he kept in his top desk drawer. After a couple hours of this, his march turned into more of a wobble, and his "Faster, faster" sounded more like "Fashter, fashter."

No one worked faster than Trinket. She was so agile with her beak and feet, and worked so quickly, that sometimes she looked like a small brown blur.

"How do you do that?" whispered Arthur. "You don't even have hands."

"As if hands were so important," she said, and poked his arm. Arthur stifled a laugh.

A bit later, when Bonegrubber was fully "in his cups," Trinket tried to broach the subject of escape once again. The sound in the room was unbearable but was the perfect thing for hatching secret plans with a friend, if only Trinket could persuade that friend to join her.

She was perched on a high stool next to him. Arthur stood leaning against the conveyor belt, working as quickly as he could, but he was tired. They had already been there for three hours and had five more to go. "This way, no one can listen in," she began. "Now, Arthur, hear me out…"

"I know what you're going to say and I don't want to t–talk about it."

She glanced at him and said nothing. They continued working, Arthur picking up beetles to examine them for flaws, then pushing them along the conveyor belt toward the Monster's mouth, Trinket doing the same with her beak.

The warning whistle blew, which meant the Monster was stuffed to the gills again. It had swelled up so much, it looked like the nuts and bolts holding it together were going to pop. The ground beneath them began to shake, and Arthur felt like a wall of sound was surging toward him like a sea loosed from a dam.

He covered his ear with one hand and cupped his other over Trinket's small brown head.

"Thanks," she said, after the shaking had stopped. Then she nudged him with her beak and said, "Arthur, please – you're the best listener in the world, but you won't listen to me. Can't you hear me just this once?"

Arthur stared down at the pile of beetles before him. All of a sudden he felt terrible. She was right. He had made up his own Golden Rule of Silence. He was just as bad as Miss Carbunkle. And so this time, he listened.

They pretended to be concentrating hard on their work while Trinket explained the plan – how Arthur would escape through the hole behind the rubble while she created some kind of diversion. Then she would escape too, but another way altogether. She was rather vague about that part, though.

"It's too dangerous," said Arthur, shaking his head. "I probably won't fit through the hole. Second, you still haven't told me how you'd get out, and third, we'd most certainly get caught."

"I don't think so," said Trinket, puffing up her feathers and hopping a little on her stool. "Not with my plan, we won't."

"But—but what about the Wig's g–goggles? She can see a mile away. Trinket, why can't you just leave things as they are? It's so much nicer now that you're here. And besides, when we come of age, she'll have to let us go."

Bonegrubber emerged from his office, unsteady on his feet. He made his rounds, shouting random insults at the groundlings, then retreated to his office once again.

"Arthur, don't you see?" said Trinket.

"See what?"

She pointed with her beak to a group of older groundlings.

"Grumblers," the others called them – orphans who had been there since birth and were now nearly eighteen. They barely spoke, and when they did, they made a grumbling sound like tired old men.

"They've been here so long, they don't even flinch," said Trinket.

"We won't be here for ever," said Arthur. "Come on."

"You don't understand," said Trinket. "We're never going to leave. And *if* we do, it'll be because *she* sent us somewhere awful. Haven't you noticed that over the last couple months, some of the orphans have gone missing?"

"Yes, but..."

"But what? Explain *that*."

"Well," said Arthur, "they must have been taken in by some family, right? At least I ... I hope so. And anyway – the older ones, well, they probably just ... just went somewhere to, I don't know. To work, I suppose. And ... and when we grow up, we'll go somewhere too – w–won't we?" His voice trailed off. He had never really thought about where they would go after they came of age. "I mean," he continued, "you never see anyone over eighteen, do you? There. That proves it."

"Arthur, that doesn't prove a thing," insisted Trinket. "For all we know, the Wig turns the old Grumblers into slaves or ... or maybe she even kills them!"

"Don't be ridiculous."

"Well, what about the little ones? Five of them disappeared out of the blue last week. They broke some stupid rules and what happened? I'm sure she snatched them and they're locked up for ever somewhere. Rats are probably eating their toes off as we speak. We can't stay. We simply can't."

Arthur stared out across the room. All around him were rows upon rows of groundlings, standing on their tired feet, assembling beetle after beetle, snapping bodies and legs and antennae together. He imagined doing this for the rest of his life. Then he imagined being locked in a cell somewhere with rats making a meal of his feet. A shudder ran through him, from the tip of his ear to his toes. He stopped suddenly, dropping the beetle he had just picked up to inspect.

Because he had halted the flow of production, the widgets in front of him immediately began to pile up. He shoved the mound toward the Monster's mouth without examining them and hoped no one would notice. The whistle and steam blew, and he covered his ear and Trinket's head once again.

He thought about how Trinket was a bird groundling, even though she couldn't fly, and how she should be free, like the birds in the trees over the Wall. He thought about the sound of sap running through the trees. And he thought of something else, which caused a single tear to trickle down his face. It was the song he had heard long ago, from a time before he bore an unlucky number around his neck. The song that still glowed like a diamond in the deep red pocket of his heart.

"Arthur," whispered Trinket. "There's something else you should know. I didn't have a chance to tell you earlier."

"What?"

"17 Tintagel Road."

"What?"

"It's where you were born, Arthur. You were born eleven years ago on December twenty-fifth, at 17 Tintagel Road in Lumentown. I'm so sorry, Arthur, but your birth name wasn't in the file. Your family name wasn't either. Just the address and the date. But at least now you know where and when you were born. So do you want to find the place or not?"

That night, Arthur tossed and turned in his bed. He couldn't stop thinking about the extraordinary thing Trinket had said earlier. She had told him how, with the help of Nesbit and Snook, she had broken into Miss Carbunkle's office the night before. And how she had spent hours searching through Miss Carbunkle's files until she found his birthplace. She felt like it was the only way she could persuade him to go. She had taken a huge risk for him. What if she had gotten caught? Miss Carbunkle had been sleeping right above her. He shuddered to think about what could have happened.

As he lay there thinking about all of this, he heard a strange conversation starting up behind the wall. He could hear two congenial rats, different than the ones in the dining hall. He listened intently as they spoke:

RAT ONE: Hullo, mate! What brings you to this neck a the woods? Movin' up in the world, ain't we? Nothin' like improvin' oneself, I always say.

RAT TWO: Right you are – that's the ticket. Movin' up. Rubbin' noses with the hoity-toities, I am!

The two rats broke into unbridled squeals of laughter.

RAT TWO: Me an' the wife an' little 'uns couldn't bear it no more down in that cellar with all the goin's on, the knockin' and the bangin' about. Up to somethin', that one is.

RAT ONE: The big 'un with the nesty whatsit on her head?

RAT TWO: The very same. Buildin' more a them big monsters, she is. The wife and wee bairns can't sleep, you see. Thems like t'other 'un but three times big as can be. They say there's more a-comin' too! Buildin' a regular ol' factory, she is.

RAT ONE: Well, I never! Ain't the world changin' fast? You just pay it no mind, you hear me? That's human business, that is, not ours. Now then, when you get all settled like, you stop by an' the wife'll fix you up a nice plate, she will. Door's always open for ye. Don't even have to knock.

Arthur sat staring into darkness, holding his toy mouse and blue bundle for comfort. It was a cold, moonless night. He thought over and over about the rat's ominous words: *Buildin' more a them big monsters, she is... They say there's more a-comin' too! Buildin' a regular ol' factory...*

Hadn't he heard strange sounds coming from below for a while now? Banging and hammering and all sorts of things being knocked about? But he had brushed them away. He had been so chained to his way of thinking that he hadn't seen what was so clearly before his eyes now. Miss Carbunkle had no plans to free them when they came of age. Why should she? She had plenty of work for them here.

And somewhere out there was 17 Tintagel Road. He whispered it out loud – "Tintagel Road." It sounded like magic.

As quietly as he could, he crept to where Trinket was sleeping and shook her gently. "Wake up!" he whispered. "Trinket – you're right. We have to leave. I know we do. So what do we do next?"

CHAPTER 11

The Great Escape

OUTSIDE THE WALL, May was a hush of doves and morning dew. It was ladybirds in bright air, harebells and foxgloves blooming in the loam. It was lambs playing skip and chase in the meadows beyond the hill. May was the broad blue lift of sky above the coppice and the heath, and above the road to the Great White City of Lumentown.

And May, in all her splendour, was calling two young orphans to take flight.

Trinket had instructed Arthur to prepare a bundle of provisions for their journey. He stuffed what food he could find or barter for inside his scratchy old blanket, along with his only possessions: the blue scrap of cloth, the gold key and Merlyn, his clockwork mouse. He tied the bundle around his waist with a piece of cord and hid it inside his threadbare coat.

That Sunday, at the beginning of break time, Arthur stood in a corner below his favourite gargoyle and waited for Trinket's sign. She had said she'd hide somewhere after roll call, then slip into the courtyard at break. "I can't be seen until the last minute. You'll understand better when it's time. It's a surprise!" She'd give him the signal by creating a distraction, at which point he would sneak behind the pile of rocks and climb inside the hole, which he secretly thought of as the Hole I Definitely Will Get Stuck In. She promised to meet him on the Outside, at the exit to the tunnel.

"Trust me!" she said. "It's going to be brilliant!" Then she hopped up and down for a while, peeping excitedly, saying, "I can't wait, I can't wait!" until Arthur calmed her down by ruffling the feathers on her soft, fluffy head.

In the courtyard, it was business as usual. Miss Carbunkle and Mr Sneezeweed paced back and forth near the entrance to Kestrel Hall, keeping an eye out for troublemakers. Wire and his gang loitered in the centre, giving one another a good shove once in a while out of boredom. And the small, gentle groundlings of the Home played their small, gentle groundling games as far as possible from Wire and the rest.

It was business as usual, that is, until Trinket slipped

by Sneezeweed and the headmistress unnoticed – except, of course, by her friend, who was waiting beneath the shadow of a sad, droopy-eyed gargoyle.

When Arthur saw what his crazy, courageous companion was wearing, he broke into a huge smile. She had told him she had invented a "secret weapon," but her new suit was so extraordinary, so unique, he could scarcely believe his eyes. *I think this might actually work,* he said to himself as he watched Trinket sneak up on the group of bullies in the middle of the yard.

While Mug was boasting to his pals about hiding a dead mouse in some first year's pillow, Trinket jabbed him in the foot with her beak and dashed out of sight.

"What'd you do that for?" said Mug to Orlick, who was standing next to him.

"Do what?" said Orlick.

Trinket poked Mug again, then Orlick, then Mug again, then skittered away to jab the rest of their gang.

"You poked me with a stick, you did!"

"Did not!"

"Did so!"

And so on.

Trinket flitted about, stabbing at this one and that one, until every one of Wire's associates thought another was at fault. Wire stood off to the side and watched with amusement as pandemonium ensued.

The middle of the courtyard exploded in a flurry of tail, tooth and claw. Screeches, howls and wild yelps filled the air as Mug, Orlick and the gang pummelled one another. There was a lot of "You'll pay for this!" and "I'll get you!" and many expletives and insults all around. The little ones, such as Baby Tizer, scampered out of the way. Sneezeweed and Miss Carbunkle rushed forward, bearing paddle and cane.

This had to be Trinket's sign.

Arthur started toward the Wall, trying to appear nonchalant. As he approached the pile of rubble at the base of the Wall, his confidence began to wane. *I hope it's big enough. What if it's not big enough? What if I get stuck? What if there are snakes?* His ear began to shake. His thoughts turned to Miss Carbunkle. *What if I get caught? She'll pour boiling gruel down my ear, then she'll beat me with her cane and toss me in the Monster. Then, if I'm still alive, she'll starve me to death. Not to mention what she'll do to Trinket!*

He glanced back, wondering whether he should give up altogether. But Trinket's plan *was* working. She had created absolute chaos in just a few short minutes. And now she would use her secret weapon. *Calm down,* he told himself. *It's going to be fine.* He could hear Trinket's voice inside his head: *Be brave! Remember your namesake: Arthur, the Once and Future King.*

He looked around to make sure no one was watching, then steadied himself and slipped behind the pile of rocks. There was the hole, exactly as Trinket had described it. It looked just big enough for him to fit. And Trinket was right. There *was* a tunnel below the Wall. Who had tried to escape before him? he wondered. Did they ever make it out?

Meanwhile, in the middle of the yard, Sneezeweed was swatting random groundlings right and left with his paddle.

"This is mutiny!" cried Miss Carbunkle. "Stop, I say! Stop this instant!"

She lifted the big brass whistle from around her neck and blew long and hard. The piercing sound was excruciatingly loud. Mug and the others froze in place, looking battered and dazed, while Wire slunk out of sight.

Miss Carbunkle adjusted her wig, which had slipped a little to the left. "Who started this? Confess or you'll all be punished!"

A small voice piped up from below. "I started it, you big bully! Me, Trinket! That's who!"

Miss Carbunkle looked around to see where the voice was coming from.

"If you please, ma'am," said Sneezeweed, pointing down at Trinket. "It's that stupid little Bird creature. Hangs out with the one-eared mute, that one does. And look – it's covered in…" He bent down to take a closer look. "Well, I don't rightly know." Then he said to Trinket, "What are you playing at, knights in armour?"

"Well, don't just stand there, you idiot! Grab her!" shrieked Miss Carbunkle.

Mr Sneezeweed tried to snatch Trinket up, but she hopped just out of reach. Everyone was staring at Trinket now, including Miss Carbunkle. What they saw was a small wingless Bird covered in a bizarre suit of armour made from a mishmash of metal, leather scraps, clock parts and other odds and ends. On her chest were four buttons – red, green, yellow and blue.

"Try and catch me!" she cried, and hopped backward.

With her long curved beak, she pressed the small blue button. It made a clicking sound, and a soft, rhythmic clanking of gears began. From the top of her armoured head rose what looked like a folded-up umbrella. When Trinket pressed the green button, the umbrella opened up into a propeller.

To the amazement of all, the small flightless Bird lifted – albeit awkwardly – into the air.

Trinket hovered in front of Miss Carbunkle's face for a moment, then began flying in circles above her head. Her propeller whipped up so much air around her that Miss Carbunkle's small white hat with the hawk feather flew right off her head.

Miss Carbunkle's ghostly face flushed scarlet. She began swatting wildly at Trinket with her cane. Sneezeweed tried to hit Trinket as well, but she was too fast.

Trinket circled around and around above their heads,

111

her propeller whirring and buzzing like a giant bee. Then the shouting began.

"Hit her! Hit her! Hit her!" Mug and his gang took up the chant, just like that day when they had tried to toss Trinket over the Wall.

Arthur heard the commotion and peeked around the pile of rocks to make sure his friend was all right. He could see Trinket circling Miss Carbunkle's head. The headmistress was waving her arms around in hysterics, while Mr Sneezeweed was trying unsuccessfully to grab hold of Trinket's feet.

Good old Trinket! She'll be flying over the Wall any minute now. He tucked behind the rocks and was about to climb into the hole when he felt a sharp pair of claws digging into his shoulder, pulling him up and out.

Sewer breath. Rotted meat. Dirty socks.

"Going on holiday?" asked Wire. "My, my, we're a naughty little puddlehead, aren't we?" He dragged Arthur to the middle of the courtyard to where Miss Carbunkle and Mr Sneezeweed were battling the small armoured Bird.

"Excuse me, madam," said Wire. He gently tapped Miss Carbunkle's arm and bowed. "I found the other one. He was trying to escape under the Wall."

Trinket looked down in horror.

"You!" snapped Miss Carbunkle. "I should have known that *you* were behind all this. You always were a sneaky little flea." She turned to Sneezeweed. "Leave the flying vermin to me. You lock this one up *you-know-where*. And make sure he has lots of company, if you know what I mean."

Mr Sneezeweed grabbed the back of Arthur's neck and headed to the door.

Miss Carbunkle scrutinized the bristly grey Rat before her. Their eyes met, and in that moment, an inexplicable understanding passed between them – for like seeks like, even in darkness.

Or perhaps especially in darkness.

"Good work, groundling," said Miss Carbunkle. "I don't have my list with me. Your name is...?" The headmistress was famous for not remembering anyone's name, even the Grumblers who had been there since birth.

"My name is Wire, ma'am," said the Rat, bowing low. "At your service. Perhaps you recall the terrible, shall I say, 'mouse ear' incident? I daresay the fox groundling dishonoured you then as well."

"Unfortunately, I do remember it. Too well, in fact. Well, Wire, you might have just earned yourself a piece of fresh cheese."

"With all due respect, madam, I have no need for cheese. Just knowing I could help is reward enough." The Rat bowed again, then turned to join the crowd of spectators, for by then the entire orphanage had gathered.

As Sneezeweed dragged him toward the door, Arthur could still hear what Wire and the Wig were saying. He felt like throwing up. Since when did Miss Carbunkle offer anyone cheese? And Wire of all creatures! Arthur's imagination began to run wild. He imagined being served on a platter for Wire and a dungeon full of rats. He now believed that what Trinket had said was right – Miss Carbunkle was either keeping the groundlings in the rat dungeon for some sinister purpose or she was doing something even worse. His knees started to shake as he approached his doom.

Then something extraordinary happened.

Trinket landed right on top of Miss Carbunkle's head!

"Sneezeweed!" Miss Carbunkle bellowed.

The crowd of orphans watched from the sidelines, completely enthralled.

Mr Sneezeweed let go of Arthur, dropped his paddle, and ran to help Miss Carbunkle.

Arthur followed on his heels to help Trinket, hoping against hope that he wouldn't get caught again.

"I'll get her!" Sneezeweed cried, and grabbed Miss

Carbunkle's cane. He pressed the two hawk eyes on the handle, and out popped a long pole and net from the other end. He took a few steps back, for the cane was much longer now. "Sneezeweed to the rescue! Now, if you please, ma'am, stay very, very still…" He pushed his glasses up his nose, raised the net over his head, and took aim.

Arthur joined the crowd. He watched as Trinket clung tightly to Miss Carbunkle's wig with her feet and pressed another button on her chest armour. Her propeller began speeding up.

Miss Carbunkle clenched her teeth, and a thin strand of saliva dribbled out of her mouth. "Hurry up, you idiot!" she said, which sounded more like *Urryuhdyouidjit!* Then, more clearly, she hissed, "And be careful with that cane!"

Sneezeweed's shining moment had arrived. His face had a smug look on it, as if to say, *This is just the sort of thing one gets promoted for.*

Wire, who was standing nearby, snickered. Just as Sneezeweed took aim, Wire said under his breath, "Stupid twit," and Sneezeweed faltered.

Trinket flew off Miss Carbunkle's head the moment before the net landed. The only thing for it to catch was Miss Carbunkle's wig. A hush fell upon the crowd. In his shock, Mr Sneezeweed flung the contents of the net into the air.

The wig's departure was swift and sure.

Miss Carbunkle let out a strangled cry. As all eyes turned

skyward, she grasped wildly for her hood, yanked it over her head, and screamed "Get them!" to Sneezeweed as she fled the courtyard.

The wind, growing stronger now, caught the bright-orange wig and carried it up, up, and away. Sneezeweed ran after it, trying, but failing, to catch it in the net.

Apparently, the wig had a mind of its own.

Everyone stood gazing at the sky in disbelief as the wig soared upward. All except for one. Wire smiled as he watched Miss Carbunkle race to the door. He had caught, in a flash, a glimpse of her head before she tossed her hood over it. It was not the pink, gleaming globe that he, like all the others, had imagined. It was a pale pate covered in fuzzy grey and brown feathers, like the soft down of a baby goshawk.

This he filed away for later, and he turned to rejoin his so-called friends.

A slender figure in blue and white, her long ginger braid flying behind her, dashed past Miss Carbunkle to the centre of the yard. Nurse Linette had seen the spectacle from the infirmary window, which looked out upon the courtyard. She slipped something into the right pocket of Arthur's coat, an action unnoticed by all, including him. "Arthur, you must go!" she cried. "Now's your chance!"

Trinket hovered in the air. "Arthur," his friend shouted. "She's right. We've got to go! I can carry you until we get over the Wall. Grab on!"

"*What?*"

"My feet! Grab my feet. Now!"

"No way! I'm too heavy! We'll fall! Go on without me!"

"I'm not going without you," said Trinket. "Now,

jump on! Better to fall and die than stay here the rest of your life!"

Arthur glanced at Sneezeweed, who was still running around, jumping up and down with the net, as if he could somehow will the wig to descend. But the wig looked delighted to be dancing among the clouds. And the groundlings were so delighted about the wig that they began to clap. The clapping got louder and louder as more groundlings joined in. Some, Arthur noticed, even looked happy.

Out of the corner of his eye, he spied Wire, Mug and Orlick heading straight toward him, pushing others in the crowd out of the way. It was now or never.

He stood on his toes, reached up, and grabbed on to his friend's yellow feet.

Trinket, her propeller purring, and Arthur, his heart beating fast, made their ascent and flew high above them all toward the great stone Wall. Trinket was a bit slow and awkward from the weight of her friend, who was hanging on for dear life. But nonetheless, they were triumphantly airborne.

Before they reached the top of the Wall, Trinket and a somewhat terrified Arthur looked down at all the wayward and misbegotten creatures now staring up at them in awe.

"Goodbye! Farewell!" cried Trinket. "Try to find a way out! And don't *ever* forget to reach for the stars!"

A cheer broke out in the courtyard. To Arthur's

amazement, many of the creatures were shouting not just Trinket's name but his as well. "Go, Arthur, go!" they yelled.

They were cheering for *him*.

And they were calling him *Arthur*.

Those who had caps tossed them as high as they could. Amidst their fellow groundlings' wild happy cries, the two friends sailed over the Wall to the great Outside. And in the distance, whipping through the air, was a bright-orange wig, buoyant as a balloon. If you didn't know any better, you might mistake it for a very strange-looking bird.

It hovered for a moment, then flew upward toward the sun.

Part The Second

In Which the Wonderling Learns
Much About the Precarious Life
of Wayfarers, Peddlers,
Slyboots & Thieves

CHAPTER 12

The Secret Pet

 ISS CARBUNKLE RAN STRAIGHT to her chambers and locked herself inside. One by one, she began picking up various objects from her dressing table – each one a model of a failed invention of hers, a machine that was never built – and threw them across the room. She left only one untouched: a miniature version of the beetle widget Monster.

No one had ever tried to escape the Home before, and Miss Carbunkle was not happy about it at all.

I'll get those freaks, she said to herself. *They'll regret being born. And where is that Sneezeweed? The snivelling toad still has my cane!*

Moving quickly, she threw open the closet on her left and surveyed the contents. On one side, from floor to ceiling, rose shelf upon shelf of identical orange wigs, exactly like the one that had sailed over the Wall. On the other side were identical rabbit-fur hats. She chose a new hat and wig and shut the door.

She ignored the closet on the right, the one she hadn't opened in thirty years, and sat down on her bed. She began brushing the wig furiously, muttering under her breath, "Hooligans! Foul vermin! How *dare* they undermine my authority?"

There was a tentative knock at the door. "Madam?" said a thin, nasally voice. "Miss ... Miss Carbunkle?"

Sneezeweed stood outside the headmistress's chambers, sniffling and wringing his hands.

Miss Carbunkle strode to the door but did not open it. "Where did you put them?" she demanded, grinding her teeth. "I hope you put them in the cellar. They need to be taught a lesson! And give me my cane. NOW."

"Yes, ma'am. Right away, ma'am. Here's your cane, safe and sound. Shall I—?"

"Leave it by the door, you dung beetle! Now, tell me what you did with those creatures."

"I, well, ma'am, you see ... the thing is... I—"

"Out with it!" she spat through the door.

"If you please, ma'am..." Sneezeweed cleared his throat.

"I must admit … that I—I failed to catch them. But, if I could only explain—"

"*What?* Failed to catch them? Two stupid little groundlings? Well, what in God's name are you doing here, then? Go out and catch them! Take the carriage. Hurry!"

"But, ma'am… The cook, Bunmuncher, he took the carriage to market, and…"

"Well, take the blooming donkey cart, then! And take my dogs with you. They'll put a fright in those little monsters. We can't have this sort of thing at the Home! We need to show the rest of them that I will not tolerate insubordination of any kind. If we don't nip this in the bud, it will spread like an infection. Now, be gone with you, and don't come back until you've caught them, do you hear me?"

"But Miss Carbunkle, can't we…? I mean, surely we can acquire more groundlings for your needs. We lose two; we procure two more. They're worth nothing. Surely you know that better than anyone. Please, ma'am. I beg you…"

"Get that cart and get going! Or *you'll* end up in the dungeon!"

"B–but … but … my allergies, ma'am! I mean – donkeys! And d–dogs! And … and … *nature*! P–please, can't we—"

There was a peculiar growling sound from inside the bedroom. *What was that?* For a moment, Mr Sneezeweed wondered whether the headmistress had brought one of her mastiffs inside.

"SNEEZEWEED!"

"Yes, Miss Carbunkle?" he said meekly.

"Go and get those renegades! You're wasting my time. And leave my cane outside the door!"

Sneezeweed dropped her cane and ran down the stairs, honking all the way to the stables.

After Miss Carbunkle retrieved her cane, she placed it gently on the floor. She sat on her bed and waited for the one sound she loved even more than silence, the sound of a creature – *her* creature – unfurling itself from inside. It emerged headfirst, like a butterfly, moist and iridescent from its cocoon, twisting and writhing out of its narrow prison. It was an ancient creature with wings like leaves, veiny and forest green, and was the size of a large bobcat. Its face now appeared less like the hawk's on top of the cane and more like that on one of the gargoyles in the courtyard. It was a manticore – part human, part monster. It had a beak-like nose and a small black mouth with two rows of tiny pointed teeth, sharp as knives. The skin on its body, even on its four short feline legs and long serpentine tail that tapered to a point, looked like the bark of a tree, full of knots and burls and twigs sticking out every which way. Along its spine were sharp black tines.

Inside the tip of its tail was a reservoir of deadly poison.

When it was completely free, it shook itself off, stretched, and looked up at Miss Carbunkle with adoration, its eyes glistening. "Mistress!" it whispered in a soft, crackly voice.

It stepped over the discarded hollow cane and jumped up onto Miss Carbunkle's lap. The creature made a soft sound between a purr and a growl.

"Mardox!" said Miss Carbunkle with a sigh of relief. She stroked the creature's wings and scratched him behind his large rubbery ears. "I was terribly worried."

"There, there, Mistress," purred the manticore. "I'm here now. Why don't you tell Mardox all about it?"

Later, as evening fell, Linette knocked on Miss Carbunkle's door. "Aunt Clementine?" she called softly. "Are you all right? I brought your dinner. Hello?" But Miss Carbunkle did not answer. All Linette could hear through the door was her aunt muttering strange things. "Poor woman," said Linette. "Talking to herself again. She really needs to go on holiday."

She placed a tray of food outside Miss Carbunkle's room and went back downstairs.

Finally, when the great cuckoo clock in the Grand Hall chimed midnight and its beak gobbled up the last mechanical bird of the day, Miss Carbunkle patted her new wig lovingly, as one would pat the hand of a dear friend, and placed it on its special shelf in the closet, next to the others. She then bid good night to the creature burrowed under the covers by her feet and promptly went to sleep.

In the morning, the creature known as Mardox was back inside Miss Carbunkle's cane, its amber eyes dull and lifeless. And so, with a new orange wig atop her head, sausage curls and all, and a new white hat with a hawk feather proudly sticking out from the side, Miss Carbunkle began her day as usual – with one exception. She left instructions for Mr Sneezeweed (who still had not come back from his mission). Upon his return, he was to lock up "the two miscreants" in the cellar, then bring "that rat groundling – the one that smells like a water closet" to her chambers, for she had "a business proposition to discuss."

CHAPTER 13

On the Run

THE FIRST THING that struck Arthur about the Outside was the improbable light of spring. He had grown up in such a dim grey place that this other world seemed bathed in gold. The land actually shimmered, and the warmth of the sun, which he had barely felt in his short life thus far, surged through his body and gave him strength.

The second thing he noticed was the horizon. He had never seen one before, and at first glance, it was frightening. Everything in the distance – sheep on the hills, men and women in the fields – looked like tiny ants. The world seemed so incredibly vast that he had to close his eyes from time to time in order to adjust to its size.

Trinket flew and Arthur ran. They followed a road that cut through a lush valley dotted with small groves of trees to the top of a hill, where it met the main road northward to the Great White City. At least that's where they hoped it led. For they had no map, and Trinket had been brought to the Home from far away. Their scant knowledge of the local terrain and their intended route was based solely on the hearsay of groundlings at the Home.

They had been on the run for over an hour, and Arthur needed to rest. He stopped to catch his breath while Trinket hovered nearby. They scanned the road for Miss Carbunkle or someone else from the Home, but they couldn't see a soul.

Arthur was perplexed. Surely she would have sent someone to track them down. Sneezeweed or Bonegrubber. *Why hadn't she?* Was she watching them now from her tower? Then again – how important could he and Trinket really be? She could replace them with two other slaves in a heartbeat.

Arthur could see the stone fortress of the orphanage in the valley below and felt a pang in his chest. From a distance, his former home, which held so many bad memories, now looked like a sad, crumbling place, abandoned centuries ago. But it wasn't abandoned; the others were still trapped inside. And he couldn't do a thing about it.

Above him, Trinket's propeller hummed loudly like a swarm of angry bees. Arthur called out to her. "I think you should come down. Someone could hear you. And I can't hear as well either."

"How could I be so stupid!" said Trinket immediately. "And we should stay off the road. I'm not sure that groundlings are allowed to travel. I was too young to know all the rules back then."

"You're right," said Arthur. "We don't know anything."

"We'll stick to hedgerows and ditches once we get to the bottom of the hill. Coming down now."

Trinket pressed the yellow button on her chest with her beak. Her propeller spun slower and slower until she puttered clumsily to the ground. She landed on top of a gorse bush. "Ouch!" she squawked. Arthur helped her to her feet. "I'll keep my suit on for now, Arthur, just in case. You ready?"

"Just a minute," he said.

Arthur tied his blanket to the end of a good strong stick, making a bindle. Next, he grasped the tag stamped with the number 13 around his neck and tugged at it. But try as he might, he couldn't break it off the cord, so he pulled the whole thing over his head. He looked down at the small disk in his red furry hand. The number was nearly worn off. Who would he have become, he wondered, had he remained Number Thirteen and not escaped? "I have a real name," he said under his breath. "My name is Arthur."

He brushed away a tear and threw the medallion as far as he could over the hill. It landed somewhere in the vast green valley below. *I hope some creature finds a use for it,* he thought. *Maybe a crow will take it to her nest.*

He picked up Trinket and placed her on his shoulder so she could perch there for a while. Arthur was too tired to run, so he walked quickly instead. It was a bit prickly to have Trinket's claws digging into his shoulder, but it wasn't in his nature to complain.

Now that Trinket's propeller had stopped, Arthur could hear birds singing and small creatures running about in the fields and other lovely sounds. He could also hear what sounded like a very large animal crashing through a field.

When they got to the bottom of the hill, he discovered what it was.

"Sneezeweed!" cried Arthur, pointing to the right.

Sneezeweed and his donkey cart were barrelling through a field of tall grass, sending clumps of earth flying. They were less than a quarter of a mile away and gaining ground.

Arthur ran as fast as he could, with Trinket clinging to his shoulder. But Sneezeweed had spotted them and was now out of the field and on the road. He would surely catch up to them soon. Arthur noticed that up ahead, the road cut through a patch of wildflowers, blue and yellow blossoms swaying in the breeze. Seeing them gave him an idea.

"Trinket," said Arthur, "hang on tight!"

Arthur hopped down off the road and ran straight into the flowers.

Sneezeweed, his eyes red and swollen, and his nose dripping uncontrollably, cracked his whip to make the donkey go faster. He had no free hand with which to blow his nose and was already miserable beyond belief. He held the reins with one hand and with the other tossed chunks of steak over his shoulder to Miss Carbunkle's mastiffs inside the cart to keep them quiet. The dogs were tied to hooks, one on each side, and straining to get free.

"All right, you stupid mongrels," he muttered to them, "you'll get your dessert now. Just hold on." With one hand on the reins, Sneezeweed drove the cart into the field of wildflowers, and with the other hand reached over to untie the dogs – not an easy task in a moving donkey cart. As he fumbled with the first dog's rope, he began to feel a colossal sneeze coming on. The cart was deep in the wildflowers now, which was even worse than the tall grass he had just come through. Then, the worst possible thing happened. The donkey kicked a great cloud of pollen up into the air, and Sneezeweed exploded in a convulsion of sneezes.

The dogs, still tied to the cart, strained with all their

might in opposite directions. They began barking like mad and pulling so hard that the sides of the cart started buckling. The donkey kicked and kicked and kicked, while Sneezeweed sneezed on.

That's when he dropped the reins.

In an instant, the flimsy cart fell completely apart, the donkey took off, dragging the harness with it, and Sneezeweed tumbled to the ground. And the dogs, instead of attacking the two escapees, ran off into the field, barking wildly with glee.

Sneezeweed landed in a pile of boards and broken wheels upon a bed of flowers, where he would stay, drifting in and out of consciousness, until the next morning. There he would finally awaken – covered in dog fur, pollen and dung, with a concussion, two sprained wrists, and a broken foot.

"Oh, Arthur, that was brilliant!" cried Trinket.

"Thanks!" Arthur grinned. "We better get out of here before he wakes up, though."

"I don't think he'll be in any condition to chase us now," said Trinket.

They burst into a fit of laughter – loud, wonderful, forbidden laughter – and continued on their way, their hearts lighter than before.

CHAPTER 14

To Wish Upon a Star

AS THE ROAD WIDENED, the two travellers found themselves walking through another valley – and a dazzling array
of colours Arthur had never seen before. Trinket told him
the names of all the flowers they passed, so he would come
to know them too – bluebell, cowslip, celandine, marigold
and lilac.

The air was thick with the perfume of spring. Arthur
caught a whiff of the lilacs and plucked one. He dropped
it into his pocket as a keepsake, on top of what Linette had
placed there that morning: a tiny note wrapped around a gold
coin, a gift he had no idea was there.

It was late in the afternoon when they left the second
valley and entered farm country. Arthur inhaled the milky

breath of baby goats and lambs, the pungent dung of cows, the sweet smell of hay. He wished they could stay there, just lying in the grass, resting, listening, dreaming. There had been no signs of anyone following them since Sneezeweed and the donkey cart debacle. But they knew they had to keep moving, just in case.

Along the way, Arthur saw all manner of wondrous creatures: a pair of hedgehogs scuttling behind a bush; broad-backed horses pulling plows, stomping through the rich, damp earth; a herd of cows behind a fence, chewing cud in sleepy rhythms. Arthur stared in fascination as the cows coiled their thick black tongues like snakes around tufts of grass, their moist black muzzles snorting in the breeze. He wondered if he would ever be able to understand the language of all these creatures, the way he could the little mice and rats.

The music of the land rose and fell around him as he walked – the tinkling of cowbells, shepherds calling "Away to me, away to me" to their dogs, the low bellowing of bulls, and the distant cries of something wild from the forest beyond.

He thought he heard a crow caw in the distance and imagined his medallion tucked nicely in her nest, a shiny gift for her mate. And he thought how lovely it was to have a friend.

"Arthur," said Trinket, who was still perched on his shoulder. "I want to take this thing off. Can you help me?"

Trinket pressed a red button with her beak, and her flying

suit sprang open from a hinged seam running down her back.

Arthur helped her wriggle out of it. "How did you make this thing, anyway?" he said as he placed Trinket's suit inside his bindle.

"It's all in the beak, Arthur. All in the beak."

They looked at each other and started laughing again.

They decided that if Miss Carbunkle was going to send someone else after them, she would have done it already, so they stopped to rest in the shade of a hay bale.

"How *did* you make it, Trinket?" asked Arthur.

Trinket said that after teaching herself how to pick locks, she broke into the Widget Room late at night. There she found some scrap metal and spare parts. "I had help," she said, explaining how the smaller orphans – the rabbity twins, Nesbit and Snook, in particular – had smuggled out leather scraps and odds and ends they found in one of the workrooms. "I hid everything under that mountain of broken beetles," she said. "Bonegrubber only gets rid of that pile every other month or so."

"What would I do without you?" said Arthur.

"I told you, it wasn't just me," said Trinket. "It was Nesbit and Snook, and some of the others helped too. And they all kept my secret. *Our* secret."

Arthur didn't know what to say.

"You've always had friends. You just didn't know it. Now,

come on," she said, nudging Arthur with her beak. "Let's get going."

They started off again, sticking to the hedgerows and ditches.

The endless road lay before them, leading to mountains, cities and the sea. And to their destiny, whatever that might be. They needed to head north to where the main road split in two, which was, to the best of their knowledge, two days' journey by foot. At that point, Trinket would travel west toward the coast to search for her uncle, and Arthur would continue on to Lumentown, at least another two or three days by foot, although neither of them knew for sure. Then they would meet up in the City after Trinket visited with her uncle. At least that was the plan.

The two went on in silence. Arthur's feet were beginning to feel terribly sore, and he was dying for something to eat. "Trinket," he said, cocking his head to the right, where she was perched on his shoulder. "It feels like supper time to me."

"Let's see what time it is," she replied.

"How can we tell time now without clocks?"

"Arthur, there are lots of ways to tell time."

She explained to him about sundials, and then about dandelion clocks, and how one can tell the hour by how many breaths it takes to blow away all the seeds, and flower clocks, which tell you what time it is by what flowers open and close during the day.

And then one thought led to another, as it often does, and without warning, that dreadful place with its hundreds of clocks rose before him in his mind. Arthur thought of all the orphans he and Trinket had left behind. He imagined saving them – turning back and opening the big black gate, the heavy oak door, and letting everyone out. But he knew it was just a fantasy. And he knew, more than anything else, that he might not even be able to save himself from whatever dangers awaited him down the road. He just knew he had to keep on going.

Later, when the sun dipped low in the sky, Arthur could hear men and women calling their dogs and flocks in from the fields, and see farmers heading home for their evening meals, but still he and Trinket walked on. The birds of the day returned to their nests, making room in the sky for night birds and bats. A hush fell upon the land. It was twilight, and time to find shelter.

Arthur heard the sound of water trickling over stones. They followed a path off the main road that led them into a quiet, cool wood with a stream running through it. Arthur made Xs along the way with a stick so they could find their way back.

His mouth was so parched, he could barely speak. He knelt beside the stream and lapped the cool water like the wild thing he was – that is, the part of him that was still truly wild.

The two friends looked around for the perfect tree, carefully stepping over tiny spotted newts, thick mossy roots and mushrooms. It was difficult to avoid squashing some of the mushrooms, and the cool fungi felt soothing to his sore feet.

Finally, they found shelter beneath a large ancient oak. Trinket unwrapped a tiny red handkerchief. "It's all I could find," she said. Inside were a few crumbs of bread and a button-size piece of cheese. Arthur offered up his collection of odds and ends: three small rubbery carrots, two pieces of stale bread, and half a boiled potato from the night before. They greedily tucked into their humble meal, which Arthur feared could be their last for a while.

They nestled among the tree's thick tangled roots and found a soft mossy spot for a bed, which was, not surprisingly, softer than any bed at the Home except the ones in the infirmary. They snuggled close, for the air around them had cooled since the afternoon, and they had only Arthur's thin blanket to share between them.

They lay on their backs, staring up at the stars through a round opening in the canopy above. It reminded Arthur of the window on the wall across from his bed at the Home, and how he had stared at the moon on so many nights, his heart filled with longing.

Arthur heard a haunting sound. It was the hoot of an owl. He and Trinket watched its silhouette flash by, wings spread across the indigo sky, then disappear.

"Miss Carbunkle gives them a bad name," said Trinket. She motioned upward with her beak. "Owls, hawks, falcons and such. Even Merlyn the magician had an owl as a friend."

A gust of wind shuddered through the trees, and the two friends, a bit fearful, burrowed closer together beneath the old grey blanket. Comforted, they lay still, gazing up at the sparkling night wrapped around them.

All of a sudden, Trinket hopped out from under the blanket. "Arthur! Make a wish! Do it right now!"

"*What?*"

"Make a wish. It's the perfect night for it. Come on!"

"No, not me!" said Arthur, shaking his head emphatically. "N–not a good idea. N–not at all." He sat up and leaned against the tree. Trinket plopped down beside him.

She insisted that if he wanted something badly enough, he had to wish for it. This was a concept Arthur was unfamiliar with, and he pondered it for a while. He *had* wished for a friend, and the friend had eventually appeared. Maybe Trinket was right. But then, what should he wish for now? What did he really want?

He thought for a while until finally he said, "Okay. I think I have a wish. But … it's probably stupid."

"Don't say that! Nothing you wish for could possibly be stupid. Just pick a star. Then make a wish. It's simple. You don't even have to say it out loud."

Arthur and Trinket lay back down beneath the blanket and looked up through the canopy. There were so many stars, it was hard to choose. Finally Arthur settled on one, but he didn't know the name of it, or to what constellation it belonged, for he had never learned about constellations at Miss Carbunkle's Home for Wayward and Misbegotten Creatures. He pointed to it and said, "That one, over there."

"Well done, Arthur! You chose Sirius, the Dog Star, the brightest star in the heavens. Now make a wish with all your heart. Come on."

"Oh, all right, then," said Arthur. He swallowed hard and began, "I wish—I wish t–to know…"

He paused. There was so much he wished to know. And so much he hadn't realized he wished for. Now that he knew where he was born, he wanted to know if he still had family somewhere. And he wanted to know why he had no name, and why he had only one ear. And who had sung that beautiful song when he was but a wee pup, and why he could hear things others couldn't and why and why and why. There were just too many questions. But if he rolled them all into one, it was to know why he had ever been born.

Arthur took a deep breath and looked up at the sky. "I wish – and I *will* say it out loud, Trinket, for you are my best friend in the whole wide world – I wish—" He took another breath. "I wish to know why I'm here and what I'm supposed to do in the world – what is my destiny? There. I said it."

"Well done, Arthur, well done!"

A cool wind blew, and the two friends pulled the blanket tight around them.

"Your turn," said Arthur.

Trinket searched the sky and quickly found her star. It wasn't the first time she had wished upon it. It was twinkling in the tail of Cygnus, the Swan. She closed her eyes, chirped softly, then was silent.

"Well?" asked Arthur.

"Well what?" asked Trinket.

"Did you do it? Did you make a wish?"

"Of course I did."

"And?"

"And, Arthur…" She looked up at him, her bright eyes sparkling in the moonlight. "The wish I made was for you."

CHAPTER 15

Pinecone

THE NEXT MORNING, Arthur awoke with a start. A delicate-looking child with elfin ears was standing over him, pointing a makeshift wooden sword at his face.

The boy had a small turned-up nose, green eyes and black curly hair tangled with leaves and twigs. His shirt and trousers were patched together from scraps of patterned fabrics in various shades of green, with buttons fashioned from acorn tops, each painted a different colour. One of his front teeth was missing.

"Hullo!" the boy said brightly. Then, trying to sound stern, said, "Tinkerer, trader, forager, foe? If you're a foe, I'll fight you to the death!"

Arthur stared up at the boy while Trinket popped up from under the blanket. The boy jumped back in alarm. He looked from one to the other. "What are you? I need to know so—so I can report back to the Captain. And … and the Captain, she's killed ten thousand men!"

Arthur's eyes grew wide. He nervously patted his ear, which was starting to shake. The boy didn't look dangerous, but one never knew…

"Don't be scared!" insisted the boy, frowning. He held out a hand to help Arthur up. The elf-boy (for he didn't quite look like other humans) was the same height as Arthur.

"T–to answer your question," said Arthur, "we are…" He looked at Trinket.

"We're travellers!" she said. "Adventurers, if you really want to know. But I'm somewhat of a tinkerer myself – well, more of an inventor – at least I hope to be someday. In fact, I recently invented—"

"I like adventurers!" the child interrupted. He cocked his head, his face quizzical. "What exactly does one do?"

"A bit of this and that," said Trinket. "We travel here and there and do noble deeds and sail to unknown countries and explore them, you know, that sort of thing. But you see," she added, "adventuring requires a lot of food, and, well, we've quite run out of that."

The raven-haired boy's mouth dropped open so wide, a bird could have flown in. "I see now. You're like Robin Hood or … or … the Knights of the Round Table! In that case, brave adventurers, I'll find you something to eat!"

Arthur's face lit up at the mention of food.

The boy told the travellers not to worry about "the Captain." "She's really my nana," he said, blushing. "She's in charge at the moment. Everyone else went on a foraging trip yesterday and won't be back till tomorrow. *I* couldn't go, of course. I'm not *big* enough yet, so I have to stay here and guard the tree. Not much of a noble task, is it?" he said, sighing.

"Sounds like a noble task to me," said Trinket. "The woods can be a dangerous place."

The boy's face brightened. "My name's Pinecone, by the way. What's yours?"

"P–Pinecone?" said Arthur.

"I know. It's a stupid name." He shook his head, and bits of moss fell out of his hair onto the ground. "We're all named like that – Chestnut, Barkley, Ash, Hazel, Buckthorn – I call him Bucky – and Pinecone, that's me. You get the picture."

"She's T–Trinket and I'm—I'm Arthur."

"*Arthur?* Like the famous king? Blimey! Pleased to meet you both! Get your things. Home's right here."

Arthur looked up at the oak Pinecone had pointed to and its magnificent umbrella of leaves. The tree seemed to go on for ever into the sky. Birds flitted here and there while squirrels chased one another from branch to branch. Now that he was really paying attention, he could even hear the sap flowing like a river in the tree's heart's core. This marvel of a thing was someone's home.

While Arthur and Trinket gathered their belongings, Pinecone pulled up some pale-orange mushrooms and stuffed them into his pocket. "My grandma – I mean *the Captain* – she's going to like these! You ready?" He reached up and touched the tree, sliding his hand behind a thick jumble of ivy until he found what he was looking for. Then he whispered, "Nana says, 'Always thank the tree.'" He closed his eyes for a moment, as if in prayer, and pressed on an acorn carved into the bark. And a heavy arched door, far taller than they were, creaked open.

Pinecone gestured for them to come in. "Welcome!" he said proudly. Then, to someone inside, "Nana! We got visitors! Come and see!"

They stepped into a round, spacious room that had been hollowed out of the huge trunk to make a cozy home. The tree, which was massive to begin with, appeared to be even larger inside. It smelled of things Arthur had never smelled before: pine wreaths, cedar chests, rosemary and mushrooms from deep within the woods. There was a feeling, though, of that strange sensation people call déjà vu – as if he had been there, or a place just like it, before. It felt safe and familiar and simply marvellous.

Despite its hollowed-out base, the tree was very much alive. Arthur could hear the branches groaning in the wind. He stepped into the centre of the room. *So this is what a home really is.* He stood, speechless, while Trinket bounced about the place, exploring.

There were several cubbyholes for sleeping, with curtains sewn from the same green patches of cloth that made up Pinecone's clothes. Along the wall that curved around the room were several pictures painted on bark, some of different kinds of trees, some of children wearing green patchwork clothes. There was one of Pinecone when he was a baby, sucking on a small birch burl as a pacifier. In the centre of the room was a large round table with polished tree stumps for chairs.

Pinecone noticed Arthur looking at the picture of him and said, "Mum's the artist in the family. Pa's a bit of this and that – forager, peddler, carpenter. Bit of a tinkerer too."

Although they were standing inside a tree, the house wasn't dark at all. There were small luminaries in the shape of squirrels and birds scattered throughout the room. Near the ceiling and along the curved bark wall, several holes had been cut to let the light in. There were bark awnings on the outside to keep the rain at bay.

Opposite the entrance was a large fireplace, with various tools fashioned from wood and tin hanging above the mantel. An iron pot hung from a chain over the fire. Pinecone lifted the top and stirred what was inside. The room suddenly filled with the enticing smells of leeks, potatoes, mushrooms and cheese.

A plump little person with frizzy white hair who was wearing a patchwork apron walked out from one of the cubbyholes. "Don't you touch that soup, Pinecone! That's for supper, that is."

"Nana, these are my new friends and … and they're adventurers!" Then, under his breath, he said to the visitors, "That's the Captain. She's never really killed anyone, though – at least I don't think she has."

"Oh," said Arthur, relieved. He made a little bow before Nana, who seemed quite pleased by this.

Pinecone tugged at his grandmother's apron and begged, "Can they stay for breakfast, please, oh please?"

Nana tousled Pinecone's hair and nodded to Arthur and Trinket. "Of course they can, you silly little pine nut."

Pinecone jumped up and down with excitement. "You heard the Captain! You can stay for breakfast and elevenses too and lunch and … and teatime and dinner and bedtime snacks, and tomorrow we can go on an adventure, because I'm an adventurer too… I just haven't been anywhere yet, but I *will* go on an adventure really soon – but now we can just play.

What do you like to play? I mean, will I need my sword or should we play Find the Acorn, Tree Tag, Catch the Squirrel, or Stick and Toss?" All of a sudden, he stopped jumping and frowned. "I only know *tree* games," he said, and sighed. But his face brightened once again. "I bet you know lots, though. What's your favourite?"

Arthur could only stammer out, "It's ... it's lovely! Your house, I mean."

The boy beamed and looked at his grandmother, who said, "'Tis a humble place but 'tis *our* place, and that's all right by me. Now, sit yourselves down, you three."

Nana set out a large mushroom tart, a pitcher of fresh cold milk, and a bowl of pumpkin seeds on the large round table. "Soup's not ready yet, littl'uns. Have to make do with this. Now, tuck in; there you go."

Trinket perched on the edge of the table, since the chairs were too big for her. She became very excited about the seeds and proceeded to stuff herself with them. While they ate, Nana bustled about at the hearth, and Pinecone chattered on and on about his life in the forest – the animals, foraging, his brothers and sisters.

After breakfast, Trinket, who had been unusually quiet, asked Nana, "Do you know the best way to the Great White City – to Lumentown? Arthur's going to seek his destiny there, and I'm going west to find my uncle." She glanced at her friend reassuringly. "But then we're going to meet up after that. *Right* after that."

"Pinecone, go get that old map," said Nana. "Mind you," she said, turning to Arthur, "it's so old; it mightn't be up to date."

The boy rummaged around in a big cedar chest and returned with a long scroll tied with a leather cord. He pushed their dishes aside and spread the map out on the table. It was made of very old parchment and tattered around the edges. Arthur, Trinket and Pinecone leaned over the map, studying it carefully. Arthur had never seen a map before but found it surprisingly easy to figure out. Trinket pointed her beak at a spot in the north.

"That's where we're going," she said. "Looks like the road splits off there." She tapped her beak on another spot. "One road to the sea, the other to the City."

"B–but the City—" said Arthur. "It looks—it's so far. Isn't there a sh–shorter way?"

The road that led to Lumentown was indeed a long one, much longer than he and Trinket had first thought. The road curved around the edge of a great forest. He could tell by the map's legend that it was definitely not a two- to three-day journey. It would take at least another week to get there on foot, maybe more. "I won't make it," he said, sitting down. He buried his head in his hands. He felt like crying.

Nana put her hand on his shoulder and gave it a kindly squeeze. "There, there, I'm sure you'll find a way."

"You can come with me, then," said Trinket. "We can look for my uncle together! Then we'll go to the City after that. Together, Arthur. I can help you look for Tintagel Road."

"What's that?" asked Pinecone.

"It's where I ... I *think* I was born," said Arthur.

"Oh," said Pinecone. "I was born inside this tree!"

Arthur looked at Pinecone, then at Trinket. What if he did go with her? What then? He was quiet for a while, the thought churning through his head. If he went with her, then they wouldn't have to split up at all. But then – he felt a strange sense of urgency. All these years he had had no idea where he was from, and now that he did, he wanted to go there right away. He wanted to say with certainty, like Pinecone just had, *I am from this house, this street, this town. This is who I am.*

And maybe if he understood that, he'd understand his destiny.

Finally, he said, "I *have* to go, Trinket. I just do." He ruffled the feathers on top of her little brown head. She had been such a good friend to him. He hoped with all his heart that she was right – that they would see each other very, very soon.

"Wait a minute," said Pinecone, still thinking about Arthur's problem. "I know what to do! See that big forest on the map? You can cut through it! It's called the Wild Wood, but not to worry. Pa used to go that way all the time when he did his peddling in the City. Always came home in one piece."

"That's right," said Nana. "He did at that."

Trinket poked Arthur in his armpit. He cracked a smile. She said, "There you go, Arthur. You see? Things always work out in the end. You'll probably get to town even before I reach my uncle's."

Pinecone took out a piece of birch bark, made a rough copy of the map for the travellers, then rolled up the old map and placed it back in the chest. "Here you go," he said, handing the bark map to Arthur, who tucked it safely in his bindle.

Pinecone's face was scrunched up in thought. "I remember now," he said. "My pa said something to a traveller who came here a couple years ago. The traveller, he was…" He glanced at Arthur. "A bit like you."

"A groundling?" asked Arthur.

Pinecone shrugged. "I guess. Anyway, Pa told him that if he always wore a hat and kept his head down, he'd be right as rain. There was some other bit too, that I can't remember."

Arthur's ear quivered. "Thanks for the advice," he said. "But I'll have to do without. I don't have a hat."

Arthur looked longingly at the pot of soup over the fire, wishing they could stay for a while. Trinket caught his eye. He could tell she thought they should get on the road now too. Just because Miss Carbunkle and Company hadn't followed them after Sneezeweed toppled down into the valley, it didn't mean they were out of harm's way. Who knew what the Wig still had up her sleeve?

"I'm sorry, Pinecone, but we really must go," said Arthur, picking up his bindle. The boy looked crestfallen.

"Don't be sad! We'll see you again!" said Trinket. "I mean – you being an adventurer yourself and all. Adventurers always run into each other when they're out … adventuring."

That seemed to cheer Pinecone up just fine.

Nana gathered food for the travellers, enough to last a couple days or more – nuts, berries, seeds, chestnut bread and some fresh goat cheese. "Now, keep your wits about you," she said.

"Wait a second," said Pinecone, touching Arthur's sleeve as he and Trinket were heading out the door. "Take this, just in case."

He pulled a red woollen cap from a hook in the wall and handed it to Arthur. "It'll fit right over your… Well, you know what my pa said: Keep your head down and you'll be right as rain! Bye!"

Arthur thanked him and the Captain and tucked the hat into his bindle. Then he and Trinket started off.

They made their way through the woods, following the Xs Arthur had marked in the dirt. In no time at all, they were back on the road that would lead one of them north to the Great White City and the other west to the sea.

CHAPTER 16

A Parting of Friends

THE TRAVELLERS said very little that day as they made their way northward past farms and fields. They passed a few donkey carts going to market, a handful of horse-drawn carriages, and one large white-and-gold stagecoach pulled by six white horses. If Trinket and Arthur saw someone approaching, they quickly hid behind hay bales or hedges or anything they could find, for they still had no idea how the world on the Outside looked upon groundlings.

The land began to slope upward. When the two came to a quaint village of thatched-roof houses and small shops, they wished they could stop but kept out of sight and hurried on. The last thing they wanted was to be sent back to Miss Carbunkle's Home.

It was late in the afternoon when they finally arrived at the dreaded fork in the road. Arthur helped Trinket put on her flying suit and began dividing what was left of their food.

"Just the seeds, Arthur," she said. "They're all I want." He picked her up, and she sat in the palms of his hands the way she had that first time they met in Kestrel Courtyard. She looked up at his tired, anxious face. "Oh, Arthur, please don't worry! It will all turn out fine. You'll see."

Arthur looked away for a moment, afraid he might cry.

"You sure you don't want to come with me first? You don't have to go alone, you know."

"I know," he said. "It's just ... I feel like I have to go to the City to find out who I am before I do anything else. I can't explain it. But I'm just afraid ... that we..." The rest of his sentence got stuck in his throat, but Trinket knew what he was going to say.

"We *will* see each other again, Arthur. I promise it won't take that long to get to my uncle's, and I'll send word as soon as I can. Then we'll make a plan for me to join you in the City."

"But how, Trinket? How will you find me in such a big place?"

"After all we've been through together, you think I can't figure out something as simple as that?"

Arthur tried to smile but couldn't.

"No sad faces allowed," said Trinket. "I want to see you

smile when I'm airborne. That's the picture I want to take with me into the west."

He smiled, but felt as if his heart would break in two.

After they said their goodbyes, Arthur watched his friend, in full armour, hop a little, then rise clumsily into the air, her propeller whirring, stirring up the leaves and dirt around him.

"Arthur," she called down to him, "be brave! And don't forget: Never, ever lose hope! I'll see you soon, I promise!"

Arthur waved goodbye and stared up at Trinket until she was a speck in the sky, just a bird flying west to the limitless sea.

Without Trinket, the rest of the day felt unbearably quiet. He missed her terribly. And yet something kept him going.

He couldn't explain it, but it was always there – the song he had heard when he came into the world, the one that floated among the stars. He carried it with him as he walked the long road that day alone, and when his mind grew dark and wandered back to the Home and Miss Carbunkle, and Sneezeweed, Bonegrubber, Bunmuncher and Wire.

He felt it rise to the surface when he noticed, despite his sorrow, a thing of exquisite beauty: a bird, a tree, or a simple flower beside the road.

By nightfall, thanks to Pinecone's map, he had found the entrance to the great forest. He curled up at the base of a tree, burrowed beneath his blanket, and listened. Alone in the darkling wood, he felt the songs of night were like an outpouring of longing: toads and mice rustling in the leaves, moles scrabbling below the earth, bats swooping in the air, woodchucks, hedgehogs and voles – all of them seemed to be calling their loved ones to *come home, come home, come home.*

He travelled two more days in the Wild Wood, wondering if he would ever get out, for the path Pinecone had shown him on the old map must have disappeared over time. But on the third day, he saw, to his relief, sunlight pouring through an opening in the forest. Through the opening was a tree in a sunlit field. He had seen a tree like this only once before, that time in the infirmary. In the picture, it had been heavy with the weight of apples. This one was thick with pink blossoms.

He made his way out of the dark wood through the orchard to the road, and at midday, Arthur, mud-spattered and weary, arrived at the Great White City of Lumentown.

CHAPTER 17

The Great White City

THE CITY sat high on a hill.

From a distance, it shimmered in the sun – a vision of gleaming white towers and spires. In ancient times, the City had been built from *lumenstone* – a stone so pure that people believed it had been born of light. The stone was thought to be indestructible, and it seemed to glow from within.

Arthur stood before the massive white arch – the gateway to the City – and stared up at the words inscribed at the top:

LUMENTOWN
IN LUCUS A NON LUCENDO

The words carved below the name of the City made no sense to him. He had never learned Latin at the Home, only "useful" things like how to wash a shirt in cold, dirty water and make it come out clean, or how to count beetle widgets really fast, or how to spell important words like *servitude, silence* and *obey.* Maybe someone would explain these words to him. Maybe somewhere in this strange new place he would find a friend.

He stood beneath the arch, one foot inside and one foot outside the city gate, unsure of what to do next.

Before him, about a hundred feet away, was an open square; in the centre of it stood a soaring white obelisk so tall that its pointed top disappeared in a cloud. Carved into its base was a circle of hunched-over creatures, animals and ground-lings alike, who looked as if they were struggling to hold the column up on their collective backs. On either side of the obelisk was a fountain with a statue in the middle. To Arthur's left it showed a man slaying a dragon; to his right, a man shooting an arrow into a griffin's heart.

Arthur couldn't tell which was more frightening – the stone men or the monsters. He also wondered if he had completely lost his mind by coming here. He moved off to the side of the arch so he could observe things first before venturing forth.

Across the square was a grand boulevard, the main artery

of Lumentown. The boulevard and streets branching out from it had also been built from white stone and sparkled in the afternoon sun. The dazzling effect was almost too much to bear, and Arthur had to shield his eyes with his hand in order to see.

Rising from both sides of the boulevard were magnificent white buildings with soaring spires. Some had hanging gardens, their bright-red flowers spilling over balconies, blossoms falling like drops of blood on the white stone streets below.

The buildings had friezes carved on them, narrative scenes from a mythic time of battles between humans and animal gods. There were gargoyles too, grimacing from above. Arthur thought of the sad, neglected gargoyles at the Home, tears of rain dripping from their mournful eyes. But the shining white gargoyles of Lumentown looked both terrifying and beautiful to the young orphan, who stood transfixed, penniless and alone.

People milled about in the square and streets, but no groundlings walked among them. Ladies wore bejewelled snoods and large complicated bonnets adorned with flowers. They held parasols or pushed prams with chubby babies inside, or walked arm in arm with their husbands or friends. Arthur noticed that some of the women wore elaborate wigs beneath their hats. He thought of Miss Carbunkle and shuddered.

The men wore tall white hats and fancy cream-coloured coats, and strolled along smoking long ivory pipes. Perched at the top of each man's hat was a little white dove, one leg attached to the brim with a thin golden chain. From where he was standing, Arthur couldn't tell if the birds were real or not. He immediately thought of Trinket and wished she were there too.

Some of the people were walking sleek white cats on diamond-studded leashes. The cats, regal and aloof, pranced in tandem with their human companions. Arthur tried to imagine what kinds of conversations the cats had in private. Perhaps someday, he thought, he might be able to understand them, as he could the mice and rats. He might even be able to talk to them and other animals. He had no idea what his gift meant or how it would change over time – only that it seemed to be part of his destiny to find out.

All of a sudden, a man passed right by him, riding the most curious thing. It was a bicycle – a phenomenon Arthur had never witnessed before. It was an odd contraption, with one enormous wheel in front and a very small one in back, and it seemed to Arthur to be terribly strange and fast. Then, just a few feet away, he saw another man with an even stranger machine. His bike had a steam-powered engine in back, and when he pulled on a lever attached to the handlebars, the bicycle lifted into the air. Arthur watched in awe as the man ascended, flying high above the promenade of lords and ladies below, a cloud of steam trailing after him.

Arthur took a deep breath and patted his ear. He

remembered Pinecone's words of advice. He pulled out his new red cap and placed it on his head. It was warm out, but better to be hot and uncomfortable than to run into trouble, for he was sure he would find enough trouble without flaunting that red furry ear of his. He was used to far worse things than wearing a wool cap on a hot day in May.

He took off his jacket, rolled it up, and stuck it inside his bindle. Where he would go after he walked through that gate, he had no idea. But he could hear Trinket's reassuring, bell-like voice in his head, telling him to be brave.

Arthur came out of his hiding place, pulled up his collar, and, keeping his head down, walked straight through the gate, into the Great White City of Lumentown.

Somewhere, hidden in this powerful city of light, was his destiny. He hoped that he would find it – and be right as rain.

CHAPTER 18

The Heart of the City

ARTHUR CUT ACROSS THE SQUARE and headed north, toward the heart of the City. He was nervous at first, but oddly enough, no one seemed to notice him. It was as if, after all those years of pretending he was invisible, he finally was. The gentlemen and ladies appeared lost in thought or polite conversation, while the children, all of them quiet and well behaved, busied themselves with balloons or kites, or giant lollipops larger than their heads. Everyone's face had a contented, dreamy look as they strolled along the gleaming promenade.

The only creature that paid Arthur any mind was a cat. When she and her master passed him on the street, the cat narrowed her eyes at him and hissed. Although he couldn't understand the language of cats, at least not yet, he knew from the sound she made that a hiss did not mean "Hullo, nice to meet you!" and so he moved on.

From the boulevard, he followed a peaceful side street lined with fragrant trees. Except for a rumbling sound a few streets away and a faint *thud thud thud* from somewhere below, all was quiet. There wasn't a soul in sight.

The road was lined with great pillared mansions built of pink and white marble. Each yard was enclosed by a wrought-iron gate as fine as filigree. In front of each house was a manicured lawn with tidy flower beds and topiaries trimmed into the shape of cats. *Why cats?* he wondered.

He paused in front of a rose-coloured house and peeked through the gate. It was the most beautiful house on the street, with scalloped turrets, stained-glass windows, carved cantilevers and balconies overflowing with flowers. On each balcony sat a large golden cage filled with songbirds. Arthur stood motionless, mesmerized by the chorus of birds.

Suddenly, the rumbling he'd heard before grew louder. He turned to see a great horse-drawn carriage thundering toward him. When the driver saw Arthur, he pulled hard on the reins and came to an abrupt halt.

"Oi!" the coachman shouted. "Whot ya up to, snoopin' 'round these parts?"

"I–I'm looking for a house, sir," Arthur blurted out. "17 Tin… Tintagel Road. D–do you—?"

"Better have a tag on ye, groundlink, or yer in trouble," interrupted the driver.

"If you p–please, sir," said Arthur. "I d–don't know what you mean."

"Don't know what I mean, do ya?" replied the coachman. "Very funny! Now, you listen up good. You're on the wrong side of the City, you are! So g'won with ya, afore you get caught!"

Arthur opened his mouth to ask what side of the city he *should* be on, but the coach was already racing around the corner, and in a flash, it was gone.

Marble streets gave way to cobblestone roads and tall stone buildings, then redbrick houses four storeys high with fancy shops in front offering things Arthur had never even known existed. One store sold only automatons, large and small, each fashioned for a specific task: thistle trimmer, trophy polisher, moustache waxer, cat groomer, corset tightener and so on.

One shop in particular caught his eye. The sign above read TRUNDLEBEE'S TRAINS & TOYS FOR TINY TOTS.

He stretched up as tall as he could and peered into the window. Before him was a wonderland of dolls and dollhouses, stuffed animals of all kinds, jack-in-the-boxes, marionettes and miniature theatres, train sets, board games, music boxes, rocking horses and china rabbits dressed in lace petticoats. Arthur had no idea what most of these toys were, but they were so enchanting that if the shopkeeper hadn't chased after him with a broom, he could have stayed, peering into that window for ever.

He ducked into an alley and came out in a different kind of street altogether – a bit shabbier but more lively. There was something about the enormous green building across the street that drew him to it. He made his way to the other side, dodging carriages, carts and bicycles. In front of the building were three majestic arched entrances with massive pillars. Above the middle one was a large sign that read THE ROYAL MUSIC HALL. He remembered Trinket telling him about music halls once, but he hadn't quite been able to believe what she'd said at the time, for it had seemed so fanciful, the idea that people would flock to a place to hear someone sing, an act so forbidden at the Home.

The building was plastered with playbills announcing upcoming shows featuring opera singers, popular song-and-dance acts, magicians, mentalists, contortionists, acrobats and so on. Arthur didn't know what most of these things were, but the place intrigued him. He looked around to make sure no one was watching and tried one of the doors. It was locked. He looked up at the sign again and vowed that he'd come back some other time.

Next to the music hall was a spirited place called the Dancing Crow Saloon; a sign sticking out above the door was painted with a black crow with a top hat and cane. Next to that was a pub called the Pig & Pickle; next to that, one called the Brass Carp.

A man stumbled out of the last place and looked as if he was going to be sick. Arthur cautiously approached him. "Ex–excuse me, sir... I... I'm looking for a place called T–Tintagel Road. Have you heard of it?"

The man grabbed Arthur's arm. "Whot? Whot you doin' here?" he said in a slurred voice not unlike Mr Bonegrubber's. He cocked his head to the right. "Tha' away, groundlink, that-a–away! Thish ain't the place for yoush. G'won, git!" The man gave Arthur a little shove and went back inside.

Arthur walked in the direction the man had pushed him – deeper into the heart of the city. The air was ripe with horse dung and coal smoke billowing from tall chimneys on every roof. A carriage sped by, and then another, splattering a smelly mess all over Arthur's face and clothes. He wiped his face off as best he could and kept going.

Everywhere he looked, he saw clocks. Clocks over every entrance, clock towers on every corner. Clocks were even strapped to people's wrists, or pulled out from men's pockets, or dangling from gold chains. *No dandelion or flower clocks here*, thought Arthur, thinking of Trinket.

The noise, smell, and commotion grew more intense. There were so many cabmen, drawing horse and carriages, calling out for passengers, and cracking whips; and steam-powered omnibuses packed full of people; farmers leading herds of animals to market; chimney sweeps and shoe-shiners singsonging a penny for this, a penny for that; street sweepers weaving in and out of traffic; men with makeshift tables, gambling or performing magic tricks; pushcart peddlers hawking wares; clowns on stilts, juggling oranges; flower girls selling violets and daisies; and men selling ha'penny songs printed on long scrolls of parchment.

Oh, how the world exploded with sound! Arthur's red cap barely muffled the noise of it all. He pressed his hand over his ear to help block it out. Standing on every corner and along the street were musicians playing all sorts of instruments: flutes and fiddles, harps and harmoniums, bagpipes, accordions, whistles, horns and drums. There were children singing for pennies, and organ-grinders with monkeys, sometimes three in a row, each playing a different song in a different key. It was so chaotic that Arthur couldn't even hear that they were actually playing *music,* the most heinous crime of all, at least to Miss Carbunkle. And below this raucous symphony was the ceaseless *click clack clack* of hooves on cobblestone streets. Above it all, the din of a hundred church bells ringing on the hour, their chiming sounds carried on the wind.

It was perilous to walk at times, especially crossing the street. Arthur had to dart among carts and carriages, farm animals, and the double-deck omnibuses that rattled down the road. He saw very few groundlings, except for ones hauling huge baskets of rocks and bricks on their backs or on top of their heads, their faces tired and grim. *Where were all the others?*

He had no idea which way to go. But at that moment, he cared more about finding something to eat than finding the house he was born in. When a delicious scent drifted by, he followed his nose. He rounded a corner, and there, between two enormous pillars, was Lumentown Market.

Arthur breathed it all in: the fresh-baked crumpets, scones, and buns; the almond cakes, gooseberry pies, cherry tarts, roasted apples, gingerbread and strawberry cream; the rich, tasty cheeses, roasted meats and every other eatable and drinkable thing you could imagine. There were fruits and vegetables as far as the eye could see: mountains of turnips, greens, cabbages and beans; and piles of chestnuts, apples, oranges and bundles of leeks.

A man pulling an enormous cart loaded to the hilt with bright-orange fingers of carrots passed by, chanting, "Car-rots an' peas, car-rots an' peas! A penny a bunch, my car-rots an' peas!"

Oh, if only I could have a carrot right now! Or bread. Oh, Nurse Linette's bread and butter! Oh, if only I could taste a pie!

Then he saw the cart.

It was bright red and yellow. And the sign on it said only one word: PIES.

A stout blonde woman with a grease-stained apron was pulling her pie cart through the throng of people, heading right in his direction. "Puddin' an' pies, puddin' an' pies, come 'n' taste me puddin' an' pies!" she belted out over the crowd. "Mince, quince, apple, an' berry. Savoury, sweet, an' tart as a cherry!"

Arthur couldn't believe his luck! A mountain of pies, steam rising from the tops, surrounded by a circle of tasty fruit puddings, like a castle surrounded by a moat. He hurried over to her cart. "Ex–excuse me, ma'am," he said. "If–if you p–please."

The woman ignored him and kept singing her wares, every now and then cranking the handle on the pie steamer to keep it going. A customer came and went. Arthur tugged at her skirt and tried again. "If you p–please, ma'am."

"What the—?" She looked down and saw the groundling in muddy clothes and cap staring up at her. The woman tried to yank her skirt away, but Arthur held on.

"P–please," he said. "I just want—"

"Let go a me! Don't give handouts to beggars, do I?"

"S–sorry," he said, releasing her skirt. He made an awkward bow. "I'm not a b–beggar. I'd like to make a trade, fair and square. P–please."

She cocked her head and put her hands on her hips. "Let's see, then. An' 'urry up. Don't have all day."

He hastily untied his ragged bundle and placed the blanket on the ground with Merlyn, Trinket's clockwork mouse, along with Pinecone's map and a cluster of colourful stones he had found along his journey. He held up his jacket so the pie lady could examine it. "M–my jacket for a p–pie. It's—it's all I have and I'm so hungry."

She grabbed him by the collar and shook her fist in his face. "That filthy scrap for one a' my pies? What cheek! Good as gold, my pies! Do I look like a filthy-clothes monger? Now, g'won with ye or I'll call the constable, I will!"

From out of nowhere, a ragamuffin of a boy appeared, his face and clothes black with coal dust. In one swift movement, he scooped up the blanket and its contents from the ground. In a moment he was swallowed by the crowd.

"Hmmmf!" the woman snorted. "Justice!" And she gave Arthur a sharp kick in his shin, causing him to tumble into her cart, jarring the steamer below the pies.

The great pyramid of pies shuddered.

It rumbled and shook.

And then it exploded into the air.

It was a cascade of pies, a Vesuvian eruption of pies, an annihilation of fillings and buttery crusts and puddings, splattering all over the ground and anyone within five feet, including the pie lady, who began screaming at the top of her lungs for the police.

At that moment, Arthur did something contrary to his untarnished heart. He grabbed an unbroken pie from the ground, threw his jacket over it, and fled.

He tore through the crowded market, crawling under carts and pushing past throngs of people and animals, darting between the stilts of juggling clowns. But just as he reached the other side of the square, he tripped over a carrot and fell, smashing the pie into oblivion.

He was so tired and hungry, he didn't know what to do. *Let them catch me. I can't take another step.* He slumped down next to a lamppost, buried his face in his sticky, berry-stained jacket and began to cry.

And then a kind voice. "Poor little duck; poor, poor little duck." A short rosy-cheeked woman wearing a baker's hat and apron leaned over and gently touched his arm. She placed a warm roll in his lap. She was standing beside a cart piled high with rolls and loaves of bread. He looked up and tried to thank her, but the words got stuck behind the old rock in his throat.

"There, there, my lovey. Eat up. Soon you'll be right as rain, you will." His heart lightened a little when she said this.

She watched as he tore the roll in half, put one portion in his pocket for later (an old habit from Cheese Sunday at the Home), and gobbled up the other.

"Poor little lamb. Here's one for the road."

"Th–thank you," he said. He was so grateful, he was afraid

he would cry again. "Do you—do you know where Tintagel Road might be? My family used to live there."

"Don't rightly know, my lamb. But head to the river. There you'll find your way."

He forced a smile, bade her farewell, and got up to go.

She caught his arm and bent down close. She told him to watch out for something called the "Dog-sea." He imagined an ocean of barking dogs like the drooling mastiffs at Miss Carbunkle's Home. "If you see 'em, run as fast as you can. Promise me you'll do that?"

He had no idea what she was talking about, but he promised her just the same.

"There's a good lamb," she said. "Now, hurry on your way. Follow that street just ahead." She pointed to a narrow street off the square. "Good luck. And remember what I said – don't forget to run."

Arthur followed the street away from that chaotic and captivating place full of peddlers, thieves – and dangerous pies.

Arthur wandered for hours, taking this street and that, sometimes going in circles until he realized that any street going down led to the river, and any street going up led to the white towers at the top of the hill. He tried asking directions to

Tintagel Road, but every time he did, the person either ignored him, pushed him away, or told him to "go back to the other side where you belong." By the end of the day, his feet were so blistered and bruised from walking on hard cobblestones that he was desperate to find shelter.

The sky paled in the east, and a clammy mist crept into the city. Arthur put on his jacket, buttoned it up, and forged ahead. As he passed cozy homes warmly lit by candlelight, he could hear piano music from parlours wafting through the air, parents calling "Good night, good night" to children saying their sleepy prayers. What would it be like, he wondered, to be so comfortable, so cozy, safe and warm?

Throughout the city, lamplighters lit gaslights in rich and poor neighbourhoods alike. Arthur crept in shadows like a thief, afraid of the mysterious Dog-sea. *Which way now?* he wondered, and just kept moving down, down, down.

CHAPTER 19

The Moon and a Song

HE HEARD THE RIVER before he saw it.

He smelled it too.

It stank like wet cloth on Wash Day at the Home; it reeked of dead fish and all manner of other disgusting things. It was dirty brown and glistened with oil, rubbish and sewage floating on its waves.

Was this the glorious river that Trinket had told him about, the one with wooden boats with bright-coloured sails?

Along the riverbank, small groups of men, women, and children gathered around fires they had made from paper, kindling, and broken lumps of coal. The ghostly flames rose up, illuminating their sad, gaunt faces.

As night fell, they huddled together in shadowy corners, or over manhole covers where steam rose from deep below, or against abandoned boats along the shore. These were the lost souls of the city, with no place to go, no work, no family, no home – only the warmth of one another to keep them alive through the cold, damp nights.

Arthur searched for a place to bed down for the night. No cover now – just his jacket and his baby-blanket scrap and gold key hidden in his shirt pocket against his heart. He spied a rotting skiff someone had begun to rip apart for kindling and plopped down next to it on the damp ground.

He took out the other half of the roll the kind baker had given him and made swift work of it. He was about to devour the second roll when he noticed a group of people piled up together near an abandoned boat. From where he was sitting, they looked like the shadow of a large lumpy beast, with a dozen pairs of eyes flashing yellow beneath the gaslight streaming in the wind.

One of them, a man with crooked teeth, stared at Arthur and held out his hand. Arthur tentatively approached the group. He offered the roll to the man, who snatched it and immediately tore it into six small pieces, one for each person.

"Thanky, thanky," the man mumbled. "Bless yer heart."

Arthur nodded to the man and returned to his spot. He could hear one of the group – an elderly woman in rags – talking in a faraway voice: "Hearts? World 'tain't made for people with hearts no more." She muttered to herself for a while until she finally fell asleep. Then all was quiet.

Arthur pulled his dirty jacket tight around him and lay down on the ground, pressing his back against the old skiff.

He watched shadows of ships in the night, dark shapes upon the water, bobbing up and down. One boat went back and forth across the river a couple times, a gloomy red light glowing from the bow. He could make out figures disembarking from it and searching for something along the shore; for what, he did not know. He wondered if they were lonely too, and why they weren't home with their families. He thought of Pinecone, tucked up in bed in his cozy tree, and of Trinket, safe and sound in a house by the sea with her uncle. What kind of house was it? he wondered. And was she happy there? He hoped he would hear from her soon. And the orphans at the Home, he thought of them as well, and for one brief moment, he wished he were back there, back in that terrible place of cruelty and clocks. At least there he had had a bed, a blanket, and a bowl of cold porridge to count on.

He lay still, listening to the rhythmic lapping of the waves, like the beating of his unsettled heart. He had never seen a river before, and he thought, despite its stink and sad neglect, it had a kind of grandeur about it. When the wind shifted, Arthur could even smell the sea beyond the City.

The place where Trinket must be by now, he thought. It was a fresh, salty smell – the scent of hope and adventure. Of other lands and ships and seabirds and stories and dolphins flying through blue-green waves.

Somewhere across the river, a woman began singing a lullaby to a child: *"Sleep, my baby, sleep. Dream your magic dreams and sleep…"* Her voice was sweet and clear. Arthur lay still, listening in wonder, swept away by the beauty of her song. How amazing, he thought, that here in the City, a person could sing right out in the open and not get punished for it. The idea was astounding to him.

He thought of his own lullaby from long ago and wished he could remember the words. When the song ended, Arthur gazed at the light dancing on the surface of the water and tried to lull himself to sleep. He looked up, and there, high above the City, was the moon, his old friend that had comforted him on so many nights. Where his star was, the glow from a thousand gaslights made it impossible to tell – but no matter. He closed his eyes and thought of that magical night with Trinket, when he had wished upon a star. And as he drifted off to sleep, the moon, the song, and the memory of his friend were simply enough.

CHAPTER 20

Quintus

"WELL, WELL! What do we have here? Dead or alive? I wonder, I wonder…"

The Rat – a groundling in a greasy red velveteen hat and tails – leaned over the sleeping creature and nudged him with his large brown toe. Arthur made a whimpering sound, rolled over onto his back, and began to snore.

"Sleepin' like a baby," murmured the Rat. "I loves it when they sleeps like that."

The Rat was very tall for a groundling, nearly five feet, and had leathery winglike fins that stuck out from two slits in the back of his coat. They rippled a little when the wind picked up over the river.

The Rat sniffed the air: coal smoke, fried fish and coffee. The world was waking up.

Down the street, the Knocker-Uppers were tap-tap-tapping their long poles on windowpanes, rousing the sleeping Drudgers, Fishmongers and anyone else who couldn't afford a clock or a watch. The Rat checked his own pocket watch, a shiny brass thing engraved with the words *To Lulu, my blushing bride, For ever yours, Farnsworth,* which he had tried to remove without much success. He held the watch to his ear. It had stopped an hour before. He glanced up at the clock tower behind him, then turned a small knob on the watch's side, and the gears clicked into motion.

"Time waits for no one, Quintus ol' boy. Let's get on with it."

He rubbed his bristly mitts together in greedy anticipation and got down to work.

He pulled out a small sack from the inside of his coat, which was full of hidden pockets, odd little tools, and an ivory-handled jackknife. He bent down closer to the sleeping creature, his eyes suddenly fixed on his hat. "What's this, what's this? Oh, Quintus, how you do love a fine red cap!" He started reaching for the hat but stopped himself. "You knows the Rules, Quintus! Wrote 'em yerself, ya did."

And so he sang a little song while he pilfered Arthur's pockets.

Pockets an' pennies an' pretty things first;
Fill yer sack till it's ready to burst.
High hats an' trilbies, them's next to be nicked.
Bonnets an' bowlers – ripe fruit to be picked!
Then off to the pub for mutton an' ale
Till it's back on the street in top hat an' tails.

First, the Rat felt around in Arthur's left jacket pocket. Nothing. Next, he checked the right one. "What have we here?" he whispered to himself. He carefully extracted the contents: one crushed lilac, three small stones, a tiny piece of lichen – nothing of use to him, so he tossed them on the ground. But wedged in the bottom of the pocket was a prize – a little piece of paper wrapped around— *What luck, what luck, Quintus!* – a solid-gold coin. "Bright as a button, this," he muttered excitedly, biting the edge of the coin, then pocketing it. He pulled an eyepiece from his waistcoat and scanned the note from Nurse Linette. The Rat's eyes brightened.

"'Tis yer lucky day, Quintus. Yes, indeed! Yer lucky day."

He tucked the note into his waistcoat and continued his search.

Arthur woke up just as the Rat was reaching for his shirt pocket, where his small blue bundle was hidden. He let out a garbled cry and covered his face with his hands. "P–please don't eat me! Please, I beg of you!"

"Eat you? What you goin' on about?" said the Rat. "I mean no harm! Came to help ya, like, honest." He cleared his throat and said, puffing up his chest, "Saw a thief goin' through yer pockets a whiles back. Chased him away, I did."

Arthur peeked at the Rat through his hands. It *was* a Rat, but it wasn't Wire.

"Come on, now," said the Rat. "No need to be a-feared. Here, let me help you up; there's a good lad."

Arthur let the Rat help him up. He felt a bit woozy and ached all over. He brushed himself off and took a step back. "You're—you're a rat g–groundling … with … with *wings*?"

The Rat let out a laugh, which did not seem unkind. "First of all, thems are fins, not wings, and second – yer a funny little fox person with no tail. What of it? Ain't we all the same, really? Now, come, come, m' boy, I'm only trying to help you. An' you look like you can use a mate in this town. 'Specially with them thieves running about."

"I didn't have anything to steal anyway," said Arthur, shrugging. He remembered the pie he had stolen the day before and felt a wave of shame.

The Rat raised one eyebrow. "Hmmm… Nothin' to steal, you say? Not even a brass farthin'?"

"I wouldn't know one if I saw it," said Arthur.

"Well, well," said the Rat. "Nothin' lost, nothin' gained. But look at you! Half starvin', an' me talkin' about thieves."

He took a stale crust of bread and a small piece of cheese from one of his pockets and handed them to Arthur. "Got a nice morsel for ya. There's a good lad – tuck in."

Arthur gobbled up the food in seconds.

"Th–thank you," he said, embarrassed. "I—I was quite hungry."

"I can see that," said the Rat. "Hmmm." He scratched a spot below his brown bristly snout. "Now, whatchu about?"

"What do you mean?"

"What's a nice young pup such as yerself doin' in this great big city all by yer lonesome?"

"I'm looking for a place. It's called Tintagel Road. Do you know it?"

"Tintagel, is it? Got family there, do ya?"

"N–not exactly," said Arthur. "I mean, I don't th–think I do anymore. B–but I'd like to find it just the same."

"Well, I don't exactly know it, but I can help ya find it – if ya like."

"You can?" Arthur's eyes lit up. "Please, sir, if you wouldn't mind. I'd be much obliged."

The Rat looked thoughtful and pulled on one of his whiskers. "I do believe that there street – iffen it's the one I'm thinkin' of – 'tis rather hard to find. An' in a dangerous place, mind you. Can't go alone, that's fer sure. Need a guide. Ya see, m' boy, 'tain't easy gettin' 'round the City on yer own. There's lots fer you to learn afore you go ramblin' 'bout the place."

Arthur's face fell.

The Rat said, "Cheer up, lad! I'll help ya! But first things first. You need a hot plate an' a fine mug – that's what you need. Then we can figure out what to do with you. Might take a while to find that place a-yours, an' I bet ya'd like a nice bed for the night. Wouldn't that be grand, now? Feather bed an' pillow, fit for a king?"

Arthur's eyes grew wide.

"Listen, lad," continued the Rat. "These are devilish times, these are, devilish times. Best to have a friend in tow, if you know what I mean."

Arthur stared up at the Rat, uncertain, hopeful and still very hungry.

"Why, where's me manners?" exclaimed the Rat. He took off his hat and made a sweeping bow. "Quintus is the name; tradin' is the game. And what might your name be, young sir?"

Arthur wasn't sure what to say. His name could be anything in this city of strangers. He could even make up a new name for himself if he wanted. But he didn't want to. In his mind's eye, he saw Trinket's bright face and sapphire eyes. He stammered out, "M–my name is Arthur." He hesitantly took off his hat, bowed, and put his hat back on.

The Rat raised one eyebrow when he saw Arthur's ear but said nothing about it. "AR–thur," he said slowly, as if it were a foreign word, and one he found a little unpleasant. "Arthur, Arthur… Not much of a name, is it? Well, what's in a name, anyway? Let's get you a proper breakfast, Arty m' boy. I know just the place. This a-way, follow me."

Arthur wasn't sure. Should he trust this Rat? What would Trinket do? Be brave, she'd say; he knew that much. This Rat had said he'd help him find Tintagel Road. Maybe this Rat was part of his destiny. How, he couldn't imagine. But stranger things had happened to him.

Then the Rat said the magic words. "Listen, Arty – have you ever had yerself a *cheese toastie*?"

Arthur's ear perked up. "No, sir! I haven't!" he said. "B–but if you please, sir, I'd like that very much!"

"All right, then, a cheese toastie you shall have! An' Quintus always keeps his word!"

Arthur turned toward the street, but Quintus grabbed his arm.

"Not that a-way," he whispered. "Want to cross Stinkbottom Bridge, we do. Follow me an' do as I say; there's a good lad." He linked Arthur's arm in his. "City's a dicey place, mind, if you don't have a friend. Oh, by the way," he added, "best to hold yer nose till we gets to the other side."

At the entrance to the bridge was a big boxy police officer, a billy club hanging from his belt. Quintus tipped his hat to the man and winked. "Top o' the mornin' to ya, Constable

Floop," said Quintus as he slipped a coin into the man's palm.

The officer nodded, tapped his finger on the side of his nose, and said under his breath, "Word a-caution, mate. Winds of change a-blowin'. Watch yer back."

"Right, then," said Quintus, raising his eyebrow ever so slightly. He tipped his hat once more, and he and Arthur went on.

CHAPTER 21

High Hats and Huddlers

THE SUN ROSE over the city as Arthur and the Rat made their way across the bridge. All along the railing were flocks of wood pigeons and crows, fighting over bits of dead fish. It was a sad, neglected bridge, with the same soot-blackened statue on either side – a creature with a woman's face and the body and wings of a swan.

"Thirteen bridges, m' boy, thirteen, but this here one's the only one groundlinks can cross; don't forget that. Consequences would be quite nasty."

"All right," said Arthur, who couldn't help feeling there was some connection to his own destiny in the fact that there were thirteen bridges. Was it good luck or bad?

Quintus told him that farther upstream, the water was fresh and clear. But the water that flowed below Stinkbottom Bridge was the colour of mud, and at that moment, smelled like it had the night before – a fetid odour of dead things, garbage and grease.

The smell reminded Arthur of Wire's breath, but he pushed the thought away.

"Qu–Quintus, sir," said Arthur, "what's the river called?"

Quintus let out a laugh. "Same as this ol' bridge: Stinkbottom River. 'Twasn't always called that, though. Don't rightly know what the old name was. Lost its name long ago. But the bridge, I remember its old name. Years ago, 'twas called the Golden Swan Bridge. See them swan ladies? Underneath all the muck, that's solid gold, that is!"

When they reached the other side, a mean little man with a head the shape of a teacup was waiting for them. Around his waist was a brass box attached by a leather strap, and on his shoulder sat a mechanical monkey. The monkey jumped out in front of them and began screeching, "Pay the toll! Pay the toll! Pay the toll!"

"You 'eard the monkey," snapped the man. "Pay the toll. Don't have all day." Quintus reluctantly withdrew two ha'pennies from his waistcoat and tossed the coins into the monkey's paw, which clamped shut in an instant. The monkey scampered up the man's leg, opened the box, threw the coins in, then jumped back onto his shoulder.

"Toll monkeys," said Quintus, pulling Arthur away. "Can't say I likes the little dodgers."

They didn't have to walk far for food. Along the river's edge was a run-down building that bowed out like a ship, with a faded sign that said THE SWAN & WHISTLE. On the door was a crude painting of a golden swan. The entire base of the building was stained green from algae, as if someone had just plucked it from the bottom of the river and plopped it down on the shore.

Everything inside had a swan theme – swan lamps, swans carved on every table. Even the crockery had swans on it. The place was grimy and dark, but Arthur didn't care. He could smell potatoes frying, bread baking and all manner of other good things wafting from the kitchen. Best of all – in the corner, three musicians were striking up a reel on fiddle, harp and drum. Just as he had the night before when he heard the woman's lullaby, he drank the music in, letting it flow through his body like a child deprived too long of water or air.

"You all right?" asked Quintus.

"It's just … I like … I like the music. You see, where I come from—" He paused. "Never mind. It's lovely," he said, smiling. "Thank you."

It was early morning, and the place was full of Drudgers,

Fishmongers, and the like, catching a quick bite before work. But there wasn't a groundling in sight.

"Is—is it all right that I'm…?"

"That yer eatin' in this place?" Quintus laughed. "'Course 'tis. Look at Liza over there," he said, gesturing to the plump barmaid heading toward their table.

Arthur saw that she had a porcine nose and tiny pink ears.

"Even gots a tail," said Quintus. "Quite proud of it, she is, too. Why, look at me – look at these here fins on me back. Do I hides 'em? No. Proud of 'em I am. An' you can take that hat off, mate. No one gives a hoot on this side a the river iffen you gots one ear or twenty." He glanced around the room and lowered his voice: "Long as you pay yer way, that is. Then yer golden, m' boy, golden. And," he added with a wink, "ya make yerself friends in 'igh places, if ya knows what I mean." Arthur nodded, but the Rat's meaning was completely lost on him.

Quintus ordered an extravagant breakfast: fried eggs and potatoes, mushrooms, beans, fried tomatoes, kippers, toast, and, to top it off, cheese toasties. "Listen, pet," he said to the barmaid, flashing the stolen coin for a second, then tucking it back into his pocket. "You makes them cheese toasties strong an' bitey, mind. This here lad's a connoisseur of cheese, he is."

"Oh, ain't we chuffed," said Liza. "Quintus's gots his luck

on today, I see." She winked at the Rat, who winked back at her and grinned.

When their breakfast came, Arthur took his hat off and tucked in. The food was greasy, the eggs runny, the potatoes undercooked. But to Arthur, it was pure ambrosia. Especially the cheese toasties. They were so hot they burned his tongue, but he didn't care. They were creamy, and definitely strong and bitey, and were the best thing he had ever tasted in his life.

Arthur, full and content, told the Rat a little of his journey – how far he had walked and how he had come from such a terrible place. Quintus was visibly impressed and kept saying, "G'won, g'won, I'm all ears, I am" or "Brave lad you are, to go all alone an' such – into the *Wild Wood!*"

Arthur didn't say a word about Trinket. He wasn't sure why he left her out of his story. Maybe because he liked being called brave, or maybe because he knew from experience that some things were best kept hidden, even if you didn't yet know why.

When it came time to pay, Quintus took out the coin he had removed from Arthur's jacket and settled the bill in a grand manner.

"Now, that's a High Hat breakfast, that is," said Quintus as they were leaving.

"High Hat? What's a High Hat?"

"'What's a High Hat,' he says! Listen ta him! Everyone

knows what a High Hat is – well, I'll be a rat's tail; don't tell me ya don't know what a Huddler is neither?"

"H–Huddler? No," said Arthur, shaking his head. Quintus sighed.

"So much to learn, so little time. First lesson o' the day: High Hats, them's the ones in white hats as tall as yer standing. The hoity-toities that lives on the top o' the hill in shiny white houses an' homes pretty an' pink as can be. But look over yonder." Quintus pointed out the window to a shadowy place on the bank below the bridge. "See thems that crouches in the dark? Them's 'uddlers, them is. Lowest of the low in Lumentown. Don't wants to be one a them. Not never, not on yer life, unnerstand? An' there's worse things even than that, believe you me."

Arthur thought of the night before, and the people huddled together on the dock. He remembered the kind baker who had given him the rolls, and how she had warned him about the Dog-sea. How was he going to learn everything he needed to know? Clearly, the City was a mysterious and complicated place; he knew he needed help. And then, as if Quintus had read his mind, the Rat leaned in close and said, "What you need is a guide; a teacher, like. An' I'm just the chap to learn ya. What say ya, Arty, m' boy?"

"Really? I'd like that very much, sir. But…"

"Yes, m' boy? Whot is it? Gots reservatations, do ya?"

"It's just that... Do you promise you'll help me find that street? You see, it's very important I find it."

"'Course I will! A man o' my word, I am. But first you needs to get all trained up. There's rules in this here city, an' if ya don't know how to get along, you'll never find that Tintintangley Road or any other for that matter. So whot do ya say? Ya comin' with me or shall I leave you on yer lonesome to fend fer yerself?"

"I—I would like to come with you, Quintus. Can I really?"

Quintus slapped Arthur on his back. "There's a smart lad! Mark my words – with my help, you'll know the ways of the City like the back of yer hand in a week. Not a stone unturned. Let Quintus be yer guide. But fer now, we best be getting to Wildered Manor."

"Wildered Manor?" said Arthur.

"That's m' home, m' boy. *Home.* An' iffen you play yer cards right, 'twill be yours as well."

CHAPTER 22

Pigeons and Dust

QUINTUS CHECKED his pocket watch, made a *tsk-tsk*ing sound, and told Arthur to put his hat back on. Arthur followed the Rat through a maze of narrow streets lined with dark, low houses, half obscured by fog. On the other side of Lumentown, there were no street sweepers, and the roads and houses were covered in dust. Everything – even people, groundlings, and animals – was covered in a thick layer of white powdery dust mixed with soot. Here, on this side of the river, the world was exceedingly grey – just like Miss Carbunkle's Home.

There were pigeons everywhere too, flying from every roof, rookery, windowsill, and chimney top. Wherever Arthur looked, he saw pigeons and dust, pigeons and dust.

Quintus whistled a little tune as he led Arthur past empty stores with faded signs that said SHOP TO LET, their doors padlocked, windows shuttered, walls dirty and decayed. Those shops that were open looked neglected and dark inside.

They crawled over a low stone wall and cut through an abandoned park, overgrown with weeds, then made their way past poorhouses and redbrick tenements with rags hanging from railings, past people laden with bundles and groundlings pulling heavy carts. The foggy air was filled with the mingled smells of rotten fruit and fish. Along the malodorous streets, clocks *tick tick tick*ed on every corner and every building wall.

On one street, they passed a man in grimy grey hat and tails, cracking a whip at a large black bear chained to a wall, forcing it to dance a slow, clumsy waltz for a gathering crowd. Arthur wanted to help the poor beast somehow, but Quintus pulled him away, saying, "'Urry up, my dear. Nothink we can do. Come along."

"Quintus," said Arthur after they had walked for quite some time, "where do the groundlings live?"

"You'll see," said the Rat. "Almost there, almost there."

Soon after, they came to a gloomy area surrounded by a barbed-wire fence with one tall tenement after another painted the same dull grey; on the roofs were rows of makeshift chimney stacks billowing black smoke. The buildings were made completely from discarded objects – scraps of wood and metal, pieces of pipe, old shoes, pottery shards and broken toys and pots. The only creatures Arthur could see were a couple of furry faces peeking out from the small narrow windows up above.

"Where are we? And where is everyone else?" asked Arthur.

"Breakin' their backs somewheres across the river, I reckon. And them's the lucky ones!"

Here, at the entrance to the "neighbourhood" (for lack of a better word) was a large sign that read BLOOMINTOWN. Arthur squinted at the small print below.

It said D.O.G.C.

He said the initials out loud, confused. Then he said them all together, like a word, and gasped. *D.O.G.C.* was *Dog-sea*! Or maybe it meant "Dog *see*," and there was a giant dog monster with one big eye that could see him wherever he went, just like Miss Carbunkle's panoptic tower.

He remembered the baker woman's warning about that dreadful word: *Don't forget to run.*

So he did.

Arthur ran this way and that until finally, after an exhausting chase, Quintus found him hiding under a donkey cart. It took a while for the Rat to coax the poor creature out, but he finally did. "Listen, m' boy," he said. "There's a few things ya need to know."

Quintus explained that D.O.G.C. simply meant the Department of Groundling Control, and that they were the High Authorities of the Land. "Used to be they was just in charge of groundlinks' affairs, and the police, they was in charge of the humans, but times have changed."

Quintus went on to say that now the only thing higher than the D.O.G.C. was an elite group of High Hats – five brothers who held all the power in the City and the Land. Even the police and governmental departments had to answer to the D.O.G.C., including the Department for the Protection of Wayward and Misbegotten Creatures.

"I know who *they* are," said Arthur. *Cheese Sunday.*

Arthur asked if Wildered Manor was in the place with the crooked grey buildings and the barbed-wire fence, which they had by now left behind.

"Bloomintown? Bless my soul, not in a million years! Mind you, when I was yer age, 'bout thirty years back, that place was pretty as a picture – a field of flowers far as the eye could see, it was. But ya wouldn't find the likes of me livin' there now, not on yer life ya wouldn't."

"Why not?" asked Arthur.

"Second lesson o' the day: Not all groundlinks lives in big grey houses sinkin' in the dust." He put his arm around Arthur's shoulder. "There's worse, a *lot* worse, an' there's better. An' where I lives is the very best o' the best, just you wait an' see."

They turned a corner, and another, until finally, on the street formerly called Wiggins Lane, only one house remained: Wildered Manor.

CHAPTER 23

Wildered Manor

AT FIRST GLANCE, the place looked abandoned, for it was a house that had been left to its own devices. The house had invited the trees and bushes in, and the squirrels and opossums, birds and mice. Then other animals came, and groundlings with no place to go who despised the crooked grey buildings beneath the sign that said D.O.G.C.

The outside was blanketed in ivy, bird nests and wasp nests, and all manner of plant and vine crept into every window and door, blocking most of the sunlight except on the very top floor. There once had been a sign over the entrance-way that said WILFRED MANOR, but someone had crossed out the F and inserted a D and an E above.

Quintus bent down and gripped Arthur firmly by the shoulders. He looked him straight in the eye and said, "Now, when yer inside, whatevers I say, follow my lead, unnerstand? An' do us a favour. Try not to fumble yer words an' do that shakin' thing with that there ear when you take off yer hat. Most unbecomin' like. Gotta stand tall, lad. Don't wanna end up 'neath Stinkbottom Bridge – or someplace worse."

Arthur quivered a little and nodded. "I'll ... I'll do my best, Quintus. Promise."

"Good boy," said Quintus. "That's the ticket!" He unlocked the door with an old rusty key and pulled Arthur in. He led him down a long dark hallway to a rickety set of stairs overgrown with leafy vines. Arthur could hear dozens of minute creatures scuttling about in the dark. "Careful where you step," said Quintus. "We keeps the downstairs dark. Keeps the nosey parkers out of our business."

Someone had fashioned a candlestick from a giant turnip and set it on the bottom step. Quintus picked it up and motioned for Arthur to follow him upstairs. "Might want to keep yer mitts off that there railin'," he said, pointing to the dozens of tiny eyes glowing in the dark.

At the top of the stairs, Quintus turned right into a very large room. In the centre sat a large rectangular table. Above it was a crystal chandelier covered in cobwebs and grime.

Quintus let out a high-pitched whistle. Immediately a

scuffling sound came from every corner as a ragtag gang of creatures scampered out of the shadows.

"Gather 'round, my dears, gather 'round."

The group made a semicircle around Quintus and Arthur. They were a motley crew of all shapes, sizes and ages, although none of them looked as young as Arthur. There was a rather corpulent mole-porcupine groundling, a white weasel groundling, a groundling who was part English setter, an ant-eater groundling, a raccoon groundling, a stern-looking rabbit person and a creature in a bottle-green trilby. Arthur had never seen such a peculiar-looking groundling. He had the face of an aye-aye[♦] and the body of a small hunched-over man.

"Here's my faithful lot a good-for-nothin's," Quintus said with obvious pride and affection. He gestured to the groundling in the green trilby and said, "Goblin, will you do us the honours?"

In the glow of turnip light, everyone's shadows loomed larger than life on the wall, hovering over Arthur like some kind of ghostly shadow play. He shuddered and took a deep breath.

The hunched-over creature named Goblin made a stiff bow and said, in a very unenthusiastic tone, "Yes, Master

---

♦ An aye-aye is a nocturnal primate that lives in Madagascar. It does not, however, wear a trilby, which is a special kind of hat. In Lumentown, aye-aye groundlings were rare indeed.

Quintus, I'd be delighted." The groundling had enormous bulging eyes and a twisted, squished-up sort of face that looked as if a very large person had just sat on him. His leathery black ears were enormous too, as were the two yellow teeth protruding from his tiny pink mouth, which was slightly curled into a smile. Arthur couldn't tell if the smile was sinister or kind.

"Right, then," said Goblin, who proceeded to introduce the others, pointing at each one with a long knobby finger. They each bowed as Goblin said their names. "This here's Thorn and Throttle," he said, gesturing toward the Mole-Porcupine and the Raccoon, "Houndstitch and Squee to your left," he motioned to the dog boy and weasel groundling. "Cruncher to your right." The rabbit person narrowed her eyes at Arthur and cracked her knuckles loudly. "She's what you might call the strong an' silent type," said Goblin. "An', oh – that 'un over there, that's Bone, that is." The tall white anteater groundling squinted at Arthur with milky eyes and grimaced, revealing a long pink tongue coiled up like a snake inside her mouth. "That's it. Them's the lot."

Arthur thought, *When in doubt, bow.* So he did.

Quintus cleared his throat.

"Oh, lordy me," said Goblin, his voice tinged with sarcasm. "I forgot me manners! And you are…?"

Arthur opened his mouth to speak, when Quintus said,

"All in good time, Goblin." He nudged Arthur and said, "Take off yer hat, laddie. Show 'em what yer made of. No need to be shy."

Arthur didn't know whether they were going to pat him on the back, beat him up, or eat him. Or worse. Maybe *they* were the D.O.G.C. But it was too late to run. He slowly removed his red hat.

Quintus did pat him on the back, then put his arm around him as if they were old friends.

"Now, listen up," Quintus said. "This is a special one, this is. Part fox – can see that right away. Them's crafty an' clever like, foxes. An' see that there ear, nice an' fluffy an' all?" The group moved in closer to observe Arthur's ear. "Lost t'other in a fight, he did." The creatures made various sounds of approval. "Show 'em yer teeth now," said Quintus. "Go ahead. Open up." Arthur, bewildered but obedient, opened his mouth – what else could he do? "Sharp as a razor, them is," continued the Rat. "Good teeth, good nose, battle scar or two. Not to mention—" he paused for effect—"this one escaped from a high-security *prison,* then walked all the way by his lonesome from the hinterlands and through … wait for it … the *Wild Wood.*"

"My word," said Squee, pulling on one of his whiskers. The Weasel was clearly impressed. "That's a long way, that is. And dangerous too." The others grunted in approval, all except for Goblin, who looked incredibly bored. He began picking nits out of his fur and eating them.

"Now, listen up, you lot," continued Quintus. "He's new to the game, but he's brave. An' I do believe he's worthy of the work. Who's in favour of him a-stayin', say aye."

Work? What kind of work? wondered Arthur. *And what about the house on Tintagel Road?*

Everyone raised a hand or paw and said "Aye." Goblin hesitated a moment before he rolled his eyes and croaked, "Very well. Aye."

"Bravo!" said Quintus. "Take a bow, Spike old boy, take a bow!"

Arthur looked around for the creature named Spike, but not a single one bowed. Quintus gave him a little push forward. "Go ahead, *Spike.* Do us the honours."

Then he knew.

Sorry, Trinket, he thought. Arthur took a deep breath and bowed before Quintus and the others, bidding farewell to his beautiful name – born of legend, camaraderie and love.

CHAPTER 24

If Tables Could Talk

ON THE ROAD TO LUMENTOWN, inside the heart of an ancient tree, sits a large round table made of oak. There are deep marks carved all around the edge. They are from a language no one speaks anymore, a language known only to trees. A family dressed in patchwork green has just finished their evening meal and are sitting at the table, talking. One of the children, the smallest, is so tired from his day at play in the woods, he falls asleep in his chair. The boy dreams of adventure, of two brave friends he hopes to meet once again: a fox groundling and a wingless bird.

To the north, across a great winding river, is a house exhaling forgetfulness and dust. In a room as wild as a forest sits another table, built of mahogany, inlaid with mother-of-pearl. Long ago, the table held lavish feasts on silver platters; it held cups and saucers made of gold. For generations a family gathered there, their faces lit beneath a crystal chandelier. They sat around the table, dining on quail eggs and caviar and peacock pie, entertained by magicians and musicians from faraway lands. But now the table is scratched with claw marks and covered with grease and mould, and plays host to slyboots, hornswogglers and thieves.

To the west, in a quiet town by the sea, sits another table. The table is small and sturdy, round as a nest, built from driftwood, sea glass, metal scraps and shells. Around its edge runs a perching place for birds. It sits in a tree house full of gears and pulleys and all manner of bird-size tinkering things. It's the only tree for miles along a windswept coast.

Night has fallen. In a room lit by fireflies and glowworms, two small feathered creatures tell stories as they hammer and forge a new invention into being with agile beaks and feet. The younger one hops up and down with excitement when she comes to the part in her story where she and her friend – the one she misses with all her heart – sail over a giant stone wall to freedom. She has told the story to her uncle many times, but each time she adds a new embellishment or twist to her tale. "Soon as we're done with this," she reminds her uncle, "I'll find him. You'll see."

*　*　*

The last table is shiny steel and brass, and cold to the touch. Its edges are so sharp they could cut you. The table rests in the centre of a sterile room; etched onto the top is the silhouette of a hawk. A tall woman in an orange wig spreads a map across it. She and her two companions lean in to get a closer look. One, a pale, twitchy man in an ill-fitting suit, finally releases the sneeze he has been trying desperately to hold back. A single droplet from his nose splashes silently onto the map, smearing the ink. When the woman knuckles him sharply on the top of his head, the rat groundling squatting on a stool next to her flashes a secret, triumphant smile at the man. The Rat, who once emitted a fetid odour, smells like a sickly sweet bouquet of lilies now. Around his neck, a yellow silk scarf, a gift from his new patron with the bright-orange hair.

"There," says the woman, tapping a spot on the map. "Find it and bring it back. And bring the plans too. Without the plans, it's useless."

"But ... if I may have a word, ma'am," says the man with the runny nose. "How will we know where she hid it?"

"That is your job, you twit, not mine. Just be quick and don't be seen." She raises one eyebrow, her nostrils flaring. "And destroy whatever – or whoever – gets in your way. Understand?"

211

Before the man can answer, the Rat bows his head to the woman and says, "I understand perfectly well, my lady. It is the greatest honour to serve you. I shall do my very best."

When he says this, the sniffling man glares at him, while the eyes of the hawk's head on top of the woman's cane blink, then glow a ghostly green.

CHAPTER 25

Game of Thieves
(Wildered Manor)

ARTHUR WAS SITTING with the others in the common room at Wildered Manor, finishing up his breakfast of the hot cross buns Goblin had "procured" from the market that morning. Quintus had cut away all the vines from the upstairs windows – a never-ending task in summer, apparently – and the early-June sun poured into the room that had looked so nightmarish the day before. Arthur could see now that the once elegant mansion was knee-deep in filth. *Nothing a little cleaning can't fix,* he thought. If he had learned anything at all at the Home, it was how to scrub, dust and sweep. It was the least he could do for Quintus.

Just a week before, he had been trapped inside the Home.

Now he had a place to live, food to eat and new friends. And someone to teach him the ways of the world. The only thing missing was Trinket. *Soon,* he told himself. *She'll send word, and then we'll make a plan.*

Quintus had told Arthur that there was a world of adventures to be had in the City, but it was dangerous, and Arthur wasn't ready to go exploring just yet. Besides, as Quintus said, "If yer wantin' a place to stay, an' yer wantin' to find that street yer lookin' for, you need to be trained up proper first. An' most of all, you need to earn yer keep like everyone else."

Arthur was very eager to learn from his mentor, and was itching to explore the City and not be afraid. But most of all, he wanted to find out how to get to Tintagel Road.

"It's like a game, see?" said Quintus. Arthur and the others watched as Quintus set several objects on the table: his pocket watch and ivory jackknife, an apple, a silk handkerchief, a pair of brass candlesticks and a leather wallet.

"Now, listen up, you lot," said Quintus. "Spike wants to become a contributing member of society. You'd like to learn an honest trade, right, m' boy?" He winked at Arthur. "Am I right?"

"Yes, sir. I'd … I'd be much obliged to learn a trade."

Goblin smirked. "Wants to learn a trade, does he? Well, what can *he* do? Nothin'. Just look at the bloke. An' he's too young, to boot."

Bone, the anteater groundling, smacked Goblin on the head with her tail, knocking his hat off onto the floor. "He's green, you moron. You were green once; remember when you were green? I certainly do."

The others burst out laughing. Goblin let out an indignant *harrumph* and picked up his hat. He glared at Bone. "No one touches the trilby," he said, putting his hat back on. "*No one.*"

"*Tsk, tsk,*" said Quintus. "Come on, you two! Let's not bicker. One fer all, all fer one, as the sayin' goes. Show 'im how it's done, everyone. Come on. Let the games begin!"

The group waited in the room while Quintus hid one of the objects from the table somewhere in the house. When he returned, the race was on. The first object he hid was the apple, and they all scattered as fast as they could to find it. While they were gone, Quintus removed a small crumpled piece of paper from his waistcoat pocket. He put on his eyepiece and read the words twice. He let out a contented sigh. Ever since he had discovered the note in the foundling's pocket, he had taken such pleasure in folding and unfolding it, smoothing out its wrinkles, reading it again and again, and stashing his little secret away. *My ace in the hole, this is,* he'd say to himself. The words the woman named Linette had written were of course not meant for him. But how often did an opportunity such as this come across his lap? *'Twas meant to be,* he told himself. *Meant to be.*

Thorn, the Mole-Porcupine, brought back the apple, and Quintus, shoving the note back into his pocket, banged on a big black pot to call the others.

The game continued. Arthur couldn't find a thing until the very last object, the watch. Quintus had hidden it in a place nearly impossible to find – two storeys below, beneath a loose floorboard. But Arthur heard its soft ticking sound immediately, along with the insects scurrying over and around it. He brought it back so fast, his mentor barely had time to tuck the note back into his pocket.

Quintus eyed him suspiciously. "Did you see me hide that watch? Did you, lad? Don't lie to me, boy!" He grabbed Arthur by his shoulders and shook him. Arthur flinched, afraid he was going to be beaten. Quintus looked into Arthur's frightened and innocent eyes and let go. "Sorry, Spike. I didn't mean... Just tell Quintus the truth. I won't get mad. I promise. Just 'fess up."

"I d–didn't see you, sir," said Arthur. "I swear I didn't. It's just … sometimes I can hear things with my, you know…" He pointed to his ear and shrugged.

"Oh, I see," said Quintus, rubbing his snout thoughtfully. "Very interesting, this… I knew you were the right lad for somethink, a special job, mind. *Very* special." His voice was kind now, and before he banged on the pot to let the others know the watch had been found, he gave Arthur a coin as a prize. "Shhhh. Mum's the word," he said, and patted the foundling's head.

When the rest of them returned empty-handed and saw Arthur holding Quintus's watch, they slapped him on the back and punched his shoulder like he'd always been part of the gang. Except for Goblin, who appeared to be completely unimpressed.

The second game they played was hilarious, and it was all for Arthur's enjoyment, or so it seemed. He had no idea what any of this had to do with his learning a trade, but he decided that since he knew so little of the world, he must trust his new friends to know what was best for him.

Quintus pretended to be a High Hat gentleman strolling in the park, smoking an imaginary pipe and walking a cat on a leash. Meanwhile, each creature demonstrated his or her special talent by taking something from the Rat without him knowing. Bone snatched his wallet by lassoing it with her long snaky tongue. Thorn and Throttle worked as a team. Thorn, who was nearly blind, sniffed out the apple and motioned to Throttle, who skilfully removed it from Quintus's coat with his dexterous paws while Thorn distracted Quintus by striking up a conversation. Arthur couldn't stop laughing.

After lunch, they continued Arthur's "training" outside. June wildflowers were in bloom – foxglove, honeysuckle, dog rose, and poppy – and the vines blanketing Wildered Manor were covered with bright-red blossoms. There were bouquets of hummingbirds everywhere. It was hard for Arthur not to be distracted by the music of their rapid-fire *sip sip sip*s and the lightning thrum of their wings.

The abandoned landscape surrounding the house was the perfect obstacle course: mounds of brick rubble, broken glass, gorse bushes, weeds, tree stumps, and remnants of old stone walls. The group lined up in front of the house and waited for Quintus to start them off running. He used his pocket watch to clock their time.

The first game involved taking turns being "it" and dashing as quickly as possible away from the others, then finding a good place to hide. Whoever could hide the longest without being found won. Another game, which Quintus called "blending," took a bit more skill. On the count of ten, the groundlings had to find a wall, a patch of grass, anything that resembled the colour or pattern of his or her skin or fur. The point was to camouflage themselves against the surface as best they could and keep perfectly still. Arthur removed his shirt and pressed against what was left of a brick wall, which was the exact colour of his rust-coloured fur. His grey trousers blended in with the pile of rubble by his legs and feet. "Well done!" said Quintus when he found him. "Well done indeed!"

Another game involved climbing in and out of windows as quickly and quietly as possible. They even had to scale up and down walls – at least the ones with paws or hands good for clambering up a drainpipe, vine, or rough-hewn stone. They played racing games of one kind or another until dinner. Even Goblin seemed to have fun. And he didn't say a nasty thing to Arthur once.

Later, the groundlings went to bed, each in his or her own corner on a soft nest of rags, curled up as their ancestors had long ago, in burrows or warrens or caves. Some, like Thorn and Throttle, shared a room; others preferred solitude. There were no feather beds fit for kings, as Quintus had promised; most of the furniture had been used for kindling long ago. But Arthur's corner was cozy, and Quintus had even given him a patchwork quilt and a real pillow, which did have feathers and made him feel as though he were sleeping on a cloud.

Arthur had chosen a corner in a small room on the second floor, down the hall from the common room. He chose the room for the wallpaper, or what remained of it, for one could see faded images of a running fox and dozens of dogs and men on horseback chasing after it. He thought the fox looked very clever and fast.

Arthur was burrowed under his quilt when Quintus came in, carrying a glowing turnip. "Might I have a word, Spike?"

"Yes, sir, of course," said Arthur, and sat up.

The flickering candle lit up the foxhunting scene on the wall. Quintus glanced at it and said, raising an eyebrow, "Interesting choice, this ah … room."

Arthur grinned. "Thanks to you, Quintus, I understand the picture now. They're p–playing a game, you see. And it looks like the fox is winning! See, he's in front, and, well, he probably wins a prize in the end, like I won the coin! But the rest of the picture is missing."

"Yes, well," said Quintus hesitantly. "That it is."

"You wanted t–to speak with me, Quintus?"

"Yes, Spike, I did. Ya done good today, m' boy. You've got talents, rare talents, I can tell. Soon you'll be ready to get down to work. An' learn yer way around the City like – find that place yer lookin' fer to boot. You'd like that, now, wouldn't ya?"

"Very much so!"

"An' you'll be a good lad an' do as I say?"

"Yes, sir. I will, sir."

"That settles it, then," said Quintus. He ruffled the fur on the top of Arthur's head. "Good night, Spike. Sweet dreams."

As he was leaving, Arthur said, "Qu–Quintus."

"Yes, m' boy?"

"I … I just wanted to thank you. For being so k–kind and all. I'm ever so grateful."

Quintus cleared his throat and said, rather stiffly, "I … ah … well … yes. Good night, m' boy. Good night."

CHAPTER 26

Game of Thieves
(The Home)

IN A DISMAL ORPHANAGE far from city or town, two old friends have just finished playing an ancient board game called Latrunculi, the Game of Thieves. The glass board is "the city"; the two opponents, "twins." It is a game of strategy, deceit and war. The goal is to conquer the other twin's land and men, whatever it takes.

The woman had been the victor that night.

The winged creature had let her be the victor, just as he had every night for the past thirty years.

Rain pattered against the roof and eaves as they spoke in hushed tones. "You played quite well tonight, Mistress," said the creature crouched on the table. "As usual," he added, and grinned, revealing two rows of tiny sharp teeth. He flicked his long black tongue several times, as if tasting the air. He helped the woman put the pieces back in the box, then hopped down and scuttled over to the bed.

"Thank you, Mardox," said the woman, yawning, for it was late. In a few hours' time, she would have to stand in the pelting rain, rattling off the names of all the vile groundlings on her list. It was getting harder and harder to keep track of them, for while more arrived each day, just as many disappeared. But she knew where they were, for she had sent them there herself. Someone had to complete her work – her noble, brilliant, visionary work.

"When will the Rat acquire it?" asked her companion, who was now perched at the foot of her bed.

"Soon," said the headmistress. "Just a few more pieces to put in place, my pet. Then we'll be ready."

"Very good, Mistress. I know how much this means to you."

"You have no idea, Mardox. It means *everything*."

The woman put out the light and got into bed.

"Mistress?"

"What is it, Mardox? I really must get to sleep."

"Are you sure you can trust the Rat?"

The woman reached over to the creature and stroked its face. It made a guttural purring sound and stretched out across her feet. "Oh, Mardox, you know you're the only one I can really trust. How could you think otherwise? But we make do, don't we, my pet? We must, in order to succeed. Besides, if anything goes wrong, I won't be blamed. The Rat will. What could be better than that? We'll be safe, my love. We'll always be safe."

CHAPTER 27

Soup for Kings
(Wildered Manor)

QUINTUS COOKED every night, and "Soup for Kings" was his specialty. In fact, it was the only thing he cooked.

Everyone was bustling around the common room at Wildered Manor, getting the table ready while Thorn and Throttle, red-eyed and sniffling, chopped onions.

"Isn't it ready yet?" asked Squee, who was rubbing his paws together in greedy anticipation. "I haven't eaten since breakfast."

"Yeah, Quintus. When's it gonna be ready?" asked Houndstitch.

"Yeah, Quintus, when?" demanded the others.

Quintus ignored them and crushed a sprig of rosemary in his paw, held it up to his nose, and closed his eyes. "Ahhh," he said. He tossed it into the pot and stirred. He added a stale crust of bread, half a cabbage, a piece of suet Goblin had found in the trash, an old potato, a turnip that had been a candlestick for the last month and a long black thing that looked suspiciously like a shoelace. The soup tasted different every night, for it depended on what they had left in their larder and what Goblin had acquired at the market that day. "Borrowing" food at market was his special job.

Bone held out her paws to Quintus. They were cupped closed over something that was trying to crawl out. "Mightn't we add these?" she asked.

"What is it, then?" asked Quintus.

"Spiders," said Bone. "Lovely texture. Delicate crunch. There's a termite in there too. Good protein, that."

"Sorry, Bone. Not with rosemary. 'Tisn't right. For spiders, it's basil you need, an' basil we ain't got."

Bone shrugged and gobbled up the bugs with one slurp of her pink serpentine tongue. The rest of the gang began chanting, "Soup, soup, soup, soup, soup!"

"That's enough from you lot," said Quintus. "No one badgered the bloke who painted the *Mona Liser*, did they? Genius is as genius does."

"But we're hungreeeee," they whined.

They banged on pots and pans and stamped their feet. Throttle said that if Quintus wasn't going to feed them already, the least he could do was sing.

Quintus wrote songs for just about everything, and soup was no exception. While he cooked, he and the others sang until the soup was done. Except for Arthur. But oh, how he wanted to sing! He felt the song in his heart, his feet, his whole body. It prickled something in him that he had no name for. But the best he could do was squeeze out a barely audible hum, which sounded more like an off-key groan. Still, it was something.

Quintus's song was called "Soup for Kings," and it went like this:

A pinch o' this, a pinch o' that,
A little salt, a lot o' fat, ♦
A beet, a boot, a radish root,
Some peas an' cheese, perhaps a newt. †
That's all you need to make a soup
That's fit for kings an' queens.

A little this, a little that,
A cozy place to hang yer hat,
A mate, a plate, a spoon, a bowl,
A song to cheer yer heart an' soul.
That's all you need to make a soup
That's fit for kings an' queens.

♦ "A *lot o'* fat, mind you!" Quintus always added.

† "A newt?" someone always asked, and Quintus always replied, "Them's good eatin', newts!"

Soup for kings,
Soup for kings,
Soup for kings an' queens.
That's all, that's all, that's all, that's all,
That's all you need to make a soup
That's fit for kings an' queens.

Them that's rich an' them that's poor,
Doesn't matter who it's for,
Tastes the same to me an' you,
To man or beast or cockatoo.
So take a seat an' have some soup
That's fit for kings an' queens.

Soup for kings,
Soup for kings,
Soup for kings an' queens.
That's all, that's all, that's all, that's all,
That's all you need to make a soup
That's fit for kings an' queens.

Arthur had two servings of soup; it was absolutely deli-cious! (Except for the shoelace, which got stuck in his teeth.) They even had a chunk of lovely cheddar to share and a loaf of bread. *Bread* and *butter. I wish Trinket could be here,* he said to himself, remembering that day in the infirmary. He imagined

Trinket at Wildered Manor, jumping up and down, laughing and telling stories. *She'd get along with everyone,* he thought, *even Goblin.* He was so happy and distracted that he didn't notice Quintus nodding to Goblin, who left the room and returned a couple minutes later holding something small and shiny in his hands. He handed whatever it was to Quintus, who slipped it into his pocket.

"Come here, Spike, m' boy," Quintus said. Arthur got up and went over to where he was sitting. "You want to know the secret to my soup? Would you like to know what makes it so good?"

"Very much, sir," said Arthur. All of a sudden, everyone looked serious, and he felt as if this was a very important moment, but he didn't know why.

Quintus went on. "An' you want to git aroun' the City, see the sights an' all, with nobody givin' ya grief, am I right?"

"Yes, Quintus, I do."

"An' find that Tin-tin-tangle whatsit street a yours?"

"Yes! Very much!"

"An' ya know, for me to make this here soup, soup you like so much, we all needs to work; ain't that right, Spike?"

"Yes, sir."

"An' you want to work, like the rest of us?"

"Oh, I do, Quintus. You know I do."

"Well then, m' boy—" Quintus paused and reached into

his pocket—"you'll be needin' one o' these. This here's yer ticket to freedom. An' I do believe, from what I seen a you so far, that you've earned it fair 'n' square. You have potentiality, Spike, potentiality."

Quintus held out his hand to reveal what he had been hiding.

Arthur gasped.

It was a tin medallion, stamped with some kind of symbol. Above the symbol *was the number thirteen*. He couldn't believe it.

Everyone started to clap and whistle and shout, "Huzzah! Huzzah!"

Arthur was aghast. "What? B–but…" was all he could stammer out. He stood staring in disbelief at the medallion dangling from the cord.

"Show 'im, mates," said Quintus cheerfully. Everyone held up a tag on a cord or opened his or her top shirt button to reveal the all-too-familiar shiny tin disk. They were all smiling. *How can they be smiling?* Arthur thought. He was completely bewildered. He felt the soup rising in his throat and put his hand to his mouth just in case.

Quintus placed the cord with the medallion around Arthur's neck. It sat like a rock upon his soul.

His mentor went on to explain that without a number and the symbol below it that designated each groundling's job, he'd be scooped up by the D.O.G.C. in a flash. "That there's a feather duster, that is," said Quintus, pointing to the symbol below the number 13. "That's yer new occupation, so to speak." A couple of the groundlings snickered. "Wear it with pride, m' boy; wear it with pride. Constable Floop – 'member the bloke from Stinkbottom Bridge? – made it for you special. An' I gots a special job for you. Special job for a special lad." Quintus patted Arthur on the head and winked.

Arthur felt like someone had punched him in the chest. And some of the soup had definitely travelled from his stomach to his mouth, but he gulped it back down.

"You look like ya seen a ghost," said Quintus. "What's wrong with you?"

All Arthur could squeeze out of his throat was one single, feeble word: *"Why?"*

"Why?" said Quintus. "What do ya mean, *why?*"

Everyone was silent. They were all staring at Arthur. Finally, he got up the courage to speak. He said he couldn't understand why he needed to wear "that dreadful, hateful thing," as he called it, and why, oh why, did it have to be that terrible number?

"Has to be thirteen," explained Quintus. "I'm five, then we go up from there: Goblin's six, Thorn seven, Throttle eight, Houndstitch nine, Squee's ten, Cruncher eleven, Bone twelve. Yer thirteen, an' that's the end of it."

"Why not one or two or three or four? Or some other number, like forty-five or twenty-three or one hundred eighty-nine or…" Now Arthur couldn't *stop* talking, he was so upset. "Please, Quintus, any number but *that.*"

Quintus looked sternly at Arthur. "Can't be one to four. Me four brothers had them numbers, an' no one's to replace 'em, never. An' Floop, he made that number special, an' that's that. Already been paid for too. Now, listen, Spike, yer number thirteen an' that's that. An' the reason you need a number in this here town is if ya don't got one, you gotta, well, you gotta … go below."

A shiver ran down Arthur's spine. "B–below?"

Quintus went on. "'Member I says to ya there's even worse places to live than in one a them crookedy houses in Bloomintown?"

Arthur nodded.

"Gloomintown, we calls it. The City below the City. Wretched place. Dark, dark, m' boy. Nothin' but backbreakin' work an' misery down there. Birds with eyes as big as yer head chase ya down and eat ya up alive. Nasty eels down there, giant frogs, water spiders the size of my head, filth and muck and big black rats, not the nice kind but the kind 'twould eat his own mother if he was hungry."

Quintus told Arthur that the D.O.G.C. sent groundlings who didn't have proper numbers down below. "Hard to get a proper number these days. Have to know someone iffen ya wanna stay above. Coal pits, that's where they work down there. Darkness night an' day. 'Course, there's other jobs – factory work, sewer muckin', an' the like. But it's a livin' hell, Spike, an' you don't wanna be there. Never see the light a day again – you wouldn't want that, now, would ya?"

Quintus said he'd explain more in the morning. He was tired and it had been a long day. But he wanted Arthur to understand how important it was to have a number, and how it was a privilege. And how he had gotten his "friends in high places" to register that very same number, Number Thirteen. "All groundlinks in the City gots to have a number," he said again, emphatically. "Everyone's got to know his place. You know that, don't ya?"

Arthur felt an uncomfortable twinge in his heart, for he remembered those same words from one of the infamous dining hall signs at the Home.

Quintus put his arm around Arthur. "Spike, I promise you – as long as you work hard an' do as I say, you shall have all the food you wants an' then some. An' I'll protect you with my life, I will. So will me mates here. An' we'll help you find that place yer lookin' for. Just do as I says. An' I knows what's best, don't I, mates?" The others nodded in agreement. "We all must pull our weight, an' that's the end of it. Now, let's sing another round, shall we? Cheer up the place a bit afore bedtime?"

The group sang "Soup for Kings" once again, and banged

on pipes and pots and bowls. Everyone sang at the top of his or her lungs, except for the one-eared foundling with the medallion stamped number 13, who stood silently, staring at his feet. When the song was done, they all raised a cup to toast Arthur, the glow of turnip lights illuminating their cheerful faces.

Even Goblin looked somewhat happy that night – at least he wasn't sneering. So Arthur cracked a smile, but it wasn't a real smile; it was a mask to make everyone else happy. Because all he could think about was the familiar weight of the cord around his neck. Was *this* his destiny? The thing he had once wished for upon a star? *Oh, Trinket,* he thought. *Where are you?* And then, this thought too: *I can't let Quintus down.*

Everyone said good night and scampered off to their rooms. As Arthur turned to go, Quintus said, "By the way, Spike, you can pretend all you want that you can't sing, but I know different. I heard ya singin' in yer sleep last night. Got quite a lovely tenor, you do. Like I said, you gots potentiality. You certainly do. Now off to bed with ya, there's a good boy."

CHAPTER 28

Soup for Kings
(The Castle)

AS NIGHT FELL, the man in white gloves stared out the window, surveying the City from his castle on the hill. The man's hair and eyebrows were the colour of pale-white gold, and his eyes were a cold steel grey. At his feet was a sleek white cat wearing a diamond collar. In a corner of the room sat a narrow glass cabinet that held only one object: the man's white hat. It was the highest high hat in the Land – even higher than the hats of his four brothers – at nearly three feet tall.

The man noted the silhouette of spires standing against the vermillion sky but did not think *What a beautiful sunset* or *What a lovely night is this*. Rather, he thought about the world, how it pulsed with electromagnetic light – and dark magic.

He thought about empires, how they rise and fall in an instant. He thought about power, *his* power.

Then he thought about turtle soup.

He sat down at a long narrow table covered in stiff white linen. The cat followed him. It rubbed against the man's legs, then stretched out below the table and started to purr.

The man dipped his spoon into his bowl and began to eat. The soup was murky green. Steam rose from the top of it, fogging the man's monocle. He removed his monocle and handed it to another man, who stood discreetly off to the side. Close enough to serve but far enough to be rendered invisible. He was a servant, after all.

The servant wiped the man's monocle, handed it back, and bowed.

When the man in white gloves was finished, he took a sip of red wine and dabbed his thin lips with the corner of a white linen napkin.

"Something else, my lord?" asked the servant.

"No, Reginald. That will be all."

"As you wish, my lord. Shall I send the woman in now?"

"Wait a moment," said the man in white gloves, removing a gold pocket watch from his cream-coloured waistcoat. He wound the watch several times and put it back. He could hear the woman outside the room, pacing back and forth in the hall. After a minute or two, she stopped at the door and cleared her throat loudly.

How utterly annoying, thought the man. *Why did I ever agree to meet this woman?*

"Very well, Reginald. I suppose you must. You may send her in now."

The servant led the woman with the ridiculous orange wig into the room. She stood there, unsure of what to do next. Without turning or looking up, the man in white gloves addressed her.

"Will you please take a seat."

It was a command rather than an offer.

The woman approached the dining table, rested her cane against it, and sat down.

"What did you say your name was... Miss Carpbungle? Or was it... Fartbunkle? Barfkrumple?"

"*Carbunkle,* Your Excellency. *Miss Carbunkle.* And ... and I thank you for seeing me today. I know how busy you are and—"

The man waved his hand to silence her. "Let's get to the point, shall we, Mrs Carptinkle? Tell me, madam, why in the world do you think that my brothers and I would ever want to help *you* – a lowly headmistress – with your so-called business venture?"

"Because, my lord," said the woman, adjusting a stiff orange curl, "it would give you two things that I believe you value above all else."

"And what might those be, *headmistress?*" asked the man,

pronouncing the last word with disdain. "Who are you to presume what I would or would not value?"

"Forgive me, my lord. I spoke out of turn." She looked down at the table.

"Go on," he said impatiently. "I don't have all day."

The woman licked her thin lips and said, "Money and power, my lord. Money and power."

"Hah." The man sneered. "As if I don't have enough of those. I butter my bread with them in the morning and go to bed with them at night. Money and power, madam – that is the very air I breathe."

"Oh, but my lord," said the woman, "this is something else altogether." She leaned forward, fixed her eyes on the man, and whispered, "This is something that can change the world."

CHAPTER 29

The Gargoyles' Quickening

AS THE CITY SLEPT and worked and ate and raced along in time with clocks and speed and steam-powered machines that never stopped, the gargoyles kept watch. They kept watch atop the glowing white towers of Lumentown. They watched as creatures trudged along murky streets, carrying burdens too heavy to bear; they watched as Huddlers sought warmth in dark corners and along riverbanks; they watched and waited and felt the shifting of the earth below. The gargoyles had weathered the storms of change, of fog and darkness, of light and despair. They had been there for ever. Long before the High Hats, before the groundlings. They were ancient creatures and bore the weight of sorrow and greed in the Land.

While Lumentown breathed opulence and industry, its heart beat in shadows, far below its gleaming white streets. It beat in factories and coal pits night and day, day and night in Gloomintown, the City's dark unruly twin.

The epicentre of both realms was a castle perched high on the hill near the entrance to Lumentown. It looked like a glowing white cake, all turrets and towers; gates inlaid with precious stones. There were five who lived there, five brothers in cream-coloured suits and five white fur hats.

Here too, above the castle, the gargoyles kept watch. They watched as white peacocks and pampered cats wandered the gardens behind soaring white walls. They watched as the five men gathered, the highest of High Hats in the Land, the ones who stamped decrees and chose where some could live and some could not, who decided how much a soul was worth.

And like the poor stone creatures at Miss Carbunkle's unhappy Home, the gargoyles of Lumentown, tired of cruelty and greed and darkness, had begun to weep.

Across the river, in a house grown wild with time and neglect, a one-eared orphan could hear their tears falling in his sleep. And in his sleep, he began to form a song from their sorrow.

But he had far to go before he would sing it.

CHAPTER 30
Thief

THE MORNING AFTER Arthur received his medallion bearing the dreaded number, Quintus handed him a brand-new suit of clothes – a crisp white shirt, navy-blue trousers, coat and waistcoat. The clothes were a bit too large for him and had lots of extra pockets sewn into them, but they were stylish and well made. Quintus told him to go to his room and put them on straightaway, then come back. He had a "special job" just for Arthur.

When he returned, all dressed up, Quintus slapped him on the back and said, "Look at you, Spike – or should I say 'guv'nor'?" Arthur tried to smile but couldn't. He could feel the medallion choking him, even though the cord wasn't tight.

"Come on, buck up!" said Quintus. "Let's not grouse about what can't be changed." Arthur forced a weak smile. "There's a good boy," said Quintus. "An' take off that red hat. It's seen better days. The suit looks better without it, I do believe."

He handed Arthur a feather duster and a rucksack, and said that Arthur was to go with Goblin to the other side of town that morning and seek out the house of "a certain lady friend." While Goblin procured sustenance from the nearby market, Arthur was to, as Quintus put it, "borrow a few trinkets from the house" – whatever he could fit in his pockets and rucksack. Arthur felt a little pang when Quintus said the word *trinkets*.

Quintus said the feather duster plus the symbol and number that hung around his neck should grant him safe passage.

Arthur's face fell. "But Quintus, I—I don't quite understand."

Quintus turned to the others and said, "Look at 'im. Fresh as a daisy, he is. Perfect for the job!" He gave Arthur's shoulder a little squeeze. "Listen, lad, I'll spell it out for ya. I'm what ya call a snout. Sniff things out fer the coppers, I do, an' the coppers, they looks out fer me. They do little favours, like Constable Floop makin' me that there tag around yer neck. An' they tries to keep D.O.G.C. out of my business, see? So there's nothink to worry about. Now, be a good lad. Don't wanna bite the paw that feeds you. Do this one thing for me an' I'll help you find that place you were lookin' for."

"You—you want me to st–steal something? But Quintus, I never stole anything before," said Arthur. "I— I can't."

"You mean to tell me you never stole nothink?" Quintus narrowed his eyes. "Nothink a-tall?"

"No, never. I mean – not like *that*."

"Never went 'ungry? Had to take somethink lest you starve?"

"Well, I…"

"Never took somethink t'eat 'twasn't yours?"

"But … well…" Arthur looked down at the floor, ashamed. After a long pause, he said quietly, "Once I … I st–stole a pie… But just once!"

"'Course ya did! Had to, din't ya? Weren't a-gonna go 'ungry. All right, then, Spike. Let ol' Quintus 'splain you the ways of the world. There's thems that 'ave and thems that 'aven't. So it's up to us—" he gestured to the group—"to set things right. We does a lit'le borrowin' an' tradin', is all. Like Robin Hood an' his merry lads. Listen," continued Quintus. "This is how it works. We steals from the High Hats an' gives to the poor, an' the poor – them's us!"

The gang broke into squeals of laughter while Arthur stood wringing his hands.

Quintus told him that, most important of all, he must act like a Duster. In fact, that had been one of his training games the day before. Quintus had called it play acting. He had made Arthur pretend he was a Duster. He had showed him how to carry the feather duster against his right shoulder, which was the way real Dusters carried them, and how to walk subserviently, with his eyes lowered and his head down. He was good at that part, and everyone had clapped, which had made him happy at the time. Everything was a game, Quintus had said, but the Duster game was the most important one of all. At least for *him*.

Now he understood why.

"Right then. Off with the two of you. Here ya go, tosh fer the toll monkey, to an' fro. An' fill yer pockets, Spike. There's a good lad. Oh – an' *don't* lose that there feather duster!" Quintus patted him on the head and pushed him out the door.

When Arthur and Goblin got to Stinkbottom Bridge, Goblin paid the toll monkey, for groundlings, and only groundlings, had to pay going both ways. On the other side, Constable Floop was standing there checking the tags of the privileged few groundlings that came and went.

"A word, little man," whispered Floop to Goblin. "Got a message for your mate Quintus. You tell him a changin' o' the guards is comin' an' I don't know how much longer I can watch his back. You tell 'im that, right? He'll know what I mean." He tipped his hat and added, "Sorry, mate. New guv'nor an' all. New world order, so to speak. Ta."

"Ta to you," said Goblin, tipping his trilby. The policeman nodded, and Goblin and Arthur went on their way.

"What did he mean, Goblin?" asked Arthur.

"Never you mind," said Goblin. "Just do the job, all right? And you make sure you're in that alley by ten o'clock on the dot. You got one hour, understand?"

"I promise," said Arthur. "I'll be back in time."

The house was on a street right by the market, and while the buildings weren't made from lumenstone or marble, they were majestic all the same. The house he was to enter was very old and built from stone. It was covered with creeping jasmine that smelled intoxicating. In the front of the house was a peacock-blue door flanked by statues of winged animal gods and goddesses in tall stone niches. The front gate was open, and Arthur followed a path to the back of the house.

The yard was small but beautiful, and a little bit wild. There was an overgrown herb garden, patches of flowers randomly planted here and there, and in the centre, a blossoming apple tree in dire need of pruning. Next to the tree was a lovely stone fountain where several songbirds were splashing about.

Quintus had told Arthur that he'd find the key beneath a stone bird by the back door. When he was sure no one was watching, he lifted the bird and grabbed the key. If he had known more about birds, he would have noticed that the stone bird was a nightingale. The thing he did notice was that the lock on the door was at groundling level. At the Home, where most everyone was a groundling, not a lock was within reach.

He paused. *I don't like this,* he thought. *There could still be someone inside.* Quintus had said no one would be there. He couldn't hear anyone, but even so... What if the inhabitants were just asleep?

Arthur froze, key in hand, unsure of what to do. Then he heard a shrill voice from across the yard. "You there! Groundling! Stop this instant!"

He spun around. The voice came from a neighbour woman who had stepped out to trim her topiaries. She was wearing an absurdly large sunbonnet and carrying an enormous pair of pruning shears.

The backyard of the woman's house faced the backyard of the house Arthur was about to enter. The woman in the giant sunbonnet stomped across the row of rosebushes separating the two properties and marched across the yard over to Arthur. "Who are you and what are you doing here?" she said, pointing her shears down at his nose.

He did exactly what he had been told to do if anyone saw

him. He bowed his head and held up his feather duster. "If you p-please, ma'am. I'm—I'm the new D–Duster."

"Hah!" She sneered. "Likely story."

He tried again. "You see … I'm here to, well, to dust! Yes, that's what I'm here to do. Me being a Duster and all."

"I know full well what a Duster is, you ninny. Let's see your number, then. Come on, out with it."

He pulled his tag out from under his shirt. She grabbed the cord, yanking him forward, and examined his number and symbol. She released him in disgust. He stumbled backward, righted himself, and bowed again.

Arthur was certain the woman was going to call the police or the D.O.G.C. – he still didn't quite understand how it all worked – but instead she shooed him away like a fly and went back to trimming her large leafy cats: for every single topiary in her yard was a crouching, springing, or stretching cat.

As he fumbled with the lock, Arthur could hear the woman muttering to herself as she walked back to her yard. "Keys to groundlings! What will that dreadful woman think of next? It's the icing on the cake, it is. First, Cook gets sick and *I* must go to market. Next, the nanny quits and *I* am left to tend to Baby! Then, the gardener falls ill and *I* end up doing a labourer's work! A labourer's! And now I'm forced to talk to some hideously deformed freak! Disgusting. Right next door! There ought to be a law!"

Arthur put the key back under the stone bird, closed the door on the woman's voice, and stepped inside.

Quintus had told him to search each one of the house's three floors, every nook, cranny, and closet, and to take what he could in one hour. Take *trinkets,* he'd said. Arthur cringed. What would his Trinket think if she saw him now? He stood inside the entrance and listened; there was no one there. His thudding heart relaxed to a slow, steady beat, and he entered the parlour.

All the windows had peacock-blue shutters and were draped with plush burgundy curtains. Richly pattered rugs covered the floors. On three of the walls were rows of daguerreotypes, engravings and paintings of wild animals in faraway lands. He had seen only one real picture before, Linette's engraving of her mother and Miss Carbunkle when they were young, and it was hard not to stop and stare at these. On the fourth wall hung a giant tapestry in blue, deep crimson, and ochre. It depicted a medieval scene of magical beasts: centaurs, dryads and unicorns standing in a circle in a walled garden. Arthur recognized the unicorn from Trinket's tales of King Arthur. A white horse with a horn, she had told him. The most innocent of all creatures.

He couldn't bring himself to put any of the precious

objects in his pockets. Each was so unique and beautiful: a quill pen resting on a piece of creamy paper on a small polished table edged with gold, a clock in the shape of a swan, a set of miniature trees carved from jade that looked like they were dancing.

In the middle of the room was a piano. Arthur had no idea what it was, but he thought it must be something that made music, for it looked a little like the accordions he had seen people playing his first day in town. He climbed up on the bench and gently touched a key. A quiet note rang through the air.

His heart beat fast. He touched another. Another note sang out. Arthur took a deep breath. His hand hovered over the keys. How he wanted to stay and coax out more sounds! But he heard the swan clock ticking away and forced himself to move on.

Arthur crept through the first floor – the kitchen, dining room and other rooms branching out from the parlour – all of them lavish and full of wondrous things.

The second floor contained the library and several other rooms. Inside the master bathroom was a marble bathtub carved with sea nymphs and sea centaurs riding the waves. He ran his red furry hand over their figures. They were all animal-human hybrids, just like him.

In another room, he came upon a wooden cabinet with

many drawers. He opened one and found a walnut, inside which someone had carved a tiny city of bridges and spires. In other drawers were shells and precious stones and various treasures. On the wall across from the cabinet were shelves of relics, mostly ancient helmets, fragments of armour, cross-bows and swords. Arthur thought of King Arthur and his Knights of the Round Table, but these helmets weren't made for humans at all. They had been forged for animals: rabbits, horses, birds, elephants and even one for a fox. Or were they made for groundlings like him? He ran his finger over the fox's silver mask. *What were these for?*

Next he wandered into the library. Lining three of the walls were shelves and shelves of books going up to the ceiling. Arthur had never seen so many books in his life. In fact, the only book he remembered ever seeing was Miss Carbunkle's *Essential Manual for the Vocational Training of Errant Groundlings*. He picked one up – a leather-bound volume with gilded letters embossed on the spine. It was in a language he couldn't under-stand, with words like those above the entrance to the City. He lifted the book to his nose and breathed in its delicious papery smell.

A grand fireplace took up the remaining wall. The pil-lars framing the fireplace were creatures carved out of wood, guardian figures with horse legs and human bodies, their faces part goat, part man. Above the mantel were more standing figures, each one half human, half mammal or bird. In the centre was a coat of arms. It bore the words *House of Nightingale*. On top was a knight's helmet, shaped for a bird, with three large feathers protruding from each side. At the bottom were two entwined snakes. In the centre of the shield was a picture of a tree, and inside the tree was an ancient lyre. The inscription floating above read *Protector of the Sacred Grove*.

"What *is* this place?" he said aloud.

He climbed up a narrow staircase to the top floor and entered a room filled with light.

Arthur froze. There were musical instruments everywhere he turned. For a moment, his shoulders tensed as if he were going to be hit. He could see in his mind one of Miss Carbunkle's signs, hanging on the wall of the dining hall: *Music Is the Root of All Evil.*

"It is not!" he said aloud, as if the headmistress were in the room. "You're wrong!" Saying that felt good, and his shoulders relaxed.

He walked around the room full of instruments he didn't know the names for, defiantly touching this and that, plucking a harp string, running his hand along the back of a viola da gamba. He saw another piano like the one downstairs, but this one had a pyramid of tiny pianos on it, each one stacked on top of another, from large to small. He also saw musical inventions, like a self-playing violin with a mechanical arm holding the bow and a hurdy-gurdy that played itself.

Arthur started to leave – the clock in the room told him he had only twenty minutes left, and he had yet to put a single thing in his rucksack for Quintus – when he noticed coloured light streaming under a door in the back corner of the room.

He opened the door and walked into a rainbow.

CHAPTER 31

The Songcatcher

THE ROOM WAS SMALL, with tall, arched stained-glass windows depicting animals in elegant motion: red gazelles leaping over luminous green hills, bright-yellow birds soaring across an azure sky. The light illuminated everything, making the floor a patchwork of colours. He saw a rainbow of light glinting off something in the corner and turned to look.

It was a machine of some kind; he could tell that much. It sat on a wooden table next to a small brass clock. The base, which was about two feet long and one foot high, was a black-and-red lacquered box decorated with intricately painted flowers, leaping stags, rabbits and birds in flight. Along the edges of the base were flowers and vines painted in gold. Jutting from the top was a large scalloped brass bell like the bell-shaped horn of an old-fashioned phonograph.

Below the bell was a drawer with a word painted in beautiful gold script. Arthur touched the word. *Songcatcher.* He felt a strange tingle surge through his body. Then he noticed some kind of dial with numbers on the side of the machine. Above the dial was the word *Dreamometer.*

It was as if the machine were whispering to him, but the whisper was something he felt more than heard. The voice seemed to say one word: *Listen.*

How does it work? Trinket would know. But Trinket wasn't there. Nearby were two closets. He opened the one on the left and walked in. On one wall were hundreds of small black boxes stacked on shelves all the way up to the ceiling. Each box was numbered and labelled with a picture and the title of its contents. He perused the labels: *Waterfalls, Night Birds, Nasty Storms, Tree Music, Gregorian Chants, Ancient Celtic Drowning Ballads, Bawdy Music Hall Ditties, Mozart: The Toddler Years, Italian Operas with Tragic Plots, Italian Operas with Silly Plots, Bear Cub Waltzes, Elephant Dirges, Mouse Anthems, Frog Symphonies* and so on. Across from the shelves was an enormous cabinet of many drawers. When Arthur opened one, he saw a row of cards. The cards seemed to correspond to the boxes, as each had a number and picture as well, along with a brief explanation of the sounds contained in each box.

Hanging on the wall next to the cabinet was a framed piece of parchment; at the top, written in elegant script, were the words *The Songcatcher: How to Listen in Four Easy Steps.*

What harm was there in listening for just a minute?

The instructions to operate the Songcatcher were quite simple. The first thing Arthur needed to do was choose what he wanted to listen to by picking one of the boxes. There were so many, though, and he had so little time! After much deliberating, he finally picked a dusty one on the bottom shelf that didn't have a picture or even a number, just a red question mark and the words *Choose for Me.*

Inside the box was a hollow brown cylinder made of wax, its surface etched with fine grooves. Arthur opened the drawer on the machine inscribed with the word *Songcatcher* and placed the cylinder over a brass tube the way the instructions said to do. The tube was connected to a phonograph needle. According to the description on the wall, this was how the Songcatcher worked its magic. While the cylinder spun, the needle ran along its grooves, allowing songs and other sounds to flow into the listener's dreams – for the listener had to be asleep in order for the machine to work. Once a sound slipped inside the sleeper's mind, the memory of it remained.

The next step was to set the Dreamometer. He didn't have much time, so he turned the dial to five minutes. Next, he dragged a chair over to the table. He set it below the

Songcatcher's bell, sat down and lowered the bell so it covered his head. Finally, the last step: he reached for the hand crank and turned it three times to the right, just as the instructions said. Then he closed his eyes.

Time disappeared and the world fell away.

Arthur sank into a deep, deep sleep. The Songcatcher entered his dreams and filled him with sounds – vibrating, lulling, soaring sounds – as if he had opened his heart like a door and the world poured in.

It was one long Song of Life, flowing into him like a river. He heard the sound of a swan, its head falling toward slumber; he heard swallows grazing over the pinnacles of the City, a spider weaving a silken web. He heard the night music of a tangled wood, moist with rain. The rain became a carillon of bells, the cry of a distant seal, a crashing wave, the formation of an ice crystal on the forest floor. He heard a boy playing a shofar in the desert, its wail transforming into the plaintive howl of a wolf to its mate. He heard a creation song from a faraway land, then a simple bone flute, a woman singing an aria, and someone leafing through the pages of a book.

The music of the world entered his heart and made a place for itself: a young man's tear splashing on piano keys after he has played a sonata, the warble of a thrush rising from a creek, a snail gliding over leaves, a child humming to herself, crickets, frogs, and waterfalls. He heard someone playing an Andalusian guitar, the drumming of a thousand bat wings inside a dark cave. He heard an ancient lyre, the last leaf of autumn falling to the ground, someone whispering *I love you*. He heard the sound of wind, a beating heart, a mother saying good night to her child.

Finally, Arthur heard his own steady, beautiful breath. He let out a gasp and awoke.

He felt serene. And something else he didn't quite understand.

Arthur's heart ached. But it wasn't that he was terribly sad. It just simply ached, as if it were too full and the contents had nowhere to go.

He looked at the clock next to the Songcatcher. He couldn't believe that only five minutes had gone by. It was ten to ten. He grabbed his duster and empty rucksack and ran downstairs and out the door.

When he and Goblin returned to Wildered Manor, Arthur tried to explain to Quintus why he hadn't taken anything from the house, but he kept muddling up his words. It was as if he were in shock from so much beauty.

"I'm sorry, Quintus," he said. "I just saw one thing after another, and I didn't know what to take, and then there was this … this machine and it, well, all of a sudden I was sleeping

257

and then there were birds and the ocean and … and all kinds of songs and … and…"

Quintus cut him short. "Stop yer nonsense, Spike," he said, frowning, and put the kettle on for tea. "Don't want to hear it now."

"But, Quintus, it was…"

"No, not a word more. Tomorrow you *gots* ta take somethin' or there'll be trouble for sure, you hear me? An' I'll have no more talk about sleep machines an' the like."

Arthur let out a frustrated sigh. "All right," he said. "But if I t–take something tomorrow, Quintus, will you show me where that place is then, 17 Tintagel Road? Will you promise? Please, will you?"

"If you do right by me tomorrow, I promise I'll do right by you."

That night, after eating soup and listening to the others sing while he, as usual, only hummed along, Arthur finally crawled under his quilt and went to sleep.

He dreamed of a tapestry of sounds, sounds he had no name for – all the birds and fishes and other creatures of the world, the waterfalls, the wind – all the songs and symphonies the Songcatcher had poured into his soul. And, unbeknownst to him, he sang a melody from his dark corner of the house, and his voice, lilting and pure, floated out the window into the world.

CHAPTER 32

A Promise Kept,
a Promise Broken

THE NEXT DAY, Quintus insisted that Arthur return to the big stone house. "Our lady friend comes back soon, so you'd better do things right this time. Gots to take advantage of her generosity while she's gone."

The group found this last remark quite funny, but Arthur didn't laugh. Instead, he politely reminded Quintus of their deal – that Quintus would show him where 17 Tintagel Road was after he finished the job. It was his sixth day in Lumentown, and he still didn't know where the street was. Arthur was getting impatient.

* * *

An hour later, Arthur and Goblin were standing in the alley near Lumentown Market. From there, it was just a short walk to the big stone house with blue shutters. Arthur was dying to listen to the Songcatcher again, but he was terrified of getting caught, and he certainly didn't want to steal anything from the beautiful, magical house.

"That's just plummy, me workin' with you again," said Goblin.

Arthur didn't know what to say. He hung his head and said, "S–sorry, Goblin. I don't even want to go."

"I don't care a toss what you want to do. The point is," said Goblin, "Quintus says you need to finish the job, an' Quintus calls the shots around here. Not you, not me, understand? Now, go on; you're wastin' my time." Goblin checked his tag, making sure it was on the outside of his shirt. Then he turned to go.

"Goblin – wait. Can I ask you a question?" said Arthur.

"What is it? We gots to go!"

"Why can't one of the others go to that house? I mean – why's it have to be *me*?"

Goblin snorted. "You're dumb as a radish, aren't you?" He removed his hat and brushed off a speck of dirt. "Listen to me. You know what a cabin boy is?"

"N–no … what is it?"

"Lowest on a ship's ladder, cabin boy is."

"I'm not sure I follow you, Goblin," said Arthur.

"I'll lay it out for you in plain English," said Goblin. "If everyone's starvin' on the ship, who do you think they're gonna eat first? Think it's the captain, do ya? Well, think again. You, Daisy Face." He poked Arthur in the chest with a long knobby finger. "You're our cabin boy, you is."

"B–but—"

"No buts about it. You gots the duster tag, cabin boy." He held up his own medallion. It was stamped 6, and below was the symbol of a carrot, which meant his sanctioned "job" was to load and unload carts at the market. "We all works outside jobs, if you knows what I mean." Goblin snorted again, which was his version of a laugh but sounded more like someone coughing up a piece of food. "Now, let's get on with it. You take some nice little treasures, you hear me? And swear you'll be here on time." Goblin put his trilby back on his head and continued. "D.O.G.C. makes their rounds on the hour every hour in this part of town, an' ya don't want to get caught. Just because you and I got numbers don't mean they won't check to see if they're legit if they see us loiterin' about. You almost made us late yesterday. Now, swear to it!"

"I swear, Goblin. I p–promise. But Quintus said if I have a tag, I should be fine."

"You heard what Floop said. Changing of the guard and all that. So you just make sure you're on time – and don't lose that feather duster!"

Goblin scuttled away toward the market in his green

waistcoat and trilby, and Arthur, in his new suit of clothes, held his feather duster in prominent view, just as he'd been told. He turned in the opposite direction and began walking toward the big stone house.

When Arthur plucked the key from under the stone bird, the neighbour wasn't in her yard. But she *was* watching him; let there be no mistake. She peered at him through her spyglass from her upstairs window. After he slipped inside the door, the woman went over to her desk, took out a piece of paper, and noted the date and time of day. "Curious," she said to her husband, who was reading the paper. "Curious that one should require a duster two days in a row."

"Yes, dear," said her husband, turning a page.

"Then again … that house must be covered in filth, the way she lets groundlings in and out. That woman is an abomination! I suspect she allows the vermin to relieve themselves right on the carpet! Yes, I'm sure of it!" She put her hand up to her forehead, as if she were about to faint. "The mess in there! I shudder to think!"

"Yes, dear," said her husband, turning another page.

"Still … it *is* curious, now, isn't it, Henry? Henry? *Henry!* Are you listening to me?!"

* * *

This time, Arthur ran straight upstairs to the room with the Songcatcher. He opened the closet on the left and gazed at all the rows of boxes. There were just too many to choose from. For lack of a better idea, he closed his eyes and picked three boxes at random. They turned out to be: the Complete Works of Beethoven; Mouse Hornpipes, Airs, and Jigs; and Medieval Dance Music. He decided to listen to each for ten minutes, which gave him ample time to do what he had to do and still get back to Goblin.

He chose the Medieval Dance Music first. He knew what dancing was from Trinket, who had demonstrated how to dance one day – or at least how her people danced – which meant a lot of hopping up and down and spinning really, really fast. Which to him looked just like she always looked when she was excited, but she assured him there was a difference.

"This first one's for you, Trinket," he said.

The music was a richly textured mix of ancient instruments that Arthur had never heard of – medieval harps, rebecs, viols, frame drums, sackbuts, bells and wooden flutes – and it made his heart expand. He felt light and happy as he dreamed. It was like flying. He listened to things called saltarellos and *estampies*. They were fast and rhythmic, and without knowing it, he stamped his feet to the music as he slept.

Next, he listened to Mouse music, which was lively too, although some of it was so high-pitched that later, when he woke up, his ear felt all itchy. He ended with Beethoven. This was something profound. It left him feeling breathless, full of yearning, and full of awe. He also felt like he needed to lie down and take a very long nap.

He carefully put the cylinders back in their boxes, shut the closet door, and went downstairs. Arthur had decided that the only thing he felt comfortable taking from the house that had given him so many gifts was food. Anyway, wasn't food a kind of treasure? At Wildered Manor, it inspired songs and made good soups. He found the larder next to the kitchen on the first floor and filled his pockets and rucksack with potatoes, onions, carrots and two small bags of rice. *There*, he said to himself. *That should make everyone happy.*

Arthur arrived at their meeting place early. He was to wait for Goblin by the entrance to the alley near Market Street, where they had parted ways almost an hour before. His pockets and rucksack were stuffed with food, and although he felt guilty about taking so much, he was quite pleased with himself all the same. He hoped Goblin and the others would be too.

The alleyway was empty. And then, all of a sudden, he noticed something flying in his direction. The thing, whatever it was, was blurting out random words that sounded like *Blech!* *Meep!* and *Glah!*

Arthur moved out of the shadows to get a better look. Was it some kind of bird? A giant bug? What could it be? Curious, he started walking toward it. It began to make clicking and buzzing sounds, like gears in motion. He stopped in his tracks. *Trinket? Could it be?* He felt a sudden rush of love for his friend.

Arthur called out, "Trinket? Is that you?" and ran toward the thing.

"Blech! Shmeep! Platz!"

When he got close enough, he saw that it wasn't Trinket at all, but some kind of odd mechanical bird with a head that was too big for its body and eyes that rolled around in their sockets. It blinked an awful lot as well. The bird's metal wings jerked up and down awkwardly until it finally stabilized itself. It hovered right in front of Arthur's face and blurted out "Ploop," followed by a peep.

A peep that sounded just like Trinket.

It opened its beak and Trinket's voice came pouring out: "Dear Arthur: If you can hear this message, my experiment worked! Hurrah! I found you! I told you I would find you, didn't I?"

Arthur couldn't believe it! It was *her*!

He forgot all about the D.O.G.C. and Goblin. He stood right in the middle of the alley, not caring a toss who saw or heard him.

There was another outburst of *Blech! Shmeep! Platz!*, then the bird continued talking. Arthur listened, captivated, his heart beating fast.

"This is a messenger pigeon, Arthur! Still has some bugs to work out (like that eye-rolling thing – quite annoying, really), and sometimes it says things that don't make sense at all, but don't worry. I'll sort them out soon enough."

Trinket told him how she'd found her uncle, who was indeed a tinkerer. And that she was safe and sound, living in a tree house by the sea. But she couldn't wait to see him. "I miss you terribly, Arthur," she said. "Do you miss me? I am learning a lot from my uncle, though. He's not an inventor, really, but he's awfully good with his beak. As you know, Arthur, it's all in the beak." She began to laugh and so did he. It was as if she were right there with him.

She asked him where he was living and whether he had eaten a pie yet, and if he had found the house on Tintagel Road. She also asked if he had had any trouble in the City. She said her uncle had told her that every town made up its own rules about groundlings. "We're lucky," she said. "My uncle said some towns don't even let groundlings live there at all. The people here are nice, though. It helps that my uncle's the only tinkerer around!"

Trinket told him to follow the instructions at the end of her message so he could send a message back. "It works sort of like a player piano, Arthur, but you probably don't know what that is. When you speak into it, something inside punches little holes on a scroll and… Oh, never mind. Rather hard to explain. Just talk, and I'll get the message! And don't worry. The bird knows how to find me. And it will always be able to find you. At least I hope it will. The first experiments were disasters. I sent messages to twenty complete strangers!"

Arthur stood there grinning. Then Trinket's voice said, "Oh, by the way, I haven't figured out yet how to stop it from flying away right after my message ends. So Arthur, grab it *right now* so you can send me a message back!"

The bird began flying in circles around Arthur's head, then it flipped over and took off down the alley in the opposite direction of where he was supposed to meet Goblin. It kept squawking, "Hello, Arthur! Goodbye, Arthur! Hello! Goodbye! Blech! Meep! Gack!"

He tore after it down the alley and around the corner. He flew past donkey carts, street musicians, bicyclists and people heading to market. The bird zigzagged to the right, flew straight up, then swooped down another alley. After several minutes, he finally caught the bird. As soon as he grasped it firmly in his hands, a scroll popped out of its beak. The bird began talking again. Trinket's voice told him to insert the scroll into the side of the bird: "See the slot there, Arthur? Feed the scroll through it while you talk. The bird will do the rest!"

Then he remembered Goblin. He was going to be late.

Goblin, Trinket, Trinket, Goblin – what to do?

There was so much to say, but he kept it short because he was worried about Goblin. He would be so angry!

"Trinket," he began, "I know it hasn't been long, but I miss you so much. I can't wait till you come!"

He quickly told her where he was staying but left out the part about how he had to wear a tag again, and how he had just stolen about ten pounds of vegetables. He didn't even mention the Songcatcher. He had to get back to Goblin. "Send another message soon!" he said. "Please, you have to. And tell me when you're coming. I've got to go now."

After he finished talking, the bird set off on a crazy path down the alley, flying upside down, banging into walls, and squawking all the way until it finally turned the corner and was gone. Arthur glanced up at the clock on the building across the street. He was very, very late.

Arthur ran back as fast as he could to the place he was

supposed to meet Goblin. But Goblin was nowhere to be seen.

Arthur called out to him several times. He searched behind every rubbish bin and discarded crate and box, but still, there was no Goblin.

Then he heard a terrible sound – the sharp cry of someone in pain, followed by a steam whistle and the rattling of hooves on cobblestones.

Arthur peeked around the corner. Two men wearing thick brass goggles and black bowler hats bearing the D.O.G.C.'s insignia of a single eye were shutting the back of a large black wagon, pulled by two automaton horses. Steam billowed from the horses' nostrils and ears. Arthur could see the D.O.G.C. logo on the door, and above the letters were the words *We See All!*

And lying in the middle of the road was Goblin's beloved green trilby, flat as a pancake and covered in mud.

CHAPTER 33

The End of Music

GOBLIN WAS GONE, and it was entirely his fault.

Back at Wildered Manor, he turned over the vegetables he had taken, then, reluctantly, showed them Goblin's hat. Once he explained what had happened, no one would talk to him except for Squee, who felt sorry for him. Everyone moped about, grumbling to themselves or at one another. No one sang the soup song at dinner either, not even Quintus. They ate in silence, then went to bed.

In the morning, when they were all gathered in the common room for breakfast, Quintus told Arthur that Goblin had most likely been taken to prison or "down below," which was where Arthur would end up if he didn't bring something other than food back from that house. "Workin' in the coal pits now, I reckon," said Quintus. "He might never see the light a day again, poor sot. You let me down, Spike. I need to trust me mates. It breaks me heart – Goblin gone an' you lettin' me down."

Arthur had one more day to redeem himself before the lady who lived at the stone house returned. If he could just take one small thing, maybe Quintus would still help him find the house where he was born. Yet he knew in his heart of hearts that he would disappoint Quintus again, for how could he ever take something from that magical place? He was so anxious about it that he kept pulling on his ear.

But two beautiful thoughts existed alongside the weight of guilt and worry: Trinket's message and the wonder of the Songcatcher. When he thought about the miraculous machine, he felt light and giddy, as if he could float up to the ceiling of Wildered Manor and fly over the City's bright spires.

He couldn't wait to go back to the house with blue shutters.

And he dreaded it as well.

It was sad going alone. None of the others would go with him, not even Squee. Even though Goblin had never been that nice, Arthur sensed that he hadn't always been so grumpy. He felt so sorry for what had happened, he couldn't bear thinking about it.

When Arthur got to Stinkbottom Bridge, he paid the toll monkey, which went as well as it could go, considering the monkey screamed at him five times instead of three. But when he greeted Constable Floop, the officer didn't respond in kind. Floop looked right through him as if he weren't even there.

Strange, thought Arthur. *Very strange indeed*.

When he arrived at the house, he was so excited about listening to the Songcatcher again that he pushed the thought of stealing out of his mind completely. He dropped his duster in the foyer and ran straight upstairs. He knew exactly what he wanted to hear this time.

Lullabies. The song he had carried in his heart for as long as he could remember had to have been a lullaby. If he could find the song, he might be able to piece together the puzzle of who he really was.

But finding the right lullaby proved to be a difficult task. Apparently, there were millions of lullabies in the world. He searched the catalogue. The list was endless: Lullabies for Naughty Babies, Lullabies for Sweet & Tender Babies, Lullabies for Hedgehogs, Songs for Sleepy Lemurs, Songs for Sleepy Sloths, Snuggling Songs in the Key of C, D, E, and so on. He shook his head in frustration. Finally, he narrowed it down to only one, a box labelled simply *Lullabies*.

After he put the cylinder in place, Arthur pulled the Songcatcher's bell over his head and turned the hand crank three times. The tinkling sound of a music box lulled him to sleep, and he slipped into a dream.

It was like his old dream – his nightmare – only this time it wasn't scary; at least, the scary part hadn't happened yet. It was the same place he always saw, but he could see it much clearer now. He saw the backyard of a big white house and beyond, a grove of trees. The animals weren't running away in the dream, but walking toward him instead. There were rabbits and squirrels, birds and mice and even a fox! And there was no blazing pillar of fire, just a beautiful sky glittering with stars and an orange moon above. It was all so lovely and peaceful. In the distance, he saw the silhouettes of soaring towers and spires; it was the skyline of Lumentown.

In the dream, he was looking up at the stars. Someone was holding him, rocking him to sleep. He knew that whoever it was was about to sing the music box's song.

But Arthur never got to hear the song, or see the face of the singer, for a loud crash downstairs wrenched him from his dream. He heard the sound of glass breaking, then fervent whispering. He pushed the Songcatcher bell up and off his head. Three creatures were talking, and their voices were frighteningly familiar.

"You lot start in the front of the house. I'll check the

back," said one. Another said, "Right, Wire," and a third added, "We got this."

Wire, Mug and Orlick? What in the world were they doing here?

The fur on Arthur's neck stood up. He dashed inside the Songcatcher closet and looked frantically for a place to hide. But there were only narrow shelves of boxes, and the drawers in the cabinet were much too small to hide in. He ran back out, opened the closet on the right, and slipped inside. It was dark and cluttered, perfect for hiding. Inside the closet, hanging on a hook next to the door, was a key. He locked himself in and crawled under a pile of blankets in the corner.

He lay very, very still.

Wire, Mug and Orlick were downstairs, turning things over, throwing things about, and making a huge racket. Every once in a while, Wire would hiss at the other two to "hurry up and find it, you stupid twits!"

Arthur could hear every single horrible word.

When they finished demolishing the rooms on the first floor, they moved on to the second. They rummaged through closets, yanking out dresser drawers, throwing the contents on the floor and stomping on them. They were clearly looking for something but destroying things along the way just for fun. Arthur could hear them saying things like "Look under the bed, you clodpole" and "I already checked there, ding-dong."

Wire, Mug and Orlick started up the stairs to the third floor.

They were in the music room now, knocking all the instruments to the ground, breaking things left and right. Arthur heard the stack of miniature pianos tumble to the floor and shatter. They bashed the violin against the wall, kicked the harp down the stairs, and smashed the hurdy-gurdy to bits.

Then they were in the Songcatcher room.

"Well, look what we have here," said Wire in that cool, cruel voice of his.

"Must be it," said Orlick. "She said a big brass bell whatsit. But fer my money, don't look like much to me."

Arthur could hear Wire smacking Orlick on the side of his head. "Idiot. What *you* think doesn't matter, does it? Let's just find the plans and get out of here."

Arthur shook beneath the pile of blankets. *Why?* He said over and over in his head. He choked back tears. *The Songcatcher! What if they destroy it? What if they destroy* me?

All at once Wire was outside Arthur's closet, jiggling the handle. "Must be in here if the door's locked," said Wire. "I'll get it open. I'll kick it open if I have to." Arthur lay very still. It was stifling under the blankets, and he could barely breathe. The door shook violently as Wire tried to kick it in. But salvation came from Orlick, who called out from the other closet, "I found it! It's in here, mate! Plain as day!"

"Give it to Wire, you moron," said Mug. Arthur could hear them grunting and pulling something. It sounded like they were playing tug-of-war.

"I know! No need to be nasty like."

"Yer the one who's nasty. Take fer instance yesterday, when—"

"Will you two shut it?" said Wire. "Now, hand those plans over or I shall demonstrate how nasty *I* can be."

All three were in the other closet now, examining something. "Yes," said Wire. "This must be it. She said it was a long scroll tied with a blue ribbon. These must be the plans. This is good. This is very good. She'll be quite pleased. Now you can have one more minute of fun, then let's get out of here. Sneezeweed said he'd wait for us in the cellar. We'll have to go back the way we came, through the drainpipe again."

"Them tunnels down below give me the willies," said Mug. "An' I almost got stuck in that pipe. Me bum's still sore, if you really want to know."

"I really don't care to know about your bum right now," said Wire.

"Well, I don't like bein' Sneezy's slave."

"Me neither," said Orlick.

"Just remember – you are working for *her*, not him. And just keep thinking about all that extra cheese," said Wire. "And all those special privileges she promised."

Before they left, Mug and Orlick knocked as many cylinder boxes off the shelves as they could, then stomped on the cylinders rolling around on the floor. They yanked some of the catalogue drawers open and tossed bunches and bunches of cards up in the air, laughing demonically.

"That's enough, now," said Wire coolly. "Go pick that thing up and let's get out of here. And don't drop it!"

Arthur waited until he was sure they were gone, then crept out from under the pile of blankets.

He was about to run out of the closet when a thin beam of light from a small round window fell on a picture hanging on the wall. There, in a gilded frame, was the same hand-coloured engraving Arthur had first seen in the infirmary – two happy girls beneath an apple tree, the very same apple tree right outside the house. *It c–can't be,* he said to himself. *I don't understand.* He dragged a box over to the window and reached up to open the curtains, letting the light pour in.

The engraving wasn't the only picture hanging in the dusty closet. There were rows and rows of photographs, all of Miss Carbunkle or her twin sister, whose name, as he discovered on a label, was Phoebe Nightingale.

Arthur knew he should hurry up and go, but he just couldn't. He had to find out more.

There the twins were, together at age six, in matching pinafores and bonnets on matching ponies. And at age seven, at the zoo with their governess. Age ten, waving from the bow of a great ship. And at twelve, the girls at a picnic, dressed all in white, playing croquet. As Miss Carbunkle grew a little older, Arthur could tell her apart more easily in the photos, for while her sister's face became lovelier and more open and kind, Miss Carbunkle's grew sour and stern. And then, after age eighteen, there were no more pictures of the two together, just photographs of Phoebe Nightingale from the past thirty years. In one, she was standing in front of a music hall – the very same music hall Arthur had seen on his first day in the City! The marquee above read: *The Golden Voice of Phoebe Nightingale: One Night Only!* In others, she was waving from a hot-air balloon above the City; or on a concert hall stage, singing, her eyes closed, her hands clasped at her chest; or dressed in finery and jewels in her parlour, a fluffy white dog in her lap. There were photographs of Miss Phoebe in sailboats with friends, and on horseback, or playing the piano, or making a toast at a dinner party at her home.

On the dusty shelves, Arthur found remnants of Miss Phoebe's past: bundles of cards and letters, stacks of daguerreotypes, various kinds of tokens from her family and her life on the stage.

Arthur was absolutely bewildered. How was it that of all

the houses Quintus could have chosen for him, he had ended up in this one? And who *was* Phoebe Nightingale? And what exactly had happened when she and Miss Carbunkle turned eighteen?

It seemed impolite to look through all these personal things, but he couldn't help it. He picked up a bundle of old letters tied with a pink ribbon. He had started reading the first one – a letter from Phoebe's father to her – when he thought he heard sounds coming from the house next door. He had to get out of there *now*.

Before he ran downstairs, he glanced at the table where the Songcatcher had sat. All that remained was the clock.

CHAPTER 34

Wanted

ARTHUR RUSHED out the back door so fast that he didn't shut it tight. He ran all the way to Wildered Manor and didn't stop once except to pay the Stinkbottom toll.

He hoped against hope that the neighbour hadn't seen him come or go. But she had. She had observed his coming and going through her spyglass. She noted the open door, banging in the breeze. She noted the way he had fled from the place. She wrote her detailed observations on a piece of paper, then gathered her skirts and went out to investigate. She peeked inside the door and saw the rampant destruction. Then she found Arthur's feather duster lying in the middle of the foyer. "Aha!" she said. "Caught you in the act! I knew it, I knew it!"

She immediately sent one of her servants to fetch the police, who alerted the D.O.G.C., since the culprit appeared to be a groundling, not a human. The authorities were there within minutes.

"I knew that groundling was dodgy the moment I saw him," she said to the D.O.G.C. officer when he arrived. "He had that *look,* if you know what I mean."

"Oh, yes, madam," said the officer. "I know *exactly* what you mean."

He said that he suspected that the devious groundling was responsible for a string of robberies in the area.

"Oh, my!" said the woman. "I shudder to think what he could have done to me! Not to mention what he could have done to poor, defenseless Baby!"

"Did he appear to be dangerous, madam?" asked the officer.

"What a question! I was afraid for my life." She proceeded to offer a description of Arthur, with several embellishments, of course. And within no time at all, posters of him were plastered all over the City.

In the posters, he looked rabid, his teeth bared as though he were about to bite someone's nose off. His ear looked larger too, and his eyes looked crazy. Around the artist's rendering it said:

WANTED FOX GROUNDLING. DANGEROUS! THIEF! OUTLAW! WILD & CRAFTY! Use caution! Violent when provoked. REWARD! Contact the D.O.G.C. WE SEE ALL!

* * *

When Arthur arrived at Wildered Manor, no one was home except for Quintus, who knew something was up the moment he saw him.

Arthur frantically explained what had happened. He told Quintus everything. This time Quintus listened intently when Arthur told him about the Songcatcher. When Arthur told him about how Wire and his friends had destroyed every musical instrument in the place, Quintus winced. But when he tried to ask Quintus how he had happened to send him to Miss Carbunkle's sister's house, Quintus brushed it aside, saying, "World's full of funny coincidentalisms, lad. Don't pay it no mind."

"What if someone saw me?" asked Arthur. "What if they think *I* did it?"

"'Course they'll think you done it. But that ain't all," said Quintus gravely.

"What do you mean?"

"Listen an' listen good. Me an' Floop an' a couple t'others, we gots an unnerstandin' – a business arrangement, you might say. It's all fine an' dandy. But there's a line me an' the mates can't cross. *Never.* But the problem is, Spike – *you* crossed it."

"*I* c–crossed it? I don't understand, Quintus."

"Where's your duster, Spike?"

Arthur searched inside his rucksack. It was empty.

"As I feared. You crossed the line. 'Twasn't me who left yer duster. An' that'll lead 'em all the way here. Don't think Floop won't give ya up if D.O.G.C. breathes down his neck." Quintus took hold of Arthur's arm and looked him in the eye. "Listen, Spike – I can't lose this house, you unnerstand? I can't be harbourin' a criminal. If I do, they'll take away the house an' I'll end up like Goblin too."

"But I'm not a criminal!" said Arthur.

"I know you ain't, but D.O.G.C. will think you are, sure as I'm standin' here. What I mean to say is – you gots to go. I'm sorry, but that's the way it is. An' you gots to go *right now.*"

"B–but where can I go?" Arthur stared at the floor, trying desperately to think where he could run to. *Trinket!* "I—I have a friend by the sea," he said. "I'll—I'll leave the City. I'll go back the way I came. I'll—"

"They'll be lookin' fer ya all over Lumentown and beyond! Floop told me just last week D.O.G.C.'s been lookin' fer some groundlink who's been breakin' into houses. Now they'll think it's you, Spike. Only one place for you now, I'm afraid." He put his hand on Arthur's shoulder.

Arthur looked up at Quintus. He knew the answer before Quintus even said it.

"Below," said Quintus. "Far, far below. Now, hurry!"

Quintus told him about a secret entrance to the City below the City, a passageway through the sewers on the other side of the river. "Can't go over the bridge, mind. Gots to ferry across. An' the ferry only runs after dark."

"But, Quintus, I—"

"Ya gots to hide somewhere till nightfall, hear me? Then look for the ferry. You'll know the boat when you see it."

"Can't I just hide here? *Please.*" His voice cracked.

Quintus shook his head solemnly. He handed Arthur a coin. "Gonna need somethink to get across, m' boy. Put this an' that other one I gave ya someplace safe."

"Thank you, Quintus," said Arthur with tears in his eyes. "P–please say goodbye to the others for me, okay? Especially Squee."

He quickly threw together a bundle of things. He rolled up the suit of clothes Quintus had given him ("You can keep 'em, Spike, as a remembrance like, an' keep the rucksack too"), and he put on the clothes he had come with. He tucked his blanket scrap and gold key into his shirt pocket, along with the coins Quintus had given him.

When he was ready, he stood inside the door to Wildered Manor, clutching his red hat. He didn't know what to say to his mentor, his betrayer, his friend. All he could manage was "I—I still need to find 17 Tintagel Road... Can you—?"

Quintus gripped him by the shoulders and said, "No time for that now. Now, run! Run like the devil! Run!"

PART
THE THIRD

In Which the Wonderling Finds
That Which Once Was Lost
& Discovers the Truth About
Some Things Along the Way

CHAPTER 35

One Born With Wings, One Born Without

EMEMBER WHEN YOU FOUND ME?" asked Mardox. It was early morning, and the manticore was reclining on a cushion next to Miss Carbunkle in her observatory as she gazed out through her telescope at the courtyard below. Ever since the two groundlings had escaped, she had become more vigilant in her surveillance activities.

Her first act in reestablishing order was to abolish break time. She wondered, though, if she would miss it. Break had been the one time in her dreadfully boring, regimented week when she could relax her rules long enough to let her hair down – or would have, if she had hair. She allowed her mind to wander and thus had come up with her best inventions – inventions she still had no money to build.

Now, in place of break time, she and Sneezeweed took turns running her newly instituted Groundling Obedience Retraining Programme (otherwise referred to as G.O.R.P.). The orphans were forced to sit in the classroom for two straight hours and repeat, over and over: *I will not sing, I will not play. I'll toil in silence night and day.* ◆

"Mistress?" said Mardox.

"Sorry, my pet. I was thinking of something else. Yes, of course I remember. How could I forget?" She put down her telescope and pulled the creature onto her lap.

"Tell me the story again," begged the manticore. *"Please?"*

"But you know how it brings back bad memories, my sweet."

"Well, Mistress … if you don't want to…" He gazed up at her, his droopy eyes glistening and moist.

"Oh, Mardox. Of course I'll tell you the story." She fondly petted his rubbery snout. "It's the only bright moment from that wretched time." Her face clouded up, and she bit her thin, pale lip.

"Calm yourself, my mistress. Think of the moment we became one. Think of that!"

◆ Without intending to, however, Miss Carbunkle had written a poem. One could even say – if it had been set to music – that the headmistress had unwittingly written a song.

"You are right, as usual. But first, perhaps I should see what that incompetent assistant of mine is up to."

"Let the others do the work now, Mistress," said Mardox. "Then you and I can focus on more important matters, like the machine, and your sister and our plan. After you tell me the story, of course." He laughed, or rather, he made a peculiar noise that was a cross between a hiss, a chortle and a snarl.

"Once again, my pet, you are correct. I am done with doing servants' work! Let the Rat and the others earn their keep. And let that nitwit Sneezeweed do his job for once!"

After Trinket and Arthur's escape, the first thing Miss Carbunkle did was replace the dogs Sneezeweed had lost with another pair of mastiffs, equally drooly and dim. She thought of hiring guards from the City, but then Wire had offered up a most brilliant, not to mention inexpensive, solution. Why not use the meanest bullies at the Home to keep the others in line? Give them a little of this and that – some cheese, extra soup and bread, a new set of clothes, and, most important, an ounce of power – and they would gladly do her bidding. It was astonishing how little it took to gain their loyalty.

She placed Wire in charge of them all. That Rat was proving to be quite useful, all things considered.

* * *

Miss Carbunkle gazed out her panoptic window at the sky. It was heavy with clouds, but for once there was no rain. Soon she would travel to her second appointment with the man with the white gloves. This time they were to meet not in the castle high on the hill but in that dreadful place called Gloomintown. But no matter. She would go to the ends of the earth if it meant securing funds for her project. She hoped she would be successful in pleading her case this time around.

"Don't think of that," said Mardox, reading her mind. "Tell me the story instead."

"Sorry, my pet. Ah, yes, the story."

Mardox nuzzled his snout in Miss Carbunkle's cold white hand and purred.

The headmistress took a deep breath and began.

"It was after my father's funeral, and I went walking in the graveyard. I was sad, but more angry than sad, for a great injustice had been done to me."

Her face clouded up again, and Mardox murmured, "There, there, Mistress. Tell me the lovely part, the part when we became *one.*"

And so, in the grey morning light, Miss Carbunkle told the tale of how she found the manticore on the outskirts of a graveyard, at the edge of a barren field. She recounted how she had tripped over a root and tumbled down face-first into a ditch, twisting her ankle along the way. When she sat up, she knew she'd need help climbing out. That was when she saw the top of a cane sticking out of the earth. She saw his wooden hawk face, and their eyes met.

Just when she needed help the most, there he was, unlike her family. They had never been there for her. Not once.

"Your eyes flashed amber, and I felt something inside me. I had to free you. I knew it then."

The manticore's face brightened. "Go on, Mistress! Please tell me the rest!"

She told him that she knew how painfully he wriggled and writhed inside his wooden prison beneath the earth. She *felt* it. As though *she* were inside the cane, struggling to be free.

She felt it all. How he had waited all those years, for decades, for centuries. And then she came. The one to whom he was meant to bind his soul.

Even long after her ankle had healed and she had no need for a cane to lean on, she never took a step without it. The manticore was her confidant, and she was his protector. She rid the Home of mirrors, to prevent him from seeing his own reflection. For it was true that a manticore must never look upon himself, but only gaze at the one to whom he was bound – lest he accidentally see his own dark soul in the reflection ... and perish.

What she didn't know was that she was but a stopping place along his way. And, that as special as she was – beloved by him, one might even say – there would always be Miss Carbunkles when he needed them. And they would always need him. For he was born of old magic, which, as we all know, has a mind of its own.

After she had finished telling him the story, Mardox drifted off to sleep. Miss Carbunkle sat there, unmoving in the grey light, unable to shake her memory of that time. How she *hated* that time. The dreaded funeral, and all the horrible, cloying people clustering around her *darling, sweet sister* – that awful, awful creature, that freak. And the day before that, when she and Phoebe sat beside their father and watched him die. Even then, despite the fact that *both* of them had come to sit vigil, he still loved her sister more than he loved her.

It had always been so, her father's preference for the other twin. The *oh-so-talented, silver-tongued beauty* Phoebe Nightingale, the sister she hated with all her heart, or what was left of that small leathery sack inside her chest.

They were not identical twins, in more ways than one.

When the first twin arrived, the father sang out her name – Phoebe, named for his beloved wife. She arrived pink and beatific, with two tiny blue-black wings sprouting from each shoulder blade, just like her mother. But at the moment of the second twin's birth, something went terribly wrong.

When the baby emerged, red-faced and screaming, the mother let out a gasp, rolled her eyes heavenward, and was gone.

For days, the child remained nameless. Its father was lost in sorrow and couldn't bear to see it. A week passed, then two. Finally, after a month, the maid came into her master's study, holding the infant in her arms, and said: "If you please, sir, the wee bairn needs to be called somethin'. What abouts Clementine for a name? Look at them chubby orange cheeks – round and bright as a fruit to be plucked, they are." The infant's father whispered feebly, "Call it whatever you like; just take it away," and waved his hand for the maid and the child to leave.

And from the day of his wife's death, Clementine Carbunkle's father preferred Phoebe, who had inherited her mother's angelic voice and small fluttering wings. Wings that the family kept secret, just as they kept secret Clementine's hairless, feathery head.

Although the second twin could not carry a tune, Clementine had gifts of her own. But no one noticed.

She invented things. Extraordinary things. Just like her father, the inventor. She kept the models she made for her inventions hidden in a cabinet, along with her diagrams, sketches, and intricate building plans. For not one soul in the house paid them any mind at all.

The day both girls turned eighteen was the day their

father suddenly took ill. Within a week, it was clear he was dying. He told the maid to call the girls to his bedside. They came at once.

Phoebe and Clementine sat on the edge of his bed, one on either side.

"I don't have long, my dears, I know this now. So please listen to what I have to say." He turned his head to young Phoebe, who was weeping and clutching his hand. "There, there, my darling girl! No tears! There's a good girl. My time is short, so listen: You, my Phoebe, my little songbird, shall be a great singer. You shall take your mother's last name, the grand name of Nightingale. Certainly not mine. Carbunkle is no name for a shining star. A Carbunkle is one letter away from a pustule, a blemish, a boil. No – you, my darling…" He paused to cough violently. He took a sip of water from the glass Phoebe offered him and went on. "You, my dearest Phoebe, shall be the nightingale you were born to be, and sing to the world like your dearly departed mama, my one great love." Tears filled his eyes as he said this. "You shall sing in the grandest concert halls across the world. Your trademark shall be your name and your cloak. It shall be rich indigo, like your eyes, and it shall conceal your secret inheritance – your beautiful blue-black wings."

Their father broke into a terrible fit of coughing. When he composed himself, he turned to Clementine. "And you, my dear." He sighed and coughed again. "You must have a respectable profession, my dear Clemmy. Why not? Why should women always marry? Yes, you too shall go forth into the world and succeed."

There was an uncomfortable pause, followed by another bout of coughing. Phoebe reached for her father's hand and squeezed it hard. Her sister sat stiffly on the other side of the bed, her hands rigid in her lap.

"As you know, my child," he continued, smiling weakly, "you were not blessed with your mother's musical gift like your dear, darling sister. It *is* unfortunate. But I know you can make your way in the world somehow. At first I thought … a nurse is a fine profession or … a secretary or … a companion to a high-hatted lady…" His sallow face brightened a little. "But then I hit upon it. You shall teach! As they say: those who cannot do can always teach. And you shall!" He coughed again. It was clear it was getting more difficult for him to breathe. "My dear Clemmy." *Oh, how she hated that name! It sounded like "clammy!" And her full name, Clementine, the name of a sour fruit, given to her by a mere commoner!* "You are a smart girl," said her father. "And while you did not inherit your mother's talent—" here he paused again—"you have her strong will and … and I suppose you have a little of me as well. You have…"

She waited for him to say the magic words she had wanted her whole life to hear: *You have my gift for invention.*

Instead, he said in a feeble voice, "You have my family

name – Carbunkle – which, although it *does* sound rather like an infected boil … will help you gain access to Society. And without your sister's grace and talent, my dear—" he smiled weakly at her—"you will need all the help you can get."

He didn't notice the pained, constricted look on his daughter's face. How she pulled back from him ever so slightly, how her heart began to shrink at the very moment of his demise.

"My dear girls," he whispered hoarsely, for he was not long for this world. "Always be good, always be kind, and—" His voice broke off. He began to make terrible rasping sounds and seemed to be fading away.

"Papa!" cried Phoebe, grasping his hands in hers.

Several moments passed in silence, save for the sound of their father's laboured breaths.

Finally, with great effort, he slowly turned his face to Phoebe's, away from Clementine's, and gasped, "My darling girl … you must reach for the stars. For *you*, they shall always be within reach."

And then he died.

It was Phoebe who inherited his most miraculous invention of all: the Songcatcher. It was Phoebe who inherited the house – her mother's family home, the lavish House of Nightingale – and everything in it. She inherited her mother's gowns and her beautiful indigo cloak edged with tiny grey pearls.

Clementine inherited a large crate of textbooks and money specifically earmarked for her training as a teacher and, afterward, to start a school, or orphanage, should she desire to do something to benefit the less fortunate of the world.

When Mardox awoke from his nap, he knew from Miss Carbunkle's face what she was thinking. "Do not trouble yourself about her, Mistress! She is not worth it!"

"*She* is a constant reminder of what I do not have," said Miss Carbunkle, punctuating each word in anger, for she had been fuming about her sister for the last hour while the manticore slept. "And I mean to stop her from having what she wants."

"Yes, Mistress. You must. And you know I shall do whatever it takes to help you."

The two sat for a while in silence as Miss Carbunkle stroked the creature's ears.

"Mistress?"

"Yes, my pet?"

"When shall we astonish them all, my lady? Do something terrible and grand? You know I have waited so very long."

"I know, my pet, I know. You must have a bit more

patience. Your day will come. And when it does, you shall blaze in glory! You will reveal your power—"

"*Our* power, Mistress. For we are one."

Her thin lips curled into a smile. "Mark my words, my pet. When the day comes, together we shall unleash your – *our* – extraordinary power. I promise you that."

CHAPTER 36

The Crossing

ARTHUR DIDN'T STOP RUNNING until he came to Stinkbottom Bridge. Music poured out of the Swan & Whistle, floating over the waves. How he longed to go inside, take his hat off, and order a big plate of cheese toasties with a cold glass of milk. But it felt too risky, so he hurried down the towpath to the riverbank instead. An upturned skiff promised shelter. He grabbed hold of the gunnel, heaved up the side, and slipped below.

He waited all day beneath the skiff, drifting in and out of sleep until darkness finally fell upon the City. It was time.

Arthur crawled out from under his hiding place and stretched his stiff legs. Quintus had said he would know the boat when he saw it. When he spotted the red glow of a grease lamp coming from a weatherworn rowboat docked along shore, he wondered if it was the same vessel he had seen ferrying passengers across the river during his first night in Lumentown.

Arthur crept up to the boat; he could barely make out the hooded figure hunched at the stern. Despite the fact that it was a warm night in June, the lumpy little man was wrapped in a heavy black coat and scarf, and his face was hidden in shadow.

"P–pardon me, sir," said Arthur. "If you please. Can you take me across the river?" He added, "Quintus sent me."

The ferryman spoke in a low, croaking voice. "We are the Norahc. We ferry the nameless, the hunted and the lost."

Another voice piped up, a pitch higher, and repeated the words. "We are the Norahc. We ferry the nameless, the hunted, and the lost."

Arthur tried to make out where the other voice was coming from, but he couldn't see anyone else in the boat. The man motioned for him to climb aboard. As he settled onto the hard splintery seat, a little head, identical to but smaller than the first, popped out of the man's collar.

"Oh, h–hello," said Arthur nervously. "I see there are two of you."

The two heads said in unison, "We are the Norahc. We ferry the nameless, the hunted, and the lost."

A third head, much smaller than the other two, popped out and said, clearly annoyed, "Yes, yes. What they said." He rolled his eyes toward the other heads. "We're the Norahc, blah blah blah. Can we just get on with it?"

"Oh, all right," said the first head. He turned to Arthur. "Pay first, go second." The third head grumbled, "Them's the rules."

Arthur could now see his face – rather, all three faces. They appeared both human and amphibian: three frog-like heads with bulbous eyes and greenish skin. "How m–much is it to cross?" asked Arthur.

"Show us," said the second head.

"Reveal," said the first.

"'How much is it?' he asks," said the third head. He snorted. "Pony up."

Arthur removed the tag from around his neck. "Will this do?"

The third head bit the disk and spat on the floor of the boat. "This ain't gold or silver. What you playin' at? You know how much we risk to take you lot across?"

"It's worth a lot of money to some," said Arthur.

"Not to us," said the first head. The Norahc tossed the medallion over its shoulder. Arthur watched it sink into the water without regret. He next offered it the coin that Quintus had given him as he was leaving Wildered Manor. The first head blew on it and bit it hard, his bulging eyes gleaming in the moonlight. The Norahc slipped it into its pocket. "What else? What else?" murmured all three at once.

The Norahc finally settled on the coin and Arthur's rucksack and its contents: his new set of clothes and the red hat that Pinecone had given him. "Well," said the first head, "this will have to do."

"I suppose so," said the second.

"We gets the dregs o' the earth every time," said the third.

"Let's just push off and go," said the second head.

Arthur still had the other coin tucked away, the one Quintus had given him the day he found his pocket watch below the floorboards. It was hidden with his baby blanket scrap and key. He was certain that he'd need some money when – and if – he made it below.

The second and third heads sank back down into the coat. The Norahc grabbed a very long oar and stood up. It began rowing as if it were steering a punt in low water. But once they pushed off from shore, the river became very deep indeed.

The fog swirled around the boat as they cut through choppy waves. The Norahc was silent. Arthur listened to the waves lapping against the boat and to night sounds floating over the river. Things drifted by in the wake: a piece of wood, a dead rat, a tattered fisherman's cap, and the carcass of a pig. They passed a coal barge, a steamboat, and a cockleboat or two, causing the Norahc's boat to rock violently in the black waters.

Then a strong wind blew in from the east, and choppy waves slapped hard against the boat, tossing Arthur from side to side. He feared they might capsize and lamented the fact that he had never learned how to swim. But then, who would have taught him to swim where he came from?

"If—if you please," said Arthur. "Mightn't it be easier if you ... if you sat down?"

"The Norahc does *not* sit," said the first head.

The boat continued to rock back and forth, the gunwales dipping dangerously in the river each time.

The second head appeared. "Excuse me, but he does have a point."

The third head popped up and snapped, "Sit down or we'll never get there. Besides," he added, "we need to rest our bum."

The first head sneered. "The Norahc does not *sit* when the Norahc steers the boat."

"Well, I've never liked that rule to begin with!" said the second head.

The three heads argued back and forth, causing the boat to rock even more wildly.

Arthur suggested in a meek voice, "Ex—excuse me, not to be disrespectful or anything, but ... shall *I* row? I mean, if it would help out."

He immediately regretted this, for, along with swimming, he had never ridden a boat in his life, let alone steered one.

The three heads all stared down at Arthur, their froggish lips curling into three identical sneers.

"I take that as a no," said Arthur. He cleared his throat. "I'll just … I'll just sit here and be quiet, then." After a lengthy pause, he said, "Lovely moon out tonight, don't you think?"

But the Norahc said nothing, and the second and third heads disappeared inside the creature's coat.

The tide was strong, and the Norahc rowed hard as it approached the shore. Arthur could see the kindling fires of Huddlers along the dock and riverbank. Finally, the boat reached the other side, about a half a mile downstream from Stinkbottom Bridge. There, Arthur disembarked, hatless, nearly penniless, and dressed exactly the same as when he had first arrived in Lumentown.

"Goodbye," he said to the Norahc as it swung the boat around and started back to the other side. "Thank you for the, uh, ride. Much obliged."

But all he could hear as the night swallowed up the boat were the creature's words, drifting over the waves. "We are the Norahc. We ferry the nameless, the hunted, and the lost."

CHAPTER 37

Down, Down, Down

QUINTUS HAD SAID that when he reached the other side, he should look for a manhole near where the Huddlers gathered. Through it was the way down – the unofficial way down, that is. There was an official entrance near Lumentown Market: an entrance to a station for the subterranean trains of Gloomintown. But those trains were reserved for the ones who could come and go freely from one realm to the next – the High Hats, D.O.G.C. officials, and factory owners. Groundlings – the numberless ones, the hunted ones like Arthur, and the lost – had to find another way.

Arthur came upon a group of Huddlers sleeping near a manhole, just like Quintus had described. He could see the steam rising around their bodies from the vents. One of the Huddlers, a gaunt young man, was kind enough to open the manhole cover and help Arthur down into the hole. From there, he descended a long rusty ladder that led into a large sewer pipe. He didn't know what else to do but follow where the pipe went – down, down, down – sloshing through who knows what kind of filth.

The stench was unbearable.

He slogged through a labyrinth of pipes in pitch-darkness. The water – or whatever it was – came up to his knees and was as thick as pudding. It was so dark that Arthur couldn't even see his hands in front of him. It felt as if the darkness crept into him and settled in his soul.

The wind howled through the pipes like a wild animal caught in a trap as Arthur made his way through a series of tunnels, following the flow of the slow current. After a while, his eyes adjusted to the dark, and he saw signs of life scuttling and creeping about the sides and top of the tunnels: small white crabs, frogs, slugs, rats and bugs the size of mice.

The drainpipe Arthur was in narrowed at the exact time the flow of the water sped up, causing him to lose his foothold. He suddenly found himself carried along by the current, bobbing up and down in the dark-brown river of filth. It drew him along so fast, he feared he would drown. It tossed him this way and that, and his head kept going under. He gulped in the mucky water and choked, struggling to keep his head above the surface.

He cried out for help, but all he could hear was his own voice echoing back to him: "Help me! Help me! Please!"

At last the rushing muck spilled into a much larger pipe. The water level lowered, and the current slowed. At the end of the long rusty pipe was a dim red light. He found his feet and trudged toward it with all the strength he had left in him.

The light led to a vast tunnel lit with red grease lamps. Arthur entered the tunnel and was at long last out of the river of sewage. He was drenched to the bone, covered in stinking filth, and shivering with cold. But he wiped his face off as best he could and kept going.

The tunnel led from one gloomy passageway to another, past a series of confusing corridors and a vast network of pipes and caves, leading to a labyrinth of even more tunnels.

Arthur was terribly lost.

Something was dripping from above, making small pools of stagnant black water everywhere. He looked up at the subterranean sky of sweating black rock and saw stalactites dripping rivulets from sewers above. The walls dripped too, and the ground where he stood was damp and covered in sewage. It was as if the City below the City were weeping.

Just like the gargoyles, thought Arthur.

He wanted to curl up somewhere and cry too, but he had to keep going.

Arthur let his ear be his guide. He had never been so grateful for his gift than in that moment, for he heard voices in a corridor on his right and hurried toward the sound. As he made his way, he noticed big-eyed mice and rats sniffing and gobbling up strange fungi, clumps of algae and scuttling bugs. He wondered what he was going to eat down there, at least until he could find a way out. *If* he could find a way out.

And if not, would he ever see Trinket again?

When Arthur entered the corridor, he saw an astounding sight: hundreds of groundlings were pouring in from all directions. He had never seen so many in his life. They were all shapes and sizes and ages. Some were so old, they could barely walk. There were many young ones too, their parents trying frantically to keep families all together.

Arthur was pushed and jostled in the crowd. As he walked, a fog set in, thick as soup and brown as umber, like some primeval force conjured from the centre of the earth.

He followed the corridor to a vast, vaulted place that looked like it had once been an immense cathedral made of black stone. Some groundlings went to the left, others to the right. All of them were seeking a bridge to the other side. For before them was a wide, sluggish river, deep and black as night.

Arthur closed his eyes and cocked his ear in one direction, then another. But there was no sound that could offer him the best choice. He tried asking others which way to go, but no one knew, for they were all strangers to this place too. He decided to turn right, and after several more twists and turns, he found himself at the head of a wide, rusty bridge.

Arthur soon discovered that at the entrance to Gloomintown, no little man with a teacup-shaped head and a clockwork monkey collected tolls from groundlings desperate to get inside. Instead, there was a giant mole groundling.

The Mole stood at the entrance to the bridge in a grey overcoat and bowler hat splattered with stains from the sewage dripping from above. The large black creature sniffed the stagnant air, his whiskers quavering. He held a stick in his hand; at the end of it was a barbed wire loop, which Arthur guessed was for snatching groundlings that tried to sneak by without paying.

As others pushed past him, Arthur felt paralyzed. He looked behind at the vast labyrinth of pipes and dark passageways flooded with filthy water. He couldn't go back; he could only move forward, so he waited in an unruly queue until it was his turn to go.

He approached the Mole cautiously. "H–hullo," said Arthur. "P–please, sir. I'd like to cross the bridge." He bowed. But the Mole was quite blind and didn't notice.

"Turn out your pockets," said the Mole. It was a soft,

sinister voice and oddly mesmerizing. "I smell it, groundling. Turn out your pockets. Quickly!"

Arthur had only one coin left. The coin Quintus had given him. It was his ticket out, his payment for food and shelter in Gloomintown until he could find safe passage away from there without travelling through the City above.

And so he lied.

"I ... I don't have anything. Please. May I pass?"

"I smell something shiny," said the Mole. Arthur gasped, fearing the worst – that the Mole would take his gold key. But the Mole sniffed the air and said, "Yes, yes ... something shiny and silver." The Mole stretched the word *silver* out slowly, as though tasting it on his tongue. "Yes, yes, silver." He sniffed the air again. "Turn out your pockets!" His voice was angry now; his black furry hand tightened around the stick with the wire loop.

Arthur had no choice but to pull out the coin from his pocket and hand it over to the Mole, who snatched it up.

The Mole ran his snout over it, his whiskers quivering with excitement. "Yes, yes, lovely silver, this. Lovely, lovely. You may pass."

Arthur heaved a sigh of relief and walked over the rusty iron bridge into Gloomintown.

CHAPTER 38

As Above, So Below

A COLD RAIN pelted down upon the roof of Miss Carbunkle's Home for Wayward and Misbegotten Creatures. It was June, but the weather inside the Wall was as dismal as always. It was the middle of the night, and everyone was supposed to be in bed. But three of Arthur and Trinket's old friends – Nigel, the dachshund groundling, and Nesbit and Snook, the rabbity twins – were huddled together in a corner of the younger groundlings' dormitory in Kestrel Hall, committing the worst possible crime of all.

They were singing.

And gathered 'round them were little ones, listening with wonder.

"That's called three-part harmony, that is," whispered Nigel.

"Lovely!" murmured the twins. "Lovely," murmured the others.

"Let's try it again, shall we?" said Nigel. "With more feeling this time, but *pianissimo*. The walls have ears! Right, then. Take it from the top: a-one and a-two and a-three!"

Despite Miss Carbunkle's New World Order – the implementation of increasingly more rules and Wire's gang of thugs gleefully ready to reinforce them – the groundlings had begun to defy the headmistress in every way possible. For many of them, in particular the ones who had helped Trinket in her clandestine endeavours, had been stirred to rebellion. And they were now unstoppable.

When chalk disappeared from the headmistress's storeroom, pictures began to appear everywhere. Funny pictures of a bald Miss Carbunkle trying to catch her wig and caricatures of Mr Sneezeweed blowing his nose right off his face. There were other kinds of pictures too – Arthur and Trinket sailing over the Wall to freedom, and images from the world outside: flowers and trees and butterflies and anything and everything the groundlings could remember from the time before they arrived.

They even drew unicorns and fairies. They were inspired. But inspiration can be a dangerous thing.

Once caught, the rebels were never seen again. The disappearances that had begun that winter had only increased. And just as more and more groundlings arrived at the Home each day, more and more began to disappear.

Thus, as Nigel, Nesbit and Snook began their forbidden song, a tall rat groundling with black pebble eyes and a bespectacled man with a runny nose, bandages around both wrists, and a cast on his foot came upon them.

The Rat, proudly wearing the yellow scarf the headmistress had given him, clamped his sharp-clawed hand over the mouth of Nigel, while Sneezeweed grabbed the twins' collars. The ones who had been listening quickly scampered to their beds and trembled under the covers, fearful that they would be taken as well.

Nigel, Nesbit, and Snook's crime was a Code Red S-3 infraction, meaning it was the worst possible crime (Code Red); specifically, singing (S); with three groundlings as the culprits (3).

Sneezeweed and Wire dragged the small criminals out into the hall and shoved them forward just a few feet to their left. They stopped in front of what they had always thought was a storage closet. At the end of every hall was the same closet door, and like most of the doors at the Home, it was always locked up tight.

The hall was empty as usual. Sneezeweed unlocked

the door and shoved Nigel, Nesbit and Snook inside the closet, then lit a small lamp. Wire followed Sneezeweed and the others.

It turned out it wasn't just a closet.

"Lovely word, *dungeon,*" said Wire. "Much nicer than *cellar* or *basement,* don't you think? More poetic, *dungeon.* Sits nicely on the tongue when one says it, I daresay."

Apparently, every single hall – Kestrel, Hawk, Falcon and Owl – had a secret entrance to the cellar, and the closet at the end of Kestrel Hall was one of them. Sneezeweed reached behind some cleaning supplies on a shelf at the back and pressed what looked like a stain on the wall. The wall sprang open like a door, and he and Wire shoved Nigel, Nesbit and Snook down a dark, winding staircase, into the unknown.

Cockroaches and spiders darted over their feet as they descended into the bowels of the Home. When the prisoners reached the bottom, a horrifying sight awaited them: as far as the eye could see was a factory. It was much larger than the Widget Room in Falcon Hall, which was the largest room in the Home. This was a real factory, with dozens and dozens of beetle-eating electromagnetic Monsters. And there were other machines that Nigel, Nesbit, and Snook were certain did other ghastly things.

The three small groundlings grabbed on to one another's paws and started to cry.

"Cut your slobbering!" said Sneezeweed. He dragged them into a dim, dank room next to the factory. All along the walls were small cells like animal cages. Inside were the older orphans who had disappeared over the past four months or so, the ones everyone called Grumblers. In other cells were groundlings who had broken rules, just as they had. And groundlings they had once thought adopted or sent to another place.

This *was* the other place.

Sneezeweed pushed the three of them into a cell and said, "Good riddance!" He blew his nose and said, "Work starts tomorrow, five a.m. sharp! And here you don't get the nice porridge and pea soup you get upstairs. You get what we call 'bow-wow broth.'"

Sneezeweed informed them that they would work every day and evening, but, out of the kindness of Miss Carbunkle's heart, they were allowed Sunday nights off. "But you will remain in your cells when not at work," he said with an emphatic sneeze.

"Oh, and by the way," added Wire. "No need for a clock down here. Believe me, you'll know what time it is."

The two turned and left to report back to Miss Carbunkle.

At the top of the stairs, Sneezeweed turned to Wire and said under his breath, "This is just fine and dandy, me working with you. A *Rat*. A common, conniving, filthy, stinking sewer rat groundling. I don't know what you're playing at, Wire, but don't expect me to believe that you're in this for anything other than to serve yourself. You *will* mess up, and when you do, I, Mortimer Horatio Eloishus Sneezeweed, will personally lock you up down below, with the rest of your kind. And I shall gladly let your rodent brethren dine on your spleen."

"Is that so?" said Wire, smiling coolly. "Well, you will see, over time – *Snotweed* – just how useful I can be to Her Missus, and how useless you truly are. Oh, and by the way, as for dining on spleens – I've been known to dine on one or two myself."

That same night, far away in the City below the City, Arthur sat gloomily against a wall of sweating black rock, next to a shallow pool, and pondered his hopeless situation. He had had a brutish journey that night and had just spent his last coin to cross a bridge – and for what? He had no money, no food, no place to sleep, and there was no way he could get out of this subterranean hell without help. But he didn't know a soul. Not only that, but he never even got to see where he was born on Tintagel Road. Then there was the Songcatcher. He'd never listen to it ever again. And Trinket seemed lost to him for ever.

Arthur didn't even have the energy to cry.

The water looked black in the dim light, but who could say? Everything looked dark to him. The eternal blanket of night in Gloomintown was even worse than the eternal grey of Miss Carbunkle's Home. How was he ever going to get out of there?

He wasn't alone, however. All along the wall were hundreds of groundlings, huddled together, hungry and spent. They too had no idea what to do or where to go.

The answer came soon enough in the form of a truculent badger groundling with exceptionally large forearms, great yellowish claws and a low, gravelly voice.

"Wake up, wake up, my pretties! Who wants a job? A fine bed for the night? Food for the belly? We all wants that, don't we? Queue up, queue up, groundlinks. An' those who don't likes to work, well then, take a look to your right." Everyone turned to see what the Badger was pointing at: a dark and dilapidated graveyard a short walk away. "Not a nice way to go, starvin' to death, heh, heh, heh."

Arthur joined the other wet and weary groundlings and got in line. He was bewildered by the fact that here, in the City below the City, groundlings, rather than humans, seemed to be in charge, at least so far.

The Badger opened up a giant red ledger and removed a quill pen from his pocket. "My name is Gaffer. But guess what? You lot gots no name down here! Heh, heh, heh! Instead, you

gets a number! No need for names down here, no, not a-tall."
He cackled again, the same *heh, heh, heh,* a sound that Arthur
found quite unpleasant to his ear.

When it was Arthur's turn, the Badger looked him up and
down. His eyes fixed on Arthur's once red fluffy ear – now
matted down with brown muck – and said, "Whot, you deaf
an' dumb, groundlink? Can. You. Hear. Me? Heh, heh, heh!"

Arthur decided that maybe this time it was in his best
interest *not* to hide his secret gift. He reckoned that if this nasty
creature thought he was deaf, he might give him the worst job
ever, and Arthur needed to earn *something* in order to get out
of there.

"Actually, sir, with all due respect, I can hear quite well.
B–better than well, in fact – I can hear things very, very far off."

"Well, in that case, Foxy, I gots a job for you! Starts tomorrow morning. You'll be what we here call a Trap-Rat."

"W–what's a Trap-Rat?" asked Arthur.

"Heh, you'll find out soon enough," said the Badger.

"Will I make enough to get back to Lumentown?"

"You won't be goin' nowhere, Foxy. No one goes back.
No one. An' by the way, down here you gets a new name: one
million, three hunnerd thirteen, hunnerd thirty-one, three
hunnerd thirteen. That would be, for a dimwit such as yourself, thirteen — thirteen — thirteen — thirteen — thirteen. Got
that? Oh, an' one more thing. Lose a day of work, lose a day of
bread. Now, wait over there with the rest of 'em until I say so."

After what seemed like hours, Gaffer finally led Arthur and the others to what he called their "new digs."

"Here they are, only the best for you lot!"

Arthur looked around but couldn't see anything except a big black wall. "Ex … excuse me, but where are we supposed to sleep?"

Gaffer grinned. "Oh, it's just a little hole in the wall, but it's cozy, heh, heh." He cocked his head toward it and laughed.

Arthur's new home was indeed a little hole in the wall.

Along the sheer black expanse, dripping with sewage from above, were rows and rows of holes carved into the rock from top to bottom. A complicated system of ropes, gears, platforms, and pulleys allowed the groundlings to ascend and descend the wall.

"Crookeries, we calls 'em," said Gaffer. "Night crows, thems made 'em long times ago for their babies. Let's hope they ain't comin' back to snatch you in the middle of the night! Heh, heh, likes to eat groundlinks, them birds! Thinks you lot is tasty!"

Gaffer handed each groundling a crust of bread and assigned them all crookery holes corresponding to their numbers.

"I reckon you lot wants a nice little blankie. Who wants a nice little blankie? Don't be shy," said the Badger.

They all raised their hands and paws eagerly, as it was quite cold and damp in Gloomintown.

"Well, bless my soul," said Gaffer. "I ain't got none!"

The crowd was silent. What else could possibly go wrong on this terrible night?

Arthur stared up at the vast wall and shook his head in dismay. Compared to this, the Home's stone Wall was nothing. "If you p–please, sir," he said, "how can I tell which one is mine?"

"Up at the top, Foxy. Next to the Wombat. Second crook to the left. The one with the five thirteens." He cackled with his mouth wide open; Arthur cringed at the Badger's teeth, which were rotten, cracked and brown. Before he turned to go, Gaffer jerked his head up toward Arthur's new "home" and said, "Mind the step! Heh, heh, heh!"

Arthur climbed up the rope ladder to a rickety platform and was hoisted to the top by a loud clanking pulley. His new "home" was a small, damp, empty hole carved into the rock. It reeked of bird droppings, mould, sewage and pee. He crawled inside and tried unsuccessfully to fall asleep. He was to start work at five in the morning, which was in two hours' time. Arthur was to work fifteen-hour days, six days a week, from five a.m. till eight at night, and half a day on Sunday, in exchange for a crookery hole and two crusts of bread a day.

What did Gaffer mean when he said No one goes back? Arthur had to figure something out fast. He *had* to find Trinket. But in the meantime, he was exhausted, and there were only two hours before dawn – a dawn devoid of light.

Arthur remembered what Gaffer had said about the night crows and sat up straight, his ear tuned to the dark world around him. He hoped the Badger was lying. Instead of monstrous birds, however, he heard what sounded like the lapping tides of a river hidden behind the rock. He listened to sounds he had never heard before and didn't understand: the whistle of the Night Train shuttling fortunate humans – factory owners, High Hats, and D.O.G.C. officers – back and forth to a station above in Lumentown. He heard what he would soon learn was the rumble of scavenger carts, borne along by large mole groundlings, blind but sure-footed in this strange subterranean world. The Moles searched for clinkered refuse, objects discarded or forgotten in rubbish dumps or outside crookeries and factory walls.

And Arthur could hear life above in Lumentown.

He strained to listen through the thick rock and earth separating the two worlds. He could just barely hear the pattering rain upon the streets, rain he couldn't feel below, only the drip, drip, drip of sewage waste. In the City below the City, there was no gentle snow, no warm, golden sun, not even a thunderstorm like at the Home.

In the netherworld of Gloomintown, there was no weather at all.

CHAPTER 39

The City Below the City

ARTHUR AWOKE the following Sunday thinking of
17 Tintagel Road – the musical sound of the name, the number that (thank goodness) was *not* thirteen, and the complete
muddle he had made of his search, not to mention everything
else. He had slept poorly that night, as he had every night since
he'd arrived. The crookeries were like dovecotes, only stained
with soot and sweating with dampness. They were so cold and
miserable to sleep in that some of the smaller groundlings
abandoned their crookeries altogether and sought out holes in
factory chimneys to keep warm.

How *could* anyone sleep in a dark, damp hole with no
privacy, barely big enough to lie down in? And he still didn't

know if that Badger had been telling the truth about the night crows. Just in case, he kept his ear alert for the sound of large flapping wings.

He looked out of his hole at the vast, murky world before him: the perpetual sameness, everyone breathing the same gloomy, unmoving air, trudging toward bellowing factories and coal pits. The air felt old and full of sorrow, as if it had inherited centuries of grief. Arthur could smell the subterranean fog. It smelled like rotten eggs. The voluminous smoke from the factories had nowhere to go, so it hovered at the top of Gloomintown and drifted up a handful of vents into the Great White City above.

Was this to be his life now? His destiny?

He had to get a message to Trinket. He was sure she had made a plan by now. She *was* Trinket, after all. But how in the world was he going to reach her if he was stuck in this hellish place?

Arthur sat cross-legged on the floor of his crookery hole and took a bite of his morning's ration of bread. A mechanical monkey like the one on Stinkbottom Bridge delivered the bread, climbing up and down the wall and pelting the inhabitants with their rations twice a day. This clockwork monkey was even meaner than the one above.

"Yuck!" said Arthur, spitting out a mouthful of bread. The crust was green with mould. He tossed it out of his hole;

it fell far below, making a soft splashing sound in a shallow pool of black water.

Soon he'd have to trudge with the others to the mine. His job had to be one of the worst in Gloomintown. As a Trap-Rat, he operated the trapdoors of the mines, controlling the ventilation for the miners. He'd heard about other jobs – glue makers and bone grinders, stone breakers and grave diggers, hatmakers, fat boilers, dung scrapers and so on. And for the lucky few, there were jobs at seedy establishments along a certain nefarious passageway called Black Slug Lane. These places were set up entirely for groundling foremen and ones like Gaffer or the Mole guard who collected tolls on the bridge. Even though they were stuck there for ever in Gloomintown just like all the other groundlings, they received special perks for their higher status. They had exclusive access to the rat-fighting clubs, the freak shows, and the only groundling pub, appropriately named the Dung & Shovel.

After work, groundlings like Arthur, who had no special privileges, huddled in crookery holes, sharing their misery and morsels of food, beneath the lurid glow of smoky grease lamps or sputtering candles bartered for at the Night Market.

After only a few days, Arthur could tell which groundlings had been there a long time. They could barely breathe, and their eyes had grown larger through the years in order to adjust to the lack of light. They had a haunted, empty look about them, and rarely spoke. They reminded Arthur of the Grumblers at the Home, the older groundlings who had clearly accepted their sad lot in life.

Arthur remembered how, on his very first day in Lumentown, he had heard a thudding sound from deep below the earth. He realized now that that *deep below* was exactly where he was, and where he might stay for the rest of his life if he couldn't figure out how to escape.

But Arthur hadn't forgotten Trinket's words – *Be brave! And never, ever lose hope!* And still, nestled in his heart, was that song from long ago, and the lilting voice that floated in the stars above, *her* voice, whoever she was...

And whenever he could, he strained to hear signs of life in the light-filled world above. When he listened very, very hard, he swore he could hear the sounds of children playing.

Arthur had awoken early that morning so as to have a few moments to sit beside the black shallow pool below. He climbed down a rope ladder to the nearest platform and tugged on a lever, and the pulleys clinked into action, carrying him all the way down.

He had only a few minutes, but at least he had that, so he closed his eyes and pretended that he was back with Trinket, on the road to Lumentown, sitting beside a clear, sunlit stream. He conjured the green hills and the wildflowers and the cows and sheep dotting the landscape. He was so preoccupied with his thoughts that it took him a while to notice the creature sitting on a pile of black rubble nearby. It was a frog, watching a school of tiny silver fish wheeling near the surface of the water. Every once in a while, its tongue would zap one and slurp it up.

Arthur nodded his head politely and said, "Hello there, frog."

The frog fixed its gaze on him and croaked. It seemed to stare at Arthur with a most disapproving look.

"Hello," he said again, but the frog just stared.

"Well, what are you staring at, anyway?" said Arthur, suddenly feeling cranky and sorry for himself.

The frog blinked, then spoke. "No need to get testy! Never saw a fox person down here before, did I?" The frog croaked again and, in one nimble leap, was gone.

Great, said Arthur to himself, staring as the ripples began to settle into stillness once again on the black face of the pool. *I finally meet someone who might be able to tell me how to get out of here and I ruin it. That's just great.*

As he got up, he heard someone whisper to him from behind the wall. "Psst. You there." Arthur looked around but couldn't see a soul. "Psst!" the voice said again. "Yes, you.

Don't listen to frogs, Foxy. They're not to be trusted. If you really want to know what goes on around here, ask the mice."

Arthur looked around again, but all he saw was the wall of solid stone. The whistle sounded the start of his shift, and he hurried off to the mines.

CHAPTER 40

A Mouse's Tale

THAT NIGHT, just as Arthur was falling asleep, he heard a soft rustling sound from behind the wall. He looked up and there, peering out at him from a tiny opening in the corner of his crookery hole was a small grey mouse with pink ears. It had a friendly, inquisitive face, with long white whiskers and a pale-pink nose.

"Hello, there!" said Arthur. "Come. I won't hurt you, I promise."

The mouse crept out of its hole and drew nearer. It twitched its nose and blinked.

"Poor mouse. You must be hungry," whispered Arthur.

The mouse inched closer. Arthur noticed that it had a

rather unusual tail. The end looked bent and flattened, as if someone had stepped on it.

Arthur searched his pockets and found a handful of breadcrumbs, and placed them before the mouse. "There you go. Tuck in. I wish I had something better to give you, but I don't."

The mouse stood up on its hind legs, looked over its shoulder, and clutched its whiskers nervously. It seemed to be making sure no one was going to snatch the crumbs. Then it vigorously rubbed its paws together for a moment, looked left and right, and commenced eating. After its meal, it twitched its nose several times and let out a dainty burp. It began to groom itself, rubbing its paws over its face and the rest of its body and finally its long grey tail.

Arthur sighed. "I wish you could understand me. I'm quite fond of mice. And I could use a friend."

The mouse cocked its head, looked him in the eye, and after a moment said in a slightly condescending voice, "Well, the question is: Can *you* understand *me*? But of course you can't. They never can."

Arthur sat straight up. "But I can!" he exclaimed. "Plain as day!"

The mouse's eyes opened wide. "Excuse me? *You* can understand *me*?"

"Yes, I can understand you just fine! What's your name?

How did you get here? What – oh, bother, just tell me about yourself!"

"Why, my name is Peevil! What's yours?"

"My name is Arthur!"

"Arthur? Like … like *the* Arthur, the Once and Future *Mouse* King?" said Peevil, his eyes widening further. "And his Mouse Knights of the Round Table? This *is* a great honour, to be sure! Please – do excuse my haughtiness from before. I had no idea."

The mouse bowed graciously before Arthur. Arthur stood up and bowed to the mouse.

"It is truly a pleasure to meet you, Peevil," he said. "A pleasure indeed."

The two talked long into the night.

Peevil explained to Arthur how in the Days of Yore (although he didn't specify when that was), mice were knights and fought for honour and glory instead of cheese. He made it a point to add, "Not that I have anything against cheese, of course."

Arthur told him how he used to listen to the mice and rats talking behind the walls of the Home, how their conversations gave him solace before his friend Trinket arrived.

"I know how you feel," said Peevil. "All alone, even when

you're surrounded by so many others. It's how I've felt every day down here since I arrived."

He told Arthur his long sad story, how he had come from a wonderful and loving family, twenty siblings in all. "Very sophisticated and cultured family, mind you." He had been separated from them several months before by an awful turn of luck. They'd been on an outing at Lumentown Market, when a delicious smell distracted him. "It was Brie. I suppose you could say that cheese was my downfall."

He fell into an open manhole and got sucked right down into the sewers. "That's how I broke my tail," said Peevil. He held up the end of his tail. "Nearly drowned too." He shuddered and pulled on a whisker.

"I know what *that* feels like," said Arthur. "Not the tail bit. I don't have one. But I know how it feels to be lost and alone."

"Now I don't know how to get back home to my family." Peevil let out a mousy sigh. "Anyway, how *is* it that you can understand me? No offence, but that's not normal for a groundling or a human. Can you understand other animals as well, or just mice?"

"I can't understand all creatures," said Arthur. "And I definitely don't understand cats. Not yet, at least."

"Cats!" squeaked Peevil. His whiskers drooped. "What's to understand? They're rude, arrogant, vicious killers, and—"

"Oh, my, don't say that," said Arthur. "I'm sure there are

some good ones. And anyway, if I can understand them some-day, I'll find out more about them, and maybe talk to them, and then they won't hiss at me when I walk by."

He offered Peevil more crumbs, but the mouse said he was quite full, thank you. "Peevil," said Arthur, "you seem to be such an … an experienced, worldly sort of mouse. Do *you* have any idea why I'm the way I am?"

"The way you are?"

"I mean – why I can hear things like I do. And why I can understand at least some of the animals, ones like you."

"Well," said Peevil, "I can't say I know the answer, but there must be a reason for it."

"I wish I knew what it was," said Arthur. "Peevil … I know you said it's not normal, but do you think there are others who can understand you when you talk? And if so, does that make *you* a groundling too?"

"First of all," said Peevil, "the world is more complicated than you think. There are creatures below and above that oper-ate by different rules altogether. Second, we animals aren't what the High Hats think we are; that is to say, *stupid*. We can talk, at least among ourselves, anyway. Or most of us can. And some of us—" Peevil's eyes lit up—"*mice* to be specific – can not only talk, but recite poetry as well. But until you came along, I never met a groundling or human who could under-stand a word I said."

"I see!" said Arthur. "Well. This is all very interesting indeed, I must say."

The two sat together for a while, listening to Gloomintown's nocturnal sounds – bats swooping through tunnels, Sewer Hunters trudging through black waters full of refuse and dead things, trying to scavenge what they could. Arthur could hear the fluttering of wings near the ceiling of the underworld. He never saw any birds, only felt their presence somewhere high above the great rock wall, where strange lights flickered and glowed like stars.

"Can I ask you another question?" said Arthur.

"Ask away!" Peevil was sitting up on his haunches now, fussing with his tail again, cleaning it and smoothing it down.

Arthur thought that Peevil spent an awful lot of time grooming himself, but to each his own. He asked, "How do you get by in Gloomintown? I mean – do groundlings give you food or must you steal food down here?"

"Steal? What kind of a question is that?"

"Oh, I'm so sorry!" said Arthur. "I meant no harm. It's just that ... well, how *do* you get on down here?"

"No harm done," said Peevil. He patted Arthur's hand with his tiny paw. "To answer your question – I provide a very important service to the night crows."

"The night crows? A Badger said those crows might come back to look for their babies, and that if they find a ground-ling in their crookery, they'll eat him. I didn't know if I should believe him. Still..."

"That's a lie! They never come back once their babies have flown. They don't care about groundlings either, at least the ones I know. Their job is to guard the dead. See those lights up there?" Peevil pointed up to the ceiling of the world. "Those are their eyes. From far away, they look like stars."

Arthur looked up. For a moment, he felt as though he were outside, on the road again with Trinket. "What do you do for them?" he asked.

"I clean their tail feathers. They give me food in exchange. Their feathers get awfully full of soot and, well, other things, as you can imagine. It's a nasty business, but it keeps me honest and alive until I can figure a way out of here. Kind of like mucking out a horse stable in exchange for bread, if you know what I mean."

"Uh, not really ... but I get the picture. Aren't you afraid of them, Peevil? I mean – won't they try to eat you? Don't crows eat mice?"

"Oh, heavens, no! Not down here at least."

"Can't you just, well, you know – sneak into crookery holes and take little bits of food?"

"I told you, Arthur. I'm not a thief! I'm a – well, if you really want to know, I'm a thespian. Or a poet. A knight with a poet's soul. Or vice versa. Can't make up my mind, really."

Arthur smiled at the mouse and yawned. He was getting very tired, but he wanted to stay up as long as he could and talk to his new friend.

"Shall I recite a poem for you before you go to bed?" asked Peevil.

"Oh, yes! I'd like that very much!"

"It's called *The Once and Future Mouse King,* but I should warn you: it's quite long. Actually, it takes about five years to finish the whole thing, if one recites approximately three hours every day."

"I see," said Arthur. "Mightn't you have a shorter poem? I'm worried that if it's too long, I'll fall asleep and miss the best parts."

"Oh, they all fall asleep, even mice," said Peevil, sighing. "I'm used to it. But don't worry. I'll just pick up tomorrow where I leave off today. By the way," he added, "all great poetry must be sung, you understand."

Arthur nestled into a corner of his cold, damp hole as best he could. The mouse began to beat a steady rhythm with his tail in the dark. Arthur closed his eyes to listen as Peevil began to sing his epic tale:

"Once there were mice so happy and gay,
Singing and dancing and making their way
Around the green hedges, around the great trees.
Then came the darkness that forced them to flee.
Where is the Mouse King to sing their souls free?
Where is the Mouse King to sing their souls free?"

From the cracks in the rocks, from the crookeries and tunnel walls, Arthur heard a chorus of mice. Their high, pure voices rose up into the subterranean sky. The air was full of their song, and Arthur listened with wonder until he finally fell into a deep, bone-weary sleep.

And yet the song of *The Once and Future Mouse King* lingered in his mind long after he awoke.

CHAPTER 41

A Flash of Orange

DEEP IN THE HEART of Gloomintown, Arthur began to sing in his sleep once again. He sang Peevil's epic tale, which the mouse continued to recite to him each night before he went to bed. Some groundlings, like the Wombat next door, stayed up late just to listen. The song grew inside Arthur and sparked a glimmer of hope in him and in the others who heard it. The song caught on, and every morning, groundlings marching to factories and mines hummed its melody. Arthur's song had reached them in their own crookery holes, and their steps were much lighter for the gift he gave unawares.

One night, a pipe broke near the Crookery, and a deluge of black filthy water, dead rats and debris flooded the passageway that Arthur normally took to the mines. He had to find an alternative route the next morning. But he was so new to the place, and there were so many confusing twists and turns, that he – along with some of the others – soon became lost.

He found himself along Black Slug Lane, aptly named, for the street (which was really a giant sewer pipe) was known to be populated with thousands of large, black slugs.

A rowdy group of Badger border officers had just gotten off their shift and were about to head into the Dung & Shovel before placing their bets on the first rat fight of the day. Gaffer, the Badger who had assigned Arthur his job and hole in the wall, grabbed him by the arm. "Where you headed, Foxy? Shouldn't you be in the pit? Sneakin' away, are we? Heh, heh."

"C–Crookery Row got flooded last night, sir," explained Arthur. "I'm just trying to find another way there."

The Badger motioned with his head to go left and went into the pub, cackling away.

Arthur was about to leave, but something he saw out of the corner of his eye stopped him: a long caravan of slugs coming toward him from the right, leaving a glowing silver trail in their wake. Even in his despair, Arthur was struck by how beautiful the stream of silver light was in the midst of so much darkness.

And then, another curious thing – the slugs seemed to be carrying tiny bits of food on their backs. Where were they coming from? He had heard about the Night Market, but since he had no money to buy anything, he hadn't bothered to look for it. But now he had something to barter with. The poem about the Mouse King!

And so, instead of turning left toward the mines, he turned right and followed the slugs' silvery trail.

At the end of Black Slug Lane, the trail went down a long tunnel, up a circular set of stairs carved from black rock, and down another tunnel. From inside the tunnel, Arthur could hear the echoes of many creatures talking at once, bartering, calling out prices, and arguing about the quality of goods.

He thought, *So I miss work one day and don't get a rotten piece of mouldy bread. Maybe I'll get something better at the market anyway.* And maybe, just maybe, someone might be kind to him, like that baker woman at Lumentown Market, and offer him a nice warm roll for free.

Arthur thought of rolls and began to salivate. Then he thought of soup, and Quintus's Soup for Kings. How he wished he were back at Wildered Manor! But he pushed the thought away and followed the silver trail right into the Gloomintown Night Market.

The market was a hubbub of trade, mostly rotten food discarded from the City above and sold at black market prices. There were carts of spoiled meat, rotten fruit and decaying fish heads. A woman was selling loaves of bread, but Arthur could see that the crust was tinged with green and the loaves looked like they were made mostly from sawdust. He perused the carts pulled by beaten-down groundlings rather than horses or donkeys, and searched for something to eat.

Naturally, he looked for pies, but there weren't any to be had. There were, however, cabbages. And they didn't look half bad.

Arthur approached the cabbage seller, a short, plump man with a sour, pimply face.

"Excuse me, sir," he said politely, and made a little bow. "If you please, sir. Might I have a word?"

The man scowled at him and grunted out something resembling "Whot you want?"

Arthur asked the man if he would kindly consider trading a cabbage in exchange for an abridged recitation from the highly acclaimed *Once and Future Mouse King* – in verse form, of course, for Arthur still couldn't sing except in his sleep.

The cabbage seller stared at Arthur as if he were out of his mind. "A mouse for a cabbage? Are you loopy or what?"

Arthur was about to speak when he spied a shocking flash of orange.

A woman in a towering orange wig, followed by a tall grey Rat, ducked into a sloping passageway that branched off from the marketplace. A man Arthur didn't recognize was leading them somewhere.

What in the world were Miss Carbunkle and Wire doing in Gloomintown? They were up to no good, he was certain of that, but it was none of his business. His business was to run away before they saw him and dragged him back to the Home. He ducked under the cabbage cart, then crawled under a long table stacked high with fried sewer eels. Arthur was stealthily making his way back toward the tunnel when he caught the word *Songcatcher*. He stopped in his tracks. And then Miss Carbunkle said, in her shrill, clipped voice, "When I'm done, there won't be a single song left on this planet. Music is the root of all evil, and don't you forget it!"

Arthur had no choice but to follow them. He simply had to find out what she was talking about.

He kept his distance and crept along in shadows, which was easy to do in Gloomintown. He overheard the headmistress and the Rat speak in hushed tones about a meeting they were heading to with a very important man. Apparently Miss Carbunkle had already met him once before.

"And when His Excellency speaks, you just keep quiet and stay out of the way, understand?"

"Of course, madam. As you wish," said Wire, bowing his head.

Their guide led them down twisting pathways, through a dark, narrow tunnel that opened up into a street lined with factories.

Arthur saw them enter the back of one of the buildings. Above the door was a sign with a picture of a green hat and the name of the company: TRILBIES & NOTHING ELSE! Arthur immediately thought of Goblin and felt a pang of guilt.

He waited a few moments and followed them in. Next to the door, he found a pile of discarded hats in a rubbish bin. Arthur silently thanked Quintus for his training in "blending." He picked out the largest hat he could find. He put it on, smashing his ear down so it would fit over his head. It wasn't like his red hat from Pinecone, which had more room for his big pointy ear. But it worked just the same, and with no ear sticking out and his face and fur black from coal dust, he hardly looked like himself.

Miss Carbunkle, Wire and their guide made their way down a long hallway to the factory's assembly room. Arthur could hear the foreman berating one of the workers, who had apparently made something other than a green trilby. The foreman was screaming at the top of his lungs, as a poor wombat groundling cowered, "We have always made green trilbies! And we will continue to make green trilbies till the end of time. What *you* have made, groundling, is a big blue *CAP! With a feather in it! OUTRAGEOUS!*"

Arthur wished he could help the groundling, but what could he do? And he had to follow Miss Carbunkle.

The room was filled with hundreds of groundlings, bent

over long tables making trilby after trilby as fast as they could. While the foreman was hollering at the worker, Arthur slipped under a table and crept from one table to the next, sliding along the floor until he was at the back of the room, where Miss Carbunkle and her entourage had gone.

The headmistress and Wire waited while their guide knocked on the door of an office. Another man opened the door and ushered them in. When Arthur caught a glimpse of the headmistress as she entered the room, he cringed. Her face was just as he remembered it, a frozen expression of pinched irritation, bordering on rage. He noticed Wire, who was wearing his tag on the outside of his shirt, probably to protect himself from being snatched and kept below. But he was also wearing something else: a yellow silk scarf. *Since when did groundlings wear fancy scarves at Miss Carbunkle's Home?* He also caught a glimpse of the person they were meeting – a tall, pale man wearing a monocle and white gloves.

The smashed trilby on Arthur's head muffled the sound, so he carefully lifted the hat and let his ear work its magic.

CHAPTER 42

A Most Devious Plot

WHILE ARTHUR LISTENED intently outside the room, someone inside the room was listening with equal fascination.

Wire stood off to the side, his eyes lowered in mock submission. But his eyes saw everything. He noted the man's cat torturing a small mouse in the corner, and how the man glanced over and nodded in approval. And he watched Miss Carbunkle very carefully as she and the man discussed her business proposal, what she referred to as Operation Songcatcher, or O.S.C.◆

The man with white gloves sat down in a chair several inches higher than Miss Carbunkle's, which was so small and low to the ground that she was forced to sit with her legs sticking straight out in front of her. Miss Carbunkle was used to being higher than everyone else and shifted uncomfortably in her seat.

The man looked down at the headmistress with soulless eyes and a bored expression. "I see Reginald got you here on time, Miss Carfunkle." He checked his pocket watch and said, "May I offer you some tea?"

"No, thank you," said Miss Carbunkle. "It's ... ah ... Miss *Carbunkle,* by the way. But never mind." She cleared her throat. "And yes, your servant was quite helpful. I never would have found this—" she paused—"this *place* without him."

"Ah, Gloomintown, our charming little city with all its charming little citizens," the man said, laughing darkly. "If I had my way, these monstrous, misshapen freaks would be wiped off the face of the planet. But my brothers find the vermin useful in our factories and our mines. I suppose they have a point. But, God, I long for the day when we can eliminate them altogether and replace them with machines."

Miss Carbunkle flinched.

It was barely noticeable – just a slight movement in her right cheek and a stiffening of her neck. Wire smiled to

---

◆ Miss Carbunkle and those who governed the City shared a particular fondness for acronyms. This is clearly evident in Miss Carbunkle's infamous educational tome, *The Essential Manual for the Vocational Training of Errant Groundlings* (E.M.V.T.E.G.), which includes, among other things, a long list of acronyms for just about every activity of the day.

himself, for he knew Miss Carbunkle's deep, dark secret. That she too – at least a part of her – was one of the *vermin*: the *monstrous, misshapen freaks* of the world.

The man flicked a minute piece of dust off his lapel and went on. "I told you at our last meeting that I would consider the matter in due course. I don't have an answer for you yet. I must say, your pushiness is beginning to irritate me, Miss Carfinkle, and I do not appreciate being irritated. And I am very short on time today. I am visiting all of my factories, and I own nearly all the factories down here, so you can see, Miss Carbungle, how I am *always* short on time."

"Please, Your Excellency, hear me out. It was a long journey by coach... If you could just give me a few minutes of your time. Last we met, I didn't fully explain my plan. If I could only explain myself better, I believe you would be quite interested indeed."

The man sighed heavily, flared his nostrils, and lit a long ivory pipe. "Very well. You have exactly five minutes to speak your piece." He opened a drawer and removed a special kind of hourglass that contained only enough sand for five minutes. He turned it over and said, "Speak."

Miss Carbunkle's face flushed, and she said, "Oh, thank you, Your Excellency. Thank you!" and proceeded to discuss her plans.

*　*　*

Outside the room, Arthur listened in horror from his hiding place as Miss Carbunkle explained, in detail, how she was nearly ready with stage one of her two-part plan called Operation Songcatcher – a plan that was absolutely diabolical.

Her idea was to build thousands of Songcatchers that looked just like the original one her father had made, but the cylinders would be devilishly different. Each one would contain an electromagnetic beetle, the very same widgets Arthur and the others had helped to make at the Home. Once activated, the machine would coax the listener to sleep, just like the original Songcatcher, but instead of embedding beautiful songs and sounds in one's memory, it would efficiently erase all of the music and wonder of sound from the listener's mind.

For ever.

The listener would be left with no desire to listen to music or delightful sounds ever again, not even a bird's song, a cricket, or the patter of summer rain. No more arias or waterfalls or waltzes, no mouse hornpipes and reels or music of snow. And certainly no lullabies.

"And the wonderful thing about it," said Miss Carbunkle enthusiastically, "is that the listener won't even remember what happened. All he or she will recall is that there was something about the machine that was absolutely marvellous. I guarantee you, with my darling little beetles, our customers will tell all their friends to run out and buy one."

Miss Carbunkle explained that she would give the so-called Songcatchers and cylinders away for free to groundling orphanages and workhouses for the poor. But her greater vision was to sell them all over the world. She would destroy music for ever and make a phenomenal profit while doing it. What could be more brilliant than that?

"All I need now," she said to the man in white gloves, "is the money to finish what I started – the funds to build the fake Songcatchers – *and* the groundlings to build them. We have enough cylinders and beetles to begin. But I cannot move forward without those machines and more groundlings to do the work. Right now, the plans are gathering dust in my closet. I need slave labour *now* and lots of it."

"But you already have groundlings," said the man. "You run an orphanage, for heaven's sake."

"My lord, with all due respect," said Miss Carbunkle, "I simply do not have enough for the scope of this project. And you, most Honourable Excellency, you have told me yourself that you seek, shall we say, to *limit* the population. If the D.O.G.C. can transport more orphaned groundlings to my Home, there will be that many fewer polluting the streets of Lumentown. Perhaps acquiring them from Gloomintown would be the easiest way, since here they aren't tagged and registered. And," she added, "your financial investment would serve us both well. *Very well,* I assure you. It's a brilliant, fail-safe, and lucrative plan. That is all I have to say. I won't take up any more of your time."

"Do not dare to assume," said the man sharply, "that what *you* deem so brilliant and lucrative would be brilliant and lucrative to *me*."

"But my lord..." began Miss Carbunkle.

The man glared at her with his steel-grey eyes and hissed, "Silence!" Arthur could hear him puffing on his long pipe and walking back and forth across the room. Finally, he said, "I see from my hourglass that our time is up, headmistress. Till next we meet. Goodbye."

"Please, my lord. Wait just a moment," pleaded Miss Carbunkle. "Your Excellency is a true visionary. One who wields enormous power. Think of my project's potential. You use the groundlings you need and send the rest of them to me. Then share in the extraordinary profits. My bleeding-heart idiot of a sister's plan was to build more Songcatchers and give them away for free to the poor – groundlings and humans alike – or so her naive twit of a daughter said. That would only serve to create hope in the ... the *vermin*, as you call them. But imagine a machine that can squelch the very thing that groundlings hold most dear. We can crush it right out of them. Think what that can do! If you crush their hopes and dreams, why, they'll do anything; trust me."

Arthur listened as Miss Carbunkle thanked the man

for his time and stood up to take her leave. As she and Wire were walking out the door, the man called her back. "Wait. Perhaps … perhaps I have been a bit too hasty. It does seem possible that your plan has, shall we say, untapped potential? I shall consider your proposal, Miss Carbunkle. My brothers and I meet next Monday. I shall let you know of our decision. Have a pleasant journey back, madam. Good day."

"Good day, Your Excellency!" said Miss Carbunkle. "And thank you! Thank you ever so much!"

"Yes, yes," said the man in white gloves. He waved her away dismissively, went back into the office and shut the door.

Arthur felt as if someone had punched him in the gut. A machine that would erase all of the music in the world? Destroy hope inside everyone who ever longed for something else – for wonder, for beauty, for love? Erase the song that still, after all these years, nestled deep within his heart?

He thought of the magical Songcatcher and all of its beautiful sounds. There was only one thing to do.

He had to go back to the Home. He had to find a way to stop her.

CHAPTER 43

The Night Crow

ARTHUR WENT STRAIGHT BACK to his crookery hole, tapped on the wall near the corner, and whispered Peevil's name. After a few seconds, his friend's tiny grey face popped out of his mousehole, followed by the rest of him.

Arthur's words came tumbling out of him in urgent fits and starts until he was done. "Well, Peevil? What do you think?"

"It is quite obvious what you must do, Arthur. You must go on a quest. And I'm just the one to help you. Every mouse needs a quest, and this shall be mine."

Peevil solemnly placed his right paw on his chest and knelt before Arthur. In the cold, dark crookery hole, the mouse pledged allegiance to Arthur and his cause. "We shall save the music of the world!" cried Peevil. "We must go at once!"

Arthur was quite touched. He was at a loss for words. Finally, he spoke. "There's one small problem."

"What's that?"

"We don't know how to get out of here."

"Oh. That," said Peevil. "Definitely an obstacle. Hmmm. What to do? What to do?"

The mouse scurried back and forth until he finally stopped, pulled on his whiskers, and rubbed his paws together exceedingly fast. "I feel an idea coming on," he said.

"Well," said Arthur, "please hurry up, because I have no ideas at all. We certainly can't go the official way – on the Night Train up through Lumentown. I'm not allowed that way, and besides, as far as D.O.G.C.'s concerned, I'm a criminal, and the second I go above, they'll throw me in a groundling prison, which I hear is even worse than this place, if you can imagine."

"This *is* a conundrum," said Peevil. The mouse paced back and forth again, then sat up on his haunches. "I've got it! There's someone who might be able to help us. She definitely can lead us out of here and take us to wherever we need to go."

"Great! Who is she? Where can we find her?"

"Well," said Peevil, "it's complicated."

"What do you mean by *complicated*?" said Arthur.

"She might not want to help us," said the mouse. "And … I don't actually know her; I just work for those who do… But what I do know, well, let's just say she's gigantic, has dangerous magical powers, is terribly moody, plus she hates to travel, and she doesn't trust foxes – in fact, she doesn't like anyone other than crows – and she's got a reputation for being really, really fickle. Oh, and when she's in a temper, she just pecks your eyes out with her beak. I think that's it."

"*That's it?*" said Arthur. He sat down on the cold, damp rock, put his head in his hands and groaned.

"Oh, and there was that rumour about her eating an entire crookery of groundlings a few years ago, but that *could* just be hearsay. Other than that, she's perfect!"

"*What?*"

"I shouldn't have said that. Forget I said that. Really, I—"

"Peevil, listen. You are an optimistic mouse. A brave mouse. The bravest mouse I've ever met. But in my humble opinion, this … this creature, whatever she is, sounds like a whole lot of trouble. Maybe more trouble than she's worth, I'd say. We should probably ask someone else."

"No – I think she's the one. I've got a feeling about this. You've got to trust me, Arthur. You do trust me, don't you?"

"Yes, but—"

"Then, please, just do as I say. We'll make sure nothing goes wrong."

"How are we going to do that?"

"Before we go asking for help, you need to learn as much as you possibly can about crows."

"Why's that?"

"Because Belisha – that's her name – is the Guardian of the Night Crows, and trust me, you don't want to do anything to make her angry."

After a few inquiries, it turned out that Belisha, the Guardian of the Night Crows, had already heard of Peevil because of his excellent cleaning service, and a meeting was set for that same evening. They were to meet her in front of the gate at the graveyard, near the entrance to Gloomintown. In the meantime, the mouse spent the rest of the day teaching Arthur everything he knew about crows.

For one, they were generalists. They ate anything edible, as well as things not edible to others. But they had a certain passion for centipedes, weevils and grubs, so Peevil suggested that they collect as many as they could for their meeting that night.

Arthur also learned that night crows were very ancient birds and followed a different set of rules from those of humans and groundlings, and even crows in the world above. Belisha, whose name, Peevil said, meant "beacon of light," was the leader of all the night crows, and she wielded great powers, both light and dark.

"The High Hats call them rat-birds, or sky rats," said Peevil. "Very insulting, to be sure." He explained that humans and groundlings alike feared night crows, for it was rumoured that they could change size at will and become threateningly large, and that they could blind a person with the blazing light from their huge glowing eyes.

"Oh, I almost forgot," said Peevil. "One more thing. Night crows *love* music. Singing calms them down. Sometimes, if two night crows are fighting, another crow will sing a song to make them get along. They sing in harmony too! Lovely singers, night crows."

Peevil told Arthur that night crows even used songs to navigate the subterranean sky. "That's how they know where to go. It's almost like their melodies are lines on an invisible map."

Fortunately, Arthur remembered how to get to the entrance to Gloomintown. As he and the mouse made their way along the sewage-drenched streets, Arthur remembered what Gaffer had said the night he arrived: The Badger had pointed to the cemetery and said, "Those who don't likes to work ... take a look to your right. Not a nice way to go, starvin' to death, heh, heh, heh."

They approached the graveyard's main entrance, a pad-locked black gate even more imposing than the one at the

Home. Arthur could hear the haunting cry of a bird ripping through the hollow darkness somewhere inside. The vast abandoned graveyard was alive with the Night Crow's song, her trilling and chortling, her chaffing and scolding, her quirking and bell-like peals. Then came the sound of an infinite number of birds singing the very same song.

Arthur looked around him. Circling the gate were hundreds of black leafless trees. They looked like birches, only black as night. They were not quite dead, but not quite of the world of the living either. He felt a prickle on the nape of his furry neck.

"I don't like the look of this place, Peevil."

Thousands of souls were buried behind the cemetery gate, all of them groundlings – the numberless, the hunted and the lost. Arthur could see makeshift plaques made of black stone or scraps of wood on the graves of those who were lucky enough to have family or friends to mark their passing.

A mist set in and swirled around the graveyard. Arthur began to shiver. Peevil sat on Arthur's shoulder, trembling and pulling on his whiskers.

"Look up there!" said Peevil. They could see two beams of light coming toward them. Arthur heard a loud flapping of wings, and then, from the mist, a large black shape emerged. It swooped low to the ground and landed inside the graveyard by the gate.

The bird was the size of a horse.

"Peevil," whispered Arthur, "I don't like this. We should turn back. Right now!"

"She's our only chance," said the mouse. "We've got to try."

"You remind me of a friend of mine. She'd say the same thing," said Arthur, shaking his head. "I'm leaving anyway. This is way too scary."

But before he could run, the Night Crow turned her gaze upon him. He tried to look up, but the light from her enormous eyes was too bright, like two blazing suns.

The Crow then fixed her gaze on the padlocked gate. It swung open with ease. Arthur gulped. Peevil gave him a little pinch and said firmly, "We're going in."

"I hope you know what you're doing," whispered Arthur. He and Peevil entered, and the gate slammed shut behind them.

The Crow dimmed her eyes and motioned for them to come forward. Arthur helped Peevil down, and together they bowed before Belisha, Guardian of the Night Crows.

"Give her the grubs," squeaked the mouse.

"Right," said Arthur, and pulled out all the grubs he had collected. He placed the squirming pile of juicy white grubs before the Crow, and stepped back, knees wobbling.

Arthur said, "If you please, madam... Most High of All Crows ... we have come to ask a favour of you."

"Why should I help *you*?" she said, munching on a fat grub. "I have only granted this audience because of the mouse, who is known and well liked by the night crows. I was not told there would be a groundling here." Her voice was deep and resonant, and rumbled as if it came from the centre of the earth. "I don't trust anyone who comes from Above. And I don't trust groundlings."

"If you please ... aren't you...?" Arthur hesitated, for he did not want to insult the great bird. "Aren't *you* a groundling? I mean – can everyone understand you?"

The Night Crow narrowed her eyes in anger. "You are as ignorant as the High Hats up above. Do you think that the world is made up only of humans, groundlings and the so-called dumb beasts of land and sea and air? There are other creatures out there, Foxling. Ancient creatures. And I am one of them."

"Arthur!" squeaked Peevil. "Get to the point and let's go! Ask her!"

But Arthur ignored Peevil, for as fearful as he was, he was curious at heart. "Excuse me for asking, but ... what *are* you, then?"

"We are the listeners, and we are the eyes of night. We trick the living and guard the dead, even in our dreams. Simply put: we are night crows, and I am the Guardian. And that is all you need to know about us. There are mysteries in this place that are far beyond your understanding, Foxling."

Peevil pinched Arthur's toe, and Arthur bowed again to the Crow.

"I'm … I'm sorry for bothering you. The truth is, what we really came to tell you is that we need to get out of Gloomintown. We need to get to an orphanage far from here, and right away."

"I told you. I do not trust anyone from the world Above."

"Why's that?" asked Arthur. "I mean… Your Majesty… Excellent, Most High… Madam… Guardian… Oh, bother. I don't know what to call you. Sorry." He hung his head, embarrassed.

"Belisha," she boomed. "The name is Belisha. And I do not trust the ones Above because there, we crows are treated with cruelty and disrespect."

"What do you mean?" asked Arthur.

"Do you know what they call us up there when we get together in a group? When we are talking or dining or singing together?"

"No…"

"A 'murder.' Yes, it's true. Up there, they say, 'Oh, look at the murder of crows eating that dead squirrel,' or 'Oh, look at that murder of crows stealing our corn,' and so on. So you can see why some of us have chosen to go Below. At least down here we get respect. *That* we have. And besides, I shall not help you simply because foxes and crows do not mix. They never have and never will."

"What do you mean?"

"We have a long history, Foxling. Your people and mine. Always trying to out-trick one another. Or, one could say, *out-fox* one another." She laughed, which seemed completely out of character. Her laugh sounded like several short caws, followed by *kek kek kek kek*.

Peevil stepped forward and said in his loudest mouse voice, "Please, Belisha, we are on a quest, and we really need your help."

"Yes, please," implored Arthur. "If you don't help us, in a few months' time, all the music of the world could disappear. Think about it – no more singing, no more beautiful songs. All of it, gone for ever."

"What? What do you mean by this?" The Crow's eyes glowed more brightly, and the two had to turn away. "Is this a lie? Are you trying to trick me, Foxling?"

Arthur told her of Miss Carbunkle's plan. He told her all about the miraculous Songcatcher, and how it had been stolen, and how, if Belisha didn't help them out of Gloomintown, not only would music disappear from the world above; it would disappear from the world below too.

"It's only a matter of time," said Arthur. "And we have to hurry. We have to go *now*."

The Night Crow was silent. Her feathers fluttered in the chilly graveyard air. She shook her great blue-black head.

"This is a terrible, terrible thing," she said. "An evil thing."

Arthur could feel the Crow's deep sorrow at what they had told her.

She said nothing for a few moments, then spoke. Her voice was a mixture of anger and sadness. "I understand now. We crows love music like life itself. This monstrous creature, this Carbunkle, must be stopped. Yes, Foxling, I will help you. I will take you there."

Thus, they struck a deal, Arthur, Peevil and the Crow. They now had a way to Pinecone's house, where they could get food and hopefully some more help. Then they would travel to the Home under cover of night.

"You should know one thing, though," said Belisha as Arthur and Peevil were leaving.

"What's that?" asked Arthur.

"You will pay a price."

Arthur had nothing left. "I can't pay you," he said. "I have no money. But I can get you grubs, lots of them! Fat ones! And weevils, and anything else you like."

The Crow laughed again: *"Kek kek kek, carack, kek kek kek carack, wok wok wok!"*

"What's so funny?" asked Arthur in his innocent way, for,

despite everything that had happened thus far, he still had an innocent heart.

"I will take something from you," said the Crow. "Something good or something bad. Night crows do not judge in that way."

"What will it be?" asked Arthur.

"*Kek kek kek!* That is for both of us to find out."

CHAPTER 44

Flight

ARTHUR AND PEEVIL were to leave the next day, after Arthur's shift at the mines, so he could at least receive his ration of bread to take on their journey. He had already missed a day of food and was weak from hunger. But when he and Peevil returned to Arthur's crookery hole, they were alarmed to find three weasel groundlings sitting around playing cards.

"Uh, excuse me," said Arthur, politely. "I—I believe you're in the wrong place? Perhaps I can help you find the right one?"

"Ain't this number 1,313,131,313?" said the largest of the weasels.

"Yes," said Arthur.

"Then we got the right place. The Badger said the groundling livin' here didn't show up to work and that's that. We got the hole now, so you just scram, all right? We'd like a little privacy, if you don't mind. We start at the mine tomorrow early."

"But…" began Arthur. Then all three Weasels bared their teeth at him and hissed. Arthur and Peevil dashed out of the hole and climbed back down.

The two had no recourse but to return to the graveyard in hopes that Belisha would take them that very night. But when they got there, she was gone. They plopped down on the cold, wet ground in front of the gate.

"I suppose we'll just have to spend the night here and wait around until tomorrow," said Arthur.

"I could recite more of *The Once and Future Mouse King* if you like," said Peevil. "Shall I begin?"

"Wait. I think I hear something."

His ear flicked this way and that. Arthur could hear the flutter of wings, but they were too small to be Belisha's. He searched the dark cemetery for signs of her, but he could only see the shapes of hundreds of small black birds with large glowing eyes, wheeling above the graves. They were singing a haunting song with very complex harmonies. Arthur could almost make it out, as if it were in a foreign language he had forgotten long ago.

"What if she doesn't come?" asked Arthur.

"You mean tomorrow night?" asked Peevil.

"I mean *ever*. You said she was fickle. What if she just never comes?"

But Belisha did come. She came in a flurry of black feathers and light.

"How did you know to come back?" asked Arthur.

"Didn't you hear them singing?" said Belisha. "They were calling me. They did it for your little friend here," she added, motioning to Peevil.

After they had gone over the plan one more time, Belisha said, "All right, you may climb aboard now. But absolutely no kicking. I'm not a horse, you know."

The great Crow bowed her head and body as low as she could so Arthur and Peevil could scramble up onto her back. Arthur placed Peevil in his shirt pocket and held fast to Belisha's soft feathery neck. The Night Crow let out a harsh cry and lifted into the air.

Arthur was afraid Peevil would fall, so he tried to make him stay inside his pocket. But the mouse kept popping his head out so he could see everything and feel the wind on his face. He told Arthur that he wanted to be wide awake the moment the three of them rose up into the world of light.

"You just be careful, you hear me?" Arthur called out to the mouse, who was clearly having the time of his life.

"Wheeeeeee!" cried Peevil, clinging tightly to the top of Arthur's pocket with his tiny paws.

They flew through the dark world below the luminous City, through subterranean tunnels and mines, through black rock caverns, past factories sputtering smoke. They wove their way through the labyrinth that led toward the way out, the light from the Crow's bulging eyes cutting a path through the darkness.

Along one wall, they came upon a cavernous chamber about fifty feet high, supported by pillars, arches and buttresses, with gargoyles jutting out from every corner. It was an underground cathedral that obviously had once been grand. It looked like the vaulted entryway into Gloomintown but smaller and more intact. Arthur could hear bats inside the cathedral, their wings humming and quivering with song. As they passed through it and out, the light from Belisha's eyes shone on faded frescoes of animal gods and goddesses, and carvings of strange birds and trees.

They soared over the black winding river, which Belisha told them was called the Serpentine. From above, Arthur could see how long and wide it was, and he thought of Stinkbottom River and the first time he crossed the bridge with Quintus in Lumentown. And once again, his mind drifted to 17 Tintagel

Road. *And now look,* he said to himself. *Instead of there, I'm here, going back to that dreadful, dreadful place.*

But he had to go back. He knew it. For if he didn't, what would happen to all the songs?

After they had been flying for several hours, Arthur dozed off, clinging to the Night Crow's neck. A sudden burst of air jolted him awake. He felt a strong breeze rising up around them. He turned his head and saw that the breeze was coming from Belisha's wings. She was twisting them this way and that so as to stir the air. She was going much faster now, and Arthur feared for Peevil, who was so light, he could be sucked right out of his pocket. He put his hand inside his shirt and touched the mouse's head. Peevil was huddled at the bottom of Arthur's pocket, hanging on for dear life.

"I'm all right," said Peevil. "But tell her to slow down!"

"Belisha!" cried Arthur. "Please slow down! You're going too fast!"

But the Crow said nothing.

She went faster, and the air swirled around her as if she were the eye of a storm.

Arthur felt the wind tug hard at his shirt. It felt like invisible fingers, and the fingers were coaxing something out of his pocket, something precious to him, something he kept

close to his heart. But it wasn't Peevil; it was something else –
it was the blue blanket scrap and tiny gold key.

It wasn't the wind. He knew it now. It was the Night
Crow. She was taking the only thing he had left. Arthur held on
to Belisha's neck with one hand and clutched his shirt pocket
with his other. But the churning wind was too strong, and he
watched in horror as it forced his hand away and wrenched his
blue bundle right out of his shirt pocket.

The small tattered scrap with faded gold thread opened in
the air, and it and the key simply hovered there, buoyed along
by the wind.

"Stop! Please!" he cried to the Crow, but she did nothing. Arthur moved to reach for them but nearly fell off trying.
The key and blanket scrap bobbed along with the current for a
moment, then tumbled down into the abyss.

Arthur let out a strangled cry and buried his head in the
Crow's neck in despair. He could feel Peevil, inside his pocket
against his chest, patting him with his tiny paw through his
shirt, trying to console him.

At last, the Crow slowed, and the wind died down too.

Finally, Belisha spoke.

"That is the price for your journey, Foxling. Your debt is paid."

"But why? Why did you have to take *that*?" He was crying bitterly now, his tears swept away by the dying wind.

"Because, young groundling – you have all you need." She paused, then said, almost kindly, "Except for one thing more. And that I cannot give you."

They flew until it was nearly dawn. At last, they passed through a tunnel that opened up into a large underground cave. Arthur understood now that the world below was much bigger than he had thought – not just a city under the City, but a whole subterranean land.

Arthur could smell the damp moss above and heard creatures lumbering among the twisted roots of ancient trees.

"This is where I leave you," said the Crow. "If you keep going straight, you should find an animal den you can exit through. But I must go. Soon, daylight will come, and I cannot fly in the day. And I do not know the way underground to this 'Home' of which you speak. I must return."

"B–but you said you'd help us!" said Arthur. "I thought you'd take us *all* the way. You said you'd take us there. You said…"

"I said I would take you *there*. But I never said where

there was, did I, Foxling? My eyes cannot take the bright world Above. For night crows, even the moon is almost too much to bear."

"But please, Belisha, we're never going to get there in time. It'll take us at least two more days of walking from here. Can't you see?"

"I am sorry, Foxling. I have never flown by day and I am not about to start. We are the beacons of the Underworld, not meant to be blind, helpless birds Above. Goodbye, Arthur. Goodbye, Peevil. Good luck."

They had no choice but to keep going. Maybe Pinecone's family would know what to do. They walked through the cave and in less than an hour, found themselves inside an animal den, just as Belisha had said.

"Time to go up," said Peevil. "I want to go there on my own four feet, if you know what I mean."

"I do," said Arthur.

He found the way out by ear: a trickle of fresh, clean water dripping down a round opening into the den.

"It's this way," said Arthur. They had begun to scramble up a large root toward the opening when Arthur heard a sniffing sound behind him. He turned around to look.

It was a fox.

It was so beautiful it took his breath away.

The fox was fiery red, with large pointy ears, just like his one special ear, alert to the world. It approached him tentatively, then stopped about five feet away. The animal stared deep into Arthur's eyes.

Arthur slowly reached his hand out to the creature. But the fox sniffed the air, gave him a parting glance, and fled into the dark.

Arthur took a deep breath, turned back around, and climbed.

And under the cloak of night, just before dawn, Arthur and the mouse exited the Dark World and emerged once again into a world of moonlight and glittering stars.

CHAPTER 45

The Gathering

THE DEN was right by Pinecone's house, and Arthur easily found his way to the ancient old oak. He felt for the acorn carving behind the tangle of ivy and touched it with gratitude. "This is it," he said to Peevil. "It's still dark out. I feel bad about waking them up. But it can't be helped."

He scooped the mouse up, tucked him into his pocket, and knocked on the tree trunk.

A woman with elfin ears and long raven hair opened the door. She had a broad smile on her face; she knew exactly who he was. Her son hadn't stopped talking about the one-eared adventurer and his Bird friend for the past three weeks. "You must be Arthur!" she said, motioning him inside. "I'm

Mrs Oakley, but you can call me Cathleen. My husband's up, but Nana and the children are still asleep. Please, come in. Blimey, did you travel here all by yourself?"

Arthur nodded and said, "C–Cathleen? I thought … I mean – you're not named for a tree?"

Mrs Oakley laughed. "Everyone asks me that. Markus – that's my husband – and I always knew we belonged to the forest, and when we moved here and started a family, we decided every child should be connected to the trees. It seemed silly for us to change *our* names, though. We've always been us, you see? So I'm still Cathleen and he's still Markus. And Nana, well, Nana will always be Nana Eunice, and it's no good suggesting to her otherwise. But what's in a name, eh?"

Just then, Peevil popped his head out of Arthur's shirt pocket. "Oh, this is Peevil," said Arthur. "He can understand everything you say. It's just that no one can understand him, so I'll translate."

"I see," said Pinecone's mother, raising one eyebrow. "You can understand mice, can you? Very interesting, yes, indeed." She extended a finger to Peevil, who placed a tiny mouse kiss upon it. "Oh, my!" she said. "You are a gallant mouse, aren't you!"

Peevil's ears blushed a deep pink.

Arthur took in the cozy round room – the bark walls, the glowing luminaries, the paintings of green-garbed children and trees, the kettle at the hearth, the handmade tools hanging over the mantel. "Boy, am I glad to be here," he said. There was that feeling of familiarity and safety he had felt the first time he came. He sighed happily and breathed in the scent of rosemary and freshly baked bread. Then he promptly collapsed in a chair. He hadn't realized till then how tired he was.

"Look at you! Half asleep and hungry, to be sure," said Cathleen. "But first things first! There's someone here you'll want to see straightaway. And you might want to have yourself a bath while you're at it. You don't have to… It's just a suggestion, mind, but … you do smell a bit ripe, if you know what I mean."

Arthur laughed. It had been ages since he'd thought something was funny. "I'm sure I smell exactly like where I've been living the past two weeks," he said. "In the sewers. I'd love a bath, Mrs Oakley. And of course I'd like to see Pinecone too."

"Lovely. But please call me Cathleen. My husband will show you where to go." She poked her head inside one of the cubbyholes and said, "Markus, you dressed yet? Come out and show our guests where to go. They'll be needing to freshen up before breakfast. And you-know-who is anxious to see Arthur, so get a move on, husband!"

"Right!" said a voice from behind the curtain, and a short, stout man with wild red curly hair appeared. "Follow me, if you please. Name's Markus, by the way. No formalities allowed at the Ol' Oakley Inn!"

Mr Oakley led Arthur and Peevil to a bubbling hot spring not far from their tree. "It's shallow, so don't worry none," said Pinecone's father. "You won't sink. Here's a towel, and something clean to change into. They're Pinecone's and should fit you. And take your time. There'll be breakfast waiting for you when you return."

It was almost dawn and still dark outside, but the spring was lit up with the last fireflies of night and bioluminescent moths circling above. And someone had put bunches of lavender in the water, which made it smell divine. But to Arthur, the best thing of all was seeing who was splashing around in the middle of the spring. It wasn't a small boy in patchwork green but a brown wingless bird with a long yellow beak, squawking with delight.

"Trinket!" cried Arthur. He dashed to the water's edge and hopped right in, clothes and all, with Peevil still inside his pocket.

"Yikes!" Arthur screamed, and scrambled back out. "That's hot!"

"No kidding!" squeaked Peevil. "Let me down right now! My tail's on fire!"

"Oh, sorry, Peevil!" said Arthur. He placed the mouse gently on the ground.

"Arthur!" said Trinket. "I can't believe it's you! You made it!" She added, "Just go slowly. You'll get used to the heat, don't worry. It's quite lovely once you do! And you got yourself a pet! What a cute little mouse!"

"She thinks I'm—I'm a *pet*? And cute? I'll show her how cute I can be!" said Peevil, fuming.

"How simply adorable! It's squeaking!" said Trinket with delight. "I love that. Do you still have Merlyn, the one I made you?"

"It's a long story. I'll tell you later," said Arthur. "But first, Peevil's not my pet. He's a very brave and noble mouse. And you should know that he can understand everything you say."

"I certainly can!" piped up Peevil.

"She meant no harm," said Arthur to Peevil. "Really."

"Oh, my! Please tell him I didn't mean it at all!" said Trinket. "I'm terribly sorry."

Arthur introduced his two friends properly and said he would happily translate from then on to prevent any further misunderstanding.

Peevil was still sulking and refused to go back in the water. He sat by the edge of the spring and cleaned himself off with a moist fern frond and a pawful of pine duff. Afterward, he lay on his back and stared up at the stars, which helped his mood a little.

"How did you get here?" Arthur asked Trinket, as he eased himself slowly into the bubbling water. "How did you know where I'd be?"

"It all started with your friend Quintus," said Trinket.

"Quintus?"

"I got your message, so I knew where you lived – by the way, how'd you like that invention, Arthur? I think the pigeon my uncle and I built is champion, don't you? Anyway, after I went to Wildered Manor, I searched for you in Gloomintown."

"You went to *Gloomintown*?"

"Well, I certainly wasn't going to let my best friend get stuck in a sewer, was I? That is the worst, most disgusting place in the whole wide world! I don't know how you lasted as long as you did."

Arthur listened intently while Trinket went on with her story, splashing about with her winglets at the most exciting parts.

Quintus had told her how Wire and his minions destroyed Phoebe Nightingale's house and stole the Songcatcher, and how Arthur had been accused of the crime. "There are wanted posters for you everywhere!" said Trinket. "They're calling you a rabid, violent criminal! It's awful. Anyway, Quintus told me there were only two ways to get to Gloomintown. I went through the train station. No way was I going to fly down a drainpipe! People just thought I was a regular old bird. It was actually quite easy, now that I have a new flying suit. I can't wait to show it to you later!

"By the time I found the dreadful place where you were staying – I had to bribe some truly awful Badger, by the way – there were three Weasels in the hole, and you were long gone. I didn't know what else to do, so I flew here. I figured it was worth a try."

After Gloomintown, Trinket sent a message via her mechanical pigeon to Wildered Manor. "I told Quintus where I was going and promised I'd let him know whether I found you. He was pretty worried. I told him about Miss Carbunkle's plot too. I found out about it from the Wombat in the hole next to yours. Lucky for us he likes to eavesdrop on his neighbours! Anyway, Quintus sent the pigeon back saying that if this thing is ever cleared up, you are welcome back to Wildered Manor. He felt very bad about making you go. I know he's a Rat, but he's got a good heart."

"I know," said Arthur.

"If you're ready, let's go inside now," said Trinket. "I've been boiling in this water so long, I feel like someone is making me into soup. Peevil? Shall we go? And I am truly sorry for calling you Arthur's pet."

Peevil nodded, and all was forgiven.

After they dried themselves off, Arthur slipped behind a bush and changed into Pinecone's clothes. He loved how colourful they were, and how soft they felt against his fur compared to the rough grey cloth of his own clothes. But he'd have to return to the Home in his old ones so that he could blend in.

Dawn was breaking, and Arthur could see a patch of pink-and-golden light glinting through the forest canopy as they made their way back to Pinecone's tree.

The table was set for breakfast: scrambled eggs, fried mushrooms, toast with butter and gooseberry jam, goat cheese tarts, sliced apples – and a little bowl of seeds for Trinket. Mrs Oakley was bustling around the kitchen, while at the big round table sat Pinecone and the rest of his family: his brothers Ash, Barkley and Buckthorn (Bucky for short); his sisters Chestnut and Hazel; his father, Markus; and "the Captain," Nana Eunice.

Pinecone could barely contain himself. He jumped up on his chair and, wielding an imaginary sword, proclaimed, "Hear ye, hear ye, Knights of the Round Table! Hear ye, hear ye!"

Everyone looked up at the little boy dressed in green. He was now swinging his invisible sword in circles around his head.

"Hear ye what, you little pine nut?" said his older brother

Bucky. "Make your proclamation already so we can eat."

"Oh, okay," said Pinecone. He cleared his throat. "Welcome, gallant knights from … from afar! We shall break bread before our noble quest!"

Pinecone sat back down and stuffed a fistful of apple slices into his mouth. Everyone clapped and commenced with breakfast.

"I like this young fellow," said Peevil to Arthur. "He's got the right idea."

After the meal, Trinket showed everyone her new flying suit.

It had lightweight detachable wings that connected to a tail. She still had a propeller helmet, but her heavy clockwork armour was gone. "If there's a breeze, I don't even need the propeller at all. I can show you how it works later, but now it's time to talk about the plan. I can't wait to hear it!" She hopped up and down a couple times. "Arthur? The Plan!"

"Uh, yes. The Plan," began Arthur. "The thing is… Well, the thing is that there is no plan. No plan at all." He looked down at his feet.

"No plan?"

"I'm sorry, Trinket. All I could think of was how to get here. That was hard enough." He looked around the room at everyone. "Does anyone here have an idea what we should do? Because I certainly don't."

After a short pause, everyone began talking at once. The

main problem was still how to get from Pinecone's house to the Home in time to stop Miss Carbunkle, if they even could stop her. Without Belisha, they had no means of transport. Mr Oakley said, "We do have a small peddler's cart, and we used to have an old goat to pull it, but I pull it meself now, see?"

And then there was the problem of *how* to stop her. One thing they all agreed on was that they had to steal the Songcatcher back, nab the plans and get out of there.

Arthur and Trinket came to the conclusion that there was no way around it – they were going to have to walk all the way back to the Home. But maybe, just maybe, some kind soul in a horse and buggy or donkey cart would help them along the way.

Trinket said that once they got there, she could at least carry Arthur and Peevil long enough to fly over the Wall. Once inside the grounds, they would search for the Songcatcher and the plans.

"I have a feeling they're either in her office or the cellar," said Arthur. "So, any ideas on how not to get caught? Anyone?"

Everyone sat waiting for someone else to speak. Then, from the middle of the table, Peevil began squeaking nonstop.

"Hang on, Peevil," said Arthur. "You're talking too fast. What did you say?"

"Let's see ... I'll be needing a sword, that's for sure," said Peevil.

When Arthur translated, Pinecone got very excited and began jumping up and down, exclaiming, "It's the gathering of the Knights! At the Round Table! And I'm … I'm … Sir Galahad! Hooray!"

"Right," said Arthur. "Got that." Then, to the others, "Can someone help with Peevil's sword?"

"I'll help you, brave knight!" cried Pinecone. "For King and Country!"

"Pinecone, please keep your voice down," said his mother. She looked at the mouse. "Peevil, I have just the thing for your sword. What else do you need?"

"Tell her a helmet. I'll definitely need a helmet."

"A helmet, right. One sword and one helmet," said Arthur. "As soon as we're finished here, we can figure that out. So, any other ideas? Anyone? How will we get around the orphanage without being seen?"

"I shall slay anyone in my path!" declared Pinecone, who started running around the table, pretending he was battling numerous villains.

"Pinecone," said his mother. She looked at him sternly. "If you can't control yourself, you'll have to go to your room."

"Excuse me," piped up Peevil, although he was squeaking so intensely, he sounded to everyone else like he was being tortured by a cat. "I'll obviously need a shield too. And then…"

"Peevil," said Arthur, "can't you see we're in a bit of a

muddle here? We still don't have a proper plan. Can you please wait and tell me everything all at once when we're through?"

"Shall I write it all down in a list?" asked Peevil, a bit miffed.

"Mice can write?" asked Arthur.

"Of course we can write! We're not stupid."

Finally, they pieced together the bare bones of a plan, and then the three travellers went right to bed, even though the day had just begun. They were all very tired and had a long journey ahead of them. Mrs Oakley promised she would wake them up in time to play a little with Pinecone before they left. She assured Peevil that she would gather all of his knightly clothing before their departure. Mr Oakley was in charge of supplies and provisions. Arthur, Peevil and Trinket would have to figure out the rest on the way there.

The three would start their journey by cover of night.

"Now, off to bed with you," said Mrs Oakley, and Pinecone led his fellow knights to his cubbyhole so they could get some sleep.

Later, as promised, Pinecone's mother woke the travellers so they could play a bit before their arduous journey. Pinecone and his siblings taught Arthur and Trinket how to play his favourite tree games – Find the Acorn, Tree Tag, Catch the Squirrel and

Stick and Toss. Afterward, Arthur proudly taught everyone a couple of the games he had learned at Wildered Manor.

Peevil, however, told Arthur that this was certainly not the time to think about childish games, and spent the rest of the day contemplating what battle strategies he should use, for he was sure that a great battle awaited them at this forbidding fortress called the Home, ruled by a tyrannical monster called Miss Carbunkle.

CHAPTER 46

The Quest Begins

IT WAS A WILD MOON that night, yellow and full.

Peevil, Arthur and Trinket had decided to leave right after dinner, but it was nearly nine when they finally got ready to go. Mr and Mrs Oakley tried hard to convince them to leave the next morning, but they were determined to get on the road.

Arthur was wearing his old grey clothes, which were now fresh and clean. He hated to put them back on, but where they were going, he couldn't afford to stand out.

Mrs Oakley helped Peevil put on the padded leather suit of armour she had made. She had fashioned his helmet from an acorn and his shield from the face of an antique French watch. "See those little hooks on the side of your shield?" she said.

"You can attach them to your armour if you need more protection in the front."

For his sword, she gave Peevil a small clock hand. It was elegant, sharp and perfectly formed. He slipped it through his belt. He liked the fact that his shield was French, and was so overwhelmed with emotion about everything that he recited his favourite poem by Victor Hugo, which began: *Demain, dès l'aube, à l'heure où blanchit la campagne, Je partirai.*[◆]

When Arthur repeated Peevil's translation from French to English (he didn't dare try repeating what the mouse had said in French), Mrs Oakley, who was clearly moved, put her hand to her heart and exclaimed, "Oh, Peevil!" The mouse solemnly kissed her finger and bowed.

Everyone was truly impressed by the little mouse knight before them.

Pinecone knelt before Peevil and said, "I, Sir Galahad Pinecone ... of the ... of the Order of the Oaks ... shall serve thee till the bitter end. Forsooth! What ho! And ... and ... huzzah!"

"Oh, Pinecone," said his mother, patting him on the head. "You sweet boy."

Then the Oakley family said their sad goodbyes to the three adventurers. Pinecone broke into tears and begged

---

◆ Tomorrow, at dawn, at the moment when the countryside pales, / I shall depart.

them to take him, saying that he had a sword all ready and that he was born to be a knight, but Mr Oakley wiped his tears away and said that someday he'd get to go on such an adventure, but this was not that day. He was still too little. He scooped Pinecone up and put him on his shoulders, which seemed to calm the boy down a tiny bit.

Peevil said to Arthur, "Please tell him that someday we will fight side by side. I give him my word." When Arthur relayed the message, Pinecone managed a little smile.

Pinecone's father gave Arthur the food and other things he had prepared for their mission. He gave him a rucksack as well, since Arthur had relinquished his to the Norahc not so long ago.

"Thanks!" said Arthur gratefully.

"Arthur," said Mrs Oakley, "don't forget this." She handed him a detailed map, drawn on a piece of birch bark. "And also don't forget, you three – our home is always open to you." She hugged Arthur and kissed the top of his head. No one had ever kissed him before, and he felt tingly and warm. "Come back safe and sound," she said.

And so the three travellers took off into the night.

They made their way out of Pinecone's woods and headed south toward the lower valley. It was a lovely, clear evening, and would have been a delightful walk, save for the fact that they were in a desperate hurry to get somewhere, and not one horse and buggy, not even a donkey cart, passed by to offer them a ride. The road before them was empty and stretched on and on into the dark.

"At this rate, we'll get there by next winter," said Arthur after they had been walking for more than four hours. He was beginning to feel tired and cranky. "What if we're too late? What if she's already made a copy of the plans? What'll we do then?"

"Arthur, I really think I should fly ahead," said Trinket.

"What are you talking about?" said Arthur. "We are not splitting up. One for all and all for one, all right?"

Peevil popped his head out of Arthur's pocket. "I mean, *really*," he said. "We go together or not at all."

"What's he saying?" asked Trinket. Arthur translated.

"That mouse is a bit bossy, isn't he?" she whispered.

"I heard that!" said Peevil.

"Please, let's not squabble, okay? We have a long night ahead of us."

"Sorry," said Trinket.

"I'm sorry too," said Peevil, a bit reluctantly. "And by the way, it's actually a short night, not a long one. It's June twenty-first, the Summer Solstice – the shortest night of the year."

All of a sudden, Arthur heard a familiar sound.

High above his head, giant wings were flapping in the air. He felt a strong gust of wind, and then a bright shaft of light shone down on the travellers from above. The three of them looked up at once. The great Crow hovered for a moment, then swooped down to the ground. She landed a few feet in front of them.

"Belisha!" cried Arthur. He ran up to her and would have thrown his arms around her neck if he were tall enough. He burst out, "You came back!" He suddenly remembered protocol and bowed respectfully before the Night Crow. Trinket bowed as well, while Peevil saluted the Crow by waving his sword in the air.

Belisha bowed her head to the three companions. "I was on my way home when I thought about what you said, young Foxling – about this Carbunkle creature who is plotting to steal all the music of the world. I thought that if she could find a way to steal our songs, she could take our dreams away too. And without our dreams, we are nothing."

"But will you be okay?" asked Arthur. "I mean, what if we're still not done at dawn?"

"I will have to leave you before then," said the Crow. "What is it you creatures say? 'We will cross that bridge when we come to it.' She let out several *kek kek kek keks*, which frightened Trinket terribly until Arthur explained to her that the Crow was only laughing.

* * *

It took Belisha and the others only one hour to reach Miss Carbunkle's Home for Wayward and Misbegotten Creatures. Arthur helped navigate, using the map and his own recollection of the route. As they got closer, Arthur could make out the shape of the Home in the moonlight. An icy finger went down his spine. He would have to be very brave indeed.

They decided to stop for a minute and go over the plan one more time. Belisha landed quietly on the driveway, and the others dismounted.

"First, we have to stop the dogs from barking," said Arthur. "Then we'll fly around to the back. Belisha will take us over the Wall into Kestrel Courtyard. She'll have to hide in the shadows until we meet up there again." He paused, then added, "I still don't know what we'll do if we get caught."

"I shall defend us to the death!" said Peevil, raising his sword above his head.

"You are a very brave mouse," said Arthur, "but I'm afraid your sword will be useless against Miss Carbunkle's cane or Mr Sneezeweed's paddle."

"Humph! You'd be surprised," said Peevil.

"Just remember," said Belisha, "time is of the essence. If you are not back before dawn, I must leave you behind and quickly find a way to the world below. Otherwise, I could go blind. If that happens, I am useless both Above *and* Below."

"We understand," said Arthur as he and the others climbed up onto Belisha's back.

"Is everyone ready?" asked Belisha. "Steady, now. Up we go." And the Guardian of the Night Crows flapped her great black wings and lifted into the sky.

CHAPTER 47

The Return

THE CROW hovered above the Home's high black gate. Arthur felt a shiver down his spine when he saw the old sign clanking in the wind.

M   UNKLE'S H ME F R AYWARD AND M B TT N ET R S

The guard dogs sensed something strange above them and began to bark. Arthur tossed down the sack of bones Mr Oakley had given him for just this purpose. The dogs immediately commenced with quiet, gleeful gnawing.

"I say," said Peevil, "fine aim!"

"Th–thanks," said Arthur, somewhat dazed. "I—I don't believe it! It's incredible!"

"What is it?" asked Trinket, concerned.

"I understood every word those dogs said! I mean, up until now I could only understand mice and rats. I talked to a frog once too. But just now, I understood those two dogs!"

"Blimey, Arthur, that's amazing!" said Trinket. "What were they saying? Something ghastly, I suppose?"

"No, Trinket! All they said was something like 'Birdie? No. Mousie? *Mousie!* Eat mousie! Hungee! *Me hungee!* Scratch bum? *No, you!*' Stuff like that. It was hilarious!"

"And you don't think that 'Eat mousie' is ghastly?" asked Peevil. But before Arthur could apologize to him and translate for the others, Belisha let out a reprimanding squawk and said that now was not the time to be talking about dogs. She flapped her wings and flew to the back of the Home.

They landed with a *whoosh* in Kestrel Courtyard.

Inside the Wall, it was raining, as usual. The three companions took shelter beneath one of Belisha's wings while they went over their plan one more time.

Arthur looked around at the place that had held him captive for so long. The Wall still blocked out the beauty of the world, except for his old friend the tall white birch. Everything was still sad, dismal and grey. The only change he could see was that the pile of rubble at the far end of the courtyard was gone, and most likely the hole in the Wall behind it had been sealed up tight. He had been hoping the hole was still there in case they were not done before Belisha had to leave.

Above them, the gargoyles wept veils of tears into the muddy yard. Arthur was grateful for their tears, because the splashing would block the sound of the three of them creeping to the back door of Kestrel Hall.

Arthur remembered Miss Carbunkle telling the man with white gloves that the Songcatcher plans were "gathering dust in her closet." But the Home was full of closets, so that didn't help. As for the Songcatcher, Arthur had a hunch it was hidden in either the Widget Room or the cellar.

"Don't ask me why, but I think the Songcatcher and the plans for building it are in two different places," whispered Arthur. "I want to get both out of here. I think the Wig hid the Songcatcher in one of her factories where the other machines are. The plans could be in any closet, though. Even in her office or private chambers."

Peevil offered to slip under the office door and search inside Miss Carbunkle's inner sanctum. "I can get into places you two can't. And although I am a knight," proclaimed Peevil, "I can be, shall we say, as quiet as a mouse."

"What did he say?" whispered Trinket.

Arthur translated.

"But he *is* a mouse," said Trinket.

"Excuse me, but I am a mouse *knight* on a *quest*," said Peevil. "I think that's pretty obvious."

"Stop it, you two!" said Arthur. "We can't lose any more time! Peevil – that's an excellent idea. Are you sure you'll be all right? It's awfully dangerous."

Peevil nodded solemnly. Arthur turned to the Crow and looked up at her great round eyes. "Will you be all right out here in the rain?"

"I am a Night Crow," said Belisha. "I am not the one you should be fretting about. You have no idea what I'm capable of, Foxling. Speaking of which, I would like to offer my services in this regard. Should I run into this Carbunkle of yours, I could easily and efficiently peck out her eyes and pluck out her entrails. It would take approximately two and a half minutes to complete the task."

"Thanks for the … uh … generous offer," said Arthur, "but I think if you run into Miss Carbunkle – she's hard to miss: a tall woman with a big orange wig – perhaps just pick her up and drop her in the middle of a field somewhere, then come back for us. That should suffice. Much obliged, though."

Arthur checked his pockets for the things Mr Oakley had given him for the job: candles, matches, rope and a couple other odds and ends. "I think I have everything. Trinket, would you do the honours?"

Trinket hopped up and down with enthusiasm. "Yes! Let the games begin!"

When they got to the door from the courtyard to the hall,

Arthur lifted her up so she could work her magic. She had her new flying suit on, but she would use it only if necessary, as it was a bit noisy.

"You know," said Arthur, "you'd make a pretty good thief if you put your mind to it."

Trinket peeped good-naturedly and inserted her beak into the keyhole. But to their surprise, the door was already unlocked.

"I bet it's always been unlocked," said Arthur. "Who needs a lock when you make everyone so afraid to leave?"

Trinket scuttled beside Arthur while Peevil followed close behind. The dim glow from the gaslight sconces cast eerie shadows along the silent corridor of Kestrel Hall.

"First things first," whispered Arthur. "Let's wake up Nurse Linette. She'll help us, I'm sure of it. Follow me, but be very quiet. Sneezeweed's quarters are behind that door!"

Sneezeweed's chamber was right next to the entrance to Kestrel Courtyard, across the hall from the two dormitory rooms. The infirmary was next to his room, and next to that was Linette's room. The three intruders crept up to Linette's door. Arthur reached up high and tried the handle to see if it was locked, but the door swung right open.

The three intruders peeked in. No one was there.

They tried the infirmary. That was empty too.

"That's strange," said Arthur. "Maybe she went on holiday. But I don't know. I have a funny feeling…"

"I do too, Arthur," said Trinket. "But we better move on."

They hurried down Kestrel Hall to the Grand Hall, the point where all four corridors met. The giant cuckoo clock struck two a.m. just as they reached Miss Carbunkle's office. The mechanical yellow bird danced out of the door, and as it chirped its lively song, the big beak popped out and swallowed it up with a sinister *snap!*

Arthur's ear quivered. He reached up and patted it, his old way of soothing himself when he was frightened. He would have reached for his blanket scrap and key, but they were lying somewhere in the subterranean world below.

Trinket nudged Arthur's foot with her beak. "You okay?" she asked.

He smiled down at her. "I'm fine. Really. We need to hurry. Follow me."

He motioned behind the clock. "I saw a repairman go inside the clock once. There should be a door – ah, there it is. Come on." The three slipped inside the base of the clock and shut the door. It was surprisingly roomy, at least for two small groundlings and a mouse.

"Peevil," said Arthur, "I'm pretty sure the Songcatcher's in the cellar, but just in case, it's easy to recognize. It looks like a big scalloped bell on top of a box, with a hand crank on the side. As for the plans – I've never seen them, but I think they're rolled up like a scroll and tied with a blue ribbon. And please. Do *not* try to do anything crazy. If you find either of these two things, just let us know where they are, and we'll take it from there. Got that?"

"I shall complete the mission, my liege, and report back immediately. I am at your command."

"My brave little friend," said Arthur, misty-eyed.

Arthur decided that they should all meet back inside the clock in one hour. If something went wrong, or any of them couldn't get to the clock, they were to return to Kestrel Courtyard and wait with Belisha.

"Arthur," whispered Trinket, "do you really think it's safe meeting right by her office? It seems crazy to me."

"That's the last place Miss Carbunkle would look for intruders, if she even wakes up. It's two in the morning; she has to be asleep, right? Besides, if Peevil finds the plans or the Songcatcher in there, we'll be close enough to get them. I just hope that they're in her office and not upstairs in her bedroom."

"Don't forget," said Trinket. "Her office and chambers are soundproof. Even for you. For all we know, she could be wide-awake."

"It's a chance we have to take."

The three of them crept out from their hiding place inside the cuckoo clock.

"Good luck, Peevil," said Arthur. "You are the most courageous knight I have ever known."

Trinket nodded in agreement and bowed low to the mouse in armour.

Peevil stood at the ready, his watch-face shield strapped to the front of him, his paw on the hilt of his sword. "I shall go forth bravely and with honour," said the mouse. He scampered off toward the office and in an instant was gone.

"I hope he'll be okay," said Arthur, wringing his hands. He took a deep breath and said, "We should check out the Widget Room in Falcon Hall first. She might have hidden it there. If not, we'll look in the cellar. Let's go."

CHAPTER 48

An Urgent Matter

UPSTAIRS IN HER CHAMBERS, Miss Carbunkle was indeed wide-awake. Mardox had just finished trimming the downy feathers on her head with his sharp black tines. It was a complicated business, as you can imagine.

"We really shouldn't wait so long next time," said the creature. "You know how itchy your scalp gets when those feathers start growing back in!"

Their conversation was cut short by a sound downstairs – three soft raps and one sharp one – Wire's signature knock. The headmistress hastily swept the downy feathers under her dresser and donned her orange wig, while Mardox slithered back inside the cane.

Ever since she had installed the Rat in his own private room in Hawk Hall as a reward for his help, he had made several impromptu appearances at very odd hours. This was highly unpleasant and, moreover, annoying. But Wire, for some inexplicable reason, had a powerful influence over her, despite the fact that he was a groundling and that he possessed a distinctly rodential nature.

Miss Carbunkle opened her office door and ushered Wire upstairs. "This better be important, Rat."

"My deepest apologies, madam. But I saw your light upstairs, and I do believe this is an urgent matter."

"Can't this wait till tomorrow?" said Miss Carbunkle, her thin eyebrows forming an angry *V.*

"I fear it cannot," said Wire. "It's Sneezeweed. I'm afraid he's a traitor. Not only that, he's also spreading vicious rumours about you to the staff. Shall I go on?"

"*A traitor?* What are you talking about? Sit down and tell me all you know. But be quick about it! I wish to go to bed."

CHAPTER 49

Caught

THE DOOR TO THE WIDGET ROOM was locked, but Trinket opened it with ease. Arthur lit a candle. The light fell on the giant Monster in the middle of the room, casting a menacing shadow on the wall behind it.

"To think," whispered Arthur, "that we actually helped her with her evil plot by working in here. I can't bear it."

"Don't think about it, then," said Trinket. "Let's just get the job done and get out of here."

After nearly an hour of digging through piles of discarded beetles and looking under tables and conveyor belts, and even in Mr Bonegrubber's messy office – full of empty bottles, old cabbages, sacks of half-eaten pork rinds and a pile of papers going all the way up to the ceiling – they couldn't find a thing. They dashed back to the Grand Hall and slipped inside the cuckoo clock to tell Peevil that they were going to search in the cellar next.

But Peevil wasn't there. It was nearly three a.m. If he didn't show up soon, they'd have to move on to Plan B: Go back to the courtyard and wait for him.

"What was I thinking?" said Arthur. "As if we'd be able to find anything in an hour. I'm so stupid! Poor Peevil!"

"Arthur, I'm sure he's okay. No one will see him. I told you – we little ones can get into places others can't."

"Trinket! I can hear someone coming this way, so forget Plan B right now. Let's search the cellar."

"Okay. Let's go. Which way?"

"There's just one problem," whispered Arthur. "I don't know how to get there."

"*What?*" said Trinket. "How are we supposed to find the Songcatcher, then?"

But before he could answer, the clock chimed three.

The sound was agonizingly loud to the two creatures hiding inside the clock. Trinket felt dizzy, and her whole body vibrated. She curled up in a quivering ball and rolled into a corner inside the clock. Arthur, who was completely stunned, staggered against a set of gears and fell right into the chimes.

At that very moment, a certain snivelling man who

happened to be limping by on his nocturnal rounds heard a commotion from inside the giant clock and went to investigate. His foot was still in a cast from the unfortunate donkey cart incident and made a clomping sound as he walked.

"You!" snapped Sneezeweed, grabbing Arthur by the scruff of his neck. "Come back to torment me? Missed the Home, did you? We'll see how you like your new digs now, *Number Thirteen*." He spat out Arthur's old name with disgust. "We don't have far to go – the door's right below my feet."

Sneezeweed took a step back and pressed a button on the wall to his right. A secret trapdoor sprang open where he had been standing moments before. He shoved a very dizzy Arthur down into the opening and followed him in.

Arthur stumbled along as Sneezeweed pushed him down the steep, dark staircase leading from clock to cellar. Arthur could hear rats and mice scampering and chattering on the steps and behind the walls. *If only they could help me!* he thought.

At the bottom, they turned to the right down a long narrow passageway. At the end was a rusty metal door that opened into a grim, cavernous room. It was an enormous factory, twenty times larger than the Widget Room upstairs.

Unbeknownst to both of them, however, a small birdlike creature hopped along behind them at a short distance.

The room was full of beetle machines even more monstrous than the original Monster upstairs. There was also a row of some other kind of machine, equally as monstrous, and piles and piles of brown wax cylinders next to it. *All she needs now is to build the Songcatchers, using those plans,* thought Arthur. As they passed through the factory to another room, Arthur caught a glimpse of a large brass bell.

The Songcatcher!

It was just sitting on a table in the middle of the room.

Sneezeweed dragged Arthur through a door into a smaller room with a low ceiling, covered with rusty dripping pipes and cobwebs.

The room was dimly lit by a single red grease lamp. The air smelled dank and foul, nearly as bad as Gloomintown. Arthur felt as if he were back in the underground city, heading to his cramped hole in the black rock wall.

Sneezeweed shoved Arthur into a cell, locked it, and hung the key back on its hook. "You'll pay for this, you foul little maggot," he said. "For all the humiliation you caused me. You'll pay for that wig. You'll pay for the donkey and the dogs. You'll pay for my broken foot, and the night I spent outside with the worms and bugs. When Miss Carbunkle finds out who I have waiting in the dungeon, she will turn you into bow-wow broth and feed you to the rats. Good night!"

Hidden in a crack between the cold stone floor and the grimy factory wall, Trinket held her breath.

CHAPTER 50

The Bravest Knight

AFTER A USELESS SEARCH OF Miss Carbunkle's office, Peevil scampered up the spiral staircase and slipped under the door into the headmistress's private chambers. He scurried silently along her bedroom wall toward the two closets across from her bed and dresser. He had to be very careful – for if his shield touched the floor and made a sound, that would be the end of him.

While Wire and Miss Carbunkle were talking, Peevil slipped under the door of the closet on the left. But after a perfunctory search, it was clear that the only things in there were dozens of hats and ridiculous-looking wigs.

He scampered right under their noses into the other closet.

This one looked much more promising. Every shelf was packed with dusty memorabilia. It was as if the headmistress had taken an enormous box of photographs, letters, old toys and other objects from the past, tossed them into the closet willy-nilly and shut the door.

Peevil had to be careful where he stepped, for on the floor was a broken frame and shattered glass. Next to the mess was a picture of two girls in bonnets, standing beneath an apple tree, but the face of one of the girls had been scratched out. *Curious*, thought the mouse. *Curious indeed.*

Peevil leaped from shelf to shelf, moving swiftly over the stacked photographs of Miss Carbunkle and what appeared to be her twin sister – at the zoo, playing croquet, picking flowers in a garden, and waving from the bow of a great ship. *Nothing useful here,* thought Peevil. That is, until he scaled the very top shelf. There, wedged behind a row of antique china dolls, was a long scroll of parchment tied with a bright-blue ribbon. Scrawled on the outside of the scroll was one word: *Songcatcher.*

Peevil couldn't help himself. He did what he always did when he got excited: he rubbed his whiskers very fast, tugged on his ear, and let out a little squeak.

"What's that sound?" Miss Carbunkle said immediately. "That … that sounds like … like a mouse! In my closet!"

"Have no fear, Madam! I shall look right away," said Wire.

Peevil heard the door creak open; there was no time to

hide. He looked down at the watch face on his chest. *Brilliant!* he said to himself. He stood upright on his back two feet, one paw resting on the hilt of his sword, the other at his side, and tried very hard not to breathe.

Wire surveyed the closet full of old memories – "Interesting find, this," he murmured to himself. More information to file away. For now, though, there was this mouse to find and kill. But all the Rat could see were old, dusty things and some stupid childhood toys.

He shut the door and rejoined Miss Carbunkle. *Sentimentality will be her downfall,* he decided, and put on his most humble smile.

Meanwhile, Peevil pondered the completely unrealistic, possibly insane idea of dragging the scroll out of the closet alone. The main problem he could see was opening the closet door, not to mention the door to Miss Carbunkle's chambers. He sat back down on his haunches and considered the pros and cons of his harebrained plot.

"Well, *was* there a mouse?" demanded Miss Carbunkle.

"No, my lady. Not a real one. Just a silly little clockwork mouse – a treasured toy from childhood, perhaps?"

"A *what?*"

"Some kind of windup clockwork toy," said Wire. "A mouse with a suit of armour. I suppose you could say it was a mouse *knight.*" He stifled a laugh.

"I never, I repeat *never*, had a clockwork mouse! I despise all mice, even toy ones."

"Oh. I see," said the Rat. "I'll take care of it straightaway, Mistress."

When Wire opened the door again, Peevil struck another pose. Wire pushed a chair next to the shelves and climbed up so he could reach the top. The Rat narrowed his eyes at the mouse. He and the mouse were nearly nose to nose now. "Well, mousie," said Wire, his mouth curled into a sharp-toothed grin. "The game is up."

In a flash, Peevil grabbed his sword, stabbed Wire right in the snout, and scrambled down the shelves. He scurried out of the closet and headed toward the door.

"Kill it!" screamed Miss Carbunkle, who was now standing on her bed.

Peevil was almost at the door when Wire stomped down hard on his tail. The mouse squealed in pain. Wire picked Peevil up by the tip of his rebroken tail and dangled him upside down (the most humiliating position in the world for a mouse, just so you know).

"I shall dispose of this filthy thing, madam. Worry not. And my apologies for bothering you at this late hour. I bid you good-night."

"Make sure it's dead! Good night!"

As soon as Wire had left, Miss Carbunkle whispered for her manticore to come out. She had noticed that the hawk eyes on her cane had not stopped flickering for several minutes. Something felt wrong.

As soon as the door had fully shut, Mardox leaped into Miss Carbunkle's arms. He was growling and clearly disturbed.

"What is it, my pet? Calm yourself. Tell me."

"Something is here," said the manticore. "We must find it and kill it right away!"

"What is here, my pet?"

"Something from the world Below. One of the Ancient Ones. A creature with the old magic, like mine. We must destroy it. *Now.*"

"Then we shall," said Miss Carbunkle. "This could be your moment of glory, my pet! We shall kill it, I promise you! Where is it? Where shall we go?"

"In the courtyard, mistress. Kestrel Courtyard. It is waiting there. It knows I am here. We must hurry."

CHAPTER 51

The Battle Begins

WIRE LEFT Miss Carbunkle's office, still holding Peevil by his tail. As he was musing on how best to torture and dispose of the mouse with the acorn on its head – just the sort of thing he enjoyed contemplating – he ran right into Sneezeweed, who was on his way to see the headmistress. Sneezeweed was stroking the downy patch below his nose in a most imperious fashion, and his face looked particularly smug.

"Oh, if it isn't *the Rat*," said Sneezeweed. "I see *you* caught an intruder." He looked at the mouse dangling from Wire's bristly grey mitt and snickered. "What a coincidence. I caught one too. But I do believe that mine is worth quite a bit more than yours."

"What are you talking about, Snotweed?" asked Wire.

"We'll see who she favours now, after she finds out who *I* have locked up in the cellar," said Sneezeweed. He whipped out his handkerchief, blew his nose, and continued. "Do you recall that deviant Fox groundling who escaped last month with his freaky little Bird friend? Well, I caught him single-handed! Found him right inside here." He pointed to the cuckoo clock. "Locked him up in the dungeon. He was looking for something. Now, what do you suppose he was looking for? I'd bet a year's salary it's that machine she's got down there. How did he find out about that? Hmmm. Let me see. Miss Carbunkle has been confiding in a rat groundling. And this intruder is a groundling too. I say that's awfully suspicious, don't you?"

"How can you be so stupid?" said Wire. "I don't even know what you're talking about, and frankly, I don't care. It's late. I'm going to exterminate this mouse, then go straight to bed. You can think whatever you like. It doesn't matter to me."

But it did matter to Wire. Not that Sneezeweed suspected him of conspiring with some idiot one-eared groundling, but the fact that there was something very funny going on: a mouse in armour that looked suspiciously like he was trying to snatch those plans, and now that puddlehead Fox snooping about. *They're up to something,* he said to himself, *and I'm going to find out what it is. This is just the kind of thing to win her total trust.* Wire was going to have a little chat with that plonker Number Thirteen.

Just then, the headmistress burst out of her office. "Haven't you killed that thing yet?" she said to Wire, then she turned to Sneezeweed. "Why don't you get out of the way and … and go do something useful for once?"

Before Wire could say, "As you wish, madam," Miss Carbunkle was running down the hall in the direction of Kestrel Courtyard. Mr Sneezeweed hobbled slowly after her, while Wire slipped into the clock and headed to the cellar.

Down below, Trinket emerged from the shadows, activated her flying suit, and fetched the key from the hook. She dropped it inside Arthur's cell so he could let himself out.

"Thanks, Trinket! Glad he didn't catch you too! Trinket, listen. I saw it! The Songcatcher is here! It's in the next room!"

"I saw it too!" said Trinket. "Let's grab it and get out of here. We don't have time to look for the scroll. It's going to get light soon, and I'm worried about Belisha. *And* Peevil. But first we need to help the others! There are a bunch of groundlings sleeping in those cells." Trinket pointed her beak toward the row of cells along the wall.

Arthur peered inside the cell next to him. "Oh, no! Trinket, you're right. I thought I heard breathing," said Arthur, "but I was scared. I can't hear as well when I'm scared."

Inside the tiny dark cells, groundlings slept in corners, curled up on the damp ground. Arthur pointed to a reptile groundling whimpering in her sleep. He whispered, "I remember her! That's the one who set Miss Carbunkle's desk on fire last year." He paused. "She had a name. It was … I think it was Nancy. It *was* Nancy."

In the next row of cells were all the Grumblers – the older groundlings they assumed had left the Home after they came of age. And then, in another cell, they saw their good friends Nesbit, Nigel and Snook, their sleeping faces sad and looking older than their years.

"We have to help them!" cried Trinket.

"I know," said Arthur. "Let's let these three out, and they can help the others while we grab the Songcatcher. It'll just take a second. There may be an exit nearby for Kestrel Hall. I saw Sneezeweed go back a different way, and Kestrel's right above our heads."

Their friends woke up as their cell was being unlocked. "Arthur! Trinket!" cried the three prisoners, and everyone embraced.

"Nurse Linette," said Nigel. "She's here too! Over there! Quick."

Across from Nigel's cell were more cells, including Linette's. Arthur looked inside. There, lying in a fetal position, was the nurse. She was barely recognizable. Her ginger hair was filthy and undone, and her face was white as a ghost's. The cell was much too small for her, and it looked as if someone had just stuffed her in there and thrown away the key.

"Linette!" said Arthur. "Wake up!"

Linette opened her eyes wide, smiled weakly, and in a barely audible voice whispered Arthur's and Trinket's names.

Arthur unlocked her cell and Linette crawled out.

Her voice was so faint, they could barely hear her. She told them how, late one night, she had spotted Wire and Sneezeweed carrying the Songcatcher down Kestrel Hall to the storage closet, then disappearing inside. She secretly followed them and discovered the factory, the cells, everything. When she confronted her aunt, Miss Carbunkle hit her over the head with her cane. "The next morning, I woke up inside this cell," said Linette. "I've been here ever since. I'll tell you more later, but we've got to get everyone out of here. *Now*."

"I think the exit is off the passageway just up through that other door," said Arthur. "Go to Kestrel Courtyard. We'll be there soon, then we'll find a way out together. Don't worry about the Crow. She'll help us get out – I know she will."

Linette and the others freed the rest of the orphans, while Arthur and Trinket ran into the factory to get the Songcatcher.

★ ★ ★

In the courtyard the Night Crow kept watch.

She was perched on the Wall at the far end of the yard. In less than two hours, it would be dawn, and she was beginning to worry.

When Miss Carbunkle ran out into the rain, shaking her cane at the Crow like a madwoman, Belisha shone her blazing eyes down at her and laughed: *kek kek kek kek!* "You must be the Carbunkle I have heard so much about. Well, Carbunkle, what can a little cane like that do to a big crow like me?"

"I'll show you exactly what it can do!"

"I am not afraid of your silly stick."

The Crow was worried, however. There was some kind of dark magic afoot here, and she wasn't sure what it was. When the woman with the orange hair had appeared, the magic rumbled all around her. Belisha could feel it in the Wall circling the place. She could feel it resonate throughout the ancient stone building and the earth below.

But Belisha merely tossed her head back and laughed again.

Miss Carbunkle whispered to the creature hidden inside her cane, "This is our hour of glory, my pet! We shall astonish them all!"

She did exactly what Mardox had told her to do before they left her chambers: she closed her eyes and recited the dark, ancient words he had given her. Then she held her cane above her head and released her manticore into the sky. The creature shot out of its wooden prison in a burst of blue smoke.

Through the cuckoo clock and down into the dungeon the Rat went, carrying Peevil by his tail. When Wire reached the bottom of the stairs, he headed to the cells where Sneezeweed had locked up the one-eared Fox. But instead of his nemesis cowering behind bars among dozens of other groundling slaves, he found, to his surprise, row upon row of empty cells.

The groundlings were silently escaping through another exit, up to Kestrel Hall.

Wire pinched Peevil's tail hard, and he let out a desperate squeak. "Shut up, you stinking little bottom-feeder," said the Rat. "I know your friends are here, and you're going to help me find them. Just watch."

In the factory next door, Arthur struggled to carry the heavy Songcatcher in his arms while Trinket guided him toward the door.

Arthur stopped. "Trinket," he whispered, "it's Wire! I can hear him! And he's got Peevil! Let's hide and see what he does next. We'll surprise him at the right moment. Come on!"

He clumsily set the Songcatcher down on one of the worktables, and he and Trinket quickly scooted under it.

"Come out, come out, wherever you are," said Wire. "I have your little friend. He's having a grand old time, aren't you, my little mousie-mouse?" The Rat began to swing Peevil in circles by his tail. Peevil squeaked out in pain.

"Why, I think this mouse deserves a little jolt of something special."

Wire flipped a switch, and a terrible roar started up. Then, with a blast of steam and a screech of the whistle, the Monster's gears clicked into motion.

Arthur scrambled out from under the table. "Fly out of here and get help!" he cried to Trinket.

But try as she might, Trinket couldn't get her mechanical wings to open. Something was stuck. Arthur and Trinket watched in horror as Wire dropped Peevil onto the conveyor belt heading straight toward the Monster's mouth.

The wide belt slowly creaked forward, then began to speed up. Peevil tried desperately to run, but the best he could do was scamper in place, moving closer and closer to his doom.

Arthur tried to get to Peevil, but Wire blocked his way at every turn, taunting him, hissing and dancing from side to side. Arthur glanced around for something, anything, to fend off the Rat. He spied a cartload of beetle widgets at the tail end of the Monster and dashed to it. He shoved the cart as hard as he could at Wire. But the Rat jumped out of the way, and instead, the cart flew right into the Monster, which started shaking violently, sending out a cascade of bright-blue sparks.

Wire backed off. He took one glance at the Monster, which looked like it was going to explode any moment, and fled from the room.

Arthur ran forward and snatched up his friend just in time. "Run, Peevil! Help the others! Go! We'll be right behind you."

Arthur had one hand on each side of the Songcatcher and was about to lift it once again when the Monster began to roar like a beast, a deep rolling sound that made the very ground tremble beneath them. The glass "eyes" of the Monster blazed a bluish white, and a blast of steam and sparks flew out the top.

Then, in an instant, the Monster exploded into flames, sending beetles, gears, and bits of metal flying every which way, including straight at Arthur's head. A beetle hit him between the eyes, and Arthur toppled to the floor under the Songcatcher and passed out cold. Trinket hopped back and forth, trying to dodge the flying debris. Then fire spread through the factory room in seconds.

The dungeon was in flames.

CHAPTER 52

The Battle Above

IN THE COURTYARD, Miss Carbunkle anxiously watched her manticore as he battled the Night Crow high above her, near the top of the Wall. Belisha was much larger, and she could use the light from her eyes to distract the beast. She could attack him with her beak and claws as well. But Mardox had a couple things in his favour.

The end of his tail was deadly. And it was nearly dawn.

Belisha bore down upon the beast, catching him by the middle in her great claws. She tried to snap off his head with her giant beak, but Mardox flattened the tines along his back and slipped away, then came at her again and again with his tail. He pushed the Crow closer and closer to the great stone Wall.

They fought there in the driving rain, as the head-mistress, drenched to the bone, called out encouraging words to her beloved pet and hurtled insults at the Night Crow.

Mardox wanted to drive the Crow into a corner, then attack her straight on with the poisonous tip of his tail. And it looked like his plan was going to work.

But just when the manticore had forced Belisha into the very same corner where Arthur used to hide, below the weeping gargoyle with the drooping eyes, Wire appeared in the courtyard.

What is this? wondered the Rat, taking in the shocking scene: two monstrous creatures battling in the air, and the headmistress below, cheering one on. But there was no time to even think about this, for they were all in danger.

He quickly told Miss Carbunkle about the fire, and about the intruders who were trying to steal the Songcatcher at that very moment. "Sneezeweed, the coward, ran off. I told you he was disloyal, my lady."

Before she could say anything, they both heard a sputtering sound above their heads.

"It's D.O.G.C.!" exclaimed the headmistress. "Help is on the way!"

She shouted up at what appeared to be three D.O.G.C. officials in their signature black bowler hats, riding steam-powered flying bicycles above the courtyard. One looked as if he had a white cat clinging to his back. "The intruders are in the cellar! There's an entrance at the end of the hall! Break the door down if you have to!"

The officials landed in front of the door and rode their bicycles right inside. Miss Carbunkle called after them, "And alert the fire brigade! The orphanage is on fire!"

"Already did," one of the officials shouted back. "Saw the smoke on our way in, ma'am."

The rain dwindled to a drizzle, and a pink light began to glow on the horizon. Wire and Miss Carbunkle stared up at the two fiercely determined creatures, who were now easier to see in the approaching dawn.

Mardox still had the Crow backed into a corner, right in front of Arthur's old gargoyle. The manticore grinned, his tiny sharp teeth gleaming. "I shall kill you, Crow, and oh, how deliciously slow and painful it will be!"

Belisha twisted this way and that, trying to dodge the creature's tail.

And then the sun began to rise.

"Kill it!" cried Miss Carbunkle. "Kill it now! We shall triumph together!"

Mardox twisted his tail around and hovered in the air, his stinger poised near the great Crow's face. "After I kill you," hissed Mardox, flicking his black tongue, "I shall eat you, beak and all! After that, I'll do the same to your friends. Tonight, I will feast."

Plink, plank, plunk. Behind Belisha's head, the last drops of rain dripped onto the roof and buttress above, and then, *plink, plank, plunk,* the sad-eyed gargoyle's tears stopped.

The last tear fell from the gargoyle's eye.

The solstice sun rose in the sky and shone, in all its glory, directly onto the great Crow's face. She shut her eyes tight and let out a wretched, ancient cry – a crow's caw mingled with the howl of a wolf. She twisted her head away from the light and cried once more.

But when she moved aside, Mardox saw the gargoyle face-to-face. It looked just like him.

The gargoyle blinked. And in the ways of the old magic when twin meets twin, the manticore began to turn to stone.

Mardox's poisonous stinger and tail were first to change. His mistress could see him writhing in the air, screeching in pain and anger. "My pet! What's wrong? What is it?"

For years, she had kept her beloved away from mirrors so he could not see his reflection, but now he had seen his droopy-eyed stone twin – the twin that had always been there, waiting for him to come.

Mardox's four feline legs transformed, became heavy, and crumbled off. Then his body, the sharp black tines along his back, and his face – his beak-like snout, his droopy eyes, first the left, then the right – and finally his large rubbery ears became granite. His leafy green wings were the last to turn to stone.

He crashed to the ground and broke into hundreds of pieces.

"Nooooo!" cried Miss Carbunkle. She ran to him and crouched over his broken body, now a pile of rubble. The headmistress wept for the first time in thirty years.

The Rat placed his grey bristly hand on her shoulder and in a silky voice said, "There, there, mistress. It will be all right. Wire will take care of things; don't you worry a bit."

As the Rat comforted his human companion, a strange rumbling like thunder began beneath the earth. Wire and Miss Carbunkle lost their balance and fell. Then the Wall – ever so slightly – shook.

CHAPTER 53

The Wonderling

WHEN ARTHUR AWOKE, he was alone in the dungeon. He called out for Trinket, but there was no answer. He was certain Trinket had died in the fire that was now raging around him. The smoke was so thick, he couldn't see a way out. He was trapped and terrified, and began to cry.

And then he began to howl.

Arthur wailed into the tongues of flame that licked the factory walls, wailed into the crumbling dungeon choking with smoke. And his painful cry turned into the word *"why"* – the word that had always burned inside him. Why had he been born? Why couldn't he remember who he was? Why had he been brought to this terrible place, and escaped it only to return? And why, oh why, had he been given a gift, only to have it taken away? For he would surely die that night, alone.

And the word *"why"* became a long, sorrowful note, and the note a wordless song from his parched and aching throat.

It was a wailing song of loss, and he sang it out into the burning room in his clear, sweet voice.

The song was sad, and ancient, and wild. He sang it with all his heart, with every ounce of life in him. He sang it until he couldn't sing anymore.

And when he was done, he remembered everything.

His mother, her voice, the stars. How she sang to him, how she held him up to the sky that night and said, softly, proudly, "You are the Wonderling. We have been waiting such a long, long time."

He remembered the animals that gathered around him in a circle. He remembered their voices too. He understood every word they said.

And he remembered a family. *His* family. Mother, father, and three sisters.

Then he remembered how the people came bearing torches. They were burning down the grove of trees behind a big white house. And all the animals that had gathered around – he remembered how they scattered, running from the towering flames. One tree had burned particularly bright, then crashed down in a blaze of red. It was the giant fire monster from his dream, but it wasn't a monster at all. It was a great oak tree. And inside the tree was his family's home.

Then he remembered a box – a music box with a little golden key. It had a bird on it and smelled like roses. On the box was a W – for *Wonderling*. Just like the W embroidered in gold thread on his blue baby blanket. The W he had thought was an M.

Moments before the fire, his mother had turned the key and a melody had flowed out from the box. It was the lullaby he had carried with him all his life. "Someday, you shall sing," she said to him, kissing the top of his head and then his ear, for he *was* born with only one (a sign, just like the white-leaf shape on his russet chest, just like his gift of listening, of understanding).

Then her face came to him in all its singular beauty, and he felt her heart beat against his as she sang her lilting song.

As Arthur struggled to breathe in the smoke-filled room, he heard his mother's voice inside his head, saying the words she had spoken moments before the fire destroyed his home and consumed the rest of his family: "You are the Wonderling.

It is your destiny. You must sing to the lonely, comfort the frightened, and awaken the love in sleeping hearts."

Then, in an instant, she was gone.

Now he had nothing left but his memory, and the song. What good were they to him now? He was meant to sing. He knew it as surely as he knew his hands were both human *and* fox. *This* was his destiny.

But it was too late. A plume of smoke engulfed him, and the world faded from his eyes.

CHAPTER 54
Day of Destiny

ARTHUR AWOKE to something plopping into his lap.

"Trinket!" he cried. "I thought I'd lost you for ever!"

Trinket had simply dropped out of the Songcatcher's bell, where she had hidden to dodge the flying debris. But when a beetle widget hit the crank, it activated the machine and the Dreamometer, lulling her to sleep as she listened to the same set of military marches over and over again. "Thank goodness that bell thing got so hot," said Trinket. "Otherwise, I'd still be asleep in there; gone crazy from all those marches!"

The room was filling up with smoke and getting hotter. Trinket and Arthur burst out coughing at the same time.

"We have to get out of here," cried Arthur. "Can you fly?"

"I can't! My wings are broken," said Trinket. "And the propeller's not working either."

"Okay – we'll try to run out. I'll grab the Songcatcher. Maybe it'll block the flames. Get inside my shirt. Let's go!"

Arthur held the heavy machine in front of him and staggered through the leaping flames. The heat was unbearable, but they made it safely to the next room. They were heading to the Kestrel Hall exit when Arthur heard a sound.

Inside one of the cells were two very small groundlings huddled in a corner, protecting an even smaller one who had been too scared to leave. It was Baby Tizer, the one who refused to grow larger than a hedgehog.

Arthur was struggling not to drop the Songcatcher. He held on tightly to the beautiful machine that had given him the gift of so many sounds and songs. The machine that was, truly, a miracle. He had to save it.

And yet…

His friends would surely die if he did.

In the end, the choice wasn't hard at all.

Arthur dropped the Songcatcher, and as it crashed to the floor, he scooped up the three groundlings and ran. As they ran, Arthur breathlessly told Trinket that he remembered his mother, and what she had said before she died.

"You were born to sing, Arthur! *That's* been your destiny all along!"

"I know!" said Arthur, who felt the strangest thing – happy about knowing the truth and yet terrified that he and the others might die.

When they got to the top of the stairs and Arthur pushed open the door, they gulped in smoke. The fire in the cellar had begun spreading to the rest of the Home.

"Arthur, look!" cried Trinket. There were three figures on flying bicycles heading in their direction. Arthur could see a big eye on each of their black bowler hats.

"Oh, no!" cried Arthur. "It's the D.O.G.C.!"

Before they could escape, the three bicycles sputtered, burped a blast of steam, and landed right in front of them. Then Arthur heard a familiar friendly voice. "Hullo, Spike, m' boy!"

Quintus, Bone and Squee (who was wearing a white cat mask) were piled one on top of the other on the first bike, inside a giant overcoat, with Quintus's face partially hidden beneath his oversize hat. Thorn and Throttle were on the second bike, and, to Arthur and Trinket's surprise, sitting on the third bike, on Cruncher's rabbity shoulders, was a raven-haired boy with elfin ears, a wooden sword hanging from his belt.

"Pinecone!" cried Arthur and Trinket at the same time. The little boy was grinning from ear to ear and not showing an ounce of fear.

"Crikey," said Quintus, "that's one big bird!"

"How did you know to come?" Arthur exclaimed. "And Pinecone? How—?"

"Listen," said Quintus. "Short story is your mate sent a message sayin' some lady was gonna destroy all the music in the world, an' I says, if there ain't no music, I might as well be dead. So I procured these here bicycles, an' the rest, as they say, is history. When we shows up at this lad's house—" he gestured to Pinecone—"an' found 'im cryin' in the woods, sayin' you lot forgot 'im, I had to bring 'im along, didn't I? Now, let's get you two out of here! We just flew past by t'other end – the front of the building's on fire too."

Arthur looked at Trinket and knew just what she was thinking: How would they get everyone out now? But there was no time to think. He and the others scrambled up onto the bikes and rode straight out the door into Kestrel Courtyard.

The courtyard was a whirlwind of chaos. Nurse Linette, who had led everyone outside and then gone back in to wake up the sleeping groundlings in Kestrel Hall, was now tying a large sheet around Belisha's eyes to protect her from the light. Sneezeweed (whom the prisoners had tied up) was sitting in a puddle on the ground, honking into his handkerchief, saying over and over again, "It wasn't my fault! It wasn't my fault!"

while next to him, Mug and Orlick, who had slept through most of the ordeal, grumbled, "Whatever it was, I didn't do it!" The local police had arrived and were trying to maintain order while volunteer firefighters were relaying buckets and hoses down a ladder propped up against the Wall. With all the other ancient doors besides Hawk Hall having been sealed by Miss Carbunkle long ago, the one and only exit to the Home was now utterly impassable.

And the fire continued to spread.

Miss Carbunkle and Wire stood in the middle of the courtyard. The headmistress was in shock, staring at the pile of stones that had once been Mardox. She was so stunned by grief, she didn't even notice the chaos around her until Wire nudged her and whispered, "Look over there, madam. We've been taken for fools." He pointed at Quintus, Arthur and the others.

Quintus was pointing out the headmistress and her partner-in-crime to a pair of policemen. The officers began striding toward them, wielding billy clubs. "Is there another way out?" Wire asked under his breath.

"Yes! But we must go back inside to get there."

"Run in a zigzag," said Wire. "It'll throw them off. Go!"

As she and Wire zigzagged past Quintus and the officers, Wire, who had always fancied having a cat of his own – for if anything, he was a Rat who aspired to greatness – snatched up Squee, who was still disguised as a cat.

At that moment, a ginger-haired woman in an indigo cloak was climbing down the firefighters' ladder and into the courtyard, frantically calling out her daughter's name. "Linette! Linette! Where are you?"

"Over here, Mama! I'm safe," cried Linette, waving her arms. The woman started toward her daughter but stopped. Heading straight for the door were her very own sister and a very large Rat.

Phoebe Nightingale ran – arms open, tears streaming down her face – toward the sister she had not seen in thirty years, her cloak billowing out behind her.

"Clemmy! Stop! Please! Clementine!"

But Miss Carbunkle did not turn back. Instead, she and Wire, who was dragging poor Squee by the scruff of his neck, dashed right into the burning building.

And then Arthur watched in horror as a tiny mouse with an acorn helmet and sword scurried right after them.

"Peevil!" screamed Arthur. He tried to follow, but a burly fireman held him back.

"Place is gonna burn down," said the fireman. "We gotta get you lot up and over that ladder fast."

Inside Kestrel Hall, Miss Carbunkle and Wire dashed down to her office. "I know a way out, but first I must get those plans!" she cried. Just as they reached the Grand Hall, though, flames shot up from the cellar door inside the clock, and all at once, it burst into flames. The fire began to spread toward Miss Carbunkle's glass office. "I must get those plans!" she shrieked again, and fumbled in her pocket for her key. But when she tried the lock, the door, which was burning-hot now, wouldn't budge. She kicked and kicked it, trying to break it down, then started beating the door with her now-hollow cane, but the door stayed just as unyielding as she had built it.

She was so furious, she raised her cane over her head and threw it at the burning clock. It blazed a brilliant red for a moment, then was consumed by fire.

Wire shouted at her to follow him and pulled her away.

Thus, the woman with the bright-orange wig and the Rat with the black pebble eyes disappeared through a secret passageway only she knew about, to a tunnel far below the burning cellar and far, far away from the Home.

And the orphanage, which had been built centuries ago in the shape of a giant cross and had been so many things – a monastery, a prison, a workhouse and a sorrowful home for wayward and misbegotten creatures – went up in flames.

The whole of Kestrel Courtyard began to fill with choking smoke. Even if Belisha – blindfolded and exhausted – could carry some of the groundlings, and Quintus and the others could carry some on bicycles, with only the one ladder it was doubtful that everyone could get over the Wall in time.

But still, they tried. The firefighters and police officers, along with Quintus, his friends, and Linette and Phoebe, threw themselves into action – helping groundlings up the ladder, onto bicycles, and onto Belisha's back.

Arthur and Trinket were watching the door, hoping against hope that Peevil would appear. Tongues of fire were bursting through the infirmary window now. Arthur strained to listen for a mouse's squeak but could hear only the fire roaring inside.

"Arthur," said Trinket. "Look!"

She was motioning with her beak at all the groundlings huddled around them. There were more than a hundred, way too many to save. The orphans seemed doomed.

"What can we do?" asked Arthur, his heart sinking fast.

"I don't know, Arthur! Look at them, the poor things. They're frightened to death."

Arthur stared at all the orphans sitting together on the ground, dressed in tattered grey pyjamas, clinging to one another and crying. Their crying pierced his heart and every fibre of his being.

He was at a loss at what to do and so just stood there shaking his head.

And then an idea came to him – an idea so simple it seemed ridiculous. And it certainly wouldn't save them – he wasn't so arrogant as to think that. But he thought it might help in some small way.

If he had to die, he decided, he would die singing. And doing what he knew now was his destiny: *to sing to the lonely, comfort the frightened, and awaken the love in sleeping hearts.*

And so Arthur began to sing. It was the lullaby his mother had sung to him that night under the stars, the song that had comforted him and kept him alive all those years:

"In every tree and every forest,
birds are singing a hopeful chorus…"

The groundlings looked up at the one-eared orphan's red furry face and his chestnut eyes flecked with gold, the groundling they had known as Number Thirteen. And just as the voice of the beauty of the world had flowed from the Songcatcher into him, his song now flowed into them. As he sang in his pure, sweet voice, their spirits began to lift and they felt less afraid. And as their hearts lightened, Arthur's song floated over the courtyard, and over the Wall to the tall white birch on the other side. And then a twittering began, and a chirping and cooing from the birds who nested there, and their song spread to other trees, and soon the valley beyond the Wall was filled with song. As the air reverberated with music, a dark force began to lift from somewhere deep below. The flames that moments before were consuming the building began to smoulder, then die.

The Wall started shaking, just as it had when the manticore turned to stone, and a dark mist rose up all around it, shrouding it in blackness. Then, in an instant, the mist drifted up and away into the clear, cloudless sky.

"Look!" cried Trinket and the others. They were all pointing at the Wall now, to where the ancient arched door had once been. The stones that Miss Carbunkle had used to cover it up thirty years before began falling away, one by one, until before them was a beautiful arched door made of oak and decorated with a tree filled with birds. There was no need for a key now; the door swung open by itself.

No one could speak, they were so wonder-struck. As Quintus, Trinket, and Arthur ushered the little ones to the open door, Arthur heard a jubilant and victorious squeak. There, scampering out of the charred building, was Peevil, the bravest of knights, along with fifty or more mice and rats, carrying the scroll of Songcatcher plans on their backs. Arthur let out a wild cheer, and everyone joined in, crying "Huzzah! Huzzah!" for Peevil and his comrades.

"Well, I never," Quintus said to Arthur. "If rats an' mice can work side by side, I reckon there's hope for us all."

CHAPTER 55
Endings and Beginnings

IT WAS CHRISTMAS EVE DAY, and Phoebe Nightingale's house was swirling with festivities. Phoebe was wrapping presents with her friend Mr Pitch, while Linette was putting up last-minute decorations. The cook was hard at work in the kitchen, preparing an extraordinary feast in honour of Arthur's first birthday in his new home, and Arthur, Trinket and several of the other groundlings whom Phoebe Nightingale had taken in until things were sorted out were decorating the tree. Peevil was squeaking directions from the entrance of his new home: a well-appointed dollhouse that had been refurbished to accommodate a mouse – or, rather, a *knightly* mouse. Peevil wanted everything to look perfect because his family, whom he had finally found, was coming to spend the holidays with him.

Six months had passed since the fire at Miss Carbunkle's Home for Wayward and Misbegotten Creatures. Phoebe had declined to file any charges against her sister, but Miss Carbunkle was still on the lam. No one knew her whereabouts or, for that matter, those of her accomplice, the Rat. And Squee, Arthur's friend from Wildered Manor whom Wire had snatched in the courtyard, was still missing in action.

Still, there were so many things for which Arthur could be grateful.

For one, thanks to Constable Floop and Miss Phoebe, he was no longer a wanted criminal, and all the horrible posters had been taken down in the City. Second, he now had a new name besides Arthur and "the Wonderling." He never could recall the full name his mother had given him. But Miss Phoebe had adopted him, and he was now called *Arthur Nightingale* – and would never again be known only by an unlucky number stamped on a tin tag hanging around his neck.

Phoebe had pulled a lot of strings to adopt him, since humans were rarely allowed to adopt groundlings, but it all worked out in the end. As it happened, the official in charge of the matter was one of her biggest music hall fans. And while Arthur still had to be registered with the authorities, he had more freedom than he ever imagined.

There were more good things, like Phoebe's plans for restoring the parts of the Home that had been damaged in the fire and turning it into a free boarding school for the study and practice of the arts. All the groundlings who had lived under her sister's tyrannical rule would receive a real education. And when the building was finished, they could sing and dance and play and draw to their hearts' content.

Plus, Arthur would have a tutor! Any day now, a certain Erastus Pennywhistle, a distinguished and scholarly hare groundling, was to arrive by ship. After six months of, as Miss Phoebe put it, "Arthur's idle amusements" – touring the City with Trinket, playing countless board games, sliding down banisters, and reading everything he could get his hands on about King Arthur and the Knights of the Round Table – Arthur would finally have a real teacher. He would be instructed not only in music (which, to Miss Phoebe, was the most important subject in the world), but in philosophy, philology, archaeology, Ancient Greek, Latin, alchemy, mathematics, botany, astronomy, literature and just about every other subject under the sun.

Trinket, who was now living at Phoebe's house, had also been offered the services of Professor Pennywhistle, but she had declined. "A tutor?" she had said. "Spend my days learning Ancient Greek and Latin and other silly things when I could be inventing something no one has ever invented before?

With all due respect – and gratitude for your kind offer, Miss Phoebe – I think I'll pass."

In the parlour, a cozy fire roared and sputtered in the hearth, while a gentle snow fell on the street outside the blue-shuttered windows of the House of Nightingale. Arthur was sitting by the window, gazing out at the peaceful white street. He wondered if it was gently snowing inside the Wall too, or if the Home was still being pelted with rain. He had a feeling that from now on, the weather would only get better and better there.

He remembered something Belisha had told him that day in Kestrel Courtyard after the miraculous door appeared. He had asked her if the place had become so evil and corrupt because of the manticore, and she said – in typical night crow fashion – yes *and* no. She said that sometimes people have a strange habit of inviting hate into their house when they don't get what they want or when someone hurts them. "Don't ever let that happen to you, Foxling," she said. He hugged her neck and assured her he wouldn't.

Arthur still couldn't believe his luck. All his friends were with him now – at least most of them were. He watched as Trinket flitted around the glittering tree, adding finishing touches here and there, including a bright-gold bird at the top. Trinket had invented a very useful Christmas cranberry stringer, and Baby Tizer was making sure it made enough cranberry strands for the tree. Arthur got up and began placing tinsel all around, and Peevil (who insisted on being called Peevil the Bold ever since the Great Fire) gave persistent and unsolicited advice, which Arthur was forced to translate. Trinket, who now had her own workshop at Miss Phoebe's, promised Arthur that after the holidays, she would invent some kind of translation device so Peevil could communicate with everyone.

There was a knock at the door, and Linette went to answer it. She returned in a moment and said, "Arthur, you'll never guess who's here! I'll give you a hint: he came in whistling a tune and is wearing a fancy red hat."

Arthur ran to the foyer and threw his arms around his old friend, who was elegantly dressed in red velveteen tails, a top hat, and a black overcoat.

"Quintus! It's been so long! Why haven't you stopped by sooner? Come in, come in! Shall I put the kettle on? Can you stay for tea?" He called out to Linette to ask if there were any biscuits left from the morning.

"Yes, Arthur," she called from the parlour. "Is your friend staying for tea?"

Quintus lowered his voice and said, "Listen, lad, can't stay for tea, but can we talk private like? I needs to tell you somethink. I came on a mission. To make good on somethink I shoulda done long ago."

"Of course," said Arthur, then called out to Linette not to bother with the tea. He turned back to his old friend and looked up at him with concern. "What is it, Quintus? What's wrong?"

"I made a promise to you, lad, and I aim to keep it. But first, take this. 'Twas always meant for you, not me. Should've given it to you ages ago, but I felt too shameful like."

Quintus handed him a small piece of paper that had been crumpled up and folded many times over. It was creased and smudged with grease and dirt. Arthur opened it and read the message, which had been written quickly on the day he had escaped with Trinket from the Home:

Arthur – If you make it to the City, go to my mother Phoebe Nightingale's house. She'll be out of town until the second week of June, but the key is below the stone bird next to the back door. Make yourself at home. I'll let her know you're there.

The message ended with brief directions to Phoebe's house and the words *Love, Linette. P.S. Good luck!*

"Don't deserve forgiveness," said Quintus, "but maybe … maybe someday, you might not think of me so unkindly like. We had some good times, didn't we, Spike ol' boy?"

Arthur was stunned. So this was how Quintus had chosen Phoebe's house for their robbery: he had learned from Linette's note that the place would be empty. It was something a scoundrel would do, and Quintus was a scoundrel. But he was also Arthur's friend, and if it hadn't been for him and the rest of the gang, he and Trinket might not have survived the terrible fire.

"Oh, Quintus," said Arthur. "Of course I forgive you!" And he embraced his friend once more.

"Well, I … uh…" said Quintus, who was so choked up he couldn't talk.

Neither of them spoke for a moment. Then Quintus said, "I'll not come in today, Spike. Maybe some other time. An' if you don't mind, maybe *you* can tell Linette and Phoebe that I'm real sorry fer doin' what I did. Or I'll tell her meself next time 'round. But you need to walk with me fer a bit now, Spike. I gots somethink to show ya. Bit of a trek, but I'll get you back in one piece. Turns out it ain't too far from good ol' Wildered Manor."

So Quintus and Arthur walked through the snowy streets of Lumentown, past the great pillared mansions with their stained-glass windows, their pink and white turrets and balconies, and snow-covered topiaries trimmed into the shape of cats. They passed the market and redbrick houses, the cafés and pubs and fancy shops. They passed street musicians playing harps and hurdy-gurdies, and flutes and fiddles in the cold afternoon air.

Arthur stopped at every single one and dropped a coin into his or her cup.

The noise of the streets was muffled from the snow and the holiday hush, and everyone, even the grumpiest-looking High Hats, seemed to be in good spirits that clear, crisp day.

When they reached the river, Arthur asked Quintus to wait while he stopped by a group of Huddlers gathered around a kindling fire on the dock. "I'll just be a moment," he said.

He gave each Huddler some of what he had stuffed in his pocket before he left: some rolls, a little cheese, whatever he'd been able to fetch in a hurry. "Merry Christmas," he said to them. Then, remembering Trinket's words that day they had parted and he felt so lost and alone, "Be brave," he said, "and never, ever lose hope!"

"You're a good 'un, ya are," said Quintus. He linked his arm in Arthur's and they went on.

When they got to Stinkbottom Bridge, Arthur was glad to see Constable Floop back at his post.

"Happy holidays, good cheer, an' all that," said the policeman in his usual deadpan manner. But when Quintus tried to put a coin in his hand, the officer shook his head no and said, "G'won with ya now. An' happy New Year to ya both."

On the other side of the river, they passed the Swan &

Whistle, and Arthur told himself that he ought to go back there really soon and learn a tune or two from those musicians. Now that he knew he could sing – that he *had* to sing – he wanted to learn as many songs as he could.

He glanced down at the riverbank. Maybe, just maybe, the Norahc was waiting there for evening to come. Who would it carry across next? And what would happen to that poor lost soul?

Arthur and Quintus cut through Bloomintown, and even the ramshackle tenements looked clean and cozy in the freshly fallen snow.

Finally, they arrived at 17 Tintagel Road.

"This is it, m' boy," said Quintus. He gave Arthur's shoulder a squeeze. "Hadn't been a house on this spot back ten years, I'd say. You musta been about one year old, ain't that right?"

Arthur was speechless. Now that he was finally here, he didn't know what to feel. He stared at the burned shell of what had once been a lovely home. It looked like the remains of the houses on Quintus's street, which was only a hop and skip away. Some dwellings nearby had been rebuilt and made into cheap housing for humans.

"I asked around," said Quintus. "Used to be a fine place, this house an' this here street. But after … after whot they call the Lustrum, well… Same thing happened to me."

"The Lustrum?" asked Arthur. "I thought – well, at least I remember – a fire."

"'Days of Light,' High Hats likes to call it. Every five years, some a them 'clean up' a bit, so to speak. But it ain't Days a Light fer groundlings, no, sir. You see – the worst a the lot, they burnt down the houses a groundlings and the houses a the people that helped 'em. Random like. My family lived at Wildered Manor – 'twas Wilfred Manor back then. This was, oh, thirty years back, I'd say. I was just a runt. The Wilfreds, they was good folk. Treated me mum an' pa good, they did. They protected us. Refused to send us to the poorhouse for groundlings. That's where D.O.G.C. sent our lot before they built Gloomintown. The Wilfreds ended up dyin' – the whole lot of 'em. Along with my four brothers an' the rest a me family."

Quintus took off his hat, bowed his head, and said, "Primus, Secundus, Terius, Quartus – rest in peace, mates, rest in peace."

Arthur remembered how Quintus had told him that numbers one through four were taken, and that he had to be Number Thirteen, because Quintus's brothers would always be those numbers. Now he understood why.

Quintus sniffed a little and wiped his nose on his sleeve. He put his arm around Arthur and said, "Same thing happened to you, I reckon. Yer street – Tintagel – I asked around, an' folks say 'twas the Lustrum, 'twas. You musta been just a wee pup, poor lit'le 'un. An' the folks who lived here – I reckon they protected you like the Wilfreds did me. Must've been good folks; brave too."

The two stood there in silence until Arthur said, "Quintus, can we walk around the back? I think that's where my house was. I think we lived behind the family who lived in the house. I'm not certain, but ... but I think we lived inside a tree."

They walked around what was left of the house's foundation. There, covered in snow, were charred stumps of trees, including one old fallen oak.

The two friends stood without talking.

Arthur thought about returning in the spring, when the earth had thawed. Maybe, if he dug around a bit, he might find the music box buried below.

But then, perhaps Belisha was right. He remembered the Night Crow's words as they flew through the subterranean maze: *You have all you need.*

She had said: *Except for one thing more. And that I cannot give you.*

He knew now that the thing she spoke of was his own voice.

Arthur said goodbye to 17 Tintagel Road, to his lost family, and to the human family that had bravely tried to protect them.

"Can you walk me back to the bridge?" said Arthur, who

was shivering now and wanted to join Trinket and all the others by the fire at Phoebe's house. For he knew that Miss Phoebe's was his home now, and he hoped it would be for a very long time.

"I'll take you all the way home, lad. Come on," said Quintus.

When they finally reached Phoebe's house, Arthur again invited his friend in for tea. But Quintus was in a hurry to get back to Wildered Manor. He said he had much to do before the holiday meal. "Another time, mate. Love to pop over fer a cuppa an' a chat."

Arthur asked him what he was cooking up for Christmas Eve, but he knew the answer before Quintus even spoke. What else could it be but Soup for Kings?

"By the way, Spike – I mean *Arthur* – whatever happened to that big Crow?"

"I forgot to tell you. Belisha – the Night Crow – she went back to where she's from. She guards the graveyard in Gloomintown, you see. It took a while for her eyes to heal, but Linette says they should be almost better now."

"How'd she get back, then?" asked Quintus.

"That's the amazing part," said Arthur. "She sang her way home! That's how crows find their way, I guess. The sky is like an invisible map of songs. At least, that's what she told me. We still keep in touch by using Trinket's messenger pigeon – it works a lot better now, by the way. Belisha said that from now on, she'd try to watch out for the living too, not just the dead. There are so many groundlings down there, Quintus. I hope someday they'll be free."

"Hope so," said Quintus. "It just ain't right." They were silent for a moment, then Quintus said, "An' all the lit'le 'uns from the Home? Them's all safe an' sound?"

"Oh, they're fine. Local farmers took them in. And Phoebe, she took in a few herself."

"All's well that ends well, as they say," said Quintus. "An' I nearly forgot to tell *you* somethink." Quintus chuckled. "I aim to find that orange-haired lady an' that despicable Rat who kidnapped me mate. Settin' up a new business, I am: Quintus an' Company, private detective agency. Like the sound o' that, laddie? Me first case is trackin' down poor ol' Squee. He's out there somewheres, an' I aim to find 'im an' bring 'im back home. An' maybe we'll even find good ol' Goblin, bless his heart."

Arthur's face fell. He still felt terrible about Goblin.

"Don't be down in the dumps, laddie! We'll find 'im, I'm sure of it. So give us a good huzzah, why don't ya? There's a good boy."

"Of course I will," said Arthur, who was smiling now.

"Next time we see each other, we shall make a proper toast. A toast to new beginnings! And truly, I think your plan is just champion, Quintus! Or should I say Detective Quintus? So huzzah to Quintus, Private Detective Extraordinaire!"

The two embraced once more, and Arthur watched as the Rat in the top hat and tails headed back home.

CHAPTER 56

Home

AS NIGHT FELL upon Lumentown, Arthur sat contentedly at the dining-room table with his friends, new and old: Miss Phoebe, her friend Mr Pitch – a refined-looking man of about forty, with a dark complexion and a thin black moustache – Linette, Trinket and Peevil – who was having an after-dinner nap in Arthur's shirt pocket – along with Rufus, Snook, Nigel, Nesbit, Baby Tizer and several other groundlings from the Home. It certainly was a full house, and the next day it would be even fuller, as Pinecone and his family as well as Peevil's were coming to stay for the holidays.

They had just finished eating, and Arthur began helping Linette clear the plates from the table. When he was done, he sat back down next to Mr Pitch. Everything felt so safe and cozy. A fire blazed in the hearth, and the room sparkled with candles and the lights from the crystal chandelier above.

Phoebe looked out the window and sighed. "Oh, Clemmy! My poor, poor Clementine," said Phoebe, dabbing her eyes with the corner of her napkin. "Holidays do make me so nostalgic."

Arthur still couldn't get over how alike she and Miss Carbunkle looked, despite how pinched and angry Miss Carbunkle's face had become over the years. Arthur was very grateful that Phoebe did not wear a towering orange wig too. Unlike her sister, Phoebe was not bald; her hair was naturally ginger coloured, although now streaked with grey.

Phoebe got up and went to the window. "Where is she? I fear she is dead! She didn't even turn to look at me that day. I might never see her again! Oh, it pains me so!"

"Ahem," said Mr Pitch. He folded his hands and rested them on the table, then began twirling his thumbs. He had the longest and most elegant fingers Arthur had ever seen. "Ahem," he said again.

She turned to face him. "What is it, Mr Pitch? I can tell you are dying to say something. I do so dislike when you beat around the bush like this."

Phoebe sat back down and crossed her arms over her chest. Arthur was used to their little spats now and found them quite amusing, for Phoebe and Mr Pitch had known each other for many years, and it was clear that they were very close friends.

"With all due respect, my dear," said Mr Pitch, who was sitting across from her, "it's just that I don't quite understand what all this 'poor Clemmy' is about. I mean, your sister tortured those poor groundlings for years, and she held a grudge against you for even longer. She sent hooligans to your house to steal the thing dearest to your heart – your father's brilliant invention, destroying all your possessions in the process – then ran off with that nefarious Rat. *What* is there to sympathize with? I ask you. With all due respect, of course."

Phoebe uncrossed her arms, then crossed them again. Her face flushed red. "Mr Pitch. Sometimes I simply do not understand you at all. Must I explain everything? Very well." Phoebe shook her head and continued: "First of all, we do not know whether dear Clementine is alive or dead. She is my sister, in case you forgot! And second, don't you see how sad it all is? It's terribly, terribly sad!"

"I certainly don't. In fact, I wouldn't be sorry if the woman got the gallows for what she did."

"Mr Pitch! How could you say such a thing about my baby sister? My twin? My little Clemmy?"

Arthur had a hard time thinking of Miss Carbunkle as anyone's "little Clemmy," but then he thought about it some more. She *had* been someone's little Clemmy once. And to

Phoebe, his guardian, she still was. He cleared his throat and said softly, "If you please, Miss Phoebe … may I speak?"

Phoebe reached across the table and patted Arthur's furry hand affectionately. "Of course, my dear. You may always speak your mind at the House of Nightingale."

Everyone at the table, including Trinket, who was still pecking at a bowl of seeds, turned to look at Arthur. The other groundlings offered encouraging snorts and snuffling sounds for him to go on.

"Thank you," said Arthur. He looked up at Mr Pitch, who was sitting on his right, and said, "I think what Miss Phoebe means, Mr Pitch, is that it's important to remember that even the biggest person was, at one time, very, very small." He saw Linette beaming at him from across the table. He smiled back at her and said slowly, "And perhaps – deep inside – Miss Carbunkle is still very, very small."

Phoebe's eyes filled with tears. She jumped up from her chair, ran around the table, and threw her arms around her young ward.

Mr Pitch said, "You are wise for your age, Master Nightingale. Wiser than this old humbug, I daresay!"

"A toast to young Arthur!" cried Linette.

"Happy birthday, Arthur!" they all cheered. Then Linette hurried to the kitchen and returned carrying an enormous blackberry pie with twelve bright candles.

"But it's not till tomorrow," said Arthur.

"We don't always follow the rules here at the House of Nightingale," said Phoebe. "We can have holidays and birthdays whenever we want. And besides, this way, you get a birthday pie today and a cake tomorrow!"

"You know," said Arthur, "I just realized something. After all this time, I still haven't eaten a pie!"

"And it's about time you did!" said Trinket, jumping up and down on top of the table with delight.

And so they all sang "Happy Birthday" to Arthur – even Peevil squeaked along – and ate as much pie as their stomachs could hold.

That night, after Arthur opened his gifts – including a music box Phoebe had purchased from Trundlebee's Trains & Toys for Tiny Tots, the toy shop Arthur had longed to enter his first day in Lumentown – he went upstairs to his very own bedroom, complete with a big, warm feather bed.

He thought about that night so long ago – the lilting voice that sang to him, the soft arms that held him close, the voice that said: *You are the Wonderling. We have been waiting such a long, long time.* And while Arthur still could not remember exactly where he came from, he remembered now that he *had* been loved.

Before he fell asleep that Christmas Eve, he opened the window to breathe in the crisp night air. Then he sang a sweet and tender song. It floated out the open window, up into a sky full of stars, and sailed over the snowy streets of Lumentown.

And this time, when he sang, he was awake – his eyes, and heart, wide open to the world.

Special thanks to all my Wonderlings:
Alex, Doug, Jed & Emily, Christy, James, Judi, Mark, Robert,
Cathy, Herta, Stephanie, Sandy, Tim & Cathy Ols, Hannah,
Emma & Jude, Jane & Steve, Lisa B. & Lisa G., Jane & Heidi,
Mary & Wendy, Nat & Kerry, Jo & Nate, Sianna, Jya, Tim, Leland,
Zoey & C.E., Barbara J., Tracy Kochanski, Mary Witt,
Amelia Granger, Elizabeth Gabler, Stacey Snider,
Erin Siminoff, Fred Fierst, Michelle Weiner, Michelle Kroes,
Karen Lotz, Alice McConnell, Tracy Miracle, Chris Paul,
Jennifer Roberts, Mary Hall, Iacopo Bruno, Gregg Hammerquist,
Jennifer Gates and Chelsey Heller.